Dear Reader,

It has been a long time since [my] soldiers of fortune came along [...] go back and "revisit" them, but [...] told me they planned to rerelease all three books, *Soldier of Fortune*, *The Tender Stranger* and *Enamored*, in one volume. They also asked me to do a new SOLDIERS OF FORTUNE trilogy. I was thrilled at the prospect of doing a new series, especially since it meant that I could catch up with news of the original set of heroes. Look for updates on them in the new books, which are set in Jacobsville, Texas. That's right—they're all going to be tied in with my LONG, TALL TEXANS series, which so many of you seem to enjoy. (Thanks!)

These heroes are not modern men. They live in a world where the lines between masculinity and femininity are not blurred by technology. They are deliberately larger than life. I adore men who are strong enough to be tender, virtuous enough to abstain from vulgarity and obscenity in their speech, confident enough to walk their own road through life, and intelligent and stubborn enough to make a success of any goal they strive for. I adore men who treat women with respect and courtesy and kindness. I adore men who bristle and take action when they see women abused, children mistreated, animals tormented. Those are my sort of heroes, and the stuff of which romantic fiction is made. My heroes don't eat tofu and quiche. They eat rattlesnakes. Of course, so do my heroines. It takes a strong and fiery woman to match a hero. Especially heroes like these.

I don't write about stark reality—you can get that on the six-o'clock news. But if you like pure escapism, this trilogy may appeal to you. I hope you enjoy it. As Silhouette Books celebrates its twentieth anniversary, I also celebrate my twentieth year as a Silhouette author. As you can see by the length of our association, I am very grateful to Silhouette for giving me a chance to do the only thing I ever wanted to do in life—write books. Thank you, Silhouette editors, editorial staff, administration, artists, salesmen, executives, warehousers, wholesalers, booksellers and especially you readers, for twenty of the most wonderful years any human being could wish for. Thank you for your kindness and your generosity and your loyalty. I will continue to write books as long as Silhouette will publish them and you will read them. I am still your biggest fan.

Love,

Diane Palmer

P.S. I now have a seasonal color newsletter of upcoming releases, beginning with autumn 1999. If you'd like one, send me a stamped, self-addressed envelope care of Silhouette Books, and I'll be glad to put you on my mailing list!

PRAISE FOR DIANA PALMER

"Diana Palmer is a unique talent
in the romance industry. Her writing combines wit,
humor, and sensuality; and, as the song says,
nobody does it better!"
—*New York Times* bestselling author Linda Howard

"Nobody tops Diana Palmer...I love her stories."
—*New York Times* bestselling author
Jayne Ann Krentz

"Diana Palmer makes a reader want to find
a Texan of her own to love!"
—*Affaire de Cœur*

DIANA PALMER

SOLDIERS OF
FORTUNE

Silhouette Books

Published by Silhouette Books
America's Publisher of Contemporary Romance

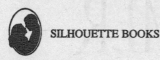 SILHOUETTE BOOKS

SOLDIERS OF FORTUNE

Copyright © 2000 by Harlequin Books S.A.

ISBN 0-373-48404-6

The publisher acknowledges the copyright holder of the individual works as follows:

SOLDIER OF FORTUNE
Copyright © 1985 by Diana Palmer

THE TENDER STRANGER
Copyright © 1985 by Diana Palmer

ENAMORED
Copyright © 1988 by Diana Palmer

Visit Silhouette at www.eHarlequin.com

Printed in U.S.A.

CONTENTS

J. D. Brettman. Eric van Meer. Diego Laremos.

They are strong, heroic, potently sexy. With nerves
of steel and a strict code of honor, these soldiers of
fortune live on the edge of danger and never let down
their guards in the pursuit of justice. And if anyone
dares to cross these merciless mercenaries, they'd
better watch out! Except now J.D., Eric and Diego
have become the unwitting targets...for love! Watch
as three spirited ladies wage a battle of their own—
to gain full possession of their beloved mercenaries'
hearts!

And if you enjoy these three books, look for a brand-
new book in the SOLDIERS OF FORTUNE series,
available in May from Silhouette Romance:

MERCENARY'S WOMAN

**She was in danger, and he fought to protect her.
But sweet-natured Sally Johnson dreamed of
spending forever in Ebenezer Scott's powerful
embrace. Would she walk down the aisle as this
tender mercenary's bride?**

Soldiers of Fortune
*In 2001, watch for more thrilling tales of men tested
by battle who become soldiers of love.*

Soldier of Fortune

For R.D.M.,
and Irene, my lovely mother-in-law

Chapter One

Gabby was worried about J.D. It wasn't anything she could put her finger on exactly. He still roared around the office, slamming things down on his desk when he couldn't find notes or reminders he'd scribbled on envelopes or old business cards. He glared at Gabby when she didn't bring his coffee on the stroke of nine o'clock. And there were the usual missing files, for which she was to blame of course, and the incessant phone calls that interrupted his concentration. There was still the heavy scowl on his broad face, and the angry glitter in his brown eyes. But that morning he'd been pacing around his office, smoking like a furnace. And that was unusual. Because J.D. had given up smoking years before, even before she had come to work for the law firm of Brettman and Dice.

She still couldn't figure out what had set him off.

She'd put a long-distance call through to him earlier, one that sounded like it came from overseas. The caller had sounded suspiciously like Roberto, his sister Martina's husband, from Sicily. Soon afterward, there had been a flurry of outgoing calls. Now it was silent, except for the soft sounds the computer made as Gabby finished the last letter J.D. had dictated.

She propped her chin on her hands and stared at the door with curious green eyes. Her long, dark hair was piled high on her head, to keep it out of her way when she worked, and loose strands of it curled softly around her face, giving her an even more elfin look than usual. She was wearing a green dress that flattered her graceful curves. But J.D. wouldn't notice her if she walked through the office naked. He'd said when he hired her that he'd robbed the cradle. And he hadn't smiled when he said it. Although she was twenty-three now, he still made the most frustrating remarks about her extreme youth. She wondered wickedly what J.D. would say if she applied for Medicare in his name. Nobody knew how old he was. Probably somewhere around forty; those hard lines in his face hadn't come from nowhere.

He was one of the most famous criminal lawyers in Chicago. He made waves. He ground up hostile witnesses like so much sausage meat. But before his entry into the profession five years earlier, nothing was known about him. He'd worked as a laborer by day and attended law school by night. He'd worked his way up the ladder quickly and efficiently with the help of a devastating intelligence that seemed to feed on challenge.

He had no family except for a married sister in Palermo, Sicily, and no close friends. He allowed no one to really know him. Not his associate Richard Dice, not Gabby. He lived alone and mostly worked alone, except for the few times when he needed some information that only a woman could get, or when he had to have Gabby along as a cover. She'd gone with him to meet accused killers in warehouses at midnight and down to the waterfront in the wee hours of the morning to meet a ship carrying a potential witness.

It was an exciting life, and thank God her mother back in Lytle, Texas, didn't know exactly how exciting it was. Gabby had come to Chicago when she was twenty; she'd had to fight for days to get her mother to agree to the wild idea, to let her work for a distant cousin. The distant cousin had died quite suddenly and, simultaneously, J.D. had advertised for an executive secretary. When she applied, it had taken J.D. only five minutes to hire her. That had been two years earlier, and she'd never regretted the impulse that had led her to his office.

Just working for him was something of a feather in Gabby's cap. The other secretaries in the building were forever pumping her for information about her attractive and famous boss. But Gabby was as secretive as he was. It was why she'd lasted so long as his secretary. He trusted her as he trusted no one else.

She was a paralegal now, having taken night courses at a local college to earn the title. She did far more than just type letters and run off copies on the copier. The office had added a computer system. She ran that, and did legwork for her boss, and frequently traveled with him when the job warranted it.

While she was brooding, the door opened suddenly. J.D. came through it like a locomotive, so vibrant and superbly masculine that she imagined most men would step aside for him out of pure instinct. His partner Richard Dice was on his heels, raging as he followed.

"Will you be reasonable, J.D.!" the younger man argued, his lean hands waving wildly, his red hair almost standing on end around his thin face. "It's a job for the police! What can you do?"

J.D. didn't even look at him. He paused at Gabby's desk, an expression on his face that she'd never seen before. Involuntarily, she studied the broad face with its olive complexion and deep-set eyes. He had the thickest, blackest eyelashes she'd ever seen. His hair was just as thick and had deep waves in it, threaded with pure silver. It was the faint scars on his face that aged him, but she'd never quite had the bravado to ask where and how he'd gotten them. It must have been some kind of man who put them there. J.D. was built like a tank.

"Pack a bag," he told Gabby, in a tone too black to invite questions. "Be back here in an hour. Is your passport in order?"

She blinked. Even for J.D., this was fast shuffling. "Uh, yes...."

"Bring lightweight things, it'll be hot where we're going. Lots of jeans and loose shirts, a sweater, some boots, and a lot of socks." He continued nonstop. "Bring that third-class radio license you hold. Aren't you kin to someone at the State Department? That might come in handy.''

Her mind was whirling. "J.D. what's going...?" she began.

"You can't do this," Dick was continuing doggedly, and J.D. was just ignoring him.

"Dick, you'll have to handle my case load until I get back," he pressed on in a voice that sounded like thunder rumbling. "Get Charlie Bass to help you if you run into any snags. I don't know exactly when we'll be back."

"J.D., will you listen?"

"I've got to pack a few things," J.D. said curtly. "Call the agency, Gabby, and get Dick a temporary secretary. And be back here in exactly one hour."

The door slammed behind him. Dick cursed roundly and rammed his hands into his pockets.

"What," Gabby asked, "is going on? Will somebody please tell me where I'm going with my passport? Do I have a choice?"

"Slow down and I'll tell you what little I know." Dick sighed angrily. He perched himself on her desk. "You know that J.D.'s sister is married to that Italian businessman who made a fortune in shipping and lives in Palermo, Sicily?"

She nodded.

"And you know that kidnapping is becoming a fast method of funding for revolutionary groups?" he continued.

She felt herself going pale. "They got his brother-in-law?"

"No. They got his sister when she went alone on a shopping trip to Rome."

She caught her breath. "Martina? But she's the only family he has!"

"I know that. They're asking for five million dollars, and Roberto can't scrape it up. He's frantic. They told him they'd kill her if he involved the authorities."

"And J.D. is going to Italy to save her?"

"However did you guess?" Dick grumbled. "In his usual calm, sensible way, he is moving headfirst into the china shop."

"To Italy? With me?" She stared at him. "Why am I going?"

"Ask him. I only work here."

She sighed irritably as she rose to her feet. "Someday I'm going to get a sensible job, you wait and see if I don't," she said, her eyes glittering with frustration. "I was going to eat lunch at McDonald's and leave early so I could take in that new science-fiction movie at the Grand. And instead I'm being bustled off to Italy...to do what, exactly?" she added with a frown. "Surely to goodness, he isn't going to interfere with the Italian authorities?"

"Martina is his sister," Dick reminded her. "He never talks about it, but they had a rough upbringing from what I can gather, and they're especially close. J.D. would mow down an army to save her."

"But he's a lawyer," she protested. "What is he going to do?"

"Beats me, honey." Dick sighed.

"Here we go again," she muttered as she cleared

her desk and got her purse out of the drawer. "Last time he did this, we were off to Miami to meet a suspected mob informer in an abandoned warehouse at two o'clock in the morning. We actually got shot at!" She shuddered. "I didn't dare tell my Mama what was going on. Speaking of my Mama, what am I supposed to tell her?"

"Tell her you're going on a holiday with the boss." He grinned. "She'll be thrilled."

She glared at him. "The boss doesn't take holidays. He takes chances."

"You could quit," he suggested.

"Quit!" she exclaimed. "Who said anything about quitting? Can you see me working for a normal attorney? Typing boring briefs and deeds and divorce petitions all day? Bite your tongue!"

"Then may I suggest that you call James Bond," he said, "and ask if he has any of those exploding matches or nuclear warhead toothpicks he can spare."

She gave him a hard glare. "Do you speak any Spanish?"

"Well, no," he said, puzzled.

She rattled off a few explicit phrases in the lilting tongue her father's foreman had used with the ranch hands back during her childhood. Then, with a curtsy, she walked out the door.

Chapter Two

Gabby had seen J.D. in a lot of different moods, but none of them could hold a candle to the one he was in now. He sat beside her as stiff as a board on the jet, barely aware of the cup of black coffee he held precariously in one big hand.

Worst of all was the fact that she couldn't think of anything to say. J.D. wasn't the kind of man you offered sympathy to. But it was hard just to sit and watch him brood without talking at all. She'd rarely heard him speak of his sister Martina, but the tenderness with which he described her had said enough. If he loved any human being on earth, it was Martina.

"Boss..." she began uneasily.

He blinked, glancing toward her. "Well?"

She avoided that level gaze. "I just wanted to say I'm sorry." Her long, slender fingers fidgeted with the skirt of the white suit she was wearing. "I know how hard it must be for you. There's just not a lot that people can do in these kinds of situations.''

A peculiar smile touched his hard features for a moment. He swallowed a sip of coffee. ''Think not?'' he asked dryly.

''You aren't serious about not contacting the authorities?'' she persisted. ''After all, they've got those special teams now, and they even rescued that one kidnap victim...''

He glanced down at her. The look stopped her in mid-sentence. ''That was a political kidnapping. This isn't. As for those special teams, Darwin, they're not infallible. I can't take risks with Martina's life.''

''No,'' she said. She stared at his hands. They were so gracefully masculine, the fingers long and tapered and as dark olive as his face, with flat nails and a sprinkling of hair, like that curling around the watch on his wrist. He had powerful hands.

''You aren't afraid, are you?'' he asked.

She glanced up. ''Well, sort of,'' she confessed. ''I don't really know where we're going, do I?''

''You should be used to that by now,'' he reminded her dryly.

She laughed. ''I suppose so. We've had some adventures in the past two years.''

He pulled out a cheroot and lit it, staring at her narrowly over the flame. ''Why aren't you married?'' he asked suddenly.

The question startled her. She searched for the right words. ''I'm not sure,'' she said. ''I suppose I just haven't bothered to get involved with anyone. Until four years ago, I was living in a small town in Texas.

Then I came up here to work for a cousin, he died, you needed a secretary..." She laughed softly. "With all due respect, Mr. Brettman, you're kind of a never-ending job, if you know what I mean. It just isn't a nine-to-five thing."

"About which," he observed, "you've never once complained."

"Who could complain?" she burst out. "I've been around the country and halfway across the world, I get to meet gangsters, I've been shot at...!"

He chuckled softly. "That's some job description."

"The other secretaries in the building are green, simply green, with envy," she replied smugly.

"You aren't a secretary. You're a paralegal. In fact," he added, puffing on his cheroot thoughtfully, "I've thought about sending you to law school. You've got a lot of potential."

"Not me," she said. "I could never get up in front of a courtroom full of people and grill witnesses like you do. Or manage such oration in a summing up."

"You could still practice law," he reminded her. "Corporate law, if you like. Or deal in estates and partnerships. Divorces. Land transfers. There are many areas of law that don't require oratory."

"I'm not sure enough that it's what I want to do with the rest of my life," she said.

He lifted his chin. "How old are you?"

"Twenty-three."

He shook his head, studying the chignon, the glasses she used for close reading and now had perched on top of her head, the stylish white linen suit she was wearing, the length of her slender legs. "You don't look it."

"In about twenty years could you repeat that?" she asked. "By then I'll probably appreciate it."

"What do you want to be?" he asked, persisting as he leaned back in the seat. His vested gray silk suit emphasized the sheer size of him. He was so close she could even feel the warmth of his body, and she found it oddly disturbing.

"Oh, I don't know," she murmured, glancing out the window at the clouds. "A secret agent, maybe. A daring industrial spy. A flagpole sitter." She looked over her shoulder at him. "Of course, those jobs would seem very dull after working for you, Boss. And do I ever get to know where we're going?"

"To Italy, of course," he replied.

"Yes, sir, I know that. *Where* in Italy?"

"Aren't you curious, though?" he mused, lifting one shaggy eyebrow. "We're going to Rome. To rescue my sister."

"Yes, sir, of course we are," she said. It was better to agree with maniacs, she told herself. He'd finally snapped. It was even predictable, considering the way he'd been pushing himself.

"Humoring me, Miss Darwin?" he asked. He leaned deliberately past her to crush out his cheroot, and his face was so close that she could smell the spicy cologne he wore, feel the warm, smoky scent of his breath. As his fingers left the ashtray, he turned his head.

That look caused her the wildest shock she'd ever felt. It was like an earth tremor that worked its way from her eyes to the tips of her toes and made them want to curl up. She hadn't realized how vulnerable she was with him until her heart started racing and her breath strangled in her throat.

"I hesitated about taking you with me," he said quietly. "I'd rather have left you behind. But there was no one else I could trust, and this is a very delicate situation."

She tried to act normally. "You do realize that what you're thinking about could get her killed?"

"Yes," he said simply. "But not to act could get her killed quicker. You know what usually happens in these cases, don't you?"

"Yes, I do," she admitted. Her gaze moved down to his broad mouth with its lips that seemed sculpted from stone and back up again to his dark eyes. He looked different so close up.

"I'm doing what I think is best," he said. His fingers nudged a wisp of hair back into place at her neck, and she felt trembly all over from the touch. "We're not sure that the kidnappers still have Martina in Italy. Roberto thinks he knows one of them—the son of an acquaintance, who also happens to own land in Central America. I don't have to tell you what a hell of a mess this could turn into if they take Martina there, do I?"

She felt weak all over. "But how are they dealing with Roberto?"

"One of the group, and there is a group, is still in Italy, to arrange the handling of the money," he answered. He let his eyes fall to the jacket of her suit, and he studied it absently with disturbing concentration. "We may do some traveling before this is all over."

"But first we're going to Italy," she murmured dazedly.

"Yes. To meet some old friends of mine," he said, his chiseled mouth smiling faintly. "They owe me a favor from years past. I'm calling in the debt."

"We're taking a team?" she asked, eyebrows shooting up. It was getting more exciting by the minute.

"My, how your eyes light up when you speak of working with a team, Miss Darwin," he mused.

"It's so gung ho," she replied self-consciously. "Kind of like that program I watch on TV every week, about the group that goes around the world fighting evil?"

"The Soldiers of Fortune?" he asked.

"The very one." She grinned. "I never miss a single episode."

"In real life, Miss Darwin," he reminded her, "it's a brutal, dangerous occupation. And most mercenaries don't make it to any ripe old age. They either get killed or wind up in some foreign prison. Their lives are overromanticized."

She glowered at him. "And what would you know about it, Mr. Criminal Attorney?" she challenged.

"Oh, I have a friend who used to sell his services abroad," he replied as he sat back in his seat. "He could tell you some hair-raising stories about life on the run."

"You know a real ex-merc?" she asked, eyes wid-

ening. She sat straight up in her seat. "Would he talk
to me?"

He shook his head. "Darwin." He sighed. "What
am I going to do with you?"

"It's your fault. You corrupted me. I used to lead
a dull life and never even knew it. Would he?"

"I suppose he would." His dark eyes wandered
slowly over her. "You might not like what you found
out."

"I'll take my chances, thanks. He, uh, wouldn't be
one of the old friends you're meeting in Rome?" she
asked.

"That would be telling. Fasten your seat belt, Darwin, we're approaching the airport now."

Her eyes lingered on his dark, unfathomable face
as she complied with the curt order. "Mr. Brettman,
why did you bring me along?" she asked softly.

"You're my cover, honey," he said, and smiled
sideways at her. "We're lovers off on a holiday."

"The way I look?" she chided.

He reached over and took the pins out of her coiffure, loosening her hair. His fingers lifted the glasses
from their perch atop her head, folded them, and
stuffed them into his shirt pocket. He reached over
again and flicked open the buttons of her blouse all
the way down to the cleft between her high breasts.

"Mr. Brettman!" she burst out, pushing at his fingers.

"Stop blushing, call me Jacob, and don't start
fighting me in public," he said gruffly. "If you can
remember all that, we'll do fine."

"Jacob?" she asked, her fingers abandoning their futile efforts to rebutton her buttons.

"Jacob. Or Dane, my middle name. Whichever you prefer, Gabby."

He made her name sound like bowers of pink roses in bud, like the softness of a spring rain on grass. She stared up at him.

"Jacob, then," she murmured.

He nodded, his dark eyes searching hers. "I'll take care of you, Gabby," he said. "I won't let you get in the line of fire."

"You meant it, didn't you?" she asked. "You're going to try to rescue Martina."

"Of course," he replied calmly. "She and I, we had a tough time as kids. Our father drowned in a bathtub, dead drunk, when we were toddlers. Mama scrubbed floors to keep us in school. As soon as we were old enough, we went to work, to help. But I was barely fifteen when Mama died of a heart attack. I've taken care of Martina ever since, just the way I promised I would. I can't let strangers try to help her. I have to."

"Forgive me," she said gently, "but you're an attorney, not a policeman. What can you do?"

"Wait and see," he told her. His eyes surveyed her quietly, approving her elfin beauty. "I'm not in my dotage yet."

"Yes, sir, I know that," she murmured.

"Jacob," he repeated.

She sighed, searching his dark eyes. "Jacob," she agreed.

That seemed to satisfy him. He glanced past her as

the plane started down, and he smiled. "The Eternal City, Gabby," he murmured. "Rome."

She followed his gaze and felt her heart lift as the ancient city came into view below. Already, she was leaping ahead to the time when she could actually see the Colosseum and the Forum and the Pantheon. But as she remembered the reason for their being in Rome, her enthusiasm faded. Of course there wouldn't be time for sightseeing, she reasoned. J.D. was going to be too busy trying to get himself killed.

The drive into Rome was fascinating. They went in on the Viale Trastevere, through the old part of the city, across the wide Tiber on an ancient bridge. The seven hills of Rome were hardly noticeable because of centuries of erosion and new construction, but Gabby was too busy gaping at the ruins they passed to notice or care.

They went right by the Colosseum, and her eyes lingered on it as they proceeded to their hotel.

"We'll find a few minutes to see it," J.D. said quietly, as if he knew how much it meant to her.

Her gaze brushed his hard face and impulsively she touched her fingers to the back of his hand. "It really isn't that kind of a trip," she said softly.

He searched her worried face. His big hand turned, grasping hers warmly in its callused strength. "We'll have to pretend that it is, for a day or so at least," he said.

"What are we going to do?" she asked nervously.

He drew in a slow breath and leaned back against the seat, handsome and rugged-looking in his vested suit. It strained against massive muscles, and she tingled at the sight. J.D. had always affected her powerfully in a purely physical way. It pleased her eyes to look at him.

"I'm working on that. But one thing we'll be doing in the hotel," he added slowly, "is sharing a suite. Will that frighten you?"

She shook her head. "I'm not afraid of anything when I'm with you, Jacob," she replied, finding that his given name was more comfortable to her tongue than she'd expected.

He cocked a heavy eyebrow. "That wasn't the kind of fear I meant, actually," he murmured. "Will you be afraid of me?"

"Why would I be?" she asked, puzzled.

He blew out a harsh breath and looked out the window. "I can't think of a single damned reason," he growled. "I hope Dutch got my message. He's supposed to call me later at the hotel."

"Dutch?" she queried softly.

"A man I know. He's my go-between with Roberto," he replied.

"Roberto and Martina don't live in Rome, do they?" she asked.

He shook his head. "In Palermo. So, for all appearances, we'll be a couple on holiday, and there won't be anything to connect us with the kidnapping."

"Will this man Dutch know if Martina is still in the country?" she asked.

"He'll know," he said with certainty.

He was obviously irritated with her, so she didn't

press him with any more questions, contenting herself
with staring at every building they passed.

Their hotel was disappointingly modern, but the
old-world courtesy of the Italian desk clerk made up
for it. He was attentive and outgoing, and Gabby liked
him at once. J.D., however, seemed to have misgivings about him. He didn't share them with her, but
he stared aggressively at the poor little man.

He had booked them a suite, with two bedrooms.
Gabby hadn't expected anything else, but J.D.'s behavior was downright odd. He glared at the elegant
sitting room, he glared at her, and he especially glared
at the telephone. He paced and smoked, and Gabby
felt as if she were going to fly apart, he made her so
nervous. She went into her bedroom and unpacked,
just to have something to do. The sudden sound of
the phone ringing startled her, but she didn't go back
into the sitting room; she waited for J.D. to call her.
Meanwhile, she changed into jeans and a silky green
top, leaving her hair loose and her reading glasses in
her purse. She did look like a tourist on holiday. That
ought to perk up J.D.

He called to her about five minutes later, and she
walked into the room to find him staring blankly out
the window. He'd taken off his jacket and vest and
opened the top buttons of his shirt. His thick, wavy
hair was mussed, and one big, tanned hand was still
buried in it. A smoking cigarette was in the other
hand, which was leaning on the windowsill.

"Jacob?" she murmured.

He turned. His dark eyes focused on her slender
figure, so intent that they missed the shocked pleasure

in her own gaze as she took in this sudden and unexpected glimpse of his body. Where the shirt was
loose, she could see the olive tan of his chest under
curls of dark hair, and rippling muscles that made her
hands itch. Her whole body reacted to his sensuality,
going rigid with excitement.

"Dutch," he said, nodding toward the phone to
indicate who his caller had been. "Martina's out of
the country."

She caught her breath. "Where?"

"Guatemala. On a *finca*—a farm—owned by a revolutionary group."

Her eyes searched his hard face. "Why would they
take her there?"

"Terrorism is international, didn't you know? They
probably have holdings all over the world, but Guatemala is in such a state of unrest it's a good place
to hide a kidnap victim." He laughed bitterly. His jaw
tautened. "They'll kill her if they don't get the
money. They may do it anyway."

"What are you going to do?"

"I've already done it," he replied. "I've given
Dutch a sum of money to buy some things I'll need.
I've also had him contact my old comrades. They'll
meet us at the Guatemalan *finca* of a friend of mine."

She cocked her head at him, uncomprehending.
"When do we leave?"

"Tomorrow," he said. "As much as I'd like to
jump on the next plane, we can't do it that way. I
need time to plan. And there's no sense in signaling
our every move. Dutch was going to speak to Roberto

for me tonight. I'll need to know the status of his fund-raising before we leave.''

"Will we fly into Guatemala?" she asked, feeling jittery.

"To Mexico," he said in answer. He smiled slowly. "As part of the holiday, of course," he added. "That will be broadcast to the right quarters."

"And now?" she asked. "What do I do?"

"We'll go see some of those ruins, if you like," he said. "It will help to pass the time."

Her eyes searched his. "I know you're worried, J.D. If you'd rather stay here…"

He moved closer to her, and the sudden proximity of his big body made her knees go weak. She lifted her face and found his dark eyes intent and unblinking.

"I don't think that's a good idea," he said quietly. He reached out and traced a slow path down her cheek to her throat, where her pulse went suddenly wild. "What would you like to see first?"

She found that her voice wobbled alarmingly. "How about the Forum?"

His dark eyes searched hers for a long moment. His fingers went to her mouth, touching it lightly, as if the feel of it fascinated him. His thumb dragged slowly, sensuously, over it, smearing her lipstick, arousing every nerve ending she had. She gasped, and her lips parted helplessly.

"The Forum?" he murmured.

She hardly heard him. Her eyes were held by his. Her body was reacting to the closeness of his in a new and frightening way. She could smell the musky cologne he wore and it made her head spin.

Her hands went to his chest in a small gesture of protest, but the feel of all that bare skin and matted hair made her jerk back.

He glanced down at her recoiling fingers with an odd expression. "It's only skin," he said quietly. "Are you afraid to touch me?"

"I've never touched anybody that way," she blurted out.

He tipped her face up to his and studied it with an odd smile. "Haven't you? Why?"

What an interesting question, she thought. What a pity she didn't have an answer.

"Don't tell me you haven't had the opportunity, Gabby," he said softly. "I wouldn't believe it."

"Mama said that it wasn't wise to do things like that to men," she told him doggedly, her chin thrust out. "She said they were hard enough to manage even when it didn't go beyond kissing."

"So there," he added for her with a faint smile. "She was right. Men get excited easily when they want a woman."

She felt the blush go up into her hairline, setting fire to her face. And he laughed, the horrible man!

She pulled away from him with a hard glare. "That was unkind," she grumbled.

"And you're delightfully repressed," he told her, but the look in his eyes was all tenderness. "You'd be pure sweet hell to initiate, Gabby."

"I don't want to be initiated," she said primly. "I want to see the Forum."

"All right, coward, hide your head in the sand," he taunted, holding the door open for her.

"It's safer that way, around you," she mumbled.

He caught her arm as she started past him, and she felt the warmth of his body like a drug. "I'll never hurt you," he said unexpectedly, drawing her stunned gaze to his face. It was hard and solemn. Almost grim. "You trust me in every other way. I want you to trust me physically as well."

"Why?" she asked.

"Because if I take you with me to Central America, I'll want you with me all the time. Especially at night," he added. "The men we'll be working with aren't particularly gentle. For all intents and purposes, you'll be my possession."

"To protect me from them?" she asked.

He nodded. "That means, in case you haven't worked it out, that you'll be sleeping in my bed."

She tingled from head to toe at the thought of lying in J.D.'s arms. It was something she'd contemplated in her own mind for a long time, and hearing it from his lips almost made her gasp. As it was, her flush told him everything anyway.

"In my bed," he repeated, searching her eyes. "In my arms. And I won't touch you in any way that I shouldn't. Even when we're back home and Martina is safe, and you're at your computer again, there won't be anything you'd be ashamed to tell your mother. All right?"

She couldn't find the words to express what she was feeling. J.D. felt protective of her. It was something she'd never expected. And uncharacteristically, she was disappointed. Did it mean that he didn't want her?

"All right, Jacob," she whispered softly.

His nostrils flared and his eyes flashed down at her. The hand holding her arm tightened until it hurt. "We'd better get out of here," he said gruffly. He let her go, turning away as if it took some effort, and opened the door.

Rome was the most exciting place Gabby had ever been. All of it seemed to be interspersed with history and crumbling ruins and romance. J.D. told her that the Colosseum, the Forum, the Ninfeo di Nerone— Nero's Sanctuary of the Nymphs—and the ruins of Nero's House of Gold residence were all near the Caelian, Capitolene, and Palatine hills. They decided to concentrate on that area of the city.

There was so much to see that Gabby's mind seemed to overload. They wandered around the ruins of the Forum first, and she just stared and stared like the eternal tourist.

"Just imagine," she whispered, as if afraid the ghosts might hear and take offense, "all those centuries ago Romans walked here just as we're walking today, with the same dreams and hopes and fears we feel. I wonder if they ever thought about how the world would be in the future?"

"I'm sure they did." J.D. stuck his hands in his pockets, and the wind ran like loving fingers through his crisp, dark hair. With his head thrown back like that, his profile in relief, he could have been one of the early Romans himself.

"Have you ever read *The Annals of Imperial Rome* by Tacitus?" she asked.

His head jerked around. "Yes. Have you?"

She grinned. "I was always a nut about Roman history. And Greek history. I loved Herodotus, even though he's been bad-mouthed a lot for some of his revelations."

"He was repeating what he'd heard or was told," he said. "But it's fascinating reading, nevertheless." He smiled amusedly. "Well, well, a historian. And I never suspected. I thought your knowledge of other countries was limited to those sweet little romance novels you read."

She glared at him. "I learn a lot about the world from those books," she said, defending herself. "And about other things too."

He cocked a dark eyebrow. "What other things?"

She looked away. "Never mind."

"We can go and see the catacombs later, if you like. They're south of here."

"Where the early Christians were buried?" She shuddered. "Oh, no, I don't think so. It's kind of an invasion of privacy. I'm sure I wouldn't want someone walking through my grave."

"I suppose it depends on your point of view," he conceded. "Well, we'll drive up to the Colosseum then."

"What was the other thing you mentioned, the Ninfeo di Nerone?"

He looked down at her with dark, indulgent eyes. "The Sanctuary of the Nymphs. You'd have fit right in, with your long, dark hair and mysterious eyes."

"I wouldn't have liked the debauchery," she said with certainty, her green eyes flashing. "The morals in Rome in Nero's time were decadent. I read that he had his wife Octavia killed, in a horrible way, after some prodding by his mistress."

"That was in Tacitus," he recalled. "A lot of terrible things happened here in the early days. But if you think about it, honey, terrible things are still happening. Like Martina's kidnapping."

"The world hasn't really changed very much, has it?" she asked sadly, watching the disturbance in his features at the thought of Martina and what she might be going through. She reached out and touched his arm gently. "They won't hurt her, Jacob," she said quietly. "Not until they get the money. Will they?"

"I don't know." He caught her arms and jerked her against his hard body, holding her there and staring intently into her eyes. "Frightened?" he asked on a husky note.

"No," she lied.

His dark eyes held hers. "We're supposed to be lovers on a holiday," he reminded her. "Just in case anyone is watching us..."

His head started to bend, and she caught her breath. Her eyes dropped to his chiseled mouth and she suddenly became breathless.

"Haven't you ever wondered?" he asked tautly, hesitating when he saw the shock on her young face.

Her eyes fluttered up to his fierce ones and back down again. "How it would be to...to kiss you?" she whispered.

"Yes."

Her lips parted on a rush of breath. She felt her breasts pressed softly against his shirtfront and was aware of the hardness of warm muscles against their hardening tips. She felt trembly all over just at the touch of his body.

His hands slid up her arms, over her shoulders, and up her throat to cup her face and look at it with searching eyes.

"For the record," he murmured quietly, "is it a distasteful thought?"

That did shock her. She couldn't imagine any woman finding him distasteful.

"It's not that at all," she said. Her fingers flattened against his shirtfront, feeling the warm strength of his body. "I'm afraid that you'll be disappointed."

His eyebrows shot up. "Why?"

She moved restlessly. "I haven't kissed a lot of people. Well, you keep me too busy," she added defensively when his eyes twinkled.

"So your education has been neglected?" He laughed softly. "I'll teach you how to kiss, Gabby. It isn't hard at all. Just close your eyes and I'll do the rest."

She did, and the first contact with that hard, persuasive mouth made her breath catch. He lifted his head, studying her.

"What was that wild little gasp about?" he asked gently.

Her wide eyes searched his. "You're my boss...."

That seemed to anger him. "For today, I'm a man." His thumbs under her chin coaxed her face up still farther. His head bent, his mouth hovering just above hers. "Relax, will you?" he whispered. "I can hear your bones straining."

She laughed nervously. "I'm trying. You make me feel...stiff. I'm sorry, I'm kind of new at this."

"Stiff how?" He pounced on that, his expression giving nothing away, his eyes narrow and unblinking.

Her lips parted. Her fingers contracted on his shirt-front, her nails biting unconsciously into his chest, and he stiffened. "Now you're doing it too," she whispered.

His face relaxed, and there was a wild kind of relief in his dark eyes. He brushed his mouth over her forehead, her closed eyes. His hands slid behind her head and into the thick hair at her nape, cradling it.

"Gabby," he murmured as he tasted the softness of her cheeks, her forehead, "that stiffness...have you felt it before with anyone?"

It was a casual-sounding question, nothing to alarm her. "No," she murmured. She liked the soft, slow kisses he was pressing against her face. She felt like a child being loved.

"Would you like me to make it worse?"

She opened her dazed eyes to ask what he meant, and his open mouth crushed down on her lips. She gasped softly, letting her eyes close again. His mouth felt odd; it was warm and smoky tasting and very, very expert. Her fingers clung to the fabric of his shirt, twisting it into wrinkles. She stood quite still, her body tense with hunger, feeling the slow persuasion of his mouth grow rougher.

He lifted his mouth away from hers, his face so close that she couldn't see anything but his lips.

"Who taught you that it was impolite to open your mouth when a man kissed it?" he whispered softly.

Her eyes went dazedly up to his dark ones. "Is it?" she whispered back, her voice sounding high-pitched and shaky.

"No," he breathed. His thumb gently tugged on her lower lip, coaxing her mouth open. "I want to taste you, Gabby. I want to touch you...inside..."

She started to tremble at the sensuality of the words and of his touch. His mouth eased hers open and slowly increased its hungry pressure. She felt the tiny bristle of a half day's growth of beard around his mouth and felt the hardness of his tongue slowly, delicately, penetrating her lips.

A tiny moan trembled in her throat.

"Don't be afraid," he whispered, his own voice oddly strained. "It won't hurt."

She did moan then, as the implied intimacy and the penetration all washed over her at once, and she drowned in the sensation of being possessed by him. He tasted of smoke and coffee, and her nails dug into his shoulders. She pressed her body into the hard curve of his and heard him groan.

"No," he said suddenly, pushing her away. He turned, walked off and lit a cigarette.

Gabby clutched her purse to her and stood staring helplessly after him, trembling all over. She'd never dreamed that it would feel like that!

Around them, a group of tourists was just entering the end of the Forum, which they'd had momentarily to themselves. Gabby got a glimpse of colorful clothing and heard murmuring voices as J.D. smoked his cigarette for several long moments before he turned and rejoined her.

"I shouldn't have done that," he said quietly. "I'm sorry."

She was struggling for composure, and it was hard won. "It's all right," she said. "I know you're worried about Martina…"

"Was I looking for comfort, Gabby?" He laughed mirthlessly. His dark eyes swept up and down her slender body.

"I'd rather it was that," she murmured, "than you needing a woman and having me get in the way."

"It wasn't that impersonal, I'm afraid," he said, falling into step beside her. He towered over her. "Gabby, I'll tell you something. I've done it in every conceivable way, with a hell of a lot of women. But up until now, I've never wanted a virgin."

She stopped and looked up at him, puzzled.

He glanced down at her. "That's right," he said. "I want you."

Her face flushed.

"You'll have to remind me at odd intervals that you're a virgin," he continued, smiling faintly. "Because I'm not really out of the habit of taking what I want."

He was angry and frustrated and probably trying to warn her off, she thought. But she wasn't afraid of him. "If you seduce me," she told him, "I'll get pregnant and haunt you."

He stared at her as if he didn't believe his ears. And then he threw back his dark head and laughed like a boy, his white teeth flashing in his dark face.

"Then I'll have to be sure I don't seduce you, won't I?" he teased.

She smiled up at him, feeling oddly secure. "Please."

He drew in a long breath as they walked, sighed and took another drag from his cigarette. "I thought this was all going to be straightforward and simple," he murmured. "Maybe I'd better put you on a plane back to Chicago, little one."

"Cold feet?" she muttered.

"Not me, lady. But you might wish you'd stayed home. I don't know where my mind was when I dragged you over here."

"You said you trusted me."

"I do. Totally. That's why I wanted you with me. The way things are turning out, I'm going to need you more than ever. When we get to my friend's *finca*," he said quietly, "someone has to stay behind to handle communications. We'll have powerful walkie-talkies and we'll need updated information. The *finca* we'll be staying at is only miles from the one where Martina is being held."

She felt uneasy as she studied his hard face. "You're not going in there alone?"

"No—with those old friends I was telling you about."

"Couldn't you stay behind at your friend's finca?"

"Worried about me?" He laughed. "Gabby, I've dodged a lot of bullets in my time. I was in the Special Forces."

"Yes, you told me," she grumbled. "But that was

a long time ago. You're a lawyer now, you sit behind a desk..."

"Not all the time," he said, correcting her. His eyes studied her quietly. "There are a lot of things you don't know about me. About my private life."

"You could get yourself killed."

"A car could hit me while I'm standing here," he countered.

She glared at him. "I'd be without work. One of the unemployed. Everything I'd do for the rest of my life would be horribly boring."

"I'd miss you too, I guess," he agreed, laughing. "Don't worry about me, Gabby. I can take it as it comes."

"Do I even get to meet this man you call Dutch?"

He shook his head. "You'll meet enough odd characters in Central America. And Dutch hates women."

"You aren't Mr. Playboy yourself," she muttered.

"Aren't you glad?" he asked, turning to look at her. "Would you like a man who had a different woman every night?"

The question shocked her. She struggled for an answer, but he'd already opened the door of the rental car and was helping her in.

The rest of the day went by in a haze. She went back to the hotel with him, her eyes full of ruins and Romans and maddening traffic. She had a bouquet of flowers that J.D. had bought from an old woman near the Fountain of Trevi. She couldn't wait to get into her room and press one of the flowers, to keep forever. She buried her nose in them lovingly.

Across the room, J.D. was speaking fluent Italian

with someone on the phone. He hung up and turned back to her.

"I have to go out for a little while," he said. "Lock the door and let no one in, not even room service, until I get back. Okay?"

She studied him quietly. "You won't go getting into trouble while I'm not around to rescue you, will you?" she said, teasing him.

He shook his head. "Not a chance. Watch yourself."

"You too. Oh, Jacob!"

He turned with his hand on the doorknob. "What?"

"Thank you for the flowers."

"They suit you." He studied her face and smiled. "You look like one of them. *Ciao,* Gabby."

And he was gone. She stared at the door for a long time before she went to put her flowers in some water.

Chapter Three

J.D. didn't come back until late that afternoon, and he was strangely taciturn. He shared a silent supper with Gabby and then went out again, telling her tersely to get some sleep. She knew he'd found out something, but whatever it was, he wasn't sharing it. Apparently his trust in her had limits. And that was disappointing. She climbed into bed and slept soundly and without interruption. Part of her had hoped for a nightmare or an earthquake that would bring him running into her room. All her wild fantasies ended with him running into her room and catching her up in his hard arms. She sighed. This was certainly not the trip she'd envisioned. It was turning into a wild tangle of new emotions. A week before, she couldn't have imagined that he would tell her he wanted her.

They flew to Mexico the following morning. Several hours into the flight Gabby shot a worried glance at J.D. He'd hardly moved in his seat since takeoff, and she'd busied herself looking at clouds and reading the emergency instructions and even the label on her jacket out of desperation.

He seemed to sense her searching gaze and turned his head to look down at her. "What's wrong?" he asked softly.

She made an odd little gesture. "I don't know," she said inadequately.

His eyebrows lifted. "I'll take care of you."

"I know that." She let her eyes fall to the vest of his gray suit. "Will we stay in Mexico City?"

"Probably not. We're supposed to be met at the airport." He reached over and took her slender hand in his big one. The contact was warm and wildly disturbing, especially when she felt his thumb moving slowly, sensuously, against her moist palm. "Nervous?" he taunted.

"Oh, no. I always go running off into the dark unafraid," she replied with a grimace. She glanced up. "I come from a long line of idiots."

He smiled at her. It was a shock to realize that he'd smiled more at her in these two days than he had in two months back at the office. Her eyes searched the deep brown of his, and the airplane seemed to disappear. He returned the look, his smile fading. His nostrils flared and the hand holding hers began to move slowly, his fingers probing, easing between hers. It was so sensuous she felt herself tremble. His hand was pressed against hers, palm to palm, fingers tightly interlocked, and when it contracted it was almost an act of possession.

Her lips parted in a soft gasp, and his eyes narrowed.

"Bodies do that," he whispered under his breath, watching her reactions intently. "Just as slowly, just as easily."

"Don't," she protested brokenly, averting her face.

"Gabby," he chided gently, "don't be a child."

She ground her teeth together and struggled for composure. It wasn't easy, because he wouldn't let go of her hand despite her token protest.

"You're out of my league, Mr. Brettman," she said unsteadily, "as I'm sure you know. Don't...don't amuse yourself with me, please."

"I'm not." He sighed and turned sideways so that his head rested against the back of the seat. Then he coaxed her face around to his. "You've never known the kind of men you'll meet when we get where we're going. I thought," he continued, smiling at her stunned look, "that it might be easier for you if we got in a little practice along the way."

"What do you mean? What will we have to do...?" she began nervously.

"I mean, as I told you in Rome, that we'll have to be inseparable for the most part. We have to look as if we can't keep our hands off each other."

She stopped breathing, she knew she did. Her eyes wandered quietly over his face. "Is that why, at the Forum...?"

He hesitated for an instant. "Yes," he said deliberately. "You were far too jumpy with me to be taken for my lover. It has to look convincing to do us any good.''

"I see," she said, fighting to keep her disappointment from showing.

He studied her eyes, her cheeks, and then her mouth. "You have the softest lips, Gabby," he murmured absently. "So full and tempting; and I like the taste of them all too much..." He caught himself and lifted his eyes. "You'd better remind me at intervals that you're off-limits."

She was so aware of him that she tingled, and the thought that he might kiss her again made her go hot all over. She smiled strangely and looked away.

"What was that about, that tiny little smile?" he asked curiously.

"I never used to think of you that way," she confessed without thinking.

"How? As a lover?" he probed.

She lowered her eyes quickly. "Yes," she said shyly.

She felt his long fingers brush her cheek and then her neck, where the pulse was beating wildly.

"Oddly enough, I've hardly thought of you any other way," he said in a deep, gruff whisper.

Her lips opened as she drew a sharp breath, and she looked straight into his eyes. "J.D....?" she whispered uncertainly.

His thumb brushed across her mouth, a tiny whisper of sensation that made her ache in the oddest places. His own breath wasn't quite steady, and he frowned, as if what was happening wasn't something he'd counted on or expected.

His eyes dropped to her parted lips and she heard him catch his breath. In a burst of nervousness, her tongue probed moistly at her dry upper lip and he made a rough sound in his throat. "Gabby, don't do that," he ground out. His thumb pressed hard against her mouth, and his head bent. "Let me…"

In a starburst of sensation, she felt the first tentative brush of his hard lips against her own.

And just as it began, it was suddenly over. The loudspeaker blared out a warning for passengers to fasten their seat belts, and the delicate spell was broken.

J.D. lifted his head reluctantly, his eyes almost black with frustration, his face pale. "The next time," he whispered gruffly, "I'll kiss the breath out of you, the way I wanted to at the Forum."

She couldn't answer him. She was swimming in deep waters, hungry for him in an unexpectedly desperate way. Her hands fumbled with her seat belt and she couldn't look at him. What was happening to them? she wondered, shaken. Just the morning before, they'd been employer and employee. And in a flash, they were something else, something frightening.

His hand caught hers, enfolding it. "Don't, please, be frightened of me," he said under his breath. "I won't hurt you. Not in any way, for any reason."

She glanced at him. "I'm all right," she said. "I'm just…just…"

"Stunned?" he asked wryly. "Join the crowd. It shocked me too."

Her eyes locked on their clasped hands. "But I

thought you kissed me to—how did you put it—make it look better for the men?''

"I did. And to satisfy my own curiosity about you. And yours about me." He tilted her face up to his. "Now we know, don't we?"

"I think I'd be better off not knowing," she muttered.

"Really? At least now you've learned how to kiss."

"You have the diplomacy of a tank!" she shot at him.

He smiled, his teeth white against that olive tan. "You're spunky, Gabby. I'm glad. You're going to need spunk."

His words brought back the reason for their trip, and she frowned. The plane started to descend and she clung to J.D.'s strong fingers, wondering if in a few weeks this would all be nothing more than a memory. He'd said they'd have to seem involved; was this just a practice session? The frown deepened. She realized quite suddenly that she didn't want it to be. She wanted J.D. to kiss the breath out of her, as he'd threatened, and mean it.

They landed in Mexico City, and Gabby's eyes widened as they walked into the terminal. She smiled, dreams of Aztecs and ancient ruins going through her mind—until she remembered poor Martina, and the fact that they weren't here to look at tourist attractions.

She looked at J.D., standing tall and quiet at her side with a smoking cigarette in his hand. He stared slowly around the terminal while Gabby shifted restlessly beside him, their two small carry-on cases beside her.

After what seemed like a long time, J.D. began to smile as a tall, devastatingly attractive man strode toward them. He was wearing a beige suit and leather boots, and he looked debonair and a little dangerous—like J.D.

"Laremos." J.D. grinned as they shook hands.

"Did you think I'd forgotten you?" the other man asked in softly accented English. "You look well, Archer."

Gabby's eyebrows lifted curiously.

"Archer," the man explained, "is the name to which he answered many years ago, during our... acquaintance. You are Gabby Darwin, no?"

"Yes." She nodded. "And you are Señor Laremos?"

"Diego Laremos, *a sus ordenes,*" he said formally, bowing. He grinned. "A dish, Archer."

"Yes, I think so myself," J.D. said casually, smiling at her as he drew her unresisting body close to his side. "Did Dutch phone you?"

The smile faded and Laremos was at once something else, something out of Gabby's experience. "*Sí.* Drago and Semson and Apollo are here now."

"No sweat. How about my equipment?"

"Apollo got it from Dutch," Laremos said, his voice low and intent. "An Uzi and a new AK-47."

J.D. nodded while Gabby tried to decide what in the world they were talking about. "We'll need some RPGs."

"We have two," Laremos said. "And eight blocks

of C-4, rockets for the RPGs, assorted paraphernalia, jungle gear, and plenty of ammo. The border is a massing point for the guerrillas these days—you can get anything if you have the money and the contacts.''

J.D. smiled faintly. ''Dutch said First Shirt has both. You made a smart move when you put him in charge of your ranch security.''

''*Sí*,'' Laremos agreed. ''It is why I survive and many of my neighbors have not. The *finca* above mine was burned to the ground a month ago, and its owner…'' He glanced at Gabby. ''Forgive me, *señorita*. Such talk is not for the ears of women.''

''I don't even understand it,'' she said, studying both men. ''What is an RP… whatever it was? And what do you mean, rockets?''

''I'll tell you all about it later,'' J.D. promised. ''Got the plane?'' he asked Laremos.

The other man nodded. ''We will have to go through customs. I assume you have nothing on you that it would be embarrassing to declare when we land; otherwise you would not have made it through Mexican customs.''

J.D. chuckled. ''Even with you along, I doubt they'd look the other way if I boarded with the Uzi slung around my neck and clips of ammunition hanging out of my pockets.''

Laremos laughed too. ''Doubtless they would not. Come. We are gassed up and ready to go.''

''Uzi?'' Gabby queried as they followed him.

J.D. pulled her against him briefly. ''An Uzi is an Israeli-made weapon. It's classified as a semiautomatic.''

"Did you use one in the Special Forces?"

He laughed softly. "No."

"Then how do you...and why...and what...?"

He bent suddenly and pressed a hard, warm kiss on her startled mouth. "Shut up, Gabby, before you get us into trouble."

As if she could talk at all, after that. Her lips felt as though they'd been branded. If only they'd been alone, and it could have been longer...

Laremos had a twin-engine plane and a pilot to fly it. He settled into one of the comfortable seats in front of Gabby and J.D. and another man, small and young, brought them cups of coffee as the plane headed toward Guatemala City.

"I have told the appropriate people that you and your friend here are visiting me," Laremos said to J.D. and laughed. "It will put you under immediate suspicion I fear, because my past is no secret. But it will spare you the illegality of having to smuggle yourself across the border. I have friends high in government who will help. Oddly enough, the terrorists who have your sister attempted to kidnap me only weeks ago. First Shirt was nearby and armed."

"First Shirt doesn't miss," J.D. recalled.

"Neither did you, my friend, in the old days." Laremos studied the older man unsmilingly.

"How many men are there in the terrorist group?" J.D. asked. "Hard core, Laremos, not the hangers-on who'll cut and run at the first volley."

"About twelve," came the reply. "Maybe twenty more who will, as you say, cut and run. But the twelve are veteran fighters. Very tough, with political ties in a neighboring country. They are just part of an international network, with members in Italy who saw a chance to make some fast money to finance their cause. Your brother-in-law is an important man, and a wealthy one. And the decision to bring your sister here was most certainly devised by one of those twelve. They took over the *finca* only a month ago. I have little doubt that the kidnapping has been planned for some time." He shrugged. "Also, it is known that the Italian authorities have been successful in dealing with this sort of kidnapping. There is less risk here, so they smuggled her out of Italy."

"Roberto is trying to borrow enough to bargain with," J.D. said. "He's determined not to go to the authorities."

"He does not know about you, does he?" Laremos asked quietly.

J.D. shook his head. "I covered my tracks very well."

"You miss it, the old life?"

J.D. sighed. "At times. Not often anymore." He glanced at Gabby absently. "I have other interests now. I was getting too old for it. Too tired."

"For the same reasons, I became an honest man." Laremos laughed. "It is by far the better way." He stretched lazily. "But sometimes I think back and wonder how it would have been. We made good *amigos,* Archer."

"A good team," J.D. agreed. "I hope we still do."

"Have no fear, *amigo.* It is like swimming—one never forgets. And you, do you keep in condition?"

"Constantly. I can't get out of the habit," J.D. said.

"Just as well that I have. Cutting through that jungle won't be any easy march. I've been keeping up with the situation down here, politically and militarily."

"What about this lovely one?" Laremos asked, frowning as he studied Gabby. "Is she a medic?"

"She'll handle communications," J.D. said shortly. "I want her at the ranch with you so that there's no chance she might get in the line of fire."

"I see." Laremos's dark eyes narrowed and he laughed. "Trust still comes hard to you, eh? You will never forget that one time that I let my mind wander..."

"No hard feelings," J.D. said quietly. "But Gabby runs the set."

Laremos nodded, "I understand. And I take no offense. My conscience still nags me about that lapse."

"Will somebody tell me, please, what's going on?" Gabby asked when she could stand it no longer.

"I've gotten together a group to get Martina out," J.D. said patiently. "That's all you need to know."

"The mercs! They're already here?"

"Yes," he murmured, watching her with a tiny smile on his face.

"Ah, I think the line of work of our *amigos* fascinates this one." Laremos grinned handsomely.

"Can I actually talk to them?" Gabby said, persisting, all eyes and curiosity. "Oh, J.D., imagine belonging to a group like that, going all over the world to fight for freedom."

"A lot of them do it for less noble reasons, Gabby," he said, searching her face with an odd intensity. "And you may be disappointed if you're ex-

pecting a band of Hollywood movie stars. There's
nothing glamorous about killing people.''

"Killing...people?''

"What in God's name did you think they did, turn
water hoses on the enemy?'' he asked incredulously.
"Gabby, in war men kill each other. In ways you
wouldn't like to know about.''

"Well, yes, I realize that.'' She frowned. "But it's
a very dangerous way to live, it's...'' She stopped
and searched for words. "Before I came to work for
you I lived a quiet, kind of dull life, J.D.,'' she said,
trying to explain. "Sometimes I thought that I'd probably never do anything more exciting than washing
clothes at the Laundromat. Those men...they've
faced death. They've learned the limits of their courage, they've tested themselves until the secrets are all
gone.'' She looked up. "I don't suppose it makes
sense, but I think I envy them in a way. They've taken
all the veneer off civilization and come away with the
reality of what they are. In a terrible way, they've
seen the face of life without the mask. I never will. I
don't think I really want to. But I'm curious about
people who have.''

He brushed the hair back from her face with a gentle hand. "When you see First Shirt, you won't have
to ask questions. You'll be able to read the answers
in his face. Won't she, Laremos?''

"But indeed.'' He chuckled.

"Is he a friend of yours?'' she asked J.D.

He nodded. "One of the best I ever had.''

"When you were in the Special Forces?'' she
asked.

He turned away. "Of course." He glanced at Laremos, and they exchanged a level gaze that Gabby didn't understand.

"You didn't want mines, did you?" Laremos asked suddenly.

"No. We could have carried in a few Claymores, but they're too much extra weight. The RPGs will be enough, and Drago can jury-rig a mine if he has to. I want to get in and get out fast."

"The rainy season hasn't started, at least," Laremos said. "That will be a bonus."

"Yes, it will. Have you still got my crossbow?"

"Above the mantel in my study." Laremos smiled. "It is a conversation piece."

"To hell with that, does it still work?"

"Yes."

"A crossbow?" Gabby laughed. "Is it an antique?"

J.D. shook his head. "Not quite."

"Is it easier to shoot than a bow and arrow?" she asked, pursuing the subject.

He looked uncomfortable. "It's just a memento," he said. "Gabby, did you pack some jeans and comfortable shoes?"

"Yes, as you saw in Italy." She sighed, beginning to feel uneasy. "How long will we be here?"

"Probably no more than three days, if things go well," he replied. "We need a little time to scout the area and make a plan."

"The hospitality of my *finca* is at your disposal," Laremos said. "Perhaps we might even make time to show Gabby some of the Maya ruins."

Her eyes lit up. "Really?"

"Don't mention archaeological ruins around her, please," J.D. muttered. "She goes crazy."

"Well, I like old things," she retorted. "Why else would I work for you?"

J.D. looked shocked. "Me? Old?"

She studied his face. It wasn't heavily lined, but there was a lot of silver at his temples mingling with his black hair. She frowned. She'd always assumed he was pushing forty, but now she wondered.

"How old are you, J.D.?" she asked.

"Thirty-six."

She gasped.

"Not what you expected?" he asked softly.

"You...seem older."

He nodded. "I imagine so. I've got thirteen years on you."

"You needn't sound so smug," she told him. "When I'm fifty, you'll hate those extra thirteen years."

"Think so?" he murmured, smiling.

She glanced away from that predatory look. "Tell me about Guatemala, Señor Laremos."

"Diego, please," he said, correcting her. "What would you like to know?"

"Anything."

He shrugged. "We have hopes for a better future, *señorita,* now that we have new leadership. But the guerrillas are still fighting the regime, and the *campanisos* are caught in the middle, as always. The warfare is sometimes very cruel. We are primarily an agricultural country, with an economy based on ba-

nanas and coffee. There is a sad lack of the things
your people take for granted. Indoor plumbing, au-
tomobiles, adequate medical facilities—these things
even the poorest of your people can expect, but
here... Did you know, *señorita,* that the life expec-
tancy in my country is only 50 years?"

She looked shocked. "Will things get better? Will
the fighting stop?"

"We hope so. But in the meantime, those who wish
to hold their land must have security. Mine is excellent. But many do not have the financial wherewithal
to hire guards. I have a neighbor who gets government troops to go with him every afternoon to check
his cattle and his holdings. He is afraid to go alone."

"I'll never grumble about paying income taxes
again," Gabby said. "I guess we tend to take it for
granted that we don't have to defend our property
with guns."

"Perhaps someday we will be able to say the same
thing."

Gabby was quiet for the rest of the trip, while J.D.
and Laremos discussed things she couldn't begin to
understand. Military terms. Logistics. She studied her
taciturn employer with new eyes. There was more
than he was telling her. It had something to do with
the past he never discussed, and he was obviously
reluctant to share any of it with her. Trust, again. At
least he trusted her enough to let her handle the communications for this insane rescue attempt. If only
he'd let those men go into the jungle and stay behind
himself. Maybe she could talk him into it. It was a

job for a professional soldier, not a lawyer. She closed her eyes and began to think up things to say, knowing in her heart that J.D. wasn't going to be swayed by any of them.

Chapter Four

Despite Gabby's unvoiced fears, they went through customs with no hitches, and minutes later were met by a man J.D. obviously knew.

The man was short and sandy blond, with a face like a railroad track and a slight figure. He was much older than the other two men, probably nearing fifty. He was wearing jungle fatigues with laced up boots. At his side was a holstered pistol; over his shoulder, a mean-looking rifle.

"Archer!" The short man chuckled, and they embraced roughly. "Damn, but I'm glad to see you, even under the circumstances. No sweat, *amigo*—we'll get Martina out of there. Apollo came like a shot when I told him what was on."

"How are you, First Shirt?" J.D. replied. "You've lost weight, I see."

"Well, I'm not exactly in the right profession for

getting lazy, am I, Boss?'' he asked Laremos, who agreed readily enough.

''Laremos said Apollo and Drago were here, but how about Chen?'' J.D. asked.

The short man sighed. ''He bought it in Lebanon, *amigo*.'' He shrugged. ''That's the way of it.'' His eyes were sad and had a faraway look. ''It was how he'd have wanted it.''

''Tough,'' J.D. said, agreeing. ''Maps and radios, Shirt—we'll need those.''

''All taken care of. Plus about twenty *vaqueros* for backup—the boss's men, and I trained 'em,'' he added with quiet pride.

''That's good enough for me.''

''Shall we get under way?'' Laremos asked, helping Gabby into a large car. He stood back to let J.D. slide in after her. They were joined by First Shirt, who drove, and another man with a rifle.

The topography was interesting. It reminded Gabby of photos of Caribbean islands, very lush and tropical and studded with palm trees. But after they drove for a while, it began to be mountainous. They passed a burned-out shell of what must have been a house, and Gabby shuddered.

''Diego,'' she said quietly, nodding toward the ruin, ''the owners—did they escape?''

''No, *señorita*,'' he said.

She wrapped her arms around herself. J.D., noticing the gesture, pulled her closer. She let her head fall onto his shoulder quite naturally and closed her eyes while the men talked.

Laremos's *finca* was situated in a valley. The house

seemed to be adobe or stucco, with large arches and an airy porch. It was only one story, and it spread out into a garden lush with tropical vegetation. She fell in love with it at first sight.

"You approve?" Laremos smiled, watching her with his dark, lazy eyes. "My father built it many years ago. The servants in the house are the children and grandchildren of those who came here with him, like most of my employees. The big landowners who hold the *fincas* provide employment for many people, and it is not so temporary as jobs in your country. Here the laborers serve the same household for generations."

They'd passed through a small village, and she remembered glimpses of dark-eyed, dark-skinned, barefooted children grouped around a big fountain, where women were drawing water in jugs. The apparent lack of modern conveniences made her grateful for her own life in Chicago.

She hadn't noticed anything unusual about the drive except that the small, dark man beside First Shirt had his rifle in his lap and kept watching the countryside. Now he stood beside the car, rifle ready, while the others went into the house.

It was dark for a moment until her eyes adjusted; then she began to see its interior. There were tiny statuettes, obviously Mayan, along with bowls of cacti, heavy wood furniture, and Indian blankets all around the big living room.

"Coffee?" Laremos asked. He clapped his hands and a small, dark woman about First Shirt's age came running with a smile on her face. *"Café, por favor, Carisa,"* he told the woman in rapid-fire Spanish.

She nodded and rushed away.

"Brandy, Archer?" he asked J.D.

"I don't drink these days," J.D. replied, dropping onto the comfortable sofa beside Gabby. "First Shirt, have you been able to get any intelligence out of the other camp?"

"Enough." The short, sandy-haired man nodded, also refusing the offer of brandy. "She isn't being mistreated, not yet, at least," he said, watching the younger man relax just a little. "They're holding her in the remains of a bunkhouse on a *finca* about six clicks away. They aren't well armed—just some AK-47s and grenades, no heavy stuff. They don't have an RPG-7 between them."

"What is a click? And what's an RPG?" Gabby asked.

"A click is a kilometer. An RPG is a rocket launcher, Russian made," J.D. explained. "It makes big holes in things."

"Like tanks and aircraft and buildings," First Shirt added. "You must be Gabby. I've heard a lot about you."

She was taken aback. Everybody seemed to know about her, but she'd never heard of any of these people. She glanced at J.D.

"So I brag about you a little," he said defensively.

"To everybody but me," she returned. "You never even pat me on the head and tell me I've done a good job."

"Remind me later," he said with a slow smile.

"Could I freshen up?" Gabby asked.

"Of course! Carisa!" Laremos called.

The Latin woman entered with a tray of coffee, and he spoke to her again in Spanish.

"*Sí, señor,*" Carisa murmured.

"I've asked her to show you your room," Laremos explained. "Archer, you might like to take the bags and go with them. Then we can talk."

"Suits me." J.D. picked up the cases and followed Gabby and the serving woman down the hall.

The room had a huge double bed. It was the first thing Gabby noticed, and she felt herself go hot all over, especially when Carisa left and she was alone with J.D.

He closed the door deliberately and watched her fiddle with her cosmetic case as she set it down on the dresser.

"Gabby."

She put down a bottle of makeup and turned.

He moved just in front of her and framed her small face in his hands. "I don't want you out of my sight any more than you have to be. Laremos is charming, but there are things about him you don't know. About all these men."

"Including you, Mr. Brettman?" she asked gently, searching his eyes. "Especially you?"

He drew in a slow breath. "What do you want to know?"

"You were one of them, weren't you, J.D.?" she asked quietly. "They're more than old friends. They're old comrades-in-arms."

"I wondered when you'd guess," he murmured. His eyes darkened. "Does it matter?"

She frowned. "I don't understand. Why should the fact that you served in the Special Forces with them matter?"

He seemed torn between speech and silence. He drew in a breath and rammed his hands in his pockets. "You don't know about the years before you met me, Gabby."

"Nobody does. It has something to do with trust, doesn't it?"

He met her searching green eyes squarely. "Yes. A lot. I've lived by hard rules for a long time. I've trusted no one, because it could have meant my life. These men—First Shirt and Laremos and the rest—I know I can trust them, because under fire they never failed me. Laremos, maybe once—that's one reason I brought you along. Against my better judgment," he added dryly. "I'm still not sure I could live with myself if anything happened to you here."

"And that's why you want me in the same room with you?" she probed delicately.

"Not quite," he admitted, watching her. "I want you in the same room because I've dreamed of holding you in my arms all night. I won't make any blatant passes at you, Gabby, but the feel of you in the bed will light up my darkness in ways I can't explain to you."

She felt her heart hammering. He made it sound wildly erotic, to be held close to that massive body all night long, to go to sleep in his arms. Her breath caught in her throat; her eyes looked up into his and her blood surged in her veins.

His fingers moved down to her throat, stroking it with a deliberately sensuous lightness. "Is your blood running as hot as mine is right now?" he asked under his breath. "Does your body want the feel of mine against it?"

He bent and tilted her face up to his, so that he could watch her expression. His mouth opened as it brushed against hers.

"Stand very still," he whispered, opening her mouth with his. "Very, very still…"

She gasped as his hard, moist lips began to merge with her own. She tasted him, actually tasted the essence of him, as he built the intensity of the kiss. His hands moved down her back, bringing her torso against his and letting her soft breasts crush against the hardness of his chest. His teeth nipped roughly at her mouth as he drew slowly away. His eyes were blazing—fierce and passionate and hungry.

"I like it hard," he said under his breath. "Will I frighten you?"

She barely managed to shake her head before he bent again. This time it was a tempest, not the slight breeze of before. He lifted her in his hard arms and she felt the heat in him as his mouth opened wide. She felt his tongue go inside her mouth in a fencing motion that made her feel hot all over and dragged a smothered moan from her throat.

She was trembling, and her body couldn't seem to get close enough to his. She clung to him, trying to weld herself to him, but before she could move, he was putting her on her feet. His eyes blazed wildly in his pale face.

"No more of that," he said heavily. He freed her abruptly, and the blood rushed back into her upper arms, making her aware of the pressure of his unconscious hold on her. "My God, you were trembling all over."

She felt naked under his glittering gaze. She'd never been vulnerable like that with anyone, but to have it happen with J.D. was terrifying.

"I feel funny," she said with a shaky laugh.

"Do you?" He took a deep breath and drew her head to his shoulder. "I'm sorry. I'm sorry, Gabby. I'm not used to virgins."

"That never happened to me before." She hadn't meant to confess it, but the words came tumbling out involuntarily.

"Yes, I felt that," he murmured. His hands, tangled in her hair, gently drew her closer to him so that her cheek rested against his chest. "Gabby, do you know what I'd like to do? I'd like to take off my shirt and feel your cheek against my skin, your lips on my body…" He groaned and suddenly pushed her away, turning on his heel. He seemed to go rigid, and his hands reached blindly for a cigarette while Gabby stood behind him and ached for what he'd just described.

"How long have we worked together…two years?" he asked in an odd tone. "And we spend two days posing as lovers and this happens. Maybe bringing you along wasn't such a good idea."

"You said you needed me," she reminded him.

He pulled out another cigarette and lit it, handing it to her with an oddly apologetic look. "It will steady you," he said gently. "Gabby, just don't tempt me, all right?"

"Do what?" she asked blankly, looking up at him with dazed eyes.

"Damn!" he growled and then sighed. "Gabby, what I'm trying to say is, let's not get emotional."

"You're the one who's cursing, counselor, not me," she reminded him coldly. "And I didn't start kissing you!"

"You helped," he reminded her, his eyes narrow. "You'd be a joy to initiate."

"I am not sleeping with you!"

His knuckles brushed her mouth, silencing her. "I was teasing. I won't do anything to you that you'll regret, Gabby, that's a promise. No sex."

She swallowed. "You scare me."

"Why?"

"Because of the way you make me feel," she confessed. "I didn't expect it."

"Neither did I. You're a heady wine, honey. One I don't dare drink much of." He lifted his hand to her hair. "You could be habit-forming to a man like me, who's been alone too long."

"Maybe I'd better resign when we get back..." she began, shaken as much by what she was feeling as by what he was telling her.

"No!" he said curtly. His fingers caught the nape of her neck and held on. "No. This is all just a moment out of time, Gabby. It's no reason to start getting panicky. Besides," he added heavily, "there's still

Martina. And God only knows how this will turn out.''

She went icy cold. "Jacob, please don't go with the others.''

"I have to," he said simply.

"You could get killed," she said.

He nodded. "That could happen. But Martina is all I have in the world, the only person I've ever loved. I can't turn my back on her, not now. I could never call myself a man again.''

What could she say to that? He touched her cheek lightly and left her alone in the room. She watched the door close with a sense of utter disaster. It didn't help that she was beginning to understand why she trembled so violently at his touch.

J.D. had always disturbed her, from the very first. But she'd assumed that it was because of the kind of man he was. Now, she didn't know. Just looking at him made her ache. And he'd kissed her...how he'd kissed her! As if he were hungry for her, for her alone.

She shook herself. Probably he just needed a woman and she was handy. He'd said not to get herself involved, and she wasn't going to. Just because she was all excited at the prospect of being part of a covert operation, that was no reason to go overboard for J.D.

She wondered at the way he'd reacted when she'd asked if he had been one of the group before. Didn't he remember that he'd told her he'd served in the Special Forces?

It was fifteen minutes before she rejoined the men,

wearing jeans and a loose pullover top and boots. J.D. studied her long and hard, his eyes clearly approving the modest gear.

She stared back at him. He seemed like a different man, sitting there in jungle fatigues and holding some small weapon in his big hands.

"The Uzi," he told her when she approached and stared at the miniature machine gun curiously. "It holds a thirty-shot magazine."

"And what's that?" she asked, nodding toward a nasty-looking oversize rifle with a long torpedo-like thing on a stick near it.

"An RPG-7 rocket launcher."

"Is that Gabby?" a short black man asked, grinning at her.

"That's Gabby." J.D. chuckled. "Honey, this is Drago, one of the best explosives men this side of nuclear war. And over in the corner, being antisocial, is Apollo. He's the scrounger. What we need, he gets."

She nodded toward the corner, where a second black man stood. That one was tall and slender, whereas Drago was chunky.

"Hey, Gabby," Apollo said without looking up.

"Does everybody know my name?" she burst out, exasperated.

"Afraid so," First Shirt volunteered, laughing. "Didn't you know Archer was a blabbermouth?"

She stared at her boss. "Well, I sure do now," she exclaimed.

"Come here, Gabby, and let me show you how to work the radio," Laremos offered, starting to rise.

"My job," J.D. said in a tone of voice that made Laremos sit back down.

"But of course." Laremos grinned, not offended at all.

Gabby followed the big man out of the room to the communications room, where Laremos had a computer and several radios.

"J.D...." she began.

He closed the door and glared down at her. "He hurt a woman once. Badly. Can you read between the lines, or are you naïve enough that I have to spell it out in words of one syllable?"

She drew in a steadying breath. "I'm sorry, J.D. You'll just have to make allowances for my stupidity. I'm a small-town Texas girl. Where I come from, men are different."

"Yes, I know. You aren't used to this kind of group."

She looked up. "No. But they seem to be nice people. J.D., it just dawned on me that you must trust me a lot to bring me here," she murmured.

"There isn't anyone I trust more," he said in a deep, rough tone. "Didn't you know?"

He stared into her eyes until she felt the trembling come back, and something wild darkened his own before he turned away and got it under control.

"We'd better get to it," he said tautly. "And when we go back out there, for God's sake, don't say or do anything to encourage Laremos, you understand? He's a friend of mine, but I'd kill him in a second if he touched you."

The violence in him made her eyes widen with

shock. He glanced at her, his face hard, and she knew she was seeing the man without the mask for the first time. He looked as ruthless as any one of those men in the other room and she realized with a start that he was.

"I'm territorial," he said gruffly. "What I have, I hold, and for the duration of this trip, you belong to me. Enough said?"

"Enough said, Jacob," she replied, her voice unconsciously soft.

His face tautened. "I'd like to hear you say my name in bed, Gabby," he breathed, moving close. "I'd like to hear you scream it..."

"Jacob!" she gasped as he bent and took her mouth.

She moaned helplessly as he folded her into his tall, powerful form, letting her feel for the first time the involuntary rigidity of his body in desire.

He lifted his lips from hers and looked into her wide eyes, and he nodded. "Yes, it happens to me just as it happens to other men," he said in a rough tone. "Are you shocked? Haven't you ever been this close to a hungry man?"

"No, Jacob, I haven't," she managed unsteadily.

That seemed to calm him a little, but his eyes were still stormy. He let her move away, just enough to satisfy her modesty.

"Are you frightened?" he asked.

"You're very strong," she said, searching his face. "I know you wouldn't force me, but what if...?"

"I've had a lot of practice at curbing my appetites, Gabby," he murmured. He brushed the hair away from her cheeks. "I won't lose my head, even with you.

"Let me show you," he whispered, and she felt his mouth beside hers, touching, moving away, teasing, until she turned her head just a fraction of an inch and opened it to the slow, sweet possession of his lips.

She could barely breathe, and it was heaven as his arms came around her, as his mouth spoke to her in a wild, nonverbal way. The opening of the door was a shattering disappointment.

"Excuse me"—Laremos chuckled—"but you were so long, I thought you might be having trouble."

"I am," J.D. said in a voice husky with emotion, "but not the kind you thought."

"As I see. Here, let me go over the sequence with you and discuss the frequencies—they are different from the ones you are familiar with, no doubt," he said, sitting down in front of the equipment.

Gabby brushed back her hair and tried not to look at J.D. She tried not to think about the long night ahead, when she'd lie in his arms in that big bed and have to keep from begging him to do what they both wanted.

The radio wasn't difficult at all. It took only minutes to learn the routine. It was the code words that took longest. She made a list and walked around the house memorizing it while the men talked in the spacious living room. At the dinner table, she was still going over it.

Only Laremos, J.D., and Gabby ate together at the table. The others carried their plates away.

"They're still antisocial, I see," J.D. murmured over his food.

"Old habits." Laremos glanced at Gabby. "And I think they do not want to disillusion this one, who looks at them with such soft eyes."

"I didn't embarrass them, did I?" she asked, contrite.

"No," J.D. said. "I think you flattered them. They aren't used to all that rapt attention." He chuckled.

"How did they come to be mercenaries?" she asked softly. "If you can tell me, I mean. I don't want to invade anyone's privacy."

"Well, Shirt was in the Special Forces, like I was," J.D. said, pausing over the sentence, as if he was choosing his words carefully. "After he got out of the service, he couldn't find anything he liked to do except police work, and he wasn't making enough to pay the bills. He had a contact in the mercenary network and he asked some questions. He was good with the standard underworld weapons and something of a small-arms expert. He found work."

"And Apollo?"

"Apollo started out as an M.P. He was accused of a crime he didn't commit, and there were some racial overtones." J.D. shrugged. "He wasn't getting any justice, so he ran for it and wound up in Central America. He's been down here ever since."

"He can't clear himself?" she asked.

"I expect I'll end up defending him one of these days," he told her with a quiet smile. "In fact, I can almost guarantee it. I'll win, too."

"I wouldn't doubt that," she murmured, tongue in cheek.

"How long have you worked with this bad-tempered one, Señorita Gabby?" Laremos asked.

"A little over two years," she told him, glancing at J.D. "It's been an education. I've learned that if you shout loudly enough, you can get most anything you want."

"He shouts at you?"

"I wouldn't dare," J.D. murmured with a grin. "The first time I tried, she heaved a paperweight at my head."

"I did not," she protested. "I threw it at your door!"

"Which I opened at the wrong time," he continued. "Fortunately, I have good reflexes."

"You will need them tomorrow, I fear," Laremos told him. "The terrorists will not make things easy for us."

"True," J.D. said as he finished his coffee. "But we have the element of surprise on our side."

"That is so."

"And now, we'd better go over the maps again. I want to be sure I know the terrain before we set out in the morning."

Gabby went on to bed, feeling definitely in the way. She took a quick bath and settled in on one side of the big double bed, wearing the long, very modest nightgown she'd brought along. Unfortunately, the material was thin, but perhaps J.D. would be too busy with his thoughts to notice.

She lay there trying to stumble through a Guate-

malan newspaper, but she couldn't concentrate. She
tingled all over, thinking of the long night ahead, of
spending it lying in J.D.'s arms. Had he really meant
that? Or had it just been something to tease her with?
And what if he did hold her in his arms all night—
would she be able to resist tempting him beyond his
control?

She tossed the newspaper onto the floor and
wrapped her arms around her knees, staring apprehensively at the door. Her long hair hung softly
around her shoulders, and she brushed strands of it
away from her face. She wanted him. There was no
use denying that she did. But if she gave in, if she
tempted him too far, what would she have? One single night to remember, and it would be the end of her
job. J.D. didn't want any kind of permanent relationship with a woman, and she'd do well to keep her
head. He was worried about his sister, justifiably nervous about tomorrow's foray into the jungle, and he
might do something insane if she pushed him.

But for just a moment she thought how it would
be, to feel his hair-roughened skin against every inch
of her, to let him touch her as he'd no doubt touched
other women. She sighed huskily. He'd be gentle, she
knew that, and patient. He'd make of it such a tender
initiation that it would surpass her wildest dreams of
belonging to a man. But it would cheapen what she
was beginning to feel for him, and it would do no
good for his opinion of her. She attracted him because
she was a virgin, untouched. And if she gave herself
to him, she wouldn't be that anymore. It was even

possible that he'd hold her in contempt for joining the ranks of his lovers.

With a weary moan, she turned out the light and burrowed under the covers. It was a lovely dream, anyway, she told herself, and closed her eyes.

She hadn't meant to go to sleep so soon, but the first thing she knew the dawn light was streaming in through the windows, bringing her wide awake.

Sleepily she stretched, and became suddenly aware of where she was. She sat up, eyes wide, and looked around for J.D. It took only a second to find him. He was standing at the window, his profile to her, looking out. And he didn't have a stitch of clothing on his body.

Her eyes were riveted on him. She'd seen men without clothes. These days, with all the explicit films, it was impossible to avoid nudity. But she'd never seen a nude man close up, like this. And she imagined that J.D. would please even the eyes of an experienced woman.

He was all powerful muscle, with dark shadows of hair feathering every inch of him. His legs were long and muscular, his hips narrow, his stomach flat. His chest was broad and bronzed and a wedge of thick black hair curled over it. She stared at him helplessly, unashamedly—until she happened to look up and saw him watching her.

Her lips trembled as she tried to speak, but she couldn't get anything out.

"It's all right," he said quietly. "If I'd found you in the same condition, I'd be staring just as hard. There's nothing to be embarrassed about.

"I don't wear pajamas," he murmured with an amused look. "I expected to be awake before you were. It was a hot night."

"Yes," she managed, choking.

He moved back toward the bed, and she sat there frozen, unable to make even the pretense of looking the other way. It didn't seem to bother him at all. He bent down, catching her by the arms, and dragged her out of the bed and against his body.

He laughed deep in his throat, the sound of it predatory, primitive. "Touch me," he dared her. His hands caught hers and ran them over his sleek hips, up his spine, and around to the matted tangle of hair over his warm chest.

Her breath was trapped somewhere beneath her ribs, and her fingers burrowed into the crisp hair over his heart.

"Yes, you like it, don't you?" he asked in a voice like rough velvet, his eyes narrow and black and hot on her face. "But not half as much as I do. I've dreamed about this, night after endless night, about how your hands would feel touching me. What do I look like to those innocent eyes, Gabby? Do I frighten you...please you? Which?"

She was drunk with the feel of him, the smell of him. Her hands roamed over his chest, his rib cage. With a long sigh she leaned her forehead on his collarbone. "You please me," she whispered. "Can't you tell? Oh, Jacob...!" Her hands pressed harder, more urgently. "Jacob, I want to do such shameless things."

"Such as?" he asked in a whisper. "Such as,

Gabby?'' He covered her hands with his own and she felt their faint tremor. ''I won't hurt you. Do whatever you want to do.''

It wasn't fair that he should have such power over her, she thought dazedly. She was too intoxicated, too hungry, to listen to the cool voice of reason. Her hands smoothed over his chest, around his back, and with an instinct she didn't even know she had, her mouth opened and pressed against the center of his chest.

He groaned harshly, shocking her. She lifted wide, curious eyes to his.

''I like it,'' he whispered huskily. ''Do it again.''

She moved closer, and his hands caught her head, guiding her mouth to the places he wanted it, while the silence lengthened and grew around them and J.D.'s breath came raggedly and in gasps. She learned so much about him all at once. That she drove him wild when she rubbed her cheek across his taut nipples, that he liked the curl of her tongue around the tangled hair. That she could nip him gently with her teeth and make him go rigid. That he wanted her badly enough to tremble.

''This isn't fair, Jacob,'' she whispered shakily, ''I'm making you miserable, I'm…''

His thumb pressed across her mouth. His face looked strained, but his eyes were blazing. ''I want it,'' he whispered roughly.

''But I'm hurting you,'' she said achingly.

''Such a sweet hurt,'' he whispered, bending. ''So sweet, so beautiful…let me make you ache like this,

Gabby. I won't seduce you, I promise I won't, but let me touch you..."

His hand moved between them and lightly touched her breast. The gown was thin, and his fingers were warm, and the sudden intimacy was shocking and pleasurable, all at once.

She gasped and instinctively caught his fingers. He lifted his head and looked down, and he smiled.

"Habit?" he whispered.

Her fingers lingered on his hairy wrist. "I...I haven't ever let..." she began.

"You'll let me." His face nuzzled hers, his cheek rubbed gently against hers and he found her mouth, cherishing it with a whispery soft pressure that was wildly exciting.

And all the while, his fingers were shaping, probing, lightly brushing until they caused a helpless reaction in her body. He drew the gown tightly around her breasts and lifted his head.

"Look," he said softly, directing her eyes down to the rigid peaks outlined under the gown. "Do you know what it means, what your body tells me when that happens?"

Her lips opened as she tried to breathe. "It means...that I want you," she whispered back.

"Yes." He brushed her lips apart with his, tracing the line of them with his tongue. His teeth caught her upper one and nibbled gently, tugging it, smiling as she reached up to do the same thing to his.

"Jacob," she whispered. Her hands crept around his neck. "Jacob..." She arched and pressed herself to him, and froze, shocked at what his taut body was telling hers.

"Body language," he whispered, coaxing her mouth open again. "Now listen. I'm going to strip you out of that gown and hold you to me, just for a second, and then I'm going to get the hell out of here before I go crazy. I don't know what we'll be walking into today. I want one perfect memory to take with me, you understand?"

She did. Because it was just dawning on her that she was in love with him. Why else would she be doing this?

She felt his hands unbuttoning the garment and she looked up because she wanted to see his face, she wanted to remember always the expression on it. In case anything happened...

He eased the gown off her shoulders and she felt it suddenly drop to the floor. She felt the whisper of the breeze against her bare skin. J.D.'s eyes blazed as he looked down at her body. And then he drew her to him, and she felt herself go rigid all over.

"I won't live long enough to forget how this feels," he whispered. "Now kiss me, one last time."

And she did, with all her heart and soul, without a single inhibition. And her arms held him and they fused together in a silence gone mad with tangible hunger.

He groaned as if he were being tortured and his arms hurt her, his lips hurt, his tongue thrust into her mouth in a deliciously fierce invasion. Finally he drew back, shaking, and put her from him.

He bent, picked up the nightgown, and gently drew it back on her without a single word.

"Worth dying for," he whispered, studying her luminous eyes, her swollen mouth, her flushed cheeks. "God, you're sweet."

"Jacob, don't go out there," she pleaded.

"I have to." He bent and retrieved his clothes from a chair where he must have flung them the night before and began to dress.

"But you're a lawyer," she persisted. She wiped away a tear and sat down heavily on the side of the bed, her green eyes wide and frightened. "You aren't a soldier."

"But I was, honey," he said as he tugged on his jungle fatigues. He turned, buttoning the shirt, his eyes dark and mysterious as they searched hers. "You still haven't worked it out, have you, Gabby?"

"Worked what out?"

He tucked in the shirt. "I served only three years in the Special Forces. I joined when I was eighteen."

She was trying to do mathematics with a mind still drugged by pleasure. "You were twenty-one when you got out."

"Yes. But I didn't start studying for my degree until I was twenty-five."

She stared at him, uncomprehending. "That means...you did something else with those four years."

"Yes." He met her searching gaze levelly. "I was a mercenary. I led First Shirt and the others for the better part of four years, in some of the nastiest little uprisings in the civilized world."

Chapter Five

Gabby stared at him as if she'd never seen him before. J.D., a mercenary? One of those men who hired out to fight wars, who risked their lives daily?

"Are you shocked, honey?" he asked, his eyes searching, his stance challenging.

Her lips parted. "I never realized...you said you served with them, but I never realized...I thought you meant in the Special Forces."

"I was going to let you go on thinking that, too," he said. "But maybe it's better to get it out into the open."

Her eyes went over him, looking for scars, for changes. She'd noticed the tiny white lines on his stomach and chest, partially hidden by the hair, but until now it hadn't dawned on her what they were.

"You have scars," she began hesitantly.

"A hell of a lot of them," he said. "Do you want to hear it all, Gabby?"

"Yes."

He rammed his hands into his pockets and went to stare out of the window, as if it was easier to talk when he didn't look at her. "I stayed in the service because it meant I made enough to keep Martina in a boarding school. We had no relatives, you see. Mama was gone." He shrugged. "But when I got out of the service, I couldn't get a job that paid enough to get Martina through school. I wasn't trained for much except combat." He fumbled in his pocket for a cigarette and lit it. "I thought I'd given this up until the kidnapping," he said absently, holding the cigarette to his lips. He drew in and blew out a cloud of smoke. "Well, Shirt was recruiting, and he knew I was in trouble. He offered me a job. I took it. I spent the next four years globe-trotting with my crossbow and my Uzi. I made money, and I put it in foreign banks. But I got too confident and too careless, and I got shot to pieces."

She held her breath, waiting for him to continue.

"I spent weeks in a hospital. My lungs collapsed from shrapnel and they thought I was going to die. But I lived through it. When I got out, I realized that there was only one way I could go from there, and it was straight downhill. So I told Shirt I was quitting." He laughed mirthlessly. "But first I went on one last mission, just to prove to myself that I still had the guts. And I came out of that one without a scratch. I came back to the States afterward. I figured that someday the guys I'd served with might need a lawyer, and I needed a profession. So I got a job and went to school at night.''

"You aren't a fugitive?" she asked.

"No. In one or two countries, perhaps, if I were recognized. But not in the States." He turned, studying her through narrowed eyes. "That's why I guard my past so meticulously, Gabby. And it's why I don't like reporters. I'm not ashamed of the old life. But I don't like being reminded of it too often."

"Do you miss it?" she asked, probing gently.

He sighed. "Yes. Part of me does. Life is so precious when you've touched death, Gabby. You become alive in a way I can't explain to you. Life is pretty damned tame afterward."

"This is why you came after Martina, isn't it, Jacob?" she asked, fitting the puzzle pieces together. "Because you knew that you and the group could succeed where a larger group might fail."

"We're the only chance she has, honey," he said quietly. "In Italy I might have stayed out of it. But down here...the government has its hands full just trying to keep the economy from failing, and there are other factions fighting for control as well. Besides all that, damn it, she's my sister. She's all I've got."

That hurt. He might want Gabby, but he didn't care about her. He'd made that perfectly clear. She lowered her eyes to the skirt of her nightgown.

"Yes, I can understand that," she said in a subdued tone.

"I had a long talk with Laremos last night," he said. "I told him that if he touched you, I'd kill him. You'll be safe here."

Her head jerked up. "I'm not afraid for myself," she said. "Only for you and the others."

"We're a good team," he said. "The way you and I have been for the past two years. Do you want to quit now, Gabby? Are you disillusioned?"

He sounded coldly sarcastic. He lifted the cigarette to his lips with a short laugh.

"Are you firing me?" she threw back, angered by the unexpected and unwarranted attack.

"No. If you leave, it's up to you."

"I'll think about it," she said.

He crushed out his cigarette in an ashtray. "You'd better get dressed. I want to go over those codes with you one last time before we get under way."

"Yes, of course," she murmured. She got up and went to find her clothes. Before she could turn around, the door opened and he'd gone out.

She got dressed and sat down on the bed and cried. To go from dream to nightmare in such a short space of time was anguish. And the worst thing was that she didn't even know what had happened.

It didn't matter to her that he'd been a soldier of fortune, she thought miserably. How could it, when she loved him?

Loved him. Her eyes pictured him, dark and solemn and strong, and a surge of warmth swept over her like fire. She would have followed him through that jungle on her knees without a single complaint. But despite his obvious hunger for her, he didn't want anything emotional between them. He'd pretty well spelled that out for her. Martina was the only person on earth he loved or would love, and he'd said so.

What he felt for Gabby was purely physical, something he couldn't help. She was a virgin and she excited him. He wanted her, but that was all. And he could have had her that morning, without a protest on her part. He must have known it too. But he hadn't taken her, because he was strong. He didn't want her getting involved with him, so he'd told her all about his past.

That was the final blow, that he'd shared his past with her, only to put a wall between them. She hid her face in her hands and tried to hold back the tears. How was she going to manage to work with him day after day now, when he couldn't help but see how she felt?

But that wasn't the worst of it. He was going out into the jungle after kidnappers who could kill him. Her heart froze in her chest. She couldn't stop him. All she could do was sit there and pray for him.

All the pleas in the world wouldn't hold him back, not when Martina's life hung in the balance. If there was a chance of any kind, he would take it. But if he died…oh, God, if he died, there would be nothing of worth left in Gabby's life. Tears welled up in her soft green eyes as she tried to imagine a world without him. She wanted to go with him, to risk her life at his side, to die with him if that was what lay in store. But even as she thought it, she knew that nothing would convince him to take her along. He might not love her, but he was fiercely protective of her. He wouldn't allow her to risk her life. And she couldn't fight him.

With a resigned sigh, she got up, combed her hair,

and went into the living room where the men were assembled. It took the last ounce of courage she possessed to smile at them. She couldn't meet J.D.'s searching gaze at all. It would cut her to the quick to see indifference in his eyes.

There was a new face in the room. It belonged to a dark, lithe man with pale blue eyes.

"Semson," J.D. told her, indicating the newcomer. "He's been out scouting for the past day or so."

"Gabby?" the new man murmured and grinned at her. "How do you stand working for this dude?"

She smiled wanly. "Oh, it has its moments," she confessed, but she didn't look at J.D. as she said it.

J.D. had picked up an automatic weapon something like a machine gun and slung it over his shoulder, but he was carrying the crossbow. Gabby stared pointedly at it and suddenly realized what it was for.

She looked up, and he seemed to read the thought in her mind.

He nodded. "Sentries," he said, confirming her suspicions. "If there are any."

She felt her throat go dry. She'd never been in a situation like this, and she could have kicked herself for coming along. It was one thing to watch an operation like this in a fictional TV show. But to realize that any one of these men, especially J.D., might never come back from the rescue attempt...that was altogether different.

"Hey, Gabby, don't look so grim," Apollo chided. "I won't let this big turkey get himself hurt."

Gabby laughed despite herself. "Thanks, Apollo," she said. "I've gotten kind of used to him."

"That works both ways. Laremos, take care of her," J.D. told the other man.

Laremos nodded. "Be assured that I will. Now, shall we double-check our coordinates and codes?"

They did, and Gabby felt her palms sweating as she rattled off the codes from memory. She knew how important they were, and that made her more nervous than ever.

"Calm down," J.D. said quietly. "You're okay."

She smiled for him. "Sure. You guys take it easy out there, okay?"

"We're sort of used to this kind of thing," First Shirt said with a wink. "Okay, guys. Hit it."

And just that quickly, they left. Gabby stood at the front door with her wide, unblinking gaze riveted on J.D.'s broad back. He didn't turn or say anything to her. It hurt terribly.

"How long will it take them to get there, Diego?" she asked the man at her side.

"At least an hour or two, Gabby," he replied. "The terrain is rugged, and they require much stealth."

She glanced up to see that his eyes were concerned. "Are you worried?"

"Of course not," he said, but he was lying and she knew it. His smile didn't reach his eyes.

"I'll get a cup of coffee, if I may, and sit beside the receiver."

He studied her closely. "Archer—you care very much for him."

"Yes," she said simply.

"Will you believe me if I tell you that of all the

men I have known, he is the most capable under fire?" he said gently. "I have seen him come back from the grave. And their opponents have traveled far, *señorita,* and are already decimated in numbers. They will not expect such an attack here. We have seen to it that their intelligence is distorted."

"But what if something goes wrong?" she burst out.

He sighed. "Then it is in the hands of God, is it not?"

She thought about that for the next three hours, pacing and sweating and worried out of her mind.

"Shouldn't we have heard something?" she asked finally, her face contorted with fear.

Laremos frowned. "It is rugged terrain," he reiterated.

"Yes, but...listen!"

The radio broke its silence, and Gabby made a dive for it. She gave the correct identification and waited.

"Panther to Red Rover," J.D.'s voice said curtly. "Bravo. Tango in ten. Out."

She keyed the mike. "Red Rover here. Alpha. Omega. Out."

The code words meant that the group had arrived undetected and would make their play in ten minutes. She'd radioed back that the message was understood and that there was no new intelligence to convey.

She looked up at Laremos, feeling her heart go wild as she realized how close the danger was. "Ten minutes," she said.

"The waiting is the hardest, is it not?" he asked

quietly. "I will have Carisa fix us another pot of coffee."

He strode away, and Gabby prayed and chewed her nails and stared at the microphone as if it held the key to salvation.

Long, agonizing minutes later, the static came again. "Panther to Red Rover," J.D. said tightly, as gunfire and an explosion of some sort sounded in the background. "Charlie Tango! Heat up the coffee. Out!"

Her fingers trembled as she returned, "Red Rover to Panther. Bravo. Omega. Out!"

She'd just signed off when Laremos came tearing into the room, eyes flashing.

"Raise them quickly! One of my men just reported that he's sighted a large guerrilla force moving toward Archer's position!"

She grabbed the mike. "Red Rover to Panther. Red Rover to Panther. Come in, Panther!"

But there was no answer. Frantically she tried again and again, and still there was no answer. Her frightened eyes went to Laremos.

"They must be under fire," he said heavily, "or they would answer. We can only pray that they spot the newcomers in time."

She stared at the mike, hating it. Her cold fingers keyed it again, and again she gave the message. There was no answer.

Her mind went wild. J.D., answer me, she pleaded silently. I can't lose you now, I can't!

As if he heard her, somewhere miles away, the radio blared. "Red Rover, we're cut off by guerrillas, lots of them," J.D. said sharply. "Going into the jungle coordinates two clicks from position Delta. Gabby, get the hell out of there, they're heading in your direction...!"

The radio went dead. Gabby stared at it helplessly and then at Laremos.

"Madre de Dios," he breathed. "I should have realized...Carisa!" he yelled. A stream of Spanish followed, and Laremos grabbed one of the weapons J.D. had called an AK-47. He thrust it into Gabby's numbed fingers.

"Carry it. I will teach you to use it when I must," he said curtly. "Come, there is no time. Aquilas!" he yelled, and the short man who'd driven in from the airport with them came running in. There was another stream of Spanish.

"My men will cover us," Laremos said curtly. "We must hurry. The guerrillas will not care who are terrorists and who are not, they will cut us down regardless. Aquilas says the government troops are not too far behind. But we cannot involve them." His wary eyes sought hers. "You understand?"

"Because of the rescue," she said, smiling wanly. "It's all right, *señor*. Just, please, get me to J.D."

He looked at her searchingly. "I understand. But do not underestimate the group, *señorita*. We were once...quite something."

He led her out of the house, and together they headed quickly into the jungle. She carried the heavy weapon with no real sense of its weight and no earthly idea of how to use it. As she followed Laremos through dense undergrowth at a breakneck pace, she wondered what her mother back home in Lytle, Texas, would think if she knew where her only daughter was.

"Quick, get down," Laremos hissed, pushing her under the dense foliage and cautioning her to be quiet.

She froze, her heart pounding painfully in her chest. She felt weak all over. What would happen if they were seen? She couldn't fire the weapon, she didn't know how! Her eyes felt as if they were going to pop out of her head, and she wished she were with J.D. Laremos would do his best, but if she had to die, she wanted to be with Jacob when it happened. Her eyes closed and she prayed silently while sweat poured down her cheeks.

There was a wild thrashing nearby, and she had a glimpse of ragged-looking men with rifles, wearing some sort of soldiers' garb. She knew without being told that they were the guerrillas Laremos had spoken about. They were muttering among themselves, but they didn't seem to be looking for anyone. They were joking and laughing, their weapons hung over their shoulders as they trailed through the jungle.

Gabby bit almost through her lower lip as she studied the weapons they were carrying. She could feel terror in her throat, strangling her. What if they were spotted? There were worse things than being killed, especially for a woman, and she remembered what she'd read about this part of the world. Her eyes closed. The bravery she'd thought she had was nowhere to be found.

It seemed to take forever for the men to march out of sight and finally out of earshot.

"Courage," Laremos whispered. "We will wait just another minute and then proceed."

"We can't go back to your *finca?*" she whispered back, hating her own cowardice.

He shook his head. "This is only a small part of the main force. Unless I am badly mistaken, the rest are camped at my *finca.*" He shrugged. "The government troops will come and drive them out. But for the meantime, we have little choice. We either try to join our comrades or risk being killed."

"I'm much too young to die," she told him with a quiet smile. "How do I shoot this thing if I have to?"

He showed her, quickly and efficiently, and she felt a little more secure as they started out again. But her eyes darted every which way, and she was so afraid that she could taste the fear in her mouth. Death seemed to lurk behind every tree.

She was learning something about courage. It wasn't being unafraid. It was being stubborn.

It was slow going. Laremos had a pedometer, a compass, and a map, and he was using all three. They had been walking for over an hour when suddenly gunfire erupted all around them.

"Oh, my God," Gabby squealed, dropping down with her hands over her head, the AK-47 falling to the ground.

"Don't panic," Laremos said tautly as he came down beside her. "Listen."

She heard bullets whizzing, but Laremos was grinning!

"What...?" she tried to ask, gathering enough

courage to grab her weapon and hold onto it with cold fingers.

"The Uzi," he whispered. "I know the sound, oh, so well, *señorita*," he said with a grin. He moved behind a tree and peered out into the jungle. All at once, he stood up. "Archer!" he yelled. "Here!"

Then there was a flurry of wild movement, crashing sounds, gunfire, and explosions, and in the middle of it came J.D., with a small, dark-haired woman under one arm and the Uzi under the other. Around him, Shirt and Apollo and Semson and Drago were covering each other and firing on the run as they joined Laremos and Gabby.

"Martina, Gabby," J.D. said as he piled in with them and let go of his sister. "Okay, honey?" he asked Gabby with a quick glance.

"Fine, now," she whispered shakily, clutching the weapon.

"They're right on our tails," J.D. said. "Apollo, got any of that C-4 left?" he yelled.

"Working on it right now, big man," came the reply. "Just enough to make a big splash. We'll have to draw them in."

"Tell me when," J.D. called back.

"The guerrillas have taken my *finca*," Laremos said. "We barely escaped in time."

"I'm sorry about that," J.D. said as he reloaded the small automatic weapon.

"Are you both all right?" Gabby asked J.D. in a quavering voice as she crawled over to Martina and clutched the frightened woman's hand.

"A few scratches, but we'll make it," he returned,

but his eyes were fierce and tormented as they searched Gabby's face. "How about you?"

"I'm learning to be a crack shot," she replied with a nervous laugh. "Laremos even told me how to cock this thing."

"If you have to fire it," J.D. said intently, "be sure you brace it hard against your shoulder so that the recoil doesn't break a bone. Take a breath, let half of it out, and squeeze the trigger, don't jerk it."

"I'll be a natural," Gabby told him, but she was trembling.

"I wish I could help," Martina whispered shakily. "But I'm so tired...!"

"God knows you've reason to be," J.D. said. He ruffled her hair. "But you're a trooper, Sis."

She managed a smile for him. "Like my big brother. I knew you'd come, I knew you would. Thank God for your Special Forces training." Martina added with a laugh, "But however did you find these other men?"

J.D. and Gabby exchanged a quiet look. "I hired them," he said blandly. "Roberto can reimburse me."

"My poor darling." Martina sighed. "He'll be so frantic."

"How are we going to get out of here?" Gabby asked J.D.

"Wait and see." He glanced toward Apollo. "Ready?" he called.

"Ready!"

"I'm going to draw them out for you. Don't let me down!"

"J.D., no!" Gabby burst out as he leaped out of the brush and started firing toward rustling noises in the undergrowth ahead.

She lost her mind. Afterward it was the only explanation she could come up with. The guerrillas came forward in a rush, and suddenly Gabby was on her feet. She saw a sniper taking dead aim at J.D.; she turned and lifted the heavy weapon and sighted it and pulled the trigger.

It was a miracle that she even hit the guerrilla's shoulder, her aim was so wide. But she did, and with terror she realized that the man had taken aim at her and was about to fire.

"Gabby!" J.D. yelled wildly.

Simultaneously she pulled the trigger again, forgetting to brace the gun in her terror. She was knocked to the ground when she fired. There was a burst of gunfire and, suddenly, a huge, horrible explosion that rocked the ground.

"All right, let's hit it!" First Shirt yelled out.

J.D. dragged Gabby to her feet, and his face showed such terrible fury that she closed her eyes. He didn't even speak. He jerked the gun out of her hands and pushed her ahead of him as he bent to lift Martina to her feet.

"Are you all right, *señorita?*" Laremos asked gently as he joined Gabby.

"My shoulder hurts a little, but I'm...I'm fine," she whispered. She started to turn around, to look behind them, but J.D. was suddenly there.

"Don't look," he said in a tone that dared her to argue. "Get moving."

He was a stranger now, a man she'd never known. His face was like stone, and there was something wild and dangerous in his eyes and in the set of his big body. She didn't say another word. She kept quiet all the long way through the jungle.

"Where are we going?" she finally asked Laremos as they kept moving through the endless jungle.

"In a circle, around my *finca*," he told her. "We have hopes that by now the government troops have rounded up the guerrillas. Apollo has gone in to check."

"So quickly?" she asked, brushing back a strand of matted hair from her sweaty face.

"So quickly," he confirmed. "Your shoulder, it is better?"

"A little bruised, that's all," she said. She felt sick to her stomach. All she wanted was to lie down and forget the past two days altogether.

"I'm so tired," Martina murmured. "Can't we rest?"

"Soon," J.D. said, gently now. "Just a little longer, honey."

"Okay, big brother. I'll trudge along. Gabby, are you holding up okay?"

"Yes, thanks, Martina."

There was a sudden crackling sound and J.D. and the others whirled with their guns leveled as Apollo came leaping through the growth, grinning.

"We're clear!" he shouted. "The government troops just marched the guerrillas away."

"What about the men in the terrorist camp?" Gabby asked.

"They scattered," First Shirt replied. "The guerrillas would have shot them if they'd found them before the government troops showed up. The terrorists have no friends here in Guatemala."

"How sad for them," Martina said, but her eyes flashed. "I do not pity them, not after the ordeal they put me through. Oh, I want my Roberto!"

"We'll send for him the minute we get to my *finca*," Laremos promised her. "The very minute."

Gabby dropped back to put a comforting arm around the smaller, older woman and smiled reassuringly. "It won't be long," she said.

"Absolutely," Laremos agreed. "There. We are home."

The *finca* looked so good that Gabby wanted to kiss it. The outside bore no marks of violence, but inside it was a different story. The furniture was wrecked, the floors scarred. Laremos's dark eyes glittered as he saw the evidence of the brief guerrilla occupation.

"I'm sorry about your house, *señor*," Martina said gently.

"*Señora*, that you are safe is the most important thing," Laremos said with pride, turning to bow in her direction. "My poor house can be repaired. But your life, once lost, would not have been restored."

"I owe you a great debt," Martina said. Her clothes were torn and her hair hung in wild strands. But she looked spunky for all that. She reached up and kissed Laremos on his tan cheek. "*Muchas gracias.*"

Laremos looked embarrassed. "My pleasure, *señora*. I regret that I could not have done more."

"Is everybody all right?" Gabby asked, looking around at the battle-scarred little group with concerned eyes.

"Gabby, you'll spoil us if you worry about us," Apollo said, chuckling.

"Not me." First Shirt glowered at Apollo. "Worry all you want, Gabby. I'll just sit here like a sponge and soak it up."

The others joined in, all except J.D. He kept to himself, looking dangerous and unapproachable until Martina and Gabby left to go up to the room Gabby had shared with him.

"A bath." Martina sighed, taking advantage of the facilities. "I feel so dirty!"

"It must have been horrible," Gabby said, digging out fresh clothes.

"Not as horrible as it could have been. I wasn't abused, at least. That surprised me." She came out of the shower minutes later, toweling her long hair dry. "Your turn. I imagine you feel as mucky as I did."

"Yes, I do." Gabby laughed. "My shoulder hurts and I feel shaky all over."

"You saved J.D.'s life," was Martina's quiet comment. "I can never thank you enough for that. But don't expect him to," she added dryly. "I think his pride's dented. He's very quiet."

"He's been through a lot. They all have. What a great bunch of guys," she said fervently.

"Tell me!" Martina laughed, and despite the weariness in her drawn face, there was joy. "I'd like to kiss every one of them twice. I can't tell you how I felt when I saw J.D. come breaking in that door! Wasn't it lucky that he had that military training?''

Obviously Martina didn't know everything about J.D.'s past, and Gabby wasn't about to betray him. "It sure was," she agreed and disappeared into the bathroom.

Her shoulder was turning blue, but she was grateful to be alive. She still couldn't believe what she'd done. It had been pure instinct when she saw the weapon pointing at J.D. Let him be angry at her—she couldn't be sorry about what she'd done. Even if the man had shot her, it would have been worth it to deflect his aim. If anything had happened to J.D., she might as well have died. She loved him—so much!

The next day, Roberto drove in from the airport and there was a wildly emotional reunion. Gabby, watching, couldn't help the twinge of jealousy she felt. Roberto was crying as he embraced his wife, and unashamedly at that. Gabby's eyes darted to J.D., who hadn't said a single word to her since they'd come out of the jungle. They'd all had a good night's sleep, Martina and Gabby sharing the big double bed this time, but his dark mood hadn't lifted. He wouldn't even look at Gabby, and that hurt most of all. She'd only wanted to save him, but it seemed that she'd committed some unforgivable sin.

Chapter Six

Roberto was very Italian, if someone who lived in Sicily could be called Italian, Gabby mused. He was of medium height and thin, with a charm that was immediately apparent when he bent over Gabby's hand.

"It is a pleasure to meet you," he said. He grinned, glancing at J.D., who was talking quietly with Apollo in the living room. "Martina's brother mentions you often."

"Does he?" Gabby asked conversationally, privately wondering whether she even had a job to go back to, now that it was all over. J.D. still hadn't looked in her direction.

"It was bad, Gabby," Martina said from her husband's side, her dark eyes meeting the other girl's green ones warmly. "Jacob and the others...well, it was a miracle that any of us got out. He'll get over it. It has been a long time since he was in the service, you know. It had to affect him.''

"Yes, of course," Gabby said, smiling faintly. She couldn't let Martina know the truth. "You look awfully good for somebody who went through what you did.''

Martina clung to her husband's arm and smiled. "I have my whole world back again. I feel good. Just a little shaken and homesick." She glanced up at Roberto. "Can we go back today?"

He inclined his head. "As soon as our pilot finishes the meal Laremos was kind enough to provide.''

"It will be good to have familiar things around me." Martina sighed. "But I do not think I ever want to go shopping alone again." She shuddered. "From now on, my husband, I will listen when you warn me against such things.''

"I had feared that it would happen," Roberto confessed, with a glance at the men scattered around the living room. "Thank God your brother and his friends knew so well what to do. I am sure that the kidnappers would never have let you live." He pulled her into his arms and held her convulsively, his eyes closed, his face contorted. "*Dio*, I could not have lived myself!" he whispered hoarsely.

"Shh," Martina said, comforting him and smiling. She clung to him, and Gabby could only imagine how if felt to be loved so possessively. She experienced a twinge of envy, because nobody had ever cared for her that way. J.D. surely hadn't. He looked as if he were frankly sick of the whole thing, especially Gabby.

"You had better spend a little time with Jacob while you can," Roberto said, releasing Martina. "It may be another year before we see him again." He smiled. "Hopefully, the next time will be under happier circumstances."

"Oh, yes," Martina said wholeheartedly. "Gabby, you must come to Palermo with him next time and visit. Our villa overlooks the sea, and it is so beautiful."

"I'd like that," Gabby said noncommittally. She was thinking that J.D. would probably never take her as far as the corner again, but she didn't say it.

Martina approached her brother, and as J.D. stood up Gabby got a glimpse of his face. It softened magically for his sister. When he smiled at her it was like the sun coming out. Gabby couldn't bear the contrast between the way he'd looked at her in the jungle and the way he looked at his sister. She turned and went toward the bedroom to finish packing.

Later, as she was folding clothes, Martina tapped at the door and entered the room quietly, smiling sheepishly.

"I hate to ask, but do you have some makeup I could borrow?" J.D.'s sister asked. "I feel like a hag."

"Yes, of course, I do," Gabby said quickly, taking her cosmetic case from the dresser. "I didn't bring much, though," she said apologetically as she handed it over, along with a brush. "I kind of figured that we weren't going to be going places that I'd need to dress for."

"Thank you," Martina said and seated herself in

front of the mirror. "There!" she exclaimed, smiling ruefully at her face. "Such pleasure, from such a mundane thing," she murmured. "Gabby, there were times when I thought I'd never live long enough to do this again."

"It must have been awful," the taller girl said quietly. "I'm so sorry, Martina."

"My own stupidity," came the reply. "Roberto warned me, but I take after Jacob, I'm afraid. I'm bullheaded and I like my own way." She sat down on the bed and studied Gabby for a long moment. "He will not speak to you, and that hurts, doesn't it?"

Gabby shrugged, taking a long time to fold a T-shirt. "A little."

"If you could only have seen his face in that split second before the recoil threw you to the ground," Martina said solemnly. "It would have been a revelation to you. In all the years of my life, I can only recall once or twice when I've seen that expression in his eyes. Once," she added quietly, "was just after our mother died."

Gabby stared at the pale garment in her hand. "I was so afraid for him," she confided. "I saw that man level his rifle at Jacob, and..." She shivered. "It all happened so quickly."

"Yes, I know." Martina stood up. "Gabby, he isn't an easy man. And he's been very restless the past few years. But I think perhaps in you he has found his future. Did you know," she added with a wicked grin, "that you're all I hear about when he calls me these days?"

Gabby laughed nervously, desperate even for crumbs. Her green eyes glowed softly as she looked at Martina. "I'd give anything to be his future," she said quietly. "But he's already said he doesn't want ties or commitment. And I'm dreadfully old-fashioned. Everybody else sleeps around and thinks nothing of it, but I'm just not built for loose affairs."

Martina pursed her lips and then grinned. "Well, well. Poor Jacob."

"Anyway," Gabby said, sighing, "it's probably just a flash in the pan. I've worked for him over two years and he's never looked twice at me until this came up." She glanced at Martina and smiled. "I'm just so glad that you came out of it all right. We were all worried about you, not just J.D."

"Roberto and I must go home today," Martina said. "But you will come and visit us one day. I believe that, even if you don't." Impulsively, she hugged Gabby. "Take care of Jacob for me. He doesn't know that he needs taking care of, so we mustn't let on. But he's so alone, Gabby."

Gabby felt as if she were choking. "Yes," she said. "I know." And it hurt to think just how alone he was, and how much it affected her.

Later, as she wandered around the house restlessly, she met First Shirt coming down the hall, and he stopped to talk to her. "Why the long face, little lady?" he asked with an affectionate smile.

"Work is going to seem like peeling onions from now on," she lied, smiling impishly at him.

He laughed heartily. "Now you know why the guys and I don't retire. Hell, I'd rather die on my feet than deteriorate behind a desk.'' He shrugged. ''But it seems to suit Archer.''

Her eyes fell. ''Yes, I suppose so.''

''Hey.''

She looked up, and he smiled at her.

''He doesn't like being helped out,'' he said knowingly. ''I ought to know. He threw a punch at me one time when I spotted a guy with a grenade and got to him first. He doesn't like making mistakes. He'll get over what happened out there.''

''Will he?'' she asked, her eyes wide and sad. ''He won't even talk to me.''

''Reaction. You have to remember, Gabby, he's been out of action for a while. This sort of thing''— he waved his hand—''you don't forget, but sometimes it brings back bad memories. He got shot up pretty bad once.''

''He told me,'' she said absently.

His eyes narrowed. ''Now, that's interesting.''

''Just to satisfy my curiosity,'' she added.

''I used to wonder if he was ever going to settle down,'' he said enigmatically. ''But there was never a special woman.''

''I suppose he liked leaving his doors open,'' she murmured, ''in case he couldn't adjust to a desk job.''

''Yes, that's what I thought,'' First Shirt said. His chest rose and fell on a deep breath. ''None of us have ties. They're too much of a luxury in this kind of work.'' He searched her wide eyes. ''I'm glad our paths crossed. Take care of Archer. He's gone too far to come back to us, but maybe he doesn't realize it yet.''

"I wish you were right, First Shirt," she said with a sad smile.

"My name—my given name—is Matthew."

She smiled. "Matthew."

"Keep in touch once in a while, will you?" he asked as he turned. "Archer's a damned bad correspondent."

"I'll do that," she promised, flattered.

Her eyes followed his lean figure down the hall. She was already thinking about Christmas. Socks, she decided. Lots of socks and gloves. She started back toward the bedroom.

It was deathly quiet after Martina and Roberto left, and one by one the men seemed to vanish. Later she learned that everybody except First Shirt had already left the country for other places, just as secretively as they'd come. She'd grown attached to them in that short space of time. Of course, the circumstances were unusual, to say the least.

Laremos was his charming self at the evening meal, but J.D. was still brooding and he wouldn't look at Gabby.

"When are we going back?" she asked J.D. finally, in desperation.

"Tonight." He bit the words off.

"I'll double-check to make sure I've packed everything." She stood up. "Señor Laremos, thank you for your hospitality. Under different circumstances, it would have been lovely. I'm sorry we didn't get to see the Mayan ruins."

"So am I, Gabby," he said sincerely. "Perhaps you may return someday, and it will be my pleasure to show them to you." He made her a handsome bow and she smiled at him as she left the room.

Minutes later, J.D. joined her, presumably to get his own things packed. He had slept downstairs with the men the night before, but his case was still in the bedroom. Gabby had considered packing for him, but she was nervous about antagonizing him any more.

She looked up from her suitcase when he closed the door. His face was still hard as granite, and his eyes glanced off hers coldly. He didn't say a word as he began to fill the small bag on the chair across from the bed.

"Are you all right?' she asked finally, when the silence became uncomfortable.

"Yes, I'm all right," he said gruffly. "Are you?"

She shrugged and smiled wanly. "It was the experience of a lifetime."

"Wasn't it, though?" he asked curtly. His eyes blazed as he studied her flushed face.

"Why are you so angry?" she asked.

He dropped his eyes to the bag and shoved his combat fatigues into it. "What makes you think I am?"

"You've barely spoken to me since we came back." She moved around the bed to stand beside him, her emotions in turmoil, her mind confused. She looked at his big body and remembered with staggering clarity how it looked without clothing, how it felt to be held by those hard arms and kissed by that mouth.

"Jacob, what have I done?" she asked softly, and touched his arm.

His hard muscles tensed beneath her touch, and when he looked down at her she had to fight the urge to back away.

"What the hell did you think you were playing at out there?" he asked coldly. "Didn't you realize that the bullets weren't blanks, that we weren't acting out some scenario from a television show? You're a dull little secretary, not a professional soldier, and if the force of the recoil hadn't knocked you down, you'd have been killed, you stupid child!"

So that was it. Shirt had been right, his pride was hurt because Gabby had seen a threat and he hadn't. "J.D., if I hadn't shot him, he'd have killed you," she said, trying to reason with him.

He slammed the bag back down. "Am I supposed to thank you?"

Her temper was blazing now too. "Don't strain yourself," she told him icily. "And I am not a dull little secretary!"

"Don't kid yourself," he said, staring at her. "You aren't Calamity Jane and you're never likely to be. You'll get married to some desk jockey and have a dozen kids."

Her face paled and his eyes narrowed when he saw it. "What's wrong, honey?" he taunted. "Were you expecting a proposal from me?"

She turned away. "I expect nothing from you."

"Liar." He caught her arm roughly and swung her around. Seconds later, she was flat on her back on the bed and he was looming over her, holding her down with hands that hurt.

"Jacob, you're bruising me!" she burst out, struggling.

He threw a long, powerful leg across hers and spread-eagled her, his hands on her wrists. "Now fight," he said coldly, "and see how far you get."

She gave up finally and lay breathing heavily, glaring up at him. "What's this supposed to prove, that you're stronger than I am? Okay, I'm not arguing."

His dark eyes wandered slowly over her body, lingering on the curves outlined by her tight jeans and the expanse of bare skin where her sweatshirt had ridden up during the struggle. Her breath caught, because she wasn't wearing a bra, and the hem of the garment was just below the curve of her breasts.

"I wanted you yesterday morning," he said bluntly. "And if you hadn't been a virgin, I'd have taken you. But any woman would have done. You were just a body to me, so if you've been weaving me into your future, forget it."

Her heart leapt in her chest. It was true, she had, but she couldn't let him see just how involved she was emotionally. Very obviously, that wasn't what he wanted from her.

"I haven't asked you for any promises, have I?" she asked quietly, searching his dark eyes. "You're safe, Jacob. I'm not trying to tie you down."

His fingers contracted. "Let's make sure of that, shall we?" he asked in a menacing tone. "Let's make damned sure that you don't ever want to try."

Her lips parted to ask the question, but he moved suddenly. One hand imprisoned both of hers above her head. The other pulled up the sweatshirt, baring her taut breasts to his eyes.

"Now, Gabby, let me show you how a real mercenary treats women."

He did, and she couldn't fight, because he was so much stronger than she was. She lay still, feeling half-afraid of him as he treated her body like a piece of used merchandise. He shamed her, humiliated her, covering her with his own taut body, while his hands touched and gripped and his body moved suggestively, making a travesty of everything she felt for him.

"Do you like it?" he growled against her bruised mouth as his hands moved lower on her pinned body and contracted, grinding her hips against his. "Because this is how it would be if I took you. Quick and rough and purely for my own pleasure. And if you're remembering yesterday morning, don't," he added. "Because that was a flash in the pan. This is the reality. This, and this…!"

He hurt her, and the crush of his mouth was as suggestive as the motion of his hard body. She tried to struggle away from him, but that only made it worse. He forced her arms down into the mattress and his body overwhelmed hers in an intimacy that made her gasp.

He laughed coldly. "Are you shocked? You wanted it yesterday. Come on, honey. I won't let you get pregnant. How about it?" And he kissed her again, cruelly, oblivious to the tears of shame and humiliation running hotly down her cheeks as he whispered graphic, crude remarks before his mouth forced hers open and penetrated it.

When he finally tired of the game and rolled away, she couldn't even move. She lay there, bruised and emotionally devastated, her face pale, her eyes closed. Tears ran in a flood down her cheeks and her body shook with sobs.

"Damn you, J.D.," she wept, flushed with fury. "Damn you!"

"That's how I am with a woman," he said coldly, ignoring the trembling of her body, the terrible hurt in her eyes. "That's how it would have been yesterday if I'd had the time and I could have coaxed you into it. Your body arouses me and I want it. But anything would have done. I just needed to forget what was ahead, the same way I've forgotten it a hundred times before with a hundred other women." His voice was bitter and he turned away. "So set your sights on some other man, and don't weave romantic daydreams around me. I've just shown you the reality. Remember it."

She didn't move. She couldn't. She was trembling too much, and she felt sick and empty. Her eyes looked up into his, bright with furious anger. Something of her pain and shame must have shown in them, because he turned away and, grabbing up his suitcase, went to the door without another glance.

"Bring your bag and let's go," he said in a harsh tone.

She watched him close the door and then she managed to get to her feet. His taunting voice would haunt her as long as she lived. She would resign, of course, but she didn't know how she was going to manage to look at him while she worked out a two-week notice. Maybe he'd let her go immediately. The only problem was that she didn't have another job to go to. Her rent and car payments wouldn't wait while she went without work.

Minutes later, wearing a fresh green pullover blouse with a matching sweater and the same jeans, and with her hair carefully pulled back in a bun, she left the bedroom, her suitcase in hand. She was still pale, but makeup had camouflaged the rest of what J.D. had done to her.

He didn't even glance in her direction as she came back into the living room. Apparently, he'd shut her out of his mind already, and she wished she had the ability to do the same with him. The scars his brutality had left on her emotions would be a long time healing. She'd loved him. How could he hurt her that way? How could he?

She tried to disguise her anguish and hoped that she succeeded. She said goodbye to Laremos and got into the station wagon with First Shirt while J.D. said his own farewells.

Shirt gave her a brief but thorough scrutiny and laid one lean, wiry hand over the steering wheel. "What did he do to you?" he asked.

She lifted a startled face. "Why...nothing."

"Don't lie," he said gently. "I've known him a long time. Are you okay?"

She shifted restlessly in the seat, refusing to let her eyes go past Shirt to J.D., who was standing apart with Laremos. "Yes, I'm okay," she said. "Of course, I'll be a lot better once I get out of his life."

"Whew." He whistled ruefully. "That bad?"

"That bad." She gripped her purse tightly in her lap.

"Gabby," he said gently, with a tiny smile, "have you ever known a fighting fish to lie down when he hit the bait? Don't expect to draw him in without a little effort."

She glared at him. "I'd like to put a hook in him, but not to land him."

"Give it a little time," he said. "He's been alone most of his life. It's new to him, needing someone."

"He doesn't need me," she said shortly.

"I'm not convinced of that," he replied. He studied her affectionately. "I think he's met his match. You're a pretty damned good shot for a lady who's never used an automatic weapon before. Laremos said you learned fast."

She pursed her lips, studying her purse. "It wasn't a hard weapon to learn," she told him. "There were only three positions to remember with the change lever—top for safety, middle for bursts and bottom for single shots. And actually, I have shot a .22-caliber rifle before. Mama and I used to hunt rabbits. But it didn't have a kick like that AK-47."

He smiled as she rubbed her shoulder. "I don't imagine so. Is your mother still alive?"

She nodded, smiling back. "She lives in Lytle, Texas. There's a small ranch, and she has a few head of cattle. It's not nearly as big as the one she and

Daddy had, but when he died, she decided to retire. Sort of.''

"And she hunts?" he asked.

"Hunts, rides, ropes, and can outcuss most veteran cowboys," she told him. "She's quite a character."

"You're a character yourself," he said. "When J.D. told me he took you along on secret meetings, I began to realize that he had an unusual relationship with you. J.D. doesn't trust anybody except his sister and me."

That wasn't bragging, either, she realized. Just a statement of fact. "He doesn't trust Laremos."

"Neither do I," he whispered, smiling.

She burst out laughing, but the amusement faded immediately as J.D. started toward the car, and she felt herself freezing up. But she needn't have worried. J.D. climbed into the back seat and slammed the door, waving to Laremos.

"Be back in a few hours, Boss," Shirt called to him. Laremos grinned and waved, and they were under way.

It was a long trip to the airport, not because of distance but because of the tension between Gabby and J.D. Despite First Shirt's efforts to keep things casual, Gabby drew into herself and didn't say a word all the way.

It was like that during the flight back as well. Gabby was relieved to find that their seats were not together. She was sandwiched between a businessman and a young girl. J.D.'s seat was farther back. Not one word had passed between them when they landed at O'Hare airport in the wee hours of the morning.

It took her a long time to find a place in the swollen ranks of departing passengers. She didn't look back to see where J.D. was either. Her only thought was to get back to her apartment. After that she'd face the thought of leaving J.D. forever, of finding another job and getting on with her life.

At last she reached the front of the terminal and stepped out into the breezy night air that carried the sound of distant car horns and city smells that had become so familiar. There was no cab in sight, but Gabby wasn't daunted. She'd just call one.

"Come on," J.D. said tersely, appearing just behind her. "I'll drive you."

She glared at him. "I'd rather be mugged."

"You might be, at this hour, alone," he said matter-of-factly. "What's the matter, afraid of me?" he taunted.

She was; he'd made her afraid. But she was too proud to let him see how much.

After a minute, she turned and followed him toward the parking lot. A little later, they were winding their way back into Chicago.

"Have you decided what you're going to do?" he asked.

She knew instinctively what he meant. "Yes. I'm going to try to find a job in the computer field. I like working with them."

He glanced toward her. "I thought you enjoyed legal work. It's too bad, to let that paralegal training go to waste."

"I'm tired of legal work," she said noncommittally. What she meant was that she couldn't take the risk of running into J.D. accidentally after she'd quit. It would be too painful.

He shrugged and calmly lit a cigarette as he drove. "It's your life. You'd better call that agency Monday morning and have them send over some applicants. I'll let Dick do the interviewing this time," he added with a cold laugh.

Her fingers clenched on her purse. She stared out of the window at the river.

"No comment?" he prodded.

"About what?" she asked indifferently.

He sighed heavily and took another draw from the cigarette. One more turn and he pulled the car into a parking spot in front of her apartment building.

She got out and waited for him to get her carry-on bag. "Don't bother walking me up," she said.

He glared down at her. "I wasn't aware that I'd offered."

Her anger exploded. "I hate you," she said in a venomous whisper.

"Yes, I know you do," he said with a cold smile.

She whirled on her heel and started toward the door of the building.

"Gabby," he called curtly.

She stopped with her hand on the door, but didn't turn. "What?"

"You'll work a two-week notice. Every day of it. Or I'll make sure you don't work again. Clear?"

She'd been thinking about not showing up at all on Monday. But when she turned and saw his eyes, she realized, not for the first time, what a formidable adversary he made. She hated to give in, but the necessity of finding a new job made her do so gracefully.

"Why, Mr. Brettman, I wouldn't miss a minute of it," she said with sweet mockery. "See you Monday."

Chapter Seven

The last thing she felt like doing Monday morning was going into the office. To make things worse, her shoulder was aching like mad. But that didn't stop Gabby. She put on a beige suit with a jazzy, multi-colored blouse, pinned up her hair, and went to work. Might as well get it over with, she told herself. She'd go back to the office, work out her notice, and get another job. Sure. Simple.

Explaining that to her mother back home in Lytle, Texas, had not been quite so simple.

"But I thought you loved your job!" her mother had gasped. "Why are you quitting? Listen, Gabby, what's happened?"

"Nothing, Mama," she'd said quickly. "It's just that Mr. Brettman may not be in Chicago much longer." She lied on impulse. "You see, he has prospects in another area, and I don't really want to re-locate.''

"Where would he go?"

"Now, Mama," she said, "you know I don't like to pry into Mr. Brettman's business."

"That Mr. Dice, his partner, why couldn't you still work for him?" her mother demanded gruffly. "Better yet, why don't you come home and get married?"

Gabby chewed on her lip so that she wouldn't say anything hasty. She had visions of her mother providing a groom, a minister, and a loaded gun for motivation. It made her want to giggle, which would have infuriated her mother.

"Gabby, you aren't in trouble?" her mother had added in a strange tone.

"No, Mama, I'm not in trouble. Now don't get upset. It may all fall through anyway."

"I like Mr. Brettman," her mother said roughly. "That one time I met him when I visited you, he seemed like a nice man to me. Why does he want to move anyway? He isn't getting married?"

"J.D.? Get married?" Gabby laughed mirthlessly. "That would make the world record books."

"He'll have to get married someday," came the curt reply.

"Think so?" Already Gabby could picture him in fatigues rushing some stronghold with Shirt and Apollo. But she couldn't tell her mother that!

"Of course. It happens to everybody. He'll get tired of living alone someday. Your father did. That's when I nabbed him." Gabby could almost see her grin.

"Are you tired of living alone?" Gabby asked suddenly. It had been ten years since her father's death. Yet her mother didn't even date.

"I don't live alone, baby. I live with my memories. I had the best man God ever made. I don't want second best."

"You're just fussy," Gabby said accusingly.

"Yes, I am. You be fussy too. Honey, think about coming home. That Chicago place is pretty big, and if Mr. Brettman isn't going to be around, I'd worry about you."

"I'll think about it," Gabby promised.

She hated thinking about it. It made her face the fact that she wouldn't be seeing J.D. again. Whether or not he went back to the old life, he'd made it impossible for her to work for him anymore. He'd forced her into resigning, whether consciously or unconsciously. And now here she was losing her boss, her job, and her heart all in the space of three days. So little time to change so much of her future. It might have been better if she'd stayed behind and never known the truth about J.D.

When she got to the office, it was clear that J.D. had not yet come in. Richard Dice was sitting on her desk with his arms folded across his chest, looking murderous.

"Morning, Dick," she said with a forced smile.

"Thank God you're back." He sighed. "That temporary girl didn't work out, and the agency hasn't called me about a replacement. Where's J.D.?"

"Don't ask me," she replied, calmly shedding her jacket and putting her purse in the desk drawer. She tucked her glasses on top of her head while she searched through the calendar for appointments that had been made by both the temporary girl and herself.

"Didn't he come back?" Dick persisted.

"Yes." She stared at him. "You mean he hasn't been in touch with you?"

"Not yet. Well?" he burst out. "What happened? How's Martina? Did they pay the ransom?"

"You're chock-full of questions." She sighed in turn. "Yes, Martina's safe. No, they didn't have to pay the ransom. And anything else you want to know, ask J.D., because I don't want to talk about it."

Dick looked at the ceiling. "You disappear for days, and all I get is one long-winded sentence?"

"You should have come with us," she said conversationally. "Then you wouldn't have to take up my time asking questions. Did you take care of Mrs. Turnbull's divorce yesterday?"

"Yes," he murmured absently. "Judge Amherst called. He wants to discuss the Landers case with J.D. before he makes a decision about the trial date."

Gabby made a note of it.

Dick was studying her closely. "You look bad."

She smiled. "Thank you. What a lovely thing to be told."

He flushed. "I mean, you look worn out."

"You try crawling through a jungle on your belly with an AK-47 and see how you look," she replied.

"Jungle? On your belly? What's an AK-47?"

She got up from her desk and started filing some folders that Dick had left there. "Ask J.D."

"But he isn't here!"

She glowered at the file folders. "Maybe he's out buying a new crossbow," she muttered.

"A what?" But she didn't hear him. He grumbled something and walked into his office, slamming the door behind him. She glanced over her shoulder. "Well, somebody's in a snit," she said to the filing cabinet.

It was a good two hours before J.D. came in, looking as neat as a pin in his vested gray suit.

"Any messages?" he asked Gabby, just as he used to.

"No, sir," she replied, and she sounded the same too, except that she wouldn't meet his eyes. "Dick took care of the Turnbull case for you, and Judge Amherst wants you to call him."

He nodded. "What have I got on the calendar for this afternoon?"

"Mr. Parker is coming by at one to get you to draw up that incorporation for him, and you have three other appointments after him."

He turned toward his office. "Get your pen and pad and let's get the correspondence out of the way."

"Yes, sir."

"Oh, there you are, J.D.," Richard called from the doorway of his own office. "Welcome back. Would you tell me what happened? Gabby's got a case of the clams."

"So have I," J.D. informed him. "Everything's okay. Martina and Roberto are back in Palermo by now, and the kidnappers were taken care of. How about lunch?"

"Sorry," Richard said, smiling. "I've got a luncheon appointment with a client. Rain check?"

"Sure."

Gabby followed J.D. into the office and left the door open. If he noticed, or cared, he didn't let on. He eased his formidable frame into the big swivel chair behind the desk and picked up a handful of letters.

He started dictating and she kept her eyes on her pad until he finished. Her fingers ached and so did her back from sitting so straight, but she didn't move an inch until he dismissed her.

"Gabby," he called as she started toward the door.

"Yes, sir?"

He fingered a pencil on his desk, and his dark eyes stared at it. "How's your shoulder?" he asked.

She shrugged. "It's still a little sore, but I can't complain." She clasped the pad tightly against her breasts. She studied his impassive face quietly. "By the way, do you need written notice, or is a verbal one satisfactory?"

His eyes came up. "Wait," he said quietly.

"I have to get another job. I can't do that if I'm obligated to you for more than two weeks," she said with remarkable calm.

His jaw clenched. "You don't have to quit."

"Like hell I don't!" she returned.

"Things will get back to normal!" he roared. "Is it too much to ask you to give it a chance? We got along well enough before!"

"Yes, we did, before you treated me like a streetwalker!" she burst out.

He saw the hatred in her eyes, in her rigid posture. His gaze fell to the pencil again. "You won't be easy to replace," he said in an odd tone.

"Sure I will," she said venomously. "All you have to do is call the agency and ask for somebody stupid and naïve who won't get too close and loves being shot at!"

His face paled. "Gabby..."

"What's going on?" Richard asked from the open door. He looked aghast. He'd never heard Gabby raise her voice in the two years he'd known her, and here she stood yelling at J.D. at the top of her lungs.

"None of your business," they chimed in together, glaring at him.

He hunched his thin shoulders and grinned sheepishly. "Excuse me, I feel a sudden urge to eat lunch. Goodbye!"

They didn't even notice his leaving. J.D. glared at Gabby, and she glared back.

"I'm too set in my ways to break in somebody new," he said finally. "And you'd be bored to death working for anybody else and you know it."

"It's my life," she reminded him.

He got up from the desk and she backed away, her eyes wide and angry and afraid. The fear was what stopped him in his tracks.

"I wasn't going to make a grab for you, Miss Darwin."

"Shall I drop to my knees and give thanks?" she asked, glaring back. "You'll never make the list of the ten top lovers, that's for sure."

"No, I don't imagine so," he said quietly. "But I

didn't realize how much I'd frightened you." He studied her closely. "Gabby, I never meant to go that far."

"I wasn't going to try to drag you in front of a minister," she said, lowering her voice. "I was curious about you, just as you were curious about me. It's over now. I don't want ties either."

"Don't leave," he said quietly. "I'll never touch you again."

"That isn't the point," she told him, shifting restlessly from one foot to the other. "I...I don't want to work for you anymore."

His dark eyes searched hers slowly, quietly. "Why?"

That was rich. Was she going to tell him that her heart would break if she had to work with him day in and day out, loving him hopelessly, eating her heart out for him? That was what would happen too. She'd go on mooning over him and never be able to date anybody else. Worse, she'd sit cringing as the days went by, wondering when he would throw it all in and rush back to First Shirt and Apollo. Now that he'd gotten a taste of the old, free life again, she had to expect that it would happen.

"There's no job security here," she said finally, putting her nameless fears into mundane words that couldn't possibly express her real feelings.

He drew a cigarette from his pocket and lit it, staring at her through the smoke. "You're guessing that I'll go back to the old life?" he asked coldly.

She shook her head. "No, J.D.—anticipating. Shirt said that you had the bug again," she confided. "I want a dull, routine employer who won't go rushing off to save the world at a minute's notice."

His jaw tightened. "It's my life. How I live it is my business."

"But of course," she said with a sickeningly sweet smile. "That's exactly what I meant. Out of sight, out of mind."

That made him angry. His dark eyes glittered as he scowled at her. "After what we shared in that room at Laremos's house?" he asked bluntly.

Her eyes narrowed. "Perhaps we're thinking of different things," she retorted. "I have a very vivid memory of being treated like the worst kind of Saturday-night pickup!"

He turned away and went to the window, his back rigid. "There were reasons."

"Of course there were!" she shot back. "You wanted to make sure that I didn't get any ideas about you just because you made a pass at me. Okay! I got the message and I'm going, just as fast as I can!" she said. "Do you really think I could forget what happened in Guatemala and go on working for you?"

He studied the cigarette in his fingers. "Maybe I'll settle down," he said after a minute.

"Maybe you will, but what concern is that of mine?" she asked. "You're my employer, not my lover."

He turned just as the phone on her desk rang. She rushed to answer it, grateful for the diversion. Fortunately, it was an angry, long-winded client. She smiled wickedly as she transferred the call to J.D.'s phone. While he was talking, she escaped to lunch, leaving him listening helplessly to the venomous divorcée on the other end of the line.

But once she was out of the office and eating a hamburger at a local fast-food restaurant, the smile vanished and gloom set in. She'd read about men who couldn't marry, who were too freedom-loving for marriage. But until J.D. came along, she hadn't known what anguish there could be in loving someone like that. Now she did, and her nights would be plagued with nightmares about hearing someday he'd died in combat. Or worse, that he was serving time in some filthy foreign jail for interfering in the internal politics of another nation.

If Martina had known the truth, maybe she could have helped talk some sense into him. But Gabby hadn't dared to tell her. J.D. would never forgive Gabby if she did.

An hour later, she dragged herself back into the office, only to find J.D. gone. There was a terse note on her desk, informing her that he'd gone to meet a client and that she was to cancel his appointments; he wouldn't be in until the next day.

She picked up the phone and started dialing. Was he really seeing a client? The thought tormented her, even after she left the office. Perhaps he'd already packed his bag and gone off in search of the sun. She cried herself to sleep, hating herself for worrying. If this was any indication of the future, she'd do well to hurry about finding another job.

The next day she forced herself to search the want ads for positions in between answering the phone, using the copier, and running the computer. J.D. still hadn't come in, and she was grateful for Dick's dictation and the hectic rush of the office. It kept her from thinking about J.D.

When he walked in the door just before lunch, it was all she could do not to jump up and throw herself into his arms. But she remembered that he didn't want ties so she forced herself to greet him calmly and hand him his messages.

"Worried about me?" he asked with apparent carelessness, but his eyes were watchful.

She looked up with hard-won composure, her eyebrows arched behind her reading glasses. "Worried? Why?"

He drew in a slow breath and turned on his heel to walk into his office. He slammed the door behind him.

She stuck out her tongue at it and picked up her purse. "Going to lunch," she said into the intercom and started out the door.

"Gabby."

She turned. He was standing in his office doorway, looking lonely and hesitant.

"Have lunch with me," he said.

She held up the newspaper. "Sorry. I'm going interviewing."

His face hardened, his eyes narrowed. "Don't."

Her soft heart almost melted under that half pleading stare. But she couldn't give in, not now. In the long run, it would be easier to eat her heart out from a safe distance. She'd die working with him, knowing that all he was capable of giving her was lust or a business relationship.

"I have to," she said quietly. "It's for the best."

"For whom?" he demanded.

"For both of us!" she burst out. "I can't bear to be in the same office with you!"

Something indescribable happened to his face. And because it hurt to see him that way, she turned and all but ran out the door. It didn't occur to her until much later how he might have taken her remark. She'd meant she couldn't bear to be with him because she loved him so, but he probably thought it was because of his brutal treatment of her at the *finca*. Well, he had been brutal. But he'd apologized, and some part of her understood why he'd acted that way. He was just trying to open her eyes to the futility of loving him. To spare her more hurt. Anyway, she told herself, her remark wouldn't faze him. He didn't care about her, so how in the world could she hurt him?

She applied for two jobs in offices a few blocks away. In one job she would be operating a computer. She knew how to do that, so it would be easy. The other was to work as a secretary for an international firm.

When she went back to the office, J.D. was gone again. Just as well, she thought. She had to get used to not seeing him. The thought was excruciatingly painful, but she was realistic enough to know that the pain would pass one day. After all, as J.D. himself had said, there was no future for her with him. He'd gone to elaborate lengths to make sure she knew that. And since she couldn't spend the day crying, she forced herself to keep her mind strictly on the job.

Chapter Eight

J.D. was so reserved after that day that he barely spoke to Gabby at all, except when absolutely necessary for business. And all the time he scowled and snapped, like a wounded animal.

"Have you heard anything about your job interviews yet?" he asked Friday morning, glaring at her over a piece of correspondence to which he had just dictated an answer.

"I hope to hear Monday about the computer job," she said quietly. "The other one didn't work out."

He pursed his lips thoughtfully. "So it may not be all that easy to find something else," he commented.

She met his level stare. "If nothing works out in Chicago, I'm going home."

He didn't move. He studied her intently. "To Texas."

She lowered her gaze to her steno pad. "That's right."

"What would you do in Texas?"

"I'd help Mama."

He put down the letter. "'Help Mama,'" he scoffed, glaring at her. "Your mother would drive you to drink in less than a week, and you know it."

"How dare you...!" she began hotly.

"Gabby, your mother is a sweet lady," he said, "but her life-style and yours are worlds apart. You'd fight all the time, or you'd find yourself being led around like a lamb."

Her breasts rose and fell softly. "Yes, I know," she said after a minute. "But it's better than the unemployment line, isn't it?"

"Stay with me," he said. "I think, if you'll just give it time, it will work out. Can't you forget how I treated you that one time?"

"Don't make it harder for me," she said.

"Is it hard, to walk out that door and never seen me again?" he asked bluntly.

Her chin trembled just a little. "You've got nothing to give—you told me so. You've left me no choice but to leave."

"Yes, that was what I said," he agreed. "I went to impossible lengths to show you just how uncommitted I was, to make sure that you didn't try to cling too closely." He sighed heavily and his hands moved restlessly on the desk. "And now I can't look myself in the mirror, thinking about the way you cringe every time I come near you." He got up from the desk and stared out of the window, stretching as if he were stiff all over. "I've never needed anyone," he said after a minute, without turning. "Not even when I was a boy. I was always looking out for Martina and Mama. There was never anyone who gave a damn about me except them. I've been alone all my life. I've wanted it that way."

"I've told you until I'm blue in the face, I'm not trying to trap you!"

He lifted his head and looked at her. "Yes, I realize that now. I want you to try to understand something," he said after a minute. "I spent a lot of my life in the military. I got used to a certain way of doing things, a certain way of life. I thought it had stopped being important to me. And then Martina was kidnapped."

"And you got a taste of it again," she said quietly, searching his face. "And now you're not sure you can be just a lawyer for the rest of your life."

"You read me very well."

"We've worked together for a long time." She stared down at the steno pad and pen in her hands, glad that he couldn't see her heart breaking. "I'll miss you from time to time, J.D. Whatever else this job was, it was never dull."

"If you stay," he said quietly, "I might be able to stay too."

"What do I have to do with it?" she asked with a nervous laugh. "My goodness, the world is full of competent paralegals. You might like your next one a lot better than you like me. I have a nasty temper and I talk back, remember?"

"I remember so much about you," he said surprisingly. "When I started trying to tear you out of

my life, I discovered just how deep the taproot went.
You've become a habit with me, Gabby, like early
morning coffee and my newspaper. I can't get up in
the morning without thinking about coming to work
and finding you here.''

"You'll find new habits,'' she said. Was that all
she was, a habit?

"I'm trying to make you understand that I don't
want to acquire any new habits,'' he growled. "I like
things the way they are, I like the routine of them.''

"No, you don't,'' she told him, glaring. "You just
said so. You want to go back to all the uncertainties
of being a mercenary, and risking your life day after
day. You want to go adventuring.''

"You make it sound like a disease,'' he said
shortly.

"Isn't it? You're afraid to feel anything. Shirt,
Apollo, Semson, all of them are men who've lost
something they can't live without. So they're looking
for an end, not a beginning. They don't have anything
to lose, and nothing to go back to. I learned so much
in those three days, J.D. I learned most of all that I
have everything to live for. I don't want that kind of
freedom.''

"You've never had it,'' he reminded her.

"That's true,'' she agreed. "But you've spent five
years working to build a life for yourself, and you've
made a huge success of it. Several people owe their
lives, and their freedom, to you. Are you really crazy
enough to throw all that away on a pipe dream?''

"Freedom isn't always won in a court of law,'' he
growled.

"How then—with an Uzi and a few blocks of C-4?" she asked. "There are other ways to promote change than with bombs and bullets!"

He drew in a short breath. "You don't understand."

"That's right, I don't. And for your information, I've lost all my illusions about the exciting life of a soldier of fortune." She stood up with her pad in hand. "I'll go and transcribe this."

He watched her walk to the door. "Wait a minute," he said.

She paused with her hand on the doorknob and watched him come around the desk. She felt a twinge of fear as he came close to her. He towered over her, his blue pin-striped suit emphasizing the strength of his muscular body.

She opened the door and moved through it, trying not to show fear, but he saw right through her.

"No," he said softly, shaking his head. "No, don't run. I won't hurt you."

"You used to say that a lot, and I listened one time too many," she said with a nervous laugh. She backed up until she got the width of her desk between them. "I have to get these typed," she added, lifting the steno pad.

His dark eyes had an oddly bleak look in them. "It's real, isn't it, that fear?" he asked.

She sat down in her chair, avoiding his piercing gaze. "I have work to do, J.D."

He propped himself on the corner of the desk with a graceful, fluid movement.

"Don't panic," he said quietly. "I'm not coming any closer than this."

She stiffened. She couldn't help it.

"I should never have hurt you that way," he said, staring down at her clenched fingers. "I overreacted. Someday I'll try to explain it to you."

"There won't be any 'someday,'" she said tersely. "You'll be off blowing things up and I'll be programming computers."

"Will you stop that?" he growled. He fumbled for a cigarette.

"Would you mind waiting until I cover my diskettes?" she asked coldly, reaching to pull them out of the double-disk-drive computer. "Smoke and dust can cause them to crash."

He waited impatiently until she'd replaced the diskettes in their envelopes and stored them in their box before he lit the cigarette.

She glared at him. "I can't transcribe your letters until I can use the computer," she said matter-of-factly.

"So the letters can wait," he said. "Gabby, I swear to God I didn't mean to frighten you that much. I was shaken by what we'd been through, I was half-crazy..." He ran a hand through his hair. "I forgot how innocent you were too. I want you to know that under ordinary circumstances it wouldn't be like that for you with a man."

"With another man, perhaps not." She bit off the words.

"Gabby, what happened the morning before the mission didn't frighten you."

She felt herself go hot all over at the reminder, at the memories that flooded her mind. She remembered the touch of his hard mouth, the feel of his body, the tenderness of the fingers that searched over her soft, aching flesh....

"You were a different man then," she shot back. "You wouldn't even speak to me when we got back to the *finca,* you wouldn't look at me. You acted like a stranger, and then you attacked me!"

He stared down at the cigarette in his hand. "Yes, I know. I've hardly slept since."

His chest rose and fell slowly. He leaned over to crush out his cigarette in the spotless ashtray on her desk. He was so close, she could see the harsh shadows under his eyes.

"Would you consider having supper with me?" he asked.

Her heart jumped, but she didn't take time to decide whether it was from anticipation or fear. "No," she said bluntly, before she had time to change her mind.

He sighed. "No." His broad, hard mouth twisted into a rueful smile. He let his eyes wander slowly over her face. "Somehow, storming that terrorist camp seems like kid stuff compared to getting past your defenses, Gabby."

"Why bother?" she asked quietly. "I'll be here only another week."

The light went out of his eyes. He got to his feet and turned back toward his office. He paused at the doorway with his broad back to her. He seemed about to say something, about to turn. Then he straightened, went on into his office, and closed the door quietly behind him. Gabby hesitated just for a minute; then she booted up the computer again and concentrated on typing the business letters he'd dictated.

Saturday morning arrived sunny and with the promise of budding flowers. Gabby hated the city on such delightfully springlike days. She was brooding in her apartment, in the midst of doing her laundry, when a knock sounded at the door.

She couldn't imagine who might be visiting, unless her mother had gotten worried and had come all the way from Lytle to see her. That thought bothered her, and she went rushing to open the door.

J.D. lifted a heavy eyebrow. "Were you expecting me?" he asked with a faint grin.

She faltered, trying to think of a graceful way to ask him to leave. While she was debating, he walked into the apartment and sat down on her sofa.

"I thought you might like to have lunch with me," he said out of the blue, studying her slender figure in faded jeans and a striped pullover knit shirt.

She realized as she stared down at him that he looked different, and then she noticed what he was wearing. She'd never seen J.D. in anything but neat suits or jungle fatigues. But now he was wearing blue jeans as worn and faded as her own, with a western-style blue chambray shirt and boots. She stood there staring at him because she couldn't help it. He was so devastatingly handsome and masculine that he made her feel weak-kneed—from a distance, at least. She was still a little uneasy being alone with him.

"I won't pounce," he said softly. "I won't make

a single move that you don't want. I won't even touch you, if that's what it takes. Spend the day with me, though, Gabby."

"Why should I?" she asked curtly.

He smiled wistfully. "Because I'm lonely."

Something in the region of her heart gave way. It must have been her soft brain, she told herself, because there was no logic in giving in to him. It would only make it harder to leave. And she had to leave. She couldn't bear staying around him, feeling the way she felt.

"You've got friends," she said evasively.

"Sure," he said, standing. He stuck his hands in his pockets, stretching the jeans flat across his muscular stomach and powerful thighs. "Sure, I've got friends. There's Shirt, and Apollo..."

"I mean...friends here in the city," she said hesitantly.

He was silent for a moment. "I've got you. No one else."

She gave in. Without another argument. How did you fight a flat statement like that, especially when you knew it was true? He'd said himself that he trusted no one except her. Friendship naturally involved trust.

"Okay," she said after a minute. "But just lunch."

"Just lunch," he agreed. And he didn't come close to her, or pressure her, or do anything to make her wary of him. He waited patiently while she closed the apartment door and locked it, and he walked beside her like a graceful giant as they left the building and got into his car.

Chapter Nine

It was an odd kind of day for Gabby. She thought she knew every one of J.D.'s moods, but that day he was different, in a way that she couldn't quite define.

He strolled beside her through the trees in the nearby park, then along the beach that edged the lake, watching birds rise and soar, watching boats sail and putter by. The wind tossed his dark hair and the sun made it glint blue-black. And Gabby thought she'd never felt like this in her life, free and yet protected and wildly excited, all at the same time. It was hard to remember that this was more of an end than a beginning. J.D. had a guilty conscience about the way he'd treated her and was trying to make amends before she left. That was all. She had to stop trying to make more out of it.

His fingers brushed hers as they walked, and he glanced down, watching her carefully.

"Looking for warts?" she asked, attempting to lessen the tension between them.

"Not really," he murmured. "I'm trying to decide what you'd do if I made a grab for your hand."

That irrepressible honesty again. She smiled and gave him her slender fingers, feeling trembly as he slowly locked them into his own. She was remembering that flight to Mexico and how he'd caressed her fingers with his own, and the remark he'd made about bodies fitting together that way. Her face burned.

He chuckled softly. "I wonder if you could possibly be thinking about the same thing I am, Gabby?" he murmured.

"I wish you'd mind your own business," she told him.

"I'm trying, but you're pretty transparent, honey. You still blush delightfully."

She tugged her fingers away and, to her disappointment, he let them go.

"No pressure," he said when she gave him a puzzled glance. "None at all. I'll take only what you give me."

She stopped, facing him. Nearby, the lake lapped softly at the shore and some children made wild sounds down the beach as they chased each other.

"What are you trying to do?" she asked.

He sighed. "Show you that I'm not a monster," he said.

"I never thought you were," she replied.

"Then why does this happen every time I come

close to you?'' he asked. His big hands shot out and caught her by the waist, dragging her against him.

She panicked. Her body twisted violently, her hands fought him. It was all over in seconds, but his face had gone white, and her own was flushed with exertion and anger.

She drew her lower lip between her teeth and bit it. J.D. looked...odd.

He gave a hard laugh and turned away. With unsteady fingers, he managed to light a cigarette despite the breeze. He took a long, steadying draw from it.

"Oh, God." He laughed bitterly. "I did a job on you, didn't I?"

Her legs were none too steady, but she managed to calm her voice enough to trust it with speech. "I'd never been handled roughly by a man before, J.D.," she told him. "And you said some pretty harsh things."

He turned, staring down at her. "Some pretty explicit ones." His dark eyes wandered slowly down her body, lingering on the soft curves as he lifted the cigarette to his mouth. "By the time I got around to that, I'd long forgotten my motives."

She blinked. "I don't understand."

His eyes found the horizon across the lake, and he smoked his cigarette quietly. "It doesn't matter," he said vaguely. He finished the cigarette and ground it out under his boot.

"You've gone back to smoking all the time," she said.

His shoulders rose and fell. "There doesn't seem much point in quitting now."

She wrapped her arms tightly across her breasts as she watched him walk down the beach. She followed him, searching for words.

"If you hadn't grabbed me like that, I wouldn't have fought you," she said curtly. She hadn't wanted to tell him that, but he looked as if her reaction to him had devastated him. Her marshmallow heart was going to do her in, she told herself when he stopped in his tracks and gaped at her.

"What?" he burst out.

She turned away, letting the wind blow her long, dark hair around. She couldn't manage another word.

He moved closer, but slowly this time. His hands came up to her face, hesitantly cupping it. Her heart pounded, but she didn't pull away.

His chiseled mouth parted as he looked deeply into her eyes. His face was rigid with control. She could feel the warm threat of his body against her, smell the musky scent of his cologne.

"Half of what I told you in that room was true," he said in a husky whisper. "In my younger days, I never gave a damn about the woman I took. But now, it matters. What I did to you, the things I said…I can't sleep, I can't eat. It haunts me."

"Why?" She, too, whispered.

His thumbs edged toward her mouth. "I…cared."

Her pupils dilated, darkening the green of her eyes. "Cared?"

He bent, and his hands were unsteady as they cupped her face. "I kept thinking about how close I came to losing you out there in the jungle," he whispered against her lips. "I wanted to purge myself of

the memory and the emotion. So I hurt you.'' His
face hardened, his heavy brows drew together. ''But
what I did to you...hurt me more.'' His hard lips
brushed hers, nibbled at them. ''You've seen me at
my worst. Trust me now, Gabby. Let me show you...
how tender I can be.''

She wanted it almost frantically. She wanted a
memory to take down the long, lonely years with her.
So she let him have her mouth, as he wanted it. And
his lips taught hers new sensations, new ways of
touching and exploring.

He moaned softly, and his hands contracted, but
his mouth was still tender even though she could feel
his big body going rigid against her.

Her eyes opened and found his watching her, passion blazing out of them, a hunger like nothing she'd
ever seen in him.

He lifted his head, his breath unsteady on her
moist, parted lips. ''Don't go cold on me,'' he whispered. ''Not yet.''

She swallowed, and her breasts lifted and fell with
her breath. ''Jacob...''

His eyes closed as though he were in pain. ''I
thought I'd never hear you say my name like that
again,'' he said harshly.

Her hands were against the front of his shirt, and
she didn't even know how they'd landed there. She
was all too aware of what was under it, of how it felt
to bury her fingers in that thick, cool mat of curling
hair.

''Don't make it difficult for me,'' she whispered
helplessly.

His hands slid around to the back of her head, tilting her face upward. "Do you think it's easy for me, letting you go?"

"Yes," she said with a trembling smile. "You said yourself that you didn't want any ties."

"Then why in God's name do I die a little every time I walk away from you?" he asked curtly. "Why do I wake up with your name on my lips?"

"I can't be your lover!" she whispered. "I can't!"

His nose brushed against hers, his lips hovered above her mouth, teasing it, coaxing it to follow his. "It would be so easy," he said softly, in a voice like dark velvet. "So easy. All it would take is ten minutes alone together with my mouth on yours and my hands under your blouse, and you'd give yourself with glorious abandon, the way you wanted to before I went to rescue Martina. Remember?" he breathed against her lips. "Remember, Gabby? You stood in my arms and let me touch you, and we rocked together and moaned…"

"Jacob." She hid her hot face against him. "Jacob, don't, please!"

His hands slid slowly down her back until they reached her hips and brought them into the curve of his, holding her there, pressing her there, so that she knew all too well what he wanted of her.

"This is a public place," she managed to say weakly, clinging to him.

"Where you're safe," he replied thickly. "Because if I did this anywhere else, I couldn't help what would happen. I want you so much."

"This is only making it worse," she told him. She

leaned her forehead against his chest. She could smell the tangy soap he used, the clean scent of the shirt he wore. Her hands spread over his hard muscles.

His breath quickened at the almost imperceptible movement. "Unbutton it." He breathed roughly. "Touch me there."

"There are people...!"

"Yes." His lips touched her closed eyelids, her forehead. "Touch me."

She could hardly breathe at all. He was drowning her in sensation, and she loved him so much it was torture. It was just going to be harder to leave him, but how could she fight this? Part of her was frightened of his strength, but a larger part remembered how it had felt when he was tender, when he'd been so careful not to hurt her.

"I won't ever hurt you again," he whispered, lifting her fingers to the top button. "Not ever. I won't overpower you, or make crude remarks to you. I'll teach you to trust me, if it takes the rest of my life. Gabby..."

She closed her eyes. Tentatively her fingers fumbled the first button free. He tensed as she found the second, and the third. She stopped there, resting against him, and eased her fingers just inside. They tingled as they came in contact with firm muscle and curling hair.

He caught his breath, shifting his chest so that her fingers slid farther under the fabric.

"You did that," he reminded her in a sensuous undertone, "when I started to touch you under your nightgown, at the *finca*. Remember? You shifted and moved so that I could touch you more easily.''

What she remembered most was the way it had felt when he'd touched her. Her eyes slowly opened, and he turned her face so that he could look into them.

His own eyes were black with desire; his face was hard and drawn, his lips were parted. ''Yes, I like that,'' he whispered as she curled her nails against him and dragged them softly over his skin. ''I like that.'' His chest rose and fell heavily and still his eyes held hers. ''If we made love, you could do that to every inch of me. And I could do it to you, with my mouth.''

She trembled. He felt it and drew her slowly into his arms. He stood like that, just holding her, in a strangely passionless embrace while the world became calm.

''Words,'' he said over her head, his tone light and solemn at the same time. ''So potent... Until you came along, I'd never made love to a woman with my mind.''

She stared out at the sailboats on the lake and involuntarily one hand pressed closer against him. ''We're at an impasse,'' she said after a minute.

His cheek nudged her dark hair. ''How?''

She laughed bitterly. ''J.D., I'm leaving next Friday.''

''Maybe,'' he said, and his arms tightened.

''Definitely.'' She pulled away from him, and he let her go immediately. She looked up. ''Nothing has changed.''

He let his eyes roam over her soft body. "At least you've stopped cringing."

"Thank you," she replied. "For removing the scars. Now I can go on to a lasting relationship."

"Why not have it with me?" he asked. "I'm well-off. I'm sexy—"

"You're unreliable," she said, interrupting him. "I want someone who doesn't know an Uzi from a blender!"

He sighed heavily, and his dark eyes were thoughtful. "I need a little time."

"Time won't help," she said. "You're hooked again. It's like the cigarettes, only worse. I can't live my life standing at windows and waiting for telephones to ring."

"You'll do that regardless."

She stopped dead and turned around, gaping at him. "What?"

"You'll do that anyway," he said matter-of-factly, watching her. He pulled a cigarette from his pocket with a what-the-hell smile and lit it. "You'll miss me. You'll want me. You're leaving the office, but the memories are portable and indestructible. You won't forget me any more than I'll forget you. We started something we haven't finished, and it's going to be between us all our lives."

"It's just sex!" she yelled at him.

Two young men walked past, grinned at J.D., and winked at Gabby, who was wishing she could sink into the sand. She hadn't even heard them approach.

She turned and fled back down the beach at a trot. J.D. was right beside her, effortlessly matching her steps and still smoking his cigarette. He finished it just as they reached the car, and he crushed it out before he joined her in the luxurious interior.

"It isn't just sex," he said, turning to face her, one arm across the back of the seat and an odd expression on his face. He smiled slowly. "But sex is going to be one big part of our relationship in the not-too-distant future."

She glared at him. "You'd be lucky!"

"No, you would," he said, cocking an eyebrow. "When I mind my manners, I'm a force to be reckoned with. What I did to you in that bed was all bad temper and irritation. What I did to you the morning before was what it's really like."

She couldn't control her heated response to that intimate remark. Her breasts tingled at the memory. His eyes dropped slowly to her breasts, and he smiled wickedly. Following his gaze, she saw why and crossed her arms over her chest.

"Too late," he murmured. "Your body will give you away every time. You haven't forgotten what we did together."

Her nostrils flared. "There are other men in the world."

"Sure," he agreed pleasantly. "But you don't want other men. You want me."

"Conceited ass," she enunciated clearly.

His fingers touched her mouth and parted her lips, as if their texture fascinated him. "You risked your life for me," he said absently. "Why?"

She laughed nervously. "Maybe I just wanted to try out the gun."

He tilted her face up and leaned over to brush his mouth tenderly across her trembling lips. "Maybe there was a reason you don't want me to know," he murmured. He drew back and looked at her. "Hungry?"

The change of topic threw her. He had switched from lover to friendly companion in seconds. She managed a smile. "Yes. What did you have in mind?"

"Cheeseburgers, of course." He chuckled and started the car.

"I like those myself."

He glanced at her. "Let's talk," he said unexpectedly. "Really talk. I want to know everything about you. What you like to read, how it was to grow up in Texas, why you've never gotten involved with a man...everything."

That sounded intriguing. It suddenly occurred to her that she knew very little about him. What he liked and disliked, what he felt. She tried to read his face.

"Curious about me too?" he asked, glancing sideways. "I'll tell you anything you want to know."

She laughed uneasily. "'Anything' covers a lot of territory."

"And requires a hell of a lot of trust on my part," he added with a smile. "Anything, Gabby."

Total honesty. She stared down at her hands and wondered why they were trembling. She wasn't sure of his motives, of where this was leading. She looked up and all her uncertainty was on her face.

He reached over and caught one of her hands, lifting it to his thigh. Her palm tingled at the contact.

"Make me stay here," he said unexpectedly.

"What?" she asked.

"Make me stay," he repeated. His eyes caught hers briefly. "You can give me something that all the unholy little wars on earth couldn't. If you want me, show me. Give me a reason, half a reason, to settle down. And I might surprise you."

She stared out through the windshield and felt as if she were floating. It was a beginning that she wasn't sure she wanted. She might hold his interest briefly, until he tired of her body. But what then? He was offering nothing more than a liaison. He wasn't talking about permanent things like a house and children. Her eyes darkened with pain. Perhaps it would have been better if he hadn't gotten rid of her fear of him.

Her troubled eyes sought his profile, but it was as unreadable as ever. The only thing that gave her hope was the visible throbbing of his pulse and the searing desire in his eyes. He wanted her so desperately that she couldn't help wondering whether he didn't feel something for her, too. But it would take time to find out, and she wasn't going to withdraw her resignation. As much as it might hurt, in the long run it would be saner to leave him than to try to hold him. Gabby wasn't built for an affair. And she wasn't going to let him drag her into one, just to occupy himself while he decided between practicing law and soldiering.

Chapter Ten

They sat in a booth at a nearby fast-food restaurant, where J.D. put away three cheeseburgers, a large order of french fries, and two cups of coffee before Gabby's fascinated eyes.

"I'm a big man," he reminded her as he was finishing the third one.

"Yes, you are," she agreed with a smile, running her eyes over the spread of muscle under his chambray shirt.

His eyes narrowed with amusement. "Remembering what's under it?" he said softly, teasing her.

She flushed and grabbed her coffee cup, holding it like a weapon. "I thought this was a truce," she muttered.

"It is. But I fight dirty, remember?"

She looked, studying his hard face. "What was it

like, those four years when you were a mercenary?" she asked.

He finished the cheeseburger and sipped his coffee, leaning back with a heavy sigh. "It was hard," he said. "Exciting. Rewarding, in more ways than just financial." He shrugged. "I suppose I was caught up in the romance of it at first, until I saw what I was getting into. One of the men I joined with was captured and thrown into jail the minute we landed in one emerging African country. He hadn't fired a shot, but he was executed just like the men who had."

She caught her breath. "But why?" she asked. "He was just…"

"We were interfering with the regime," he told her. "Despite all our noble reasons, we were breaking whatever law existed at that time. Shirt and I managed to get away. I owe him my life for his quick thinking. I was pretty new to the profession back then. I learned."

"He told me his name was Matthew," she remarked with a smile.

He cocked an eyebrow. "Be flattered. It was three years before I found that out."

She toyed with her crumpled napkin. "I liked him. I liked all of them."

"Shirt's quite a guy. He was the one who pushed me into law," he said with a laugh. "He thought I needed a better future than rushing around the world with a weapon."

"You think a lot of him," she observed.

He shrugged. "I never knew my father," he said after a minute. "Shirt looked out for me when we served in Vietnam together. I don't know—maybe he needed somebody too. His wife had died of cancer, and he didn't have anybody else except a brother in Milwaukee who still doesn't speak to him. I had Martina. I suppose Shirt became my father, in a sense.''

She cupped her hands around her coffee mug and wondered what he'd say if she told him that Shirt had said the door to the past was closed for J.D. Probably he'd laugh it off, but she decided she didn't want to find out.

He looked up. "How about your family? Any sisters, brothers?"

She laughed softly. "No. I was an only child. My father owned a ranch, and my mother and grandfather and grandmother had gone to San Antonio on vacation. Mother met Dad then and ran away to marry him over the weekend." She grinned. "My grandparents were furious."

"I can imagine." He searched her face. "You look like your mother. How about him? Was he big?"

She shook her head. "My father was small and wiry and tough. He had to be, you see, to put up with Mama. She'd have killed a lesser man, but Dad didn't take orders. There were some great fights during my childhood."

He cocked an eyebrow. "Did they make up eventually?"

She sighed. "He'd send her roses, or bring her pretty things from town. And she'd kiss him and they'd go off alone and I'd go see Miss Patty who lived in a line cabin on the ranch." She grinned. "I visited Miss Patty a lot."

He chuckled. "They say the making up can be pretty sweet."

She studied his hard face. "Yes, so I hear."

He lifted his eyes to hers. "We've had a royal falling out. Want to make up?"

She hesitated, and he concentrated on finishing his coffee and reaching for a cigarette.

"Sorry," he said quietly. "I'm rushing things."

Hesitantly, she reached across the table and touched the back of the big hand resting there. It jerked. Then it turned and captured hers in its rough warmth.

"J.D., what do you want from me?" she asked.

"What do you think I want, Gabby?" he asked in turn.

She gathered all her courage and put her worst fears into words. "I think you want to make amends for what happened in Guatemala, before you fly off into the sun. I think you want to have an affair with me."

"That's honest, at least," he said. His eyes fell to their clasped hands, and he watched his thumb rub softly against her slender fingers. "You want something more permanent, I gather."

She couldn't answer that without giving herself away. She drew her hand away from his with a light laugh. "Aren't we getting serious though?" she asked. "I need to go home, J.D. I left the laundry in the washing machine, and I've got a week's cleaning to do."

His face hardened. "Can't it wait until tomorrow?"

"Tomorrow's Sunday."

"So?"

She lifted her eyes to his. "I go to church on Sunday."

He frowned slightly. "I haven't been to church since I was a boy," he said after a minute. He studied the smoking cigarette in his hand. "I don't know what I believe in these days."

It was a reminder of the big differences between them. She frowned too, and got to her feet slowly.

"It would bother you," he murmured, watching her. "Yes, I suppose it would."

She half turned. "What would?"

"Never mind." He sighed as he put the remains of their meal into the trash can and replaced the tray in the rack on their way out. "Just a few adjustments that have to be made, that's all."

That didn't make sense, but she didn't pressure him. He didn't pressure her either, leaving her outside her apartment building with a rueful smile.

"I hate being stood up for the damned laundry," he muttered, hands in his pockets.

"New experiences teach new things," she murmured dryly. "Besides, I can't finish out the week in dirty clothes."

That put a damper on things. Her smile faded at the memory of how little time they had left together. His face grew harder.

"Well...thanks for lunch," she said awkwardly.

"We could do it again tomorrow," he said before she went inside.

Her eyes lifted. She wanted to. She wanted to, desperately. She tried to convince herself that it would be a mistake, but her body tingled and her heart surged at the idea.

"Yes," she said under her breath.

His chest rose and fell, as if in relief. "Suppose I pick you up about ten-thirty?"

She hesitated. "Church is at eleven."

"Yes, I figured it would be," he said with a rueful smile. "I hope the angels won't faint at having me in their midst."

All the color drained out of her face as she stared up at him, and she couldn't have said a word to save herself.

"Well, I won't embarrass you," he muttered curtly. "I do know not to stand up and yell 'Hallelujah' every five minutes or to snore in the front pew."

"I didn't say anything," she said.

"I still have a soul too, even if it has taken a few hard knocks over the years." He lifted his shoulders and let them fall. "I...need to go back. All the way back." His eyes held hers. "Gabby?"

"I'm Methodist," she said.

He smiled. "I used to be Episcopalian. The denomination doesn't matter so much, does it?"

She shook her head. "We can walk from my apartment."

He nodded. "See you tomorrow."

He turned to get back into the car, but she moved forward and touched his arm. The light contact of her fingers froze him. He looked down at her.

"Would you...bend down a minute?" she whispered.

Like a sleepwalker, he bent his tall frame and she stood on tiptoe to put her mouth warmly, hungrily to his.

He moaned, starting to reach for her, but she drew back with a wicked, warm smile.

"Try that again when we aren't in a public place," he said, challenging her.

Her heart jumped. "Dream on."

He lifted an eyebrow. "I've done very little else this past week," he said, letting his eyes roam over her slender body. "Gabby, have you ever thought about having children?"

She could hardly believe what she was hearing. Her face burned with pleasure, her heart sang with it. "Oh, yes," she whispered huskily.

"So have I." He started to speak, caught himself, and smiled hesitantly. "See you in the morning."

"'Bye." She stood there and watched him drive off. It was probably all some wild daydream and she'd wake up back in the office, typing. But when she pinched herself, it hurt. She went upstairs and put the clothes in the dryer and tried to convince herself that J.D. had actually said he was going to church with her.

But the next morning, she was sure she'd misunderstood him. She dressed in a pretty Gibson Girl-style white outfit with matching accessories and at precisely ten-thirty, she started out the door. Of course, J.D. wasn't going to church, she told herself firmly. What a stupid thing to...

The doorbell rang as she was opening the door. And there he was. He was wearing the same vested gray suit she'd seen him in earlier that week, but he looked different now. More relaxed, more at ease, much less rigid.

"Shocked?" he asked wickedly. "Did you expect I'd changed my mind and gone fishing instead?"

She burst out laughing and her green eyes sparkled. With her long hair piled in an old-fashioned coiffure, she seemed part of another era.

"Little Miss Victorian," he murmured, studying her. "How exciting you look. So demure and proper."

He looked as if he'd give a lot to change that straight-laced image, and she dropped her eyes before he could see how willing she felt.

"We'd better get started," she murmured, easing past him.

"I like that gauzy thing," he remarked minutes later as they walked up the front steps of the gray fieldstone church.

"You can wear it sometimes, if you like," she said teasingly.

His eyes promised retribution. She eased her hand into his, and all the fight went out of him. He smiled at her, and his eyes were warm and possessive.

J.D. paid a lot of attention to the sermon, which was about priorities and forgiveness and grace. He sang the hymns in a rich baritone, and he seemed thoughtful as the benediction was given.

"Mind waiting for me?" he asked as they rose to file out at the end of the service.

She searched his hard face and shook her head. "Not at all."

He left her and went to speak to the minister who was waiting until the rest of the congregation had left. The two men stood talking behind the rows of pews, both solemn, their voices low. Then they shook hands and smiled at each other. J.D. came back and grasped Gabby's hand warmly in his for a minute.

"I'm taking your minister to lunch instead of you," he said with a mischievous smile. "How about getting into something casual and I'll pick you up in a couple of hours?"

She looked hard at him. "Are you all right?" she asked. She was trying to see beyond the fixed smile to something deep and wounded inside him.

He drew in a slow breath and the smile faded. "You frighten me sometimes, Gabby," he said softly. "You see too much."

She couldn't think of any response to that. She touched his hand briefly and watched him walk away. Something was in the wind, a change. She frowned as she turned toward her apartment, her steps slow and deliberate. She wondered why he was taking her minister to lunch, if he had something on his conscience.

She changed into jeans and a button-up blue cotton blouse and then paced the floor for the next two hours. Wild thoughts raced through her mind, the wildest one being that J.D. might decide to chuck it all and go in search of First Shirt and Apollo.

It was three hours before he showed up. By then Gabby had consumed half a pot of coffee and chewed two fingernails to the quick. Her nerves were raw, and she actually jumped when the knock came at the door.

She let him in, too shaken to disguise the frightened uncertainty in her wide eyes.

"I thought you'd stood me up." She laughed nervously. "I was just about to give up and start watching a movie on TV. Do you want some coffee, or some cake...?"

He put a finger across her mouth to stop the wild words. His dark eyes looked into hers. "We have to learn to trust each other a little more," he said softly. "And the first thing you need to know about me is that if I ever give my word, it's good for life. I'm not going back to Shirt and the others, Gabby. That's a promise."

Tears burst from her eyes like rain from a storm cloud. She put her face in her hands and walked away.

"I'm sorry," she choked out, hating the fact that she'd given her feelings away.

He didn't say a word. He followed her, and when he caught up to her, he lifted her gently in his big arms and headed straight for the bedroom.

She had just enough sanity left to realize where they were going. She opened her mouth to protest, and his came down on it, open and moist and tenderly possessive.

"Jacob..." she whispered into his mouth.

He smiled against her trembling lips. "What?"

Her nails bit softly into his shoulders as he laid her down on the crisp white chenille bedspread. "I can't," she whispered.

"Can't what?" He sat down beside her and calmly removed his jacket, vest, and tie and then unbuttoned his shirt while she watched him, spellbound as the hard, heavy muscles came into view under that mat of crisp hair.

"I can't have an affair with you," she said.

He leaned over and began to unfasten the buttons on her blouse. "That's nice."

"Jacob, did you hear me? Will you stop that…!"

He ignored her protests and her frantic efforts to stop his fingers. "Stop what?"

"Undressing me!" she burst out with an hysterical laugh. "Jacob, I'm wearing nothing underneath, for heaven's sake…!"

"So I see," he murmured with a wicked smile, as he opened the blouse and revealed the pink and mauve rise of her breasts.

"Will you listen…" she began breathlessly.

"Shut up, darling." He bent over her and put his open mouth against one breast, letting her feel the texture of his warm lips and his tongue before he moved closer and increased the ardent pressure.

She gasped and arched and then moaned sharply, a high-pitched sound that made him lift his head.

"Did I hurt you?" he asked. "I'm sorry, I thought I was being gentle."

Her fists were clenched beside her head, and her eyes were wide with mingled fear and desire. "You know very well it didn't hurt," she whispered fiercely.

His eyes moved back down to her bareness and he smiled slowly, watching her breasts lift and fall with her quickened breathing. "Lovely, lovely creature," he said under his breath. His fingers traced her rib cage and he held her eyes, watching the recklessness come into them, the deep passion.

Her breath was coming still quicker now, and the tracing of his fingers was driving her mad. She arched her head back into the pillow, lifting her body toward him in a slow, helpless movement.

"Want me to put my mouth there again and make it stop aching?" he whispered.

"Yes," she moaned softly. "Please."

She felt the whisper of his warm breath against her skin, felt his hands go under her to slide abrasively against her bare back. He lifted her, and his mouth moved with delicate precision from one taut breast to the other. His face nuzzled her, savored her softness.

Her fingers tangled in his thick, cool hair and worked at it like a cat kneading a blanket. Pleasure washed over her in waves, waves that lifted and twisted her body.

"Jacob," she whispered as his mouth slid over hers and down to her ear, while his hands made magic on her upthrust breasts. "Jacob, teach me how to make you feel this way."

"I already do," he murmured at her ear. "Touching you like this, kissing you, makes me wild, didn't you know?"

"Really?"

He lifted his head. "Really." He rolled onto his back and eased her down over him, smiling lazily as he studied her rapt face, as his eyes wandered to where her breasts were crushed softly against his hard, hair-matted chest. His hands unfastened her hair and arranged it over her shoulders, his eyes heavy-lidded and steady as they wandered over her body.

She watched his face and moved. Just a little. Just enough to let him feel the texture of her body.

"Is that an invitation?" he asked quietly, watching her.

Her breath caught in her throat. Was it, indeed? She searched his hard face with awe and love in every line of her own. Her fingers twined in his thick hair, and she could feel his heartbeat under her.

His hands smoothed over her back. He shifted her body this time, softly rubbing her breasts against the mat of hair on his chest. He heard her catch her breath as she bent her forehead to rest it on his.

His hands shifted, so that his thumbs could tease the hard peaks of her breasts. "I ache with wanting you," he said quietly. "Shall I let you feel how much?"

"You started it," she reminded him, nuzzling her forehead against his. She moved suddenly, so that the whole soft length of her body pressed down over him, and she knew then that she wasn't going to stop him.

"Hold me like this," she whispered as she bent to put her mouth over his. "Hold me hard, Jacob."

His big hands spread at the base of her spine, moving her in a sweet, tender rotation against his hips, and he moaned deeply.

"I won't stop you this time," she whispered over his mouth. "I won't stop you, Jacob, I won't..." Her hands slid between them, into the thick cloud of hair over his chest. "Jacob...!"

"Tell me...why," he managed to say in a tortured voice.

"You know," she breathed, crushing her mouth against his in a frenzy of hunger. Her body moved against him, she trembled with unleashed desire. And suddenly he rolled her over, covering her with his crushing weight, lifting her up to him while his mouth possessed hers absolutely. She felt the wild, demanding thrust of his tongue and met it with a wildness of her own, giving him everything he demanded of her.

"Tell me," he insisted, lifting his head to let his wild eyes glitter down into her own. He shifted, grinding his hips into hers. "Tell me, Gabby!"

"I love you," she said fiercely. Her voice was trembling, but she met his eyes unafraid. "I love you, I love you!"

He seemed to stop breathing. His body was rigid above her, but his eyes were alive, burning, blazing with emotion. His hands moved slowly up her body, over her breasts, to touch her face. His big body shuddered with the effort to control his passion.

"I'm going to die from this," he told her with a faint, harsh smile. And all at once, he rolled away from her and lay on his stomach. He groaned once, as if he were hurting in unbearable ways. His body stiffened and he clenched the pillow so hard his fingers went white.

"Jacob?" she whispered, sitting up, frightened.

"Don't touch me, baby," he whispered back, his voice tormented.

She sat there watching him, a little nervous and

uncertain. He'd forced that reckless admission from her, and then he'd stopped. Why? What did he want?

Slowly his body relaxed and he sighed wearily. "Oh, God, I never thought I'd be able to stop," he murmured. "That was as close as I've ever come to losing control, except for that time at the *finca.*"

Her wide eyes studied the pale face he turned toward her. "That morning?" she murmured.

He laughed dryly. "That night," he said. "Gabby, it wasn't punishment, there at the last. It was loss of control. I very nearly took you."

Her eyebrows went up. "But you let me think…!"

"I had to," he said. "I was going out of my mind trying to decide how to handle it. In the beginning, I wanted an affair with you. But I couldn't seem to get close enough, or make you see me as a man. Then, when we were in Rome, I'd had all I could stand and I forced the issue." He laughed softly. "My God, it was the end of the rainbow, and I was floating. Until I realized you were a virgin, and I had to rethink it all. I'd decided that I'd have to fire you, and then we went into the jungle and I died a thousand deaths when that terrorist pointed his rifle at you." He rolled over onto his back and caught her fingers in his, holding them to his mouth feverishly. "That was when I realized what had happened to me. I was like a boy, all raging desire and frustration and fear. I wanted to frighten you off before I was trapped by what I felt for you. Only it backfired. I started to hurt you and went crazy wanting you instead. I can't wait anymore," he added with an apologetic smile, "and after a week from Saturday I won't have to."

"A week from Saturday?" She frowned.

"There were two reasons I took your Reverend Boone to lunch," he said. "The first was to discuss some things I had on my conscience. The second was to arrange a wedding."

She froze; her face was flushed, and her eyes were disbelieving. It was like having every dream she had ever dreamed come true at once.

He sat up, taking both her hands in his. "Gabby, the one thing I can't do is go on living without you," he said matter-of-factly.

"But...but you said you didn't know whether you could settle down."

He rubbed his thumbs over the backs of her hands and sighed. "Yes, I know. And all the while I was wondering how I'd survive if you refused me. I was trying to get a reaction out of you, to see if I'd frightened you so badly that I'd chased you away." His face hardened as he stared at her hands. "I told you once that I was used to taking what I wanted. That ended with you. I couldn't take you. It had to be a mutual wanting."

"It was," she breathed softly. "It is. I love you with all my heart."

He smiled quietly, lifting hungry eyes to hers. "Do you know what I feel for you?"

She lifted her shoulders restlessly. "You want me," she said with a shaky smile. "Maybe you like me a little."

His chest rose and fell heavily and his eyes never left hers. "I've never said the words and meant them before. It's harder than I thought."

She moved close to him and slid her arms under his, pressing her cheek against his broad chest.

His hands hesitated on her back and then slid around her, cherishing, comforting, protective. He sighed, and she felt his breath on her ear.

"I…" He nuzzled his face against her cheek and then her throat. He laid her back on the bed so that he could find her soft breasts and brush them with his lips. His teeth nipped her tenderly, his hands lifted her. With a sound like a rough, low growl, he slid his body alongside hers and kissed her until she moaned and clutched at him.

"I love you," he breathed fiercely, looming over her. His face was so taut with passion that it would have frightened her once. "Worship you, adore you. I'll go down into the dark crying your name, wanting your mouth, your voice. Is that enough?"

Tears welled in her eyes. "Oh, yes, it's enough," she said unsteadily. "But will I be enough for you?"

"Yes," he said simply. "You and the children." He bent to her mouth again. "Reverend Boone said you hadn't joined the church. I thought we'd do it together. The kids are going to need a good foundation to build on, aren't they?"

She hid her face against his throat. "I'll like having your babies," she whispered.

He trembled convulsively. "Say things like that to me, and you'll find yourself wearing scarlet at the wedding. Hush!"

She managed to laugh. "You taught me how."

"That isn't all I'll teach you. But not now." He

rolled away from her and got to his feet reluctantly, stretching as if his muscles were in torment.

She propped herself on an elbow and smiled at him wistfully. "You've got to be the sexiest man alive," she murmured. "I used to stare at you in the office and wonder what you looked like without your shirt..."

"Gabby," he said in a mock threatening tone.

She arched her body softly, wanting him, loving him, loving the way his eyes followed her movement with such obvious hunger.

"Jacob," she whispered, lying back so that the blouse slid away from her body and he could see every soft curve.

His chest rose and fell sharply. He seemed a little unsteady on his feet.

She loved that vulnerability. She'd never realized before just how much power she had over him, and it was a heady knowledge. With a small, triumphant smile, she held out her arms to him.

"I can't, honey," he whispered. "If I come back down there, I'll take you."

Her body tingled with the very thought of how it would be. She could already picture them, his hair-darkened body crushing her bare pink one down into the mattress, his voice whispering those wildly exciting things while she moaned and wept...

He reached down, and she arched toward him. And all at once, before she realized what was going on, she was out of the bed, being buttoned back into her blouse.

"And don't try that again," he murmured with a wicked smile. "Hussy."

"But..."

"When we're married," he said firmly, kissing her mouth. "Now let's go look at houses. I drove by two yesterday that looked promising. How do you feel about living on the lake?"

She slid her hand into his as they walked into the living room. "I'll like living anywhere with you," she said with feeling. "I imagine just watching television is going to be an adventure from now on."

He chuckled softly as he opened the door, his eyes narrowing. "You can't imagine the plans I have for the symphony concerts on the educational channel," he remarked with a wicked smile.

She went ahead of him out the door. "Oh, I think I might have some vague idea," she said musingly, glancing over her shoulder. "By the way, what did you do with the crossbow?"

"What crossbow?" he asked grinning.

She sighed and leaned her head against his shoulder for an instant. "Do you reckon First Shirt would give me away if we asked him?"

"I imagine he'd be pretty flattered," he said. "Want to invite the rest of the gang too?"

"Could we?"

"Sure," he told her. He smiled as they got into the elevator. "Don't look so worried. I won't try to leave with them, I promise."

"No regrets?" she asked softly.

His eyes were wistful for a moment before he sighed and drew her into his arms. "Only," he whispered, bending, "that I waited so long to tell you how I felt."

"So long?"

"Gabby," he said against her mouth, "I fell in love with you two years ago."

She started to speak, but he was kissing her, and the wildness of it made her question go right out of her head.

"You never said anything," she murmured eventually.

"I couldn't," he returned. "You were so young. I felt guilty for wanting you the way I did. But you dated, you seemed so sophisticated sometimes." He touched her hair gently. "I had too many doubts about being able to settle down to make a heavy pass at you. Too, I was afraid you might quit, and I wasn't sure I could stand that." He shrugged his broad shoulders. "It wasn't until that day in the jungle that I knew how much I cared. I spent a miserable weekend trying to convince myself that I could go back to what I was and not miss you. I failed. After that, it was a matter of trying to convince you that I wouldn't be brutal again. You can't imagine how it hurt, when you cringed away from me..."

But she could. The anguish was in his face. She reached up and kissed his closed eyes gently, tenderly. "It wasn't so much a physical fear," she confessed, "as an emotional one. I was afraid you only wanted an affair. And that you'd walk away." She laughed bitterly. "I knew I couldn't survive that. I loved you too much."

"We won't be apart again," he said quietly. "Not

ever. Even when you have the children, I'll be with you every step of the way."

Tears misted her eyes. "I'll like that."

Six days later, there was a quiet ceremony in the Methodist church. Gabby, in a street-length white silk dress, walked slowly down the aisle on the arm of a wiry little man in a new gray suit, who looked even more out of place than the other people in the church. A tall black man standing beside J.D. was tugging uncomfortably at his tight collar and tie, and several other awkward-looking men were sitting in the front pew. Gabby noticed Richard Dice and two secretaries who worked in her building casting strange glances at the assembly. Her mother seemed equally perplexed.

Gabby just grinned and walked on, feeling proud and happy as J.D. grinned at her from where he stood near the altar.

It was a brief but solemn ceremony, and at its end, after Gabby had enthusiastically kissed her new husband, she threw her arms around Matthew and hugged him.

"Thank you," she told him with a beaming smile.

First Shirt looked faintly embarrassed. "I enjoyed it. Uh, Gabby, your mother's giving us a strange look."

"Mother's always been strange, Matthew," she informed him. "I'll show you. Mother, come meet Matthew," she called while J.D.'s partner Richard congratulated him and bent to kiss Gabby's cheek.

"All the best, Gabby, J.D.," Richard said with a

grin. "What a shock, to be invited to your wedding. Especially after all that's happened the past week."

"The road to love is rocky," Gabby grinned at him. "As you'll discover someday."

"Not me," Richard retorted. "I run too fast!"

"That's what I thought," J.D. murmured with a wicked glance toward Gabby. She stuck out her tongue at him, and went to drag her mother away from the secretaries.

Mrs. Darwin, resplendent in a white linen suit and a hat that looked three sizes too big, followed her daughter slowly. She looked as out of place as Matthew and Apollo and the rest.

"I hate dressing up," she muttered, casting a curious eye at Matthew. "Give me my jeans anytime."

"I hear you shoot and cuss and ride," Matthew told her, pursing his lips.

Mrs. Darwin actually blushed. She lowered her eyes and grinned. "Well, a little, Mr...?"

"Matthew," came the reply. "Matthew Carver. Archer's...I mean, J.D.'s like a son to me." He held out his hand, took hers, and lifted it to his lips. "What a lovely mother-in-law he's getting," he murmured.

Gabby left her blushing mother and went to greet Apollo, Semson, Laremos, and Drago.

"Hi, guys," she said, grinning at them.

"Hey, Gabby," Apollo greeted her. "Good thing you know the ropes—we won't have to run you through the training course or anything."

"Now, just hold on," she informed him. "I am going on a honeymoon. My adventuring days are over. I can just see me, pregnant and crawling through underbrush with an AK-47…"

"Oh, we'd carry it for you, Gabby," he said, all seriousness.

"How gentlemanly!" She laughed.

"Unspeakable ruffian," Laremos said with a mock frown as he stepped forward to kiss Gabby's hand. "Congratulations. And of course you will not be crawling through the jungle." He grinned. "We will carry you."

Semson and Drago added their comments, and Gabby clutched J.D.'s arm, all but collapsing with laughter.

A strange man stood up farther down the pew and walked closer as the other guests paused on their way out to congratulate Gabby and J.D. He was the last. Tall, blond, and heavily muscled, he had a face as rugged as Jacob's and a tan that emphasized his sun-bleached hair.

He had brown eyes, and they studied Gabby for a long moment before he spoke. He was wearing a tan suit that looked as new as those J.D.'s men friends had on, and there was something familiar about the way he shook hands with J.D.

"I thought you hated weddings," J.D. remarked with a cool smile.

"I do. I just wanted to see who caught you." He pursed his lips and narrowed one eye, looking Gabby over in a way that made her nervous. Finally, one corner of his mouth tugged up a little and he gave a short laugh. "Well, if she can shoot and doesn't start screaming at gunfire, I guess she's okay."

"Okay?" she returned with a cold stare. "I'll have you know I'm terrific. I can even hit what I aim at."

The laugh mellowed a little and his dark eyes twinkled. "Can you?" He held out his hand. "I'm Dutch."

Her eyes widened. She remembered that he'd met J.D. in Rome and was the intelligence-gathering logistics man for the team.

"Well, miracles never cease," she murmured. "I thought you'd be bowlegged and chew tobacco."

Dutch burst out laughing. Impulsively, he drew her into a friendly embrace and hugged her. "Oh, J.D., you lucky son of a..."

"Dutch!" First Shirt burst out, interrupting him. "Where did you come from?"

"Lebanon," came the reply. "I need a few grunts. Interested?"

"Maybe," Matthew said. He glanced at the others. "Let's go talk. J.D., take care of her. And yourself." He clasped hands with the younger man. "I'll be in touch."

Gabby hugged him. "Thanks for giving me away. Let me know where you'll be at Christmas. I'll send you a box of thick socks."

Matthew kissed her forehead. "I'll do that." He leaned toward her ear. "Write down your mama's address for me too," he added in a whisper. "I like a lady who can shoot and cuss."

She laughed. "I'll do that."

The others filed out after brief goodbyes, and Gabby glanced at J.D.'s impassive face as they thanked Reverend Boone and started on their way to take Gabby's mother back to the airport.

"Call me once in a while, baby," her mother said to Gabby at the entrance to the waiting area.

"I will." She hugged the older woman. "Matthew took to you."

Her mother grinned. "I took to him too."

"There's just one thing..." Gabby began, wondering how much to tell her mother.

"He'll settle one day, just like J.D. did," came the quiet reply, and her mother gave her a knowing smile. "Some men take longer. Meanwhile, I write a sweet letter." She winked. "Come and visit."

"We will," J.D. promised, coming up to join them. He hugged his new mother-in-law and watched as she walked away with a wave.

Gabby slid her hand into the crook of his arm, and they walked back toward the parking lot.

"You've been very quiet since we left the church," he said softly. "Were you afraid I'd want to go with them?"

She was startled by his perception. "Yes, I think so. A little," she admitted.

He stopped beside the car and turned her to him, looking down into her troubled face. "I'll be honest with you, because anything less would cheat us both. I did feel a sense of loss when the others left without me, because in Guatemala I had a taste of the old, wild life and it brought back memories of days when I had more freedom than I have now. But I'm a realist, Gabby. Matthew said he told you, before we left Guatemala, that I'd gone too far to come back to them, to their way of life.'' She nodded and he touched her mouth softly with his fingers. ''He was right. I've built a future for myself, for you. I've invested too much of my life in building it to throw it away for a little excitement. Besides,'' he murmured, lifting her slender hand to his chest and pressing it hard, ''there are different levels of excitement.''

His eyes studied hers with an intensity that made her knees go weak. He slid her fingers inside his vest, against his white shirt, letting her feel the warmth of his skin and the thunder of his pulse.

''You have the same effect on me that being caught under fire does,'' he whispered huskily, moving her fingers across one hard male nipple. ''Except that you're a little less dangerous than a bullet.''

''Only a little?'' she whispered back, moving close, so that she could feel the length of his body touching hers.

His dark head bent and his mouth hovered just above hers. His hand moved between them to stroke one soft, high breast. It immediately went taut; his nostrils flared and his eyes burned with undisguised hunger.

''Are you afraid to have sex with me?'' he whispered.

Her face flushed, but she didn't drop her eyes. ''No. I love you,'' she whispered. ''And it won't be sex. It will be...loving.''

His mouth parted hers softly, sensuously. ''In broad daylight, Gabby,'' he breathed.

''Yes, I know,'' she murmured, meeting his lips

hungrily. "We can watch each other."

He looked into her eyes and saw the wildest kind of jungle there. He bent and caught her against him, kissing her hungrily and hard, feeling her response. He could hardly catch his breath when he finally lifted his head. "I don't need to go looking for adventure anymore. Not while I have you," he said gruffly. "A woman with an adventurous heart is excitement enough for me."

"Take me home, Jacob," she whispered. "Teach me."

He looked into her misty eyes and reluctantly let her go. "What an utterly delicious thought." He laughed unsteadily, and the lessons were already in his eyes. She looked at him and saw them as they would be, mouth to mouth, his body over hers, hard and warm and ardent, her eyes looking into his as they came together on crisp, cool sheets with his dark body overwhelming her soft, pink one with the same pleasure she felt when he stroked her bare flesh, only much more intimate, more intense...

She trembled softly in anticipation, wanting to be alone with him, wanting his hands, his mouth, his absolute possession. "I can hardly wait," she said, her voice trembling.

He put her into the car and paused for an instant, glancing toward the sky where a military plane was passing over. His face hardened for an instant as he stood quietly watching it until it was out of sight. But when he climbed in beside Gabby and looked at her glowing face, her bright, loving eyes, the hardness drained away. His dark eyes narrowed with the first stirrings of possession. And he smiled.

* * * * *

The Tender Stranger

To J.A. with thanks

One

The seat was much too low for his tall frame; he had barely enough room without the paraphernalia his companion was shifting in her own seat. He gave her a short glare through deep brown eyes. She flushed, her gaze dropping to her lap as she tucked her huge purse on the other side of her and struggled with her seat belt.

He sighed, watching her. A spinster, he thought unkindly. From her flyaway brown hair to the eyes under those wire-rimmed glasses, from her bulky white sweater down to her long gray skirt and sensible gray shoes, she was definitely someone's unclaimed treasure. He turned his eyes back to the too-narrow aisle. Damn budget airlines, he thought furiously. If he hadn't missed the flight he'd booked, he wouldn't be trying to fit into this sardine can of a seat. Next to Miss Frump here.

He didn't like women. Never less than now, when he was forced to endure this particular woman's company for several hundred miles from San Antonio down to Veracruz, Mexico. He glanced sideways again irritably. She was shifting books now. Books, for God's sake! Didn't she know what the baggage hold was for?

"You should have reserved a seat for them," he muttered, glaring at a stack of what was obviously romance novels.

She swallowed, a little intimidated as her eyes swept over a muscular physique, blond hair and a face that looked positively hostile. He had nice hands, though. Very lean and tanned and strong-looking. Scars on the back of one of them...

"I'm sorry," she murmured, avoiding his eyes. "I've just come from a romance writer's autographing in San Antonio. These—these are autographed copies I'm taking back for friends after my Mexican holiday, and I was afraid to trust them to the luggage compartment."

"Priceless gems?" he asked humorlessly, giving them a speaking glare as she tucked the sackful under her seat.

"To some people, yes," she acknowledged. Her face tautened and she didn't look at him again. She cast nervous glances out the window while the airplane began to hum and the flight crew began once more the tedious demonstration of the safety equipment. He sighed impatiently and folded his arms across his broad chest, over the rumpled khaki shirt he wore. He leaned his head back, staring blankly at the stewardess. She was a beauty, but he wasn't interested. He hadn't been interested in women for quite a few years, except to satisfy an infrequent need. He laughed shortly, glancing at the prim little woman next to him. He wondered if she knew anything about those infrequent needs, and decided that she didn't. She looked as chaste as a nun, with her nervous eyes and hands. She had nice hands, though, he thought, pursing his lips as he studied them. Long fingers, very graceful, and no polish. They were the hands of a lady.

It irritated him that he'd noticed that. He glared harder at her.

That caught her attention. It was one thing to be impatiently tolerated, but she didn't like that superior glare. She turned and glared back at him. Something danced briefly in his dark eyes before he turned them back to the stewardess.

So she had fire, he thought. That was unexpected in a prim little nun. He wondered if she was a librarian. Yes, that would explain her fascination with books. And love stories…probably she was starving for a little love of her own. His eyes darkened. Stupid men, he thought, to overlook a feisty little thing like that just because of the glitter and paint that drew them to her more liberated counterparts.

There was murmuring coming from beside him. His sensitive ears caught a few feverish words: "Hail Mary, full of grace…"

It couldn't be! He turned, his eyes wide and stunned. Was she a nun?

She caught him looking at her and bit her lip self-consciously. "Habit," she breathed. "My best friend was Catholic. She taught me the rosary and we always recited it together when we flew. Personally," she whispered, wide-eyed, "I don't think there's anyone up there in the cockpit flying this thing!"

His eyebrows levered up. "You don't?"

She leaned toward him. "Do you ever see anybody in there?" She nodded toward the cockpit. "The door's always closed. If there isn't anything to hide, why do they close the door?"

He began to smile reluctantly. "Perhaps they're concealing a robot pilot?"

"More likely, they've got the pilot roped into his seat and they don't want us knowing it." She laughed softly, and it changed her face. With the right cosmetics and a haircut that didn't leave her soft hair unruly and half wild, she might not be bad-looking.

"You've been reading too many of those," he observed, gesturing toward the sack of books.

"Guilty." She sighed. "I suppose we need dreams sometimes. They keep reality at bay."

"Reality is better," he replied. "It has no illusions to spoil."

"I'd rather have my illusions."

He studied her openly. Wide, bow-shaped mouth, straight nose, wide-spaced pale gray eyes, heart-shaped face. She had a stubborn chin, too, and he smiled slowly. "You're a strange little creature," he said.

"I'm not little," she returned. "I'm five feet six."

He shrugged. "I'm over six feet. To me, you're little."

"I won't argue that," she said with a shy smile.

He chuckled. "Do you have a name?"

"Danielle. Danielle St. Clair. I own a bookstore in Greenville, South Carolina."

Yes, that fit her image to a T. "I'm called Dutch," he returned. "But my name is Eric van Meer."

"Are you Dutch?" she asked.

He nodded. "My parents were."

"It must be nice, having parents," she said with unconscious wistfulness. "I was small when I lost both of mine. I don't even have a cousin."

His eyes darkened and he turned his face away. "I hope they serve lunch on this flight," he remarked, changing the subject with brutal abruptness. "I haven't had anything since last night."

"You must be starved!" she exclaimed. She began to dig in her bag as the plane jerked and eased toward the runway. "I have a piece of cake left over from the autograph party. I didn't have time to eat it. Would you like it?" she asked, and offered him a slice of coconut cake.

He smiled slowly. "No. I'll wait. But thank you."

She shrugged. "I don't really need it. I'm trying to lose about twenty pounds."

His eyes went over her. She was a little overweight. Not fat, just nicely rounded. He almost told her so. But then he remembered what treacherous creatures women were, and bit back the hasty words. He had concerns of his own, and no time for little spinsters. He leaned back and closed his eyes, shutting her out.

The flight passed uneventfully, but if he'd hoped to walk off the plane in Veracruz and forget about his seatmate, he was doomed to disappointment. When the plane finally rolled to a stop she stepped out into the aisle, juggling her luggage, and the sack containing her books broke into a thousand pieces.

Dutch tried not to laugh at the horrified expression on her face as he gathered the books quickly together and threw them into her seat, then herded her out of the aisle.

"Oh, Lord," she moaned, looking as if fate and the Almighty were out to get her.

"Most travelers carry a spare bag inside their suitcases," he said hopefully as the other passengers filed out.

She looked up at him helplessly, all big gray eyes and shy pleading, and for an instant he actually forgot what he was saying. Her complexion was exquisite, he thought. He would have bet that she hardly ever used, or needed to use, beauty creams.

"Spare bag?" she echoed. "Spare bag!" She grinned. "Yes, of course." She shifted restlessly.

"Well?" he prompted gently.

She pointed to the overhead rack.

"We'll wait for everyone else to get off," he said. "Mine's up there, too; it's all right. No big deal."

She brushed back strands of wild hair and looked hunted. "I'm so organized back home," she muttered. "Not a stick of furniture out of place. But let me get outside the city limits of Greenville and I can't stick a fork on a plate without help."

He couldn't help laughing. "We'll get you sorted out," he said. "Where are you booked?"

"Book...oh, the hotel? It's the Mirador," she said.

Fate, he thought with a wistful smile. "That's where my reservation is," he said.

Her face lit up, and the look in her eyes faintly embarrassed him. She was gazing at him with a mixture of blind trust and hopeful expectation.

"Do you know the hotel? I mean, have you been here before?" she faltered, trying not to pry.

"Several times," he confessed. "I come down here once or twice a year when I need to get away." He glanced around. "Let's go."

He got down her suitcase and helped her extricate the spare bag from the case with a wry glance at the neat cotton nightgowns and underwear. She blushed wildly at that careless scrutiny, and he turned his attention to her books, packing them neatly and deftly.

She followed him out of the plane with gratitude shining on her face. She could have kissed him for not making fun of her, for helping her out. Imagine, she thought, a man like that actually doing something for her!

"I'm sorry to have been so much trouble," she blurted out, almost running to keep up with him as they headed toward customs and immigration. She was searching desperately for her passport, and missed the indulgent smile that softened his hard features momentarily.

"No trouble at all," he replied. "Got your passport?"

She sighed, holding it up. "Thank God I did something right," she moaned. "I've never even used it before."

"First time out of the States?" he asked pleasantly as they waited in line.

"First time out, yes," she confessed. "I just turned twenty-six. I thought I'd better do something adventurous fast, before I ran out of time."

He frowned. "My God, twenty-six isn't old," he said.

"No," she agreed. "But it isn't terribly young, either." She didn't look at him. Her eyes were quiet and sad, and she was thinking back of all the long years of loneliness.

"Is there a man?" he asked without quite knowing why.

She laughed with a cynicism that actually surprised him, and the wide eyes that looked up into his seemed ancient. "I have no illusions at all about myself," she said, and moved ahead with her huge purse.

He stared at her straight back with mingled emotions, confusing emotions. Why should it matter to him that she was alone? He shook his head and glanced around him to break the spell. It was none of his business.

Minutes later she was through customs. She almost waited for her tall companion, but she thought that one way or another, she'd caused him enough trouble. The tour company had provided transfers from the airport to the hotel, but a cab seemed much more inviting and less crowded. She managed to hail one, and with her bag of books and suitcase, bustled herself into it.

"Hotel Mirador," she said.

The cab driver smiled broadly and gunned the engine as he pulled out into the crowded street. Dani, full of new experiences and delightful sensations, tried to look everywhere at once. The Bay of Campeche was blue and delightful, and there were glimpses of palms and sand and many hotels. Veracruz was founded in the early 1500s and looked as many old cities of that period did, its architecture alternating between the days of piracy and the space age. Dani would have loved to dive straight into some sight-seeing, but she was already uncomfortable in the formidable heat, and she knew it would be foolish to rush out without letting her body acclimate itself to its new environment.

As she gazed at the rows of hotels, the driver pulled into one of them, a two-story white building with graceful arches and a profusion of blooming flowers. It had only been a few minutes' ride from the airport, but the fare was confusing. And a little intimidating. Twenty dollars, just for several miles. But perhaps it was the custom, she thought, and paid him uncomplainingly.

He grinned broadly again, tipped his hat, and left her at the reservation desk.

She gave the clerk her name and waited with bated breath until her reservation was found. Finally, she had a room. Everything would be all right.

The room was nice. It overlooked the city, unfortunately, not the beautiful bay. But she hadn't expected much for the wonderfully low rates that had come with the package tour. She took off her sweater, amazed that it had felt so comfortable back in the States where it was early spring. It was much too

heavy here, where the temperature was blazing hot
even with the air-conditioning turned up. She stared
out the window at the city. Mexico. It was like a
dream come true. She'd scrimped and saved for two
years to afford this trip. Even so, she'd had to come
during the off-season, which was her busiest time
back home. She'd left her friend Harriett Gaynor
watching the bookstore in her absence. Go, Harriett
had coaxed. Live a little.

She looked at herself in the mirror and grimaced.
Live a little, ha! What a pity she hadn't looked like
that gorgeous stewardess on the plane. Perhaps then
the blond giant would have given her a second glance,
or something besides the reluctant pity she'd read in
his dark eyes.

She turned away from her reflection and began to
unpack her suitcase. There was no use kidding herself
that he'd helped her for any reason other than expe-
diency. He could hardly walk right over her precious
books. With a sigh she drew out her blouses and hung
them up.

Two

By late afternoon Dani felt up to some exploring, and she wandered the ancient streets with the excitement of a child. She'd changed into blue jeans and a loose, light sweatshirt and thongs, looking as much like a tourist as the other strangers in port. Her body was still adjusting to the heat, but the sweatshirt was simply a necessity. She couldn't bear to wear form-fitting T-shirts in public. They called too much attention to her ample bustline.

She found the stalls along the waterfront particularly fascinating, and paused long enough to buy herself a sterling silver cross with inlaid mother-of-pearl. Her pidgin Spanish seemed adequate, because most of the vendors spoke a little English. Everywhere there were colorful things to see—beautiful serapes in vivid rainbow shades, ponchos, hats, straw bags and animals and sea shells. And the architecture of the old buildings near the docks fascinated her. She stared out over the bay and daydreamed about the days of pirate ships and adventure, and suddenly a picture of the big blond man flashed into her mind. Yes, he would have made a good pirate. What was it that Dutch had called pirates—freebooters? She could even picture him with a cutlass. She smiled at her own fantasy and moved on down the pier to watch some men unloading a big freighter. She'd never been around ships very much. Greenville was an inland city, far from the ocean. Mountains and rolling, unspoiled countryside were much more familiar to Dani than ships were. But she liked watching them. Lost in her daydreams, she didn't realize just how long she'd been standing there, staring. Or that her interest might seem more than casual.

One of the men on the dock began watching her, and with a feeling of uneasiness she moved back into the crowd of tourists. She didn't want trouble, and a woman alone could get into a sticky situation.

Dusk was settling over the sleepy city of Veracruz, and the man was still watching her. Out of the corner of her eye she could see him moving toward her. Oh, Lord, she thought miserably, now what do I do? She didn't see a policeman anywhere, and most of the remaining tourists were older people who wouldn't want to be dragged into someone else's problems. Dani groaned inwardly as she clutched her bag and started walking quickly toward the hotel. The crowd dispersed still farther. Now she was alone and still the footsteps sounded behind her. Her heart began to race.

What if he meant to rob her? Good heavens, what if he thought she was looking for a man?

She quickened her steps and darted around a corner just as a tall form loomed up in front of her. She jerked to a stop and almost screamed before she noticed the color of his hair in the fiery sunset.

"Oh," she said weakly, one hand clutching her sweatshirt.

Dutch stared at her coolly, a cigarette in one hand, the other in his pocket. He was still wearing the khaki safari suit he'd worn on the plane, but he looked fresh and unruffled. She found herself wondering if anything could rattle him. He had an odd kind of self-confidence, as if he'd tested himself to the very limits and knew himself as few men ever did.

He glanced over her shoulder, seeming to take in the situation in one quick glance. His eyes were very dark when they met hers again. "You'll enjoy your holiday more if you keep out of this part of town after dark," he told her pleasantly enough but with authority in his tone. "You've picked up an admirer."

"Yes, I know, I..." She started to glance over her shoulder, but he shook his head.

"Don't. He'll think you're encouraging him." He laughed shortly. "He's fifty and bald," he added. "But if you purposely went down to the docks looking for a man, you might give him a wink and make his day."

He'd meant it as a joke, but the remark hurt her anyway. Clearly, he didn't think she was likely to attract a man like himself.

"It was more a case of forgetting where I was, if

you want the truth. I'll know better next time. Excuse me," she said quietly, and walked past him.

He watched her go, furious with her for letting the taunt cut her, more furious with himself for not realizing that it would. He muttered something unpleasant under his breath and started after her.

But she'd had quite enough. She quickened her pace, darting into the hotel and up the staircase to the second floor instead of waiting for an elevator. She made it into her room and locked the door. Although why she should have bothered was anyone's guess. He wasn't the kind of man who chased bespectacled booksellers, she told herself coldly.

She didn't bother to go downstairs for dinner that evening. Probably he wouldn't have come near her, but she was too embarrassed to chance it. She ordered from room service, and enjoyed a seafood supper in privacy.

The next morning she went down to breakfast, too proud to let him think she was avoiding him. And sure enough, there he was, sitting alone at a window table with a newspaper. He looked good, she thought, even in nothing more unusual than white slacks and a red-and-white half-unbuttoned shirt. Just like a tourist. As if he felt her eyes on him, he lifted his gaze from the paper and caught her staring. She blushed, but he merely smiled and returned his eyes to his reading. She hardly knew what she was eating after that, and she couldn't help watching him out of the corner of one eye.

He was much too sophisticated for a little country mouse, Dani told herself sternly. She'd just have to keep well away from him. He had no interest in her, despite her helpless fascination with him. He was world-weary and cynical, and looked as if she amused him...nothing more.

She made up her mind to enjoy the rest of her four-day holiday, and went to her room, where she got out a one-piece black bathing suit to wear to the beach. She pinned her irritating hair out of the way and stared at her reflection. What ravishing good looks, she thought sarcastically. No wonder he wasn't interested. Looking the way she did, it was unlikely that even a shark would be tempted.

Go to Mexico, have fun, her friend Harriett Gaynor had said. Sparkle! Attract men! Dani sighed miserably. Back home it was spring and things were beginning to bloom, and books were selling well—especially romances. And here Dani was, with nothing changed at all except her surroundings. Alone and unloved and unwanted, as usual. She glared at herself and impulsively she called the beauty salon downstairs and made an appointment to have her hair cut.

They had a cancellation, and could take her immediately. Several minutes later she sat watching the unruly locks of hair being neatly sheared off, leaving her delicate features framed by a simple, wavy short cut that curled toward her wide eyes and gave her an impish look. She grinned at herself, pleased, and after paying the girl at the counter, she danced back upstairs and put on her bathing suit. She even added some of the makeup she never used, and perfume. The result wasn't beauty-queen glamour, but it was a definite improvement.

Then she stared at her bodice ruefully. Well, there wouldn't be any miracle to correct this problem, she told herself, and pulled on a beach wrap. It was colorful, tinted with shades of lavender, and it concealed very well. She got the beach bag she'd bought in the hotel lobby and stuffed suntan lotion and her beach towel into it. Then, with her prescription sunglasses firmly over her eyes, she set off for the beach.

It was glorious. Beach and sun and the lazy rhythm of the water all combined to relax her. She stretched, loving the beauty around her, the history of this ancient port. She wondered what the first explorers would have thought of the tourist attraction their old stomping grounds made.

Feeling as if someone were staring at her, she opened her eyes and twisted her head just a little. She saw Dutch wandering along the beach, cigarette in hand, blond head shining like white gold in the sun. He was darkly tanned, shirtless, and her fascinated eyes clung to him helplessly. He wasn't a hairy man, but there was a wedge of curling dark blond hair over the darkly tanned muscles of his chest and stomach. His legs were feathered with it, too, long, powerful legs in cutoff denim shorts, and he wore thongs, as most of the people on the beach did, to protect against unexpected objects in the sand.

She turned her head away so that she didn't have to see him. He was a sensuous man, devastating to a woman who knew next to nothing about the male sex. He had to be aware of her naivete, and it probably amused him, she thought bitterly.

He watched her head turn, and irritation flashed in

his dark eyes. Why was she always gazing at him with that helpless-child longing? She disturbed him. His eyes narrowed. New haircut, wasn't it? The haircut suited her, but why in hell was she wrapped up like a newly caught fish? He'd yet to see her in anything that didn't cover her from neck to waist. He frowned. Probably she was flat-chested and didn't want to call attention to it. But didn't she realize that her attempts at camouflage were only pointing out her shortcoming?

He glowered at her. Long legs, nice legs, he mused, narrowing his eyes as he studied the relaxed body on the giant beach towel. Nice hips, too. Flat, very smooth lines. Tiny waist. But then there was the coverup. She'd said she needed to lose weight, but he couldn't imagine where. She looked perfect to him.

She was just a woman, he thought, pulling himself up. Just another faithless flirt, out for what she could get. Would he never learn? Hadn't he paid for his one great love affair already? Love affair, he thought bitterly. Never that. An infatuation that had cost him everything he held dear. His home, his future, the savings his parents had sacrificed to give him...

He tore his eyes away and turned them seaward. Sometimes it got the better of him. It had no part of the present. In fact, neither did Miss Frump over there.

He turned, blatantly staring at her, a tiny smile playing around his mouth. She was a different species of woman, unfamiliar to him. He found he was curious about her, about what made her tick.

He moved forward slowly, and she saw him out of

the corner of her eye. She felt her pulse exploding as
he came closer. No, she pleaded silently, closing her
eyes. Please, go away. Don't encourage me. Don't
come near me. You make me vulnerable, and that's
the one thing I mustn't be.

"You won't get much sun in that," he remarked,
indicating the top as he plopped down beside her. He
leaned on an elbow, stretched full-length beside her,
and she could feel the heat of him, smell the cologne
that clung to him.

"I don't want to burn," she said in a strangled
tone.

"Still angry about what I said last night?" he asked
on a smile.

"A little, yes," she said honestly.

He leaned over and tugged her sunglasses away
from her eyes so that they were naked and vulnerable.
He was worldly and it showed, and so did her fear of
him.

"I didn't mean to ridicule you. I'm not used to
women," he said bluntly. "I've lived a long time
without them."

"And you don't like them, either," she said per-
ceptively.

He scowled briefly, letting his eyes drop to her
mouth. "Occasionally. In bed." He chuckled softly
at her telltale color. "Don't tell me I embarrass you?
Not considering the type of reading material you carry
around with you. Surely every detail is there in black
and white."

"Not the way you're thinking," she protested.

"Little southern lady," he murmured, watching

her. She had a softness that he wasn't used to, a vulnerability. But there was steel under it. He sensed a spirit as strong as his own beneath shyness. "Do I frighten you?"

"Yes. I...don't have much to do with men," she said quietly. "And I'm not very worldly."

"Are you always that honest?" he asked absently as he studied her nose. There were a few scattered freckles on its bridge.

"I don't like being lied to," she said. "So I try very hard not to lie to other people."

"The golden rule?" He fingered a short strand of her brown hair, noticing the way it shone in the sunlight, as sleek as mink, silky in his hand. "I like your haircut."

"It was hot having it long..." She faltered. She wasn't used to being touched, and there was something magnetic about this man. It was unsettling to have so much vibrant masculinity so close that she could have run her hands over his body. He made her feel things she hadn't experienced since her teens, innocent longings that made her tense with mingled fear and need.

"Why are you wearing this?" he asked, and his hand went to the buttons of her shapeless overblouse. "Do you really need it?"

She could hardly swallow. He had her so rattled, she didn't know her name. "I...no, but..." she began.

"Then take it off," he said quietly. "I want to see what you look like."

There had been a similar passage in the latest book

by her favorite author. She'd read it and gotten breathless. But this was real, and the look in his dark eyes made her tremble. She forgot why she was wearing the wrap and watched his hard face as he eased the buttons skillfully out of their holes and finally drew the garment from around her body.

His breath caught audibly. He seemed to stop breathing as he looked down on what he'd uncovered. "My God," he whispered.

She was blushing again, feeling like a nervous adolescent.

"Why?" he asked, meeting her eyes.

She shifted restlessly. "Well, I'm...I feel...men stare," she finished miserably.

"My God, of course they stare! You're exquisite!"

She'd never heard it put that way. She searched his eyes, looking for ridicule, but there was none. He was staring again, and she found that a part of her she didn't recognize liked the way he was looking at her.

"Is that why you wear bulky tops all the time?" he persisted gently.

She sighed. "Men seem to think that women who are...well-endowed have loose morals. It's embarrassing to be stared at."

"I thought you were flat-chested," he mused, laughing.

"Well, no, I'm not," she managed. "I guess I did look rather odd."

He smiled down at her. "Leave it off," he said with a last lingering scrutiny before he stretched out on his back. "I'll fend off unwanted admirers for you."

She was immediately flattered. And nervous. Would he expect any privileges for that protection? She stared at his relaxed body uneasily.

"No strings," he murmured, eyes closed. "I want rest, not a wild, hot affair."

She sighed. "Just as well," she said ruefully. "I wouldn't know how to have one."

"Are you a virgin?" he asked matter-of-factly.

"Yes."

"Unusual these days."

"I believe in happily-ever-after."

"Yes, I could tell by your reading material," he said with a lazy smile. He stretched, and powerful muscles rippled all up and down his tanned body. Her gaze was drawn to it, held by it.

He opened his eyes and watched her, oddly touched by the rapt look on her young face. He'd have bet a year's earnings that she'd never been touched even in the most innocent way. He found himself wondering what she might be like in passion, whether those pale eyes would glow, whether her body would relax and trust his. He frowned slightly. He'd never taken time with a woman, not since that she-wolf. These days it was all quickly over and forgotten. But slow, tender wooing was something he could still remember. And suddenly he felt a need for it. To touch this silky creature next to him and teach her how to love. How to touch. The thought of her long fingers on him caused a sudden and shocking reaction in his body.

He turned over onto his stomach, half-dazed with the unexpected hunger. Was she a witch? He studied her. Did she know what had happened to him? No, he decided, if she did, it would be highly visible in those virginal cheeks. She probably didn't even know what happened to men at all. He smiled slowly at the searching wonder in her eyes.

"Why are you smiling like that?" she asked softly.

"Do you really want to know?" he murmured dryly.

She rolled over onto her stomach as well, and propped herself up on her elbows, looking down at him, at the hard lines of his face, the faint scarring on one cheek. She felt drawn to him physically, and couldn't understand why it seemed so natural to lie beside him and look at him.

His eyes were fixed on a sudden parting of fabric that gave a tantalizing view of her generous breasts, and when she started to move, he reached up and held her still.

"You won't get pregnant if I look at you," he whispered.

"You're a horrible man," she said haughtily.

"Yes, but I'm much safer than any one of these wily Latins," he told her. "The lesser of two evils, you might say. I won't seduce you."

"As if any man would want to." She laughed, and started to move away again. This time he let her, looming over her as she lay back, with his forearms beside her head and his eyes boring into hers at close range.

"If we weren't on a public beach, I'd give you a crash course in arousal, doubting Thomasina," he murmured. "Something just happened to me that shocked me to the back teeth, and it's your fault."

Her eyes widened as her mind tried to convince her that she hadn't heard him make such a blatant statement.

"I see you understand me," he said with a lazy smile. "What's wrong, southern belle, have you led such a sheltered life?"

She swallowed. "Yes." She studied his hard face. "Yours hasn't been sheltered."

"That's right," he told her. "I could turn your hair white with the story of my life. Especially," he added deliberately, unblinkingly, "the part of it that concerns women."

Her eyes dilated as they held his. "You...aren't a romantic."

He shook his head slowly. "No," he said quietly. "Occasionally I need a woman, the oblivion of sex. But that's all it ever is. Sex, with no illusions."

Her eyes searched his, reading embarrassing things in them. "There's a reason," she said softly, knowingly.

He nodded. "I was twenty-four. She was twenty-eight, wildly experienced, and as beautiful as a goddess. She seduced me on the deck of a yacht, and after that I'd have died for her. But she was expensive, and I was besotted, and eventually I sold everything I had to buy her loyalty." His eyes darkened, went cold with memory and rage as Dani watched. "I'd helped buy my parents a small home for their retirement with money I...earned," he added, not mentioning how he'd earned the money. "And I even mortgaged that. The bank foreclosed. My father, who'd put his life savings into his part of the house,

died of a heart attack soon afterward. My mother
blamed me for it, for taking away the thing he'd
worked all his life for. She died six months later.''

He'd picked up a handful of sand and was letting
it fall slowly onto the beach while she stared at his
handsome profile and knew somehow that he'd never
told this story to another living soul.

''And the woman?'' she asked gently.

The sand made a small sound, and his palm flattened on it, crushing it. ''She found another
chump...'' He glanced at Dani with a cold laugh.
''One with more money.''

''I'm sorry,'' she said inadequately. ''I can
understand that it would have made you bitter.
But—''

''But all women aren't cold-hearted cheats?'' he
finished for her, glaring. ''Aren't they?''

''The one boyfriend I ever had was two-timing me
with another girl,'' she said.

''What a blazing affair it must have been,'' he said
with cold sarcasm.

She searched his face, seeing beneath the anger to
the pain. ''I loved him,'' she said with a gentle smile.
''But he was more interested in physical satisfaction
than undying devotion.''

''Most men are,'' he said curtly.

''I suppose so.'' She sighed. She rolled over onto
her back and stretched. ''I've decided that I like being
alone, anyway. It's a lot safer.''

He eased onto his side, watching her. ''You disturb
me,'' he said after a minute.

''Why? Because I'm not experienced?'' she asked.

He nodded. "My world doesn't cater to inexperience. You're something of a curiosity to me."

"Yes. So are you, to me," she confessed, studying him blatantly.

He brushed the hair away from her face with strong, warm hands, callused hands that felt as if he'd used them in hard work. She liked that roughness against her soft skin. It made her tingle and ache with pleasure. He looked down at the bodice of the bathing suit, watching her reaction. The material was thin and the hard tips of her breasts were as evident as her quickened breathing.

She started to move her arms, to cover herself, but he caught her eyes and shook his head.

"That's as natural as breathing," he said in a voice that barely carried above the sound of the surf. "It's very flattering. Don't be ashamed of it."

"I was raised by a maiden aunt," she told him. "She never married, and I was taught that—"

He pressed his thumb over her mouth, a delicious contact that made her want to bite it gently. "I can imagine what you were taught." He let his dark gaze drop to her mouth and studied it slowly as he touched it, watching it tremble and part. "I like your mouth, Dani. I'd like to take it with mine."

The thought was exciting, wildly exciting. Her gaze went involuntarily to his hard, chiseled mouth. His upper lip was thin, the bottom one wide and sensuous. She would bet he'd forgotten more about kissing than she'd ever learned.

"Have you been kissed very much?" he asked.

"Once or twice," she said lightly, trying to joke.

"French kisses?" he provoked.

Her body was going crazy. She could feel her heart trying to escape her chest, and her breathing was audible. It got even worse when his hard fingers left her mouth to run down the side of her neck, across her collarbone and, incredibly, onto the swell of her breast above the swimsuit.

Her gasp whispered against his lips and he smiled. "Shocking, isn't it?" he murmured, watching her eyes dilate, her face flush as his fingers lazily slid under the strap. His body shielded her from other sunbathers, and there was no one in front of them. "No one can see us," he whispered reassuringly. He laughed softly, wickedly, as his fingers slid under the fabric with a lazy teasing pressure that was more provocative than frightening. Her body reacted wildly to being teased, and she knew that he could see what was happening. He was much too sophisticated not to know exactly what she was feeling.

"Skin like warm silk," he breathed, his mouth poised just above hers while his fingers brushed her like whispers of sensation, and she tensed and trembled as the pleasure began to grow.

She wanted more. She wanted him to touch the hard, aching tip of her breasts; she wanted to watch him do it, to see him possess her with that callused, expert hand. Her face even told him so.

His eyes were getting darker now, and the indulgent smile was vanishing as well. "If you keep looking at me like that," he said under his breath, "I'm going to slide my hand completely over you and to hell with spectators."

Her lips parted. She felt reckless and abandoned and vulnerable. Four days in which to store a lifetime of memories, she thought bitterly. Every one of her friends was married, every one of them had some happiness. But not Dani. Not ever. And now this man, who could have had any woman on the beach, was playing with her, amusing himself, because he saw how vulnerable she was…and she was letting him.

Her eyes clouded, and something deep inside the blond man stirred helplessly when he saw it.

"No," he whispered with aching tenderness. "Don't. I'm not playing."

She bit her lower lip to stop sudden tears. He saw so much, for a stranger. "Yes, you are," she protested. "You—"

His mouth lowered onto hers, just enough to let her lips experience its texture before he withdrew it. His hand, resting warmly under the strap of her bathing suit, began to move.

Her body trembled, and he whispered, "Hush," brushing his mouth tenderly over the bridge of her nose. "No one can see what I'm going to do to you." His lips went to her eyes, brushing them tenderly closed. His long fingers nudged under the fabric, farther and farther.

Her hands were on his shoulders, her fingers clinging, her breath sighing out unsteadily against his tormenting mouth. "Eric," she whispered experimentally.

He hesitated for an instant, lifting his blond head. He looked down into eyes that were full of new sensations, wide and soft and hazy. His free hand eased

to the back of her neck, stroking it softly. He held her
gaze as his hand moved slowly down, and then up,
and she felt the warm roughness of his palm against
the hard point of her breast.

"Is this the first time?" he whispered.

"Can't you...tell?" she whispered back brokenly.
Her body moved helplessly, so that she could experience every texture of his hand where it rested, and
an odd, tearful smile touched her mouth. "Thank you.
Thank..."

He couldn't bear it. The gratitude hurt him. He
moved his hand back up to her face and kissed her
mouth softly, with a tenderness he hadn't shown any
woman since he was little more than a boy.

"You speak as if you think it's a hardship for me
just to touch you," he said quietly. "If you knew
more about men, you might realize that I'm as
aroused by you as you are by me."

"Me?" she repeated, her eyes wide and bright and
full of magic.

"You, you voluptuous, exciting little virgin," he
said, his voice rough with laughter. "I ache all over."

She began to smile, and his attention was caught
by the sunniness of it, by the sudden beauty of her
face. And he'd thought her drab and dull. How odd.
He sensed a deeply buried sensuality in that voluptuous body, and he wanted it.

He propped himself up on an elbow, his free hand
still tugging absently at her short hair.

She gave her eyes the freedom to roam that powerful body, talking in its bronzed sensuousness, the
light covering of dark blond hair on his chest, his

rippling stomach muscles, his strongly muscled thighs. He even had nice feet. And his legs weren't pale, as most American men's were. They were broad and dark, and looked good.

"I like your legs, too," he murmured.

She glanced back up. "Do you mind?" she asked gently. "I know I'm gawking like a schoolgirl."

"You're very honest, aren't you?" he remarked for the second time that day. "It's vaguely disconcerting. No, I don't mind if you look at me. Except that it—"

"It...?" she persisted.

"Arouses me," he said frankly.

"Just to be looked at?" she asked, fascinated.

He smiled a little. "Maybe it's my age," he said with a shrug. "You have very expressive eyes, did you know? They tell me everything you're thinking."

"Do they really?" She laughed, looking up at him. "What am I thinking now?" she asked, her mind carefully blank.

He pursed his lips and smiled slowly, and she felt a deep, slow ache in her body that was intensified when she looked at the broad sweep of his chest.

"That you'd like to have dinner with me," he hedged. "How about it?"

"Yes. I'd like to. If you won't seduce me for dessert," she added.

He sighed softly. "I'd like to have you," he confessed. "But I couldn't quite take you in my stride, either. A virgin would be something of a rarity for me. Most of my one-night stands have been the exact opposite of virgins."

She tried not to blush, but her cheeks betrayed her.

He searched her eyes. "I wouldn't hurt you," he said suddenly. "And with you, it would have to be lovemaking, not sex."

Her body felt boneless as he searched her eyes, and there was a flash of something like tenderness in the look he gave her. "I'm sorry," she said.

"Why?"

She dropped her eyes to his chest. "Because I think...I'd have liked you...for a lover."

"Yes, I think I'd have liked you for one," he agreed softly. He tilted her face back to his and searched her eyes. "Wrong time, wrong place. We should have met ten years ago."

She smiled ruefully. "You wouldn't have liked me at sixteen," she said. "I really was twenty pounds overweight."

He drew in a slow breath. "And I was in the early days of some pretty raw living," he agreed. "What a pity." He lifted her hand and kissed the soft palm, watching her face color with pleasure. "How long will you be here?"

"Four days," she said miserably.

His teeth bit into the soft flesh. "Make some memories with me," he whispered.

"That will only make it worse..." she began.

"We'll keep it light," he said. "I won't seduce you."

"By tomorrow I'll probably beg you to," she said unhappily, studying him with helpless longing. "I'm frighteningly vulnerable with you."

His eyes went along her body and he felt himself

going rigid with desire. "Yes. I'm pretty vulnerable myself."

She had to force her eyes to stay on his face, and he smiled wickedly, knowing exactly what she was thinking.

He laughed and she rolled over onto her stomach again.

"Don't worry," he murmured as he stretched out beside her. "I'll take care of you. Don't sweat it."

She turned her eyes toward his and searched them, and then she smiled. "You're so handsome," she whispered helplessly.

"You're a knockout yourself," he said. "Flat-chested, hell." He laughed. "You're dynamite!"

"Thank you."

He searched her face appreciatively. "So innocent. J.D. would laugh himself sick at me."

"J.D.?" she asked curiously.

"An old friend." He grinned. "Close your eyes and let's soak up some sun. Later, I'll take you sightseeing." His eyes closed and then opened. "Not to the docks," he added, and closed them again.

She closed her own eyes with a smile. Miracles, she thought wistfully, did occasionally happen to lonely spinsters. These were going to be the four most beautiful days of her entire life. She wouldn't take a second of them for granted, starting now.

Three

Dani was glad she'd stopped by the little boutique in the basement of the hotel on her way up to change for dinner. She'd bought a white Mexican dress with an elastic neckline and lots of ruffles, and when she put it on she looked slightly mysterious, with her brown hair and gray eyes and creamy complexion. Her wire-rimmed glasses weren't so spiffy, she admitted, but they did make her eyes look bigger than they were. And she wasn't really fat, she told herself, smiling at her reflection. It was mostly what was on top, and the dress even minimized that. She got her small evening bag and went downstairs to meet Dutch in the lobby.

He was wearing white slacks with a white shirt and blue blazer, and he rose lazily to his feet from a plush sofa, leaving his evening paper there as he joined her.

"Nice," he said, taking her arm. "What do you fancy? Mexican, Chinese, Italian, or a steak?"

"I like steak," she murmured.

"So do I." He guided her along the hall past the family restaurant and into the very exclusive Captain's Quarters next door. White-coated waiters in white gloves were everywhere, and Dani glanced up at Dutch apprehensively as he gave the hostess his name.

"What is it?" he asked softly, guiding her along behind the well-dressed young woman with the menus.

"It's so expensive," she began, worried.

His face brightened, and he smiled. "Do you mind washing dishes afterward?" he whispered mischievously.

She laughed up at him. "Not if you'll dry," she promised.

He slid an arm around her waist and pulled her close. "You're a nice girl."

"Just the kind your mother warned you about, so look out," she told him.

He glanced down at her. "No. My mother would have liked you. She was spirited, too."

She smiled shyly, aware of envious eyes following them along the way. He was so handsome, she thought, peeking up at him. Muscular, graceful, and with the face of a Greek statue, male perfection in the finest sense. An artist would have been enchanted with him as a subject.

The hostess left them at their table, near the window, and Dutch seated Dani with a curious frown.

"What were you thinking about so solemnly just now?" he asked as he eased his tall form into the chair across from her.

"That you'd delight an artist," she said simply. "You're very elegant."

He took a slow breath. "Lady, you're bad for my ego."

"Surely you look in the mirror from time to time?" she asked. "I don't mean to stare, but I can't help it."

"Yes, I have the same problem," he murmured, and his eyes were fixed on her.

She was glad she hadn't yielded to the temptation to pull the elastic neck of her dress down around her shoulders. It was hard enough to bear that dark stare as it was.

"Shall I order for you, or are you liberated?" he asked after she'd studied the menu.

"I kind of like it the old-fashioned way, if you don't mind," she confessed. "I'm liberated enough to know I look better in a skirt than in a pair of pants."

He chuckled. "Do you?"

"Well, you'd look pretty silly in a dress," she came back.

"What do you want to eat?" he asked.

"Steak and a salad and coffee to drink."

He looked at her with a dry smile, and when the waiter came, he gave a double order.

"Yes," he told her, "I like coffee, too."

"You seem very traveled," she remarked, pleating her napkin.

"I am." He leaned back in his chair to study her. "And you've never been out of the States."

"I've been nowhere—until now." She smiled at the napkin. "Done nothing except work. I thought about changing, but I never had the courage to do it."

"It takes courage, to break out of a mold," he said. He pulled the ashtray toward him and lit a cigarette. "I hope you don't mind, but I'm doing it anyway. This is one habit I don't intend to break."

" 'I'll die of something someday,' " she quoted. "There are lots of other clichés, but I think that one's dandy."

He only laughed. "Smoking is the least dangerous thing I do."

"What *do* you do?" she asked, curious.

He thought about that for a moment, and pursed his lips as he wondered what she'd say if he told her the truth. She'd probably be out of that chair and out of his life so fast... He frowned. He didn't like that idea.

"I'm in the military," he said finally. "In a sense."

"Oh. On active duty?" she continued, feeling her way because he seemed reluctant to elaborate.

"No. Inactive, at the moment." He watched her through a veil of smoke from his cigarette.

"Is it dangerous, what you do?"

"Yes."

"I feel like a panelist on 'What's My Line?' " she said unexpectedly, and grinned when he burst out laughing.

"Maybe you're a double agent," she supposed. "A spy."

"I'm too tall," he returned. "Agents are supposed to be under five feet tall so that they can hide in shrubbery."

She stared at him until she realized he was joking, and she laughed.

"Your eyes laugh when you do," he said absently. "Are you always this sunny?"

"Most of the time," she confessed. She pushed her glasses back as they threatened to slide down her nose. "I have my bad days, too, like everyone else, but I try to leave them at home."

"You could get contact lenses," he remarked as he noticed her efforts to keep her glasses on her nose.

She shook her head. "I'm much too nervous to be putting them in and taking them out and putting them in solution all the time. I'm used to these."

"They must get in the way when you kiss a man," he murmured dryly.

"What way?" She laughed, a little embarrassed by his frankness. "My life isn't overrun with amorous men."

"We can take them off, I suppose," he mused.

Her breath caught as she read the veiled promise in his dark eyes.

"Stark terror," he taunted gently, watching her expression. "I didn't realize I was so frightening."

"Not that kind of frightening," she corrected him. Her eyes lowered.

"Dani."

He made her name sound like a prayer. She looked up.

"Seducing you is not on the agenda," he said quietly. "But if something did happen, I'd marry you. That's a promise, and I don't give my word lightly."

She began to tingle all over. "It would be a high price to pay for one mistake."

He was watching her oddly. "Would it? I haven't thought about marriage in years." He leaned back in his chair to study her, the cigarette burning idly in his fingers. "I wonder what it would be like," he mused, "having someone to come back to."

What an odd way to put it, she thought. Surely he meant someone to come *home* to. She pulled herself up short as she realized that it was just conversation. He was only amusing himself; she had to remember that. Making memories, as he'd put it. They were strangers and they'd remain strangers. She couldn't afford to mess up her whole life because of a holiday romance. That was all this was. A little light entertainment. She'd better remember that, too.

The waiter brought their food, and as they ate they talked about general things. He seemed very knowledgeable about foreign conflicts, and she imagined that he read a lot of military publications. That led to talk of the kind of weapons being used, and he seemed equally knowledgeable about those.

"My best friend's husband likes to read about weapons," Dani volunteered, remembering Harriett's Dave and his fascination with weaponry. "He has volumes on those exotic things like...oh, what is it, the little nine-millimeter carbine—"

"The Uzi," he offered. "It has a thirty-shot magazine and can throw off single shots as well as bursts. A formidable little carbine."

She laughed. "I can shoot a twenty-two rifle. That's about the extent of my knowledge of weapons."

"I know more about knives than guns, as a rule, although I've used both." He reached into his inside blazer pocket, produced a large folded knife and put it on the table.

She stared at it, fascinated. It was made of silvery metal, with a carved bone handle, and when she tugged the blade out, it was oddly shaped and had a sinister look.

"It's not a pocket knife, is it?" she asked, lifting her eyes.

He shook his head. "Although it passes for one, going through customs."

"Where did you find something so unusual?" she asked, fascinated by it.

"I made it." He picked it up and repocketed it.

"Made it?" she exclaimed.

"Sure." He laughed at her expression. "Where do you think knives come from? Someone has to make them."

"Yes, of course, but I didn't recognize... It's very formidable looking," she added.

"I don't carry it for decoration," he said. He leaned forward and sipped his coffee. "Would you like some dessert?"

"No, thank you," she said. "I don't like sweet things very much, thank God."

He smiled. "Neither do I. Let's go walk on the beach for a while."

"Lovely!"

She waited while he paid the check and then followed him out into the darkness.

The night was warm, and she took off her sandals, which she'd worn without hose, and danced in and out of the waves. He watched her, laughing, his hands in his pockets, his blond hair pale and glowing in the light from the hotel.

"How old did you say you were?" he asked when she came running back up the beach, sandals dangling from one hand.

"About ten," she laughed up at him.

"You make me feel old." He lifted a hand and touched her cheek, her lips. There were people farther down the beach, but none close enough to be more than dark shapes.

"How old are you?" she asked.

"Thirty-six," he said. His other hand came out of his pocket. He took her sandals from her nerveless fingers and dropped them down into the sand. The soft thud barely registered above the crashing surf.

"You excite me," he said in a deep, slow tone. He cupped her face in his hands and drew her closer, so that she could feel the pleasant heat of his body against hers. "Do you know how a man's body reacts when he's excited?"

Her face felt blistering hot, and she couldn't seem to move as he released her face only to take her hips in his hands and draw them against him.

Her breath caught and his open mouth touched her forehead. His breathing was audible now, and she was learning fascinating things about him, about the subtle differences in his body that she was apparently causing.

"No protest at all?" he asked quietly.

"I'm...curious," she whispered. "As you've already seen, I know very little about this."

"I don't frighten you?"

"No, not now."

His mouth smiled, she could feel it. His thumbs bit into the soft flesh of her stomach as he urged her closer. "Not even now?" he whispered.

Her legs trembled against his. She felt strange new sensations inside her, dragging sensations that left tingling pleasure in their wake. Her hands clung to his blazer because she wasn't sure her legs were going to support her much longer.

His chest rose and fell roughly against her taut breasts. "I want to be alone with you. And at the moment that's the most dangerous thing we could do."

"You want me," she whispered, realizing it with a strange sense of triumph.

"Yes." His hands moved up her body slowly to her breasts, which were bare under the dress because she hadn't wanted to suffer her hot, longline bra, which was the only strapless thing she had.

She tensed, feeling his hands lift her, cup her, so tender that she accepted them without protest. His thumbs brushed over her, feeling her instant response.

"You want me, too, don't you?" he asked gently.

The sensations his thumbs were producing made her mind go blank. She moved a little, moaning.

His face pressed against her cheek. She could feel his breath at her ear.

"Thank God we don't have an audience," he whispered huskily. "Stand very still, Dani."

His hands rose, moved to her shoulders. He eased the fabric down her arms with a slow, sinuous, achingly tender pressure. Her heart stopped beating as she felt the blood rush through her veins, felt the coolness of the salty night breeze touching her shoulders, her upper arms, and then her breasts as he slid the fabric to her waist.

She moaned again, a catching of breath that acted on him like a narcotic. He felt his own legs go weak at the wholehearted response she was giving him. Giving to him, when he knew instinctively that she'd never have let any other man do this to her.

"I wish that I could see your eyes," he whispered. He lifted his head and looked down at her shadowed face. His hands slid against her face, her throat. "You're so silky-soft," he said under his breath. His hands slid down her arms and back up, his fingers barely touching, experiencing her skin. "Like warm cream. I can feel you trembling, and it brings the blood to my head, did you know? And that little sound you made when I pulled your dress away from your breasts..." His hands moved back to her shoulders. "Sweet, sweet virgin," he whispered. "Make it easy for me. Lift your arms and let me hold you in my palms."

She stood on tiptoe as his hands began to move over her collarbone. Her hands reached up into his thick, straight blond hair as his thumbs moved down ahead of his palms and rubbed sensually at the hard tips of her breasts.

She jerked helplessly at the exquisite contact.

"I want to put my mouth on you," he whispered as his lips brushed hers and his hands slowly, achingly, swallowed her, feeling the involuntary tremors that shook her. "All of this is a natural part of lovemaking, so don't be frightened if you feel my teeth. All right?"

"Peo-ple," she moaned helplessly.

"There was only an old couple down the beach," he whispered. "They've gone inside now. Dani, Dani, of all the erotic, unbelievably sexy things I've ever done with a woman, this has to be the sweetest!"

She was arching her body toward him, blind and deaf to everything except sensation. Tomorrow, she told her conscience, tomorrow I'll worry about it.

"You want my mouth, don't you, darling?" he said, and with something like reverence he began to run his lips along her throat, down the side of her neck, over her collarbone, her shoulders. "I'm going to make a meal of you right here," he breathed, and all at once she felt his teeth on her and she stiffened and cried out.

"Eric," she moaned, frightened, her hands catching in his hair.

"It's all right," he murmured against her breast. "I wouldn't hurt you for all the world. Relax, darling, just relax. Yes, like that, Dani. Lie down. Lie down, so that I can get to you...."

He was easing her down onto the sand, and she let him, grateful to have some support under her, because the world was spinning around wildly. She clung to him, glorying in the feel of his lips, his teeth, his tongue, as he showed her how inexperienced she really was. By the time he got back to her mouth she was on fire for him.

With fierce enthusiasm she pulled his body down over hers and kissed him back with a naive but satisfying passion. He laughed delightedly against her open mouth and eased his hips over hers. She was his already.

"Eric," she ventured shakily.

"What do you want?" he asked, tasting her closed eyelids.

Her hands went to the front of his shirt, and he lifted his head. "Do you want to feel me?"

She flushed. "Yes."

"Unbutton it."

He was heavy, but she loved his weight. Overhead there were hundreds of stars. But all she knew was the unexpected completeness of his passion.

She touched his bare, hair-rough skin with hands that tingled with excitement. She'd never touched a man's body before, but she loved the feel of Dutch's. His muscles were padded, warm and strong, and she could imagine that his strength was formidable.

"Move your hands," he said seconds later, and when she did, he dragged his bare chest roughly over hers, shocking her with the force of desire the unexpected action caused in her body.

"Do you like it?" he asked as he moved sinuously above her.

"I never dreamed..." she began huskily. She was

trembling, and so was her voice. "Oh, I want you," she confessed on a sob. "I want you, I want you!"

"I want you, too, little one," he whispered, kissing her softly. "But I can't treat you like a one-night stand. I find I have too much conscience."

Tears were rolling down her cheeks. He kissed them all away, and his tongue brushed the tears from her eyelashes, and she realized suddenly that she hadn't had her glasses on for quite a while.

"My...glasses?" she falterd.

"Above your head," he said with a smile. He sat up slowly, catching her wrists to pull her up with him. She was in a patch of light that allowed him a delicious view of creamy, hard-tipped breasts in blatant arousal.

"Oh, you're something else, Miss St. Clair," he said gently. He bent and touched his mouth to the very tip of one breast.

Her breath wouldn't come steadily. She looked down at his blond head. "I...we should...that is..."

He lifted his head. "Suppose in the morning we get married?"

"M-married?"

He nodded. "Married." He pulled up her bodice with obvious reluctance. Then he reached behind her, retrieved her glasses, and put them back on her.

"But..."

His knuckles brushed one perfect breast lazily, feeling it go hard again. "This isn't going to get better," he said. "By tomorrow we'll be in such a fever that nothing is going to keep us away from each other. I haven't experienced anything this powerful since I was about fifteen. And I'm damned sure you're feeling it for the first time.''

"Yes, I know that, but we're strangers," she protested, trying to keep her head.

"We aren't going to be strangers for much longer," he said flatly. "My God, I want you," he ground out. "If you won't marry me, I'm getting the hell out of this hotel tonight, and on the next plane out of Veracruz. Because I can't bear to be around you without taking you. And I won't take you without marriage."

"But..."

"Am I so unmarriageable?" he burst out. "My God, I've had women propose to *me*! I'm not ugly, I'm well to do, I like dogs and cats, and I pay my bills on time. I'm in fairly decent health, I have friends...why in hell won't you marry me?"

"But it's only desire," she began.

"Stop trying to be logical," he said gruffly. "I'm not capable of logic when I'm aching like this. I want you. And you want me. For God's sake, put me out of my misery!"

"Would...would we have a divorce if...after we... if you...," she began.

"I'm getting older." He got to his feet and drew her up with him. "I travel a lot, you'd have to get used to that. But until now I've never had anyone of my own. I like you. I like being with you. And I think we'll set fires in bed. It's more than most people start out with. At least we aren't kids who believe in fairy tales like love and happily-ever-after. I'd rather have a woman who doesn't bore me than an infatuation that wears off.''

''And if you fell in love with someone later?'' she asked quietly, hearing her dreams die.

''I'll never love again,'' he said with equal quietness. ''But if you do, I'll let you out.'' He took her hands in his. ''Yes or no? I won't ask again.''

''Yes,'' she said without hesitation. Harriett would faint. Nobody would believe it back home, that she'd found a man like this who wanted her. All the questions she'd meant to ask went right out of her mind.

He bent and kissed her—without passion and very tenderly. ''My full name is Eric James van Meer. I was born in the Netherlands, although everyone calls it Holland, in a place called Utrecht. I lived there until I was in my teens, when I joined the service. The rest, you know, a little. Someday I'll tell you all of it. When I have to.''

''That sounds ominous.''

He put an arm around her. ''It doesn't have a lot to do with us right now,'' he said. His arm tightened. ''Do you want to be a virgin until tomorrow morning?''

Her lips parted. Her breath came wildly. Of course, she thought, and started to say it. But she couldn't. The words stuck in her throat. She thought of the long night, and her logical mind was booted out of its lofty position by a body that was in unholy torment.

''I want you so much,'' she said unsteadily.

''No more than I want you,'' he returned gruffly.

They were in the light of the hotel lobby now. He stopped, turning her toward him. His hands cupped her face and his eyes were dark and hot and full of anguish.

"I was raised a Catholic," he explained. "And in my religion, what I'm going to do to you tonight is a sin. Probably in your religion it is, too. But in the sight of God, for all our lives, I take you for my wife here, now. And tomorrow, in the sight of men, we make it right."

Tears stung her eyes as the words touched her heart. "And I take you for my husband, for better or worse, as long as I draw breath."

He bent and brushed his mouth tenderly over her wet eyes. "In Dutch, we call a married woman *Mevrouw*," he whispered.

"*Mevrouw*," she repeated.

"And darling," he added, smiling, "is *lieveling*."

"*Lieveling*," she repeated, smiling back.

"Upstairs," he said, turning her, "I'll teach you some more words. But you won't be able to repeat them in public." And he laughed at her expression.

Four

Dutch's room was nothing like Dani's. It overlooked the bay, and its quiet elegance would have suited royalty. She watched him lock the door, and nervously went to stand on the balcony where she could see a lighted ship in port.

The wind blew her hair and her dress, and she felt like a voyager on the brink of a new discovery.

"One of the passenger ships," he remarked, nodding toward the brilliantly lighted vessel. "Beautiful, isn't she?"

"Yes. I don't know much about ships, but I like looking at them."

He lit a cigarette and smoked it quietly. "I used to sail," he said unexpectedly.

She turned, looking up at the stranger who, in less than twenty-four hours, would be her husband and her lover. "Did you?"

"I moved to Chicago about eight years ago," he said. "I have an apartment on the lake, and I had a sailboat. I got drunk one night and she turned over with me. I let her sink."

Her eyes narrowed uneasily as she stared up at him, and he stared back, unblinkingly.

"I'm not an alcoholic," he said gently. "I probably sound like one to you, with these veiled references to the past. I don't drink often, but there are times when I get black moods. I won't drink around you. Ever."

It sounded as if he were willing to make any compromise, and something warm and soft blossomed inside her. She went close to him, her eyes trusting, quiet and deep. "I can make compromises, too," she said quietly. "I'll live anywhere you like."

He searched her eyes. "I don't mind readjusting."

"Yes, I know, but your work is in Chicago, I gather, or you wouldn't live there."

"My work is international," he said, and scowled. "I don't work out of Chicago. I live there because I have friends there."

"Women friends?" she blurted out.

He only smiled. He finished the cigarette, tossed it into an ashtray and drew her gently against him. "You're going to be the first woman I've been with this year," he murmured with a mocking smile. "Does that answer the question?"

She felt and looked shocked. "But...but don't you need...?" She couldn't find a delicate way to say it.

"I thought I was beyond all that, until you came along," he confessed. "I can't even remember the last time I felt this way about a woman."

"Are you sure you want to marry me?" she asked.

"Don't worry so," he told her, bending to kiss away the frown. "Yes, I want to marry you. I'll still want to marry you in the morning, too. That was no lie to get you in bed with me."

Part of her had thought that, and she lowered her eyes to his collar.

"Second thoughts?" he asked.

Her fingers toyed with the buttons on his shirt. "I'm afraid."

"Yes, I imagine so," he said matter-of-factly. "The first time was hard for me, too. I was nervous as a cat." He laughed.

"I can't imagine you being nervous," she said.

"It was forever ago. But I haven't forgotten. I'll go slowly." He bent and touched her mouth with his, very gently. "I just want you to remember two things. The first is that there are no set rules in this—it all depends on what pleases the people involved. Will you try to keep that in mind?"

She swallowed. "Yes."

"The second thing is that I'm not superhuman," he said softly. "Inevitably, there will come a moment when I lose control absolutely. Hopefully, I can bring you to that point before I reach it. But if not, I'll make it up to you afterward. Okay?"

"It all seems so mysterious," she whispered, as if even the night had ears.

"It won't by morning." His gaze went slowly over her, from head to toe and back up again, and his breathing began to change. "Rosebud," he muttered softly as he suddenly swung her up into his hard arms.

She relaxed a little and burrowed her face into his warm throat. He smelled of expensive cologne, and she loved the strength that made her seem so light in his embrace.

He laid her down on the bed gently. She expected him to start undressing himself or her immediately, and she lay there uneasily, a little frightened.

But he sat down beside her and laughed gently at the look on her face. "What are you expecting, I wonder. That I'll strip you and take you without preliminaries?"

Her eyes filmed. "I'm sorry...."

He touched her mouth with a hard finger. "Think about how it was on the beach, when I bent you back into the sand and kissed you, here." His fingers traveled down to her soft breasts. "And you threw back your head and moaned and begged me."

Her lips parted as she remembered vividly the sensations he'd aroused.

"That's how it's going to be now," he said, bending to her mouth. "Except that this time I'm not going to let you go."

His mouth opened hers with practiced ease, and his warm, callused hands were on her bare back, caressing it slowly and confidently, while all her inhibitions melted slowly away.

Seconds later the dress began to ease away from her body, and she felt his lips follow its downward movement. But she couldn't protest. The fires were burning again, and she moaned as his mouth covered her breasts, nipping at them with a tender pressure that was more arousing than frightening. His mouth followed as the dress merged with her tiny briefs and then was swept downward along with them. Shockingly, she felt his lips on her thighs, on the soft inner skin of her legs, and her body moved as the edge of his teeth followed the same path. Incredible, she thought through a fog of anguished desire, incredible that people could survive this kind of pleasure!

She wasn't even aware of what he was doing anymore; she was all sensation, all aching hunger. Her eyes were closed, her fists clenched beside her arched neck as his mouth searched her hips and her flat stomach. At the same time he was lazily divesting himself of his own clothing, making it so much a part of his seduction that she didn't even realize he'd done it until finally he slid alongside her and she felt him.

Her eyes flew open and went helplessly down the length of his body before she realized what she was doing. And then it was too late; she couldn't look away. He was glorious. Absolutely the most beautiful sight she'd ever seen, tanned all over without the slightest streak of white, as if he'd sunbathed in the nude all his life.

And meanwhile his hands touched her in a new intimate way. She started to draw away, but his mouth opened hers and his hands began a soft, tender rhythm, and soon she was weeping helplessly against his lips.

In seconds she was trembling and pleading with him. He moved, dragging his aching body into a sitting position against the headboard, his dark eyes glittering with frank desire. He lifted her over him and guided her, his body rigid with self-control, his face hard with it.

She gasped at the contact and her hands clenched on his shoulders as she found herself looking straight into his eyes.

"You do it," he told her huskily. "That way you can control the pain."

She started to argue, but she knew that it was becoming unbearable for him. She swallowed down her fear, closed her eyes, bit her lip and moved. She caught her breath and tried again.

"Help me, Eric," she begged, guiding his hands to her hips. "Please...oh!"

"It's bad, isn't it?" he ground out. "I'm sorry, I'm sorry...." His fingers contracted as his body began to fight his mind. The hunger was exploding in him. He began to tremble, his hands clenched. "Dani...!"

She opened her eyes at the new note in his voice and looked at him. The sight of his face took her mind off the pain. She watched him, fascinated. His eyes opened and found hers. Then his body seemed to take control away from his mind. His face changed, his breathing changed, the movements of his body intensified as she stared into his wild face. He arched and his face contorted, and all at once she realized what she was seeing and blushed wildly.

He was still for an instant, then he shuddered. His eyes opened slowly, looking into hers. His body still throbbed, his breathing unsteady and strained. His hands on her hips became caressing.

"I thought...you were dying," she whispered.

"I felt as if I were," he whispered back. His voice

trembled, like his body, in the aftermath. His eyes searched her face. "You were watching me. Were you shocked?"

"Yes," she confessed, but she didn't look away.

"Was it bad?" he asked.

"Yes. Until I started watching you."

He brought her fully against him, still a part of him, and held her gently, with her face against his damp chest. "I think that was what pushed me over the edge," he murmured. "I saw you watching me and my head flew off."

"You looked as though you were being tortured to death."

"And you can't imagine pleasure so intense?" he chided her gently. He laughed, but it wasn't a taunting laugh. His hands caressed her back. "When I've rested for a few minutes I'm going to watch it happen to you."

"Will it?"

"Oh, yes. You just needed a few more seconds than I could give you. The second time," he added, easing her away from him, "always takes longer, for a man."

She looked into his eyes. "You're my lover now," she declared.

He looked down where they were still joined. Her eyes followed his and she blushed furiously.

"I'm still your lover," he told her. His hands pressed against her thighs, dragging her even closer, and all at once something happened that even her inexperienced body understood immediately.

He laughed softly. "Yes, you know what's going

to happen now, don't you?'' he growled. He shifted, easing her down onto the mattress as he loomed over her.

"Now," he said hotly, blazing with renewed passion. "Now watch what I'm going to do to you. Look!''

Her eyes dilated as she watched him. But the sensations were unexpected, and she cried out helplessly, her body lifting toward him as if it recognized its master.

"Shhhh," he hissed, smiling as her face began to contort. "Yes, you're going to feel it for me this time. I'm going to make you feel it, just as it happened to me. Yes, Dani, yes, yes...!''

She throbbed with a new rhythm. She moved and twisted and tried to throw him off, and tried to bring him back; she cried and pleaded and bit and whimpered and finally threw back her head and moaned so harshly that she sounded as if every bone in her body had snapped suddenly. And then it was all free-fall. Bonelessness. Purple oblivion.

When her eyes opened again she was exhausted. He sat on the bed beside her with a warm, damp cloth in his hands, bathing her gently.

"Is it always like that for men?" she asked, needing to know.

He shook his head. "It's never been like that for me with anyone. The second time was even more intense. I cried out.''

Tears touched her eyes as she looked up at him. "Thank you.''

"Oh, God, don't," he implored her, bending to kiss

her. Once he kissed her he couldn't seem to stop. He put the cloth aside and took her into his arms, holding her, touching her face, brushing his lips over every soft, flushed inch of her face with a touch that was more healing than passionate.

She trembled in his arms, and they tightened, and she gloried in the delicious warmth of his skin against hers, the feel of her soft breasts being gently crushed by his hard-muscled chest.

"You cried out, too," he said at her ear. "Just as you felt it. I had to cover your mouth with mine so that no one would hear."

"Even in my dreams it never happened like that," she confessed.

"I'm glad it happened with me," he told her, lifting his head. "Thank you for waiting for me."

She smiled slowly. "I'm glad I waited."

"I didn't use anything," he said then. "Do you want to see a doctor tomorrow, or do you want me to take care of it until we get back to the States? A wife I can handle, but not a baby. Not yet."

"Then, could you...?" She hesitated. "I'd rather see my own doctor."

"Okay." He bent and brushed his mouth over hers.

"Do you want children eventually?" she asked because it was important.

He brushed the hair away from her eyes. "Perhaps," he said finally. "Someday."

"Too much, too soon?" she murmured dryly.

"Getting used to a wife is enough for now," he said. He let his eyes wander slowly over her. "You have a beautiful body."

"So have you."

He kissed her softly. "We'd better get some sleep. And, sadly enough, I do mean sleep." He sighed as he rose, cloth in hand. "I'm not prepared for anything else until we go into town. Unless...there are other ways if you really want..."

She blushed wildly and changed the subject. "Where are we getting married?"

"In a little chapel down the street." He grinned. "They're open at ten A.M. We'll be waiting on the doorstep."

"You aren't sorry?" she asked as he started into the bathroom.

He turned, his body open for her inspection, his face faintly smiling. He shook his head. "Are you?"

She shook her head, too. He laughed and went on into the bathroom. Minutes later she was curled up in his arms, both of them without a stitch on, the lights off and the sounds of the city at night purring in through the window.

"You can have one of my undershirts if you like," he said gently.

"I'd rather sleep like this, if it won't bother you," she murmured.

"I prefer it this way, too," he confessed. He drew her closer. "Breathing may be a little difficult, and I may die of a heart attack trying not to indulge myself a third time, but I prefer it like this. Good night, *lieveling*."

"Good night, Eric." She curled up against him with a trusting sigh and was surprised to find herself drifting off to sleep only seconds later.

Five

Dani was dreaming. She felt as if she were floating, drifting, her body bare and fulfilled. She stretched, smiling, and a voice brought her awake.

"Don't struggle, darling," a male voice chuckled. "You'll make me drop you."

Her gray eyes flew open along with her mouth, and she realized that Dutch was carrying her into the bathroom, where a huge steaming bathtub waited.

"Don't you want a bath?" he murmured dryly.

"Oh, yes," she said sleepily. "I had planned on waking up before I got in the water." She curled into his chest, snuggled her face against his throat, and closed her eyes with a sigh. "But my pillow started moving."

He laughed, realizing with a start that he'd laughed more in the past two days than in the past ten years. He looked down at her creamy body, her full breasts pressed into the rippling muscle and feathery hair of his chest. She was vulnerable with him. Yet, he sensed that she was much like him in her independence, her wild spirit.

"Wake up or you'll drown," he said.

"I thought I already had, and gone to heaven," she replied, smiling against his throat. She wasn't even surprised to find herself with him. She seemed to have dreamed about him all night long.

"We have to get married," he said.

"Going to make an honest woman of me, hmmm?" she teased, peeking up at him.

But he didn't smile. "You're already an honest woman. The first I've ever known. Hold on."

He eased her down into the warm silky water and then climbed in beside her. They soaped each other lazily, enjoying the different textures of their bodies, exploring openly.

"I feel like a child playing doctor," he told her with a wicked glance.

"It's old hat to you, I suppose," she said, watching her hands move on his muscular chest, "but I've never touched a man like this. It's all very new to me just now."

He moved her hands down, watching the flush on her face and the panic in her yes. "All right," he said gently as she resisted. "You're still shy with me. I won't insist."

"Old maids have lots of hang-ups," she said quietly.

"I'll get rid of yours before the week's out," he promised. "Want some more soap?"

She let him lather her back. Something was niggling at the back of her mind, and she glanced at him worriedly as he rinsed her.

"What is it?" he asked gently.

"Something you said last night. About…about precautions."

"There's no problem," he said carelessly. "I'll stop by a drugstore. When we get back to the States, if you'd rather not risk the pill, there's some minor surgery a man can have—"

Her eyes were horrified. The drawn look on her face stopped him in mid-sentence.

"You don't ever want children, do you?" she asked, choking on the words.

He looked hunted. "Hell," he bit off. Why had she brought up the subject! He watched her scramble out of the tub and fumble a towel around herself.

"We aren't even married yet, and you're harping about a family," he burst out, rising to his feet, his handsome face hard with anger. "What the hell do we need kids for? They're a permanent tie. A bond."

"Isn't marriage?" she asked huskily.

"Of course," he grumbled, grabbing up a towel. "But not like kids."

"You never answered me," she said quietly. "You don't ever want them, do you?"

"No," he said flatly, tired of the pretense, hating the memories the discussion was bringing back. "Not ever."

She turned and walked back into the bedroom. She didn't know him at all. And the first thing she was going to do was cut her losses. She'd go back to her room and forget him. How could she expect to live all her life without a child? What kind of man was he?

Tears blinded her. She got as far as the bed and sat down, feeling empty and sick and alone. She'd dreamed of children. Since she was eighteen she'd haunted baby shops, quietly touching the little crocheted things and imagining her own baby in her arms. She had no one of her own, but a baby would be part of her. The tears rippled down her cheeks in silvery streams, and she closed her eyes.

The man at the bathroom door, watching her, saw them, and something painful exploded inside him. She was snaring him, he thought furiously. Swallowing him up whole with her unexpected vulnerabilities. With a muffled curse he threw the towel aside and went to the bed.

He caught her by the waist, lowering her back against the rumpled covers so quickly that she gasped.

"Eric!" she called uncertainly.

His mouth covered hers, but there was none of the violence she'd expected. His lips played with hers, so gentle that she barely felt them, while his hands removed the towel and whispered over her body until she trembled.

"Draw your legs up," he breathed. He helped her, positioning his body so that they were curled together, his knees beside her, his chest on hers, his hips against her hips and thighs.

She looked up, fascinated at the look in his dark eyes.

His big, warm hands cupped her face. "Open your

mouth now," he whispered, bending, "and kiss me the way I taught you last night."

She obeyed him, liking the way her tongue tangled softly with his, liking the intimacy of this slow, tender kissing.

His knuckles brushed over her breasts, making their tips hard and sensitive, and when she gasped, his mouth took advantage of it to make the kiss even deeper. His hands searched over her, sliding under her hips to lift her to the slow descent of his body.

She felt his fingers contract on her thighs and caught her breath at their steely strength. And still he kissed her, whispery contacts that drained her of will, that made her weak. Her body trembled as he explored it with even more intimacy than the night before, each new touch intensifying her hunger for him.

He paused, hesitated, his lips touching hers. His eyes opened, holding hers, and his body lowered.

She caught her breath at the intensity of feeling she knew as he let her experience the very texture of his body with the slowness of his movement.

"Now," he said, closing his eyes, "we really make love for the first time."

She didn't understand at first. And then it began to make sense. He was so tender, so exquisitely gentle, that every movement seemed to stroke a nerve of pleasure. She clung to him, matching his tenderness, trying to give him back the beauty he was giving her. Her eyes fluttered closed and her fingers tangled in his cool blond hair, her body trembling under the expert movements of his. As the pleasure built slowly she began to writhe helplessly. And as fulfillment

came closer, she wondered if she was going to survive
it.

"Eric?" she whimpered against his mouth.

His own body was trembling, too. *"Lieveling,"* he
said huskily. *"Mijn lieveling, mijn vrouw!"*

The hands holding her clenched, and he rocked
with her, smooth, tender movements that were exquisitely soft. He whispered to her in Dutch, words that
she couldn't understand, but they were breathlessly
tender.

She kissed his tanned cheek, his mouth, his chin,
and he lifted his head for an instant, his dark eyes
glazed, his lips parted.

"Yes," he told her. "Yes, like that."

He closed his eyes and let her kiss him, savoring
the softness of her mouth on his eyes, his cheeks, his
straight nose, his lips.

She moved, trembling with need, letting him feel
her body as she drew it with smooth sweetness to
either side.

His eyes opened again, reading the intensity of
hunger in hers.

"Yes," he said. "Yes, now it happens. Now..."

His voice didn't change, but his breathing did. He
looked down at her, lengthening his movements,
deepening them, so that although the tenderness remained, the urgency grew.

Something was happening to her that she didn't
understand. Terrifying tension, hands buffeting her, a
blazing tide of warmth that speared through her like
tiny needles. Her mouth opened because she could no
longer breathe. Her body began to shudder helplessly,

tiny little shudders that matched the tenderness that was devouring her.

"I'm...afraid..." she managed, and her fingers clenched at his back as she felt her body beginning to contract.

"Hush," he said softly. His movements deepened, and still he watched. "Yes, feel it. Feel it now. There's nothing to be...afraid of, *lieveling*. No, don't turn away, let me see you...."

He turned her head back to him, and his face blurred. She thought he smiled, but she was all bursting fireworks, a flare lighting up the night sky. She felt gentle explosions all through her body, and for a moment her heart stopped, her breathing stopped. And then she cried, because it had been so beautiful, and so brief.

Even as the tears came, she felt his own body go rigid, heard the tender, surprised exclamation at her ear, and then her name....

He didn't move for a long time. Neither did she. She felt incapable of movement. What had happened surprised her. He'd said they wouldn't make love again until they got married, so why had he done it? And why that way? So tenderly, so gently, as if he cared about her.

Experimentally, her hands moved on the damp muscles of his shoulders.

He lifted his head and searched her eyes slowly. He touched her face with gentle fingers. "In my life there was never such a tender loving before," he said. "I didn't know that men and women were capable of it." He brushed away the tears. "I hurt you?" he asked.

"No." She swallowed. "It was...so beautiful," she faltered.

"Yes. For me, too." He drew away from her with exquisite slowness, watching her. He sighed heavily, and frowned. After a minute he turned back to the bathroom. "We'd better get dressed."

She got up, too, a little shaky and puzzled by his odd behavior. He'd meant to comfort her, she was certain of it. But the comfort had gotten out of hand. And the way he'd loved her...

As she dressed she wondered if she was doing the right thing, marrying a total stranger. Then he came out of the bathroom, wearing nothing except his slacks, his blond hair neatly combed, his face slowly curving into a smile. And she knew that she'd die to wear his ring, babies or no babies. She smiled back.

They were married in a small chapel, with people all around them who spoke little English. The minister beamed at them when it was over, inviting the new husband to kiss his bride.

Dutch bent and brushed his mouth softly against hers, smiling at his own folly. Well, it was done now. And it wouldn't be so bad, he told himself as he studied her radiant young face. She could wait for him at home, and they'd see each other whenever he was there. It might even be good that way. No routine to bore him. She could go on with her life, and there would be no ties. He frowned for a minute as he thought of what had happened this morning, then he shook off the instant fear of consequences. Surely to

God, he hadn't made her pregnant. He'd just have to be careful from now on. No more lapses. The thought of a child terrified him. That would make a tie he couldn't break.

Dani saw that frown, and worried about it. She wondered why he'd really married her, when he seemed the kind of man who was self-sufficient and didn't need anyone else.

"You aren't sorry?" she asked finally when they were walking back to the hotel.

He stopped, lifted his blond head and smiled, a little puzzled. "What?"

"Sorry that you married me," she continued. She searched his eyes nervously. "You've been so quiet. I know I'm not much to look at, and we don't know each other at all. I...we can always get a divorce," she finished miserably.

"I'm quiet because I have a logistical problem to work out," he said then. "Not because I'm regretting that we got married. When you know me better, you'll learn that I never do things unless I want to. I can't be pushed or coerced." He reached out and curled her fingers into his. "I like being with you," he said, meeting her eyes. "Like this, and in bed. We're both old enough to want someone to be with."

"Yes," she confessed. Tears stung her eyes and she lowered her lids before he could read her thoughts. "I never thought it would happen to me," she added. "I thought I'd be alone all my life."

"So did I." He smoothed his fingers across the back of her hand. She had pretty hands, he mused. "Do you play anything?" he asked unexpectedly.

She laughed. "The piano. Badly."

"I like piano. I play a little, too." He slid his fingers in between hers, feeling oddly possessive as he saw the bright little gold band that encircled her ring finger. "A wedding ring suits you. Feel better now about what we did last night?" he asked with a slow smile, as if he understood her uneasiness about intimacy without marriage.

"I'm old-fashioned." She sighed miserably.

"You don't have to apologize for it, not to me." His eyes gleamed suddenly as he looked at her. Short brown hair, creamy, oval face, wide gray eyes. "I liked being the first."

There was a deep, possessive note in his voice that surprised her. She smiled slowly. Her fingers squeezed his, and she looked into his eyes for so long that she flushed.

"This morning," he said softly, holding her eyes, "was my first time. I didn't realize that I was capable of tenderness. I let go with you in a way I never could before with a woman. I trusted you."

Her face was bright red, but she didn't look away. "I...trusted you." She let her eyes fall to his hard mouth, remembering with a surge of desire how it felt on her body. "One of my friends got married two years ago. She said her husband shocked her speechless on her wedding night, and made fun of her...."

His fingers contracted. "I think it would kill something in you to have a man treat you so," he remarked.

Her eyes came up, stunned at the way he understood.

He nodded. "Yes. It's that way with me, too. I don't like ridicule."

Her expression said more than she wanted it to, and she knew that he could read the worshipful look in her eyes. But she didn't care. He was her whole world.

His breath caught at that look. It bothered him, and he let go of her hand. "Don't ever try to build a wall around me," he said unexpectedly, staring at her. "I'll stay with you only as long as the doors remain open."

"I knew that the first time I saw you," she said quietly. "No ties. No strings. I won't try to possess you."

He started walking again. He wondered what she was going to do when she knew the truth about him. He glanced up, searching her face quietly. She was so damned trusting. She probably thought he was in the army reserves or something. He almost laughed. Well, she'd just have to get used to it, he told himself, because he didn't know how to change.

After they'd changed their status at the hotel desk and switched everything to his room they went downstairs for lunch. Dani picked at her food, wondering at the change in Eric. Something was on his mind, but she didn't know him well enough to ask what it was. She glanced at him with a slow-dawning mischief in her eyes. Well, she couldn't dig it out of him, but she could help him forget it.

"Hey," she called.

He glanced up, cocking an eyebrow.

"I have this great idea for dessert," she murmured, making her first attempt at being a siren.

Both eyebrows went up. "You do?"

She dropped her eyes to his throat. "I could smear whipped cream all over myself..."

"Honey tastes better."

She blushed furiously, and he laughed. He leaned forward, moving his plate aside, and lifted her fingers to his mouth.

"Do you want me?" he asked bluntly, smiling at her averted face.

"Yes," she confessed.

"Then say so. You don't have to play games with me." He got up, helped her up, and paid the check. They were back in the hotel room before he spoke again.

He backed her up against the door and pinned her there with just the threat of his body. "You can have me anytime," he said quietly. "All you have to do is tell me. That's what marriage should be. Not some kind of power game."

Her eyes narrowed. "I don't understand."

He brushed the hair away from her face and curled it behind her ear. "Bargaining, with sex as the prize."

"I'd never do that," she said. She watched him, amazed that this handsome man was actually married to her. "You were worried about something. I wanted to...to give you peace."

He seemed to freeze. His lips parted on a hard breath. "I constantly misread you, don't I?" He touched her throat with the lightest touch of his fingers and lifted his eyes to hers. "Do you want me?"

"I'll want you on my deathbed," she said shakily.

He bent and kissed her softly, tenderly. "I'm more grateful than I can tell you, for such a sweet offer. But I don't think you can take me again today, not without considerable discomfort." He lifted his head. "Can you?"

She bit her lower lip. "Well…"

"Can you?"

She dropped her eyes to his chest. "Oh, shoot!" she mumbled. "No."

He laughed softly and drew her into his arms, rocking her slowly. "That's why I was so gentle this morning," he murmured into her ear, lying a little. He didn't want to admit that she'd been the victor in that tender battle.

"Oh." That was vaguely disappointing, she mused. She slid her arms around him with a sigh, delighting in his strength, the corded power of his warm hard body. "It isn't like this in books," she concluded. She smiled as her eyes closed. "Women always can, and they never have discomfort, and—"

"Life is very different," he said. He smoothed her hair. "We'll wait a day or so, until you recuperate. Then," he added, tilting her face up to his amused eyes, "I'll teach you some more subtle forms of sensual torture."

She laughed shyly. "Will you?"

He took a deep breath. "I've never known anyone like you," he said, the words reluctant. He drew her up on her tiptoes and kissed her very softly. "Feel what's happening already?"

"Yes," she answered him.

"We'd better cool it, if you don't mind. I hate cold showers."

She laughed. "You're terrific." She sighed.

"So are you. Get on a bathing suit and let's go swim."

She started into the bathroom, met his mocking eyes, and stuck out her chin. "You're my husband," she said aloud, to remind both of them.

"Yes, I was wondering if you might remember that." He chuckled.

She undressed and he watched, his eyes quiet and full of memories. When she started to pull on the bathing suit he moved in front of her and stayed her hands.

"Not yet," he said quietly.

She looked up, hungry for him, and watched as he studied her body and saw for himself just how much she wanted him.

"How is it, for a woman?" he asked suddenly, and sounded genuinely curious. "How do you feel when you want me like this?"

"It's frightening, a little," she told him. "I get shaky and weak and I can't quite control myself. I ache…"

"Does this…help the ache?" he asked as he bent to her breasts.

She moaned. It was impossible not to, when she felt the warm moistness of his lips eating her. She didn't have a mind left after the first two seconds. She was hardly aware that he was lifting her onto the bed.

He made a meal of her body, tasting, touching,

looking at it, broad daylight streaming in the windows, while she gloried in the luxury of being married and enjoyed his pleasure in her.

"I love looking at your body," he said quietly, sitting beside her. His hands swept up and down, lingering on her soft curves. "I love touching it. Tasting it. I've never seen anything half so lovely."

"My husband," she whispered.

He looked up. "My wife."

Her body ached, and she knew he must feel the same longing she did. Her eyes asked a question, but he slowly shook his head.

"I won't do that to you," he said curtly. "Not ever will I take my pleasure and not give a thought to yours."

She ground her teeth together to stop the tears.

"And it isn't pity," he said, glaring at the look in her eyes. "I do nothing out of pity, least of all marry because of it, so you can stop looking at me that way. I want you and I'm getting irritable because I can't have you. So suppose you put on the bathing suit and I'll go have that damned cold shower and we'll swim."

He got up and she lay there, watching him as he discarded his clothing. Her lips parted as the last of the clothing came off, and she saw the urgency of his desire.

His body trembled as he looked at her, and she wanted to cry because of the torment she saw in his face.

"You said once...that there are...other ways," she ventured to ask. "Are there?"

His face hardened; his eyes glittered wildly. "Yes."

She held out her arms, her body throbbing, her blood running like a river in flood as she sensed that violence of his hunger. He hesitated only for a second before he came down beside her.

The days passed with miserable speed. They did everything together. They swam and talked, although always about general things rather than personal ones; they danced and sampled new delicacies at the dinner table. And at night he loved her. Sometimes in the early morning. Once on the bathroom floor because the strength of their desire hadn't left them time to get to bed. Sometimes he remembered precautions, but mostly he didn't, because his desire matched her own. She walked around in a sensual haze that blinded her to the future. But eventually, the day came when they had to look past Veracruz. It came suddenly, and too soon.

Six

The last day of their stay dawned unwelcomed, and Dani packed with a long face. She'd changed her plans so she could be with Dutch for his whole vacation, but at the end of the week he told her that he had a job waiting and couldn't spare any more time. She stared at him across the room as he got his own clothing together, wondering how dangerous his line of work was. A soldier, he'd said. Did that mean he was in the reserves? Probably, she told herself. That was why he wouldn't mind moving to Greenville.

She'd thought about that a lot, about picking up stakes and moving to Chicago. It wouldn't matter, although she'd miss Harriett and her friends from the bookstore. She'd have followed him anywhere. When she realized how little time they'd had together, she could hardly believe that so much had happened so quickly. It seemed like a lifetime ago that the taciturn blond giant had dropped down beside her on the airplane. And now he was her husband. Her husband, about whom she knew so little.

He seemed to feel her puzzled frown, and turned. Then he smiled at her. "Ready?" he asked as he picked up his duffel bag.

"Ready," she agreed. She drew her two bags up to where his were sitting by the door.

He glared at the smaller one and sighed. "You and your books." He chuckled softly down at her. "Well, at least now you know what they're all about, don't you?" he added.

She cleared her throat, reddening as she recalled the long, sweet nights. "Oh, yes, indeed I do, Mr. van Meer," she agreed fervently.

"No regrets, Dani?" he asked softly.

She shook her head. "Not if this were the last day of my life," she said. "And you?"

"I'm only sorry we met so late in life," he replied, searching her face. "I'm glad we found each other." He checked his watch. It was an expensive one, with dials and numbers that meant nothing to Dani. "We'd better rush or we'll miss our flight."

Dutch had made the reservation for the two of them and they had adjoining seats. She sat beside him with her heart in her throat, smiling at him with hopeless hero worship. He was so handsome. And hers. Harriett really wasn't going to believe this.

He glanced down at her, still amazed that he had a wife. J.D. and Gabby would be shocked, he thought. And Apollo and First Shirt, Semson and Drago and Laremos would never let him hear the end of it.

Dutch, married. It was incredible, even to him. But it felt nice.

It was Gabby's influence, probably, he admitted to himself. He'd heard so much about her from J.D. even before he'd met her that some of his old prejudices against women had slackened. Not much, but a little. Gabby had trekked through a commando-infested jungle for J.D. and even risked her own life to save him from a bullet. He glanced again at his companion with narrowed dark eyes. Would she do that for him? Did she really possess the fiery spirit he sensed beneath her timid manners? And how was she going to react when she learned the truth about him? That hadn't bothered him for the past few days, but it bothered him now. A lot. His gaze went to the bag of romance novels tucked under her pretty feet. Fluff, he thought contemptuously, and a smile touched his firm mouth as he thought how nearly like fiction some of his exploits might seem to the woman beside him.

Dani saw him starting at her books and shifted uncomfortably in her seat. "Well, we can't all conquer the Amazon," she muttered.

His eyebrows shot up. "What?" He laughed.

"You were giving my books contemptuous glares," she said. "And if you're thinking it's all mushy nonsense, you might be surprised." She fished down and held up a book with a cover that featured a man armed with an automatic weapon. There was a jungle setting behind him and woman beside him.

Dutch blinked. Automatically, his hand reached for the book and he scowled as he flipped through it and glanced over the blurb on the back of the book jacket.

The novel was about two photojournalists, trapped together in a Central American country during a revolution.

"Not what you expected?" she asked.

He lifted his eyes and studied her. "No."

She took the book from his hand and stuffed it back in her sack. "Most of us are armchair adventurers at heart, you know." She sighed. "Woman as well as men. You'd be amazed at how many of my customers fantasize about being caught up in a revolution somewhere."

His face hardened. He gave her a look that sent shivers through her.

"Dani, have you ever watched anyone die?" he asked bluntly.

She faltered, shocked by the icy challenge in his deep voice.

"No, of course not," she said.

"Then don't be too eager to stick your nose in some other country's military coups. It isn't pretty." He touched his pocket, reaching for a cigarette, then glanced up and noticed that the no-smoking sign was still lit as the plane climbed to gain more altitude. Then he also remembered that he'd chosen a seat in the no-smoking section to be near Dani, who didn't smoke. He said something rough under his breath.

"Have you?" she asked unexpectedly. "Stuck your nose in somebody's military coups?" she added when he lifted an eyebrow.

"That would hardly concern you," he said, softening the words with a smile.

He wasn't exactly rude, but she turned quickly

back to the window in silence. She felt uneasy, and tried to banish the feeling. He was her husband now. She'd have to learn not to ruffle him. She leaned back, closed her eyes and convinced herself that she was worrying needlessly. Surely there were no dark secrets in his past.

Someone in the seat ahead of them rang for the stewardess, and Dani closed her eyes, thinking what a long flight this was going to be. They'd planned to stop over in Greenville and then decide who would move and who wouldn't. He wanted to see where she lived, he'd said, to meet her friend Harriett and see the little bookshop she owned. She'd been flattered by his interest.

She had just closed her eyes when she heard a loud gasp and then a cry from nearby. Her eyes opened to see the stewardess being held roughly by a man in brown slacks and an open-necked white shirt. He had a foreign look, and his eyes were glazed with violence. At the stewardess's neck he was holding a hypodermic syringe. Another man who had been sitting with him got calmly to his feet, walked around the man with the syringe and went into the cockpit.

There was a loud yell and the copilot appeared, took one look at what was happening and seemed to go white.

"Yes, he's telling the truth, as near as I can tell," the copilot called into the cockpit.

There was a buzz of conversation that was unintelligible, then the captain's voice came over the loudspeaker and Dutch stiffened, his dark gaze going slowly over the man with the syringe.

"Ladies and gentlemen, this is Captain Hall." The deep voice was deceptively calm. "The plane is being diverted to Cuba. Please keep calm, remain in your seats and do exactly as you're told. Thank you."

The unarmed man came out of the cockpit, twitching his thick mustache, and fumbled around with the intercom until he figured it out.

"We wish no one to be harmed," he said. "The syringe my friend is holding to the neck of this lovely young lady is filled with hydrochloric acid." Shocked murmurs went through the crowd, especially when the shorter, bald man took the syringe to one side and deliberately let one drop fall on the fabric of the seat. It smoldered and gave a vivid impression of the impact it would have on the stewardess's neck. "So for the young lady's sake, please keep calm," he continued. "We will harm you only if you make it necessary."

He hung up the intercom and went back into the cockpit. The man with the syringe tugged the petite blond stewardess along with him, ignoring the passengers. Apparently, he thought the threat of the syringe was enough to prevent any interference.

And it seemed he was right. The other passengers murmured uneasily among themselves.

"Professionals," Dutch said quietly. "They must want to get out of the country pretty badly."

Dani eyed him uncomfortably. "Who are they, do you think?"

"No idea," he said.

"They wouldn't really use that acid on her?" she asked, her voice soft with astonishment.

He turned and looked down at her, into gray eyes more innocent than any he'd ever seen. He frowned. "My God, of course they'd use it!"

Her oval face paled. She looked past him to where one of the men was barely visible, his arm still around the stewardess.

"Can't the captain do something?" she said then.

"Sure." He leaned back in his seat and closed his eyes, clasping his lean, tough hands over his stomach. "He can do exactly what they tell him until they get off the plane. All they want is a free ride. Once they've had it, they'll leave."

She gnawed on her lower lip. "Aren't you worried?" she asked.

"They aren't holding the syringe to my neck."

His indifference shocked her. She was terrified for the stewardess. Horrified, she forced her eyes back to her lap. For God's sake, what kind of man had she married?

He closed his eyes again, ignoring her contemptuous stare. He regretted the need to shock her, but he needed time to think, and he couldn't do it if she was talking. Now he had sufficient quiet to put together a plan. They wouldn't hurt the girl if their demands were met. But glitches sometimes happened. In case one developed, he had to think of a way out. There were two men, but only one was armed. And obviously, they hadn't been able to get anything metallic through the sensors. That was good. They might have a plastic knife or two between them, or a pocket knife like the one Dutch was carrying—a knife that had special uses. His was balanced and excellent for throwing. And he had few equals with a knife. He smiled.

Dani glanced at Dutch with mingled hurt and curiosity and rage. He was asleep, for heaven's sake! In the middle of a hijacking, he was asleep! She sighed angrily. Well, what did she expect him to do? Leap up from the seat like one of the heroes in the books she read and deliver them all from the terrorists? Fat chance!

A hijacking. She sighed, nervously fingering her purse. She wondered how the poor stewardess felt. The woman was doing her best to stay calm, but it couldn't have been easy. Knowing what was in that syringe, and how quickly it would work if she were injected with it...Dani shuddered at just the thought. In her innocence she'd never believed that there were such fiendish people sharing the world with her.

Dutch opened one eye and closed it again. Dani gave him an exasperated look and clasped her hands to still their trembling. The taller of the hijackers had something in his hand that looked suspiciously like a grenade, and as the plane grew closer to Cuba, he began to pace nervously.

The shorter hijacker, the bald one who was holding the stewardess prisoner, moved into view. He forced the stewardess into the front seat, which was just one ahead of Dutch and Dani, and sat beside her, with the syringe still at her throat.

He was tiring, Dutch mused. And the other one was getting a little panicky. His dark eyes narrowed thoughtfully. He'd bet his life that the grenade was plastic. How else could they have cleared airport security? One of the magazines on covert operations ran advertisements for the fakes—they were dirt cheap and, at a distance, realistic enough to fool a civilian. Which Dutch wasn't.

He'd wait until the plane landed in Cuba. If they were granted asylum, fine. If not, he was going to put a monkey wrench into their act. He owed it to Dani, sitting so quiet and disillusioned beside him. She still believed in heroes, although God alone knew what she thought of him right now.

When the plane landed in Havana the shorter man stayed beside the stewardess while the taller one went into the cockpit. He stayed there only a few minutes, and then burst out the small doorway with wild eyes, cursing violently.

"What is it? What is it!" the smaller man demanded.

"They will not let us disembark! They will not give us asylum!" the taller man cried. He looked around wildly, clasping the forgotten grenade in his hands and ignoring the horrified looks and cries of the passengers. "What shall we do? They will give us fuel but not asylum. What shall we do? We cannot go back to Mexico!"

"*Cuidado!*" the older man cautioned sharply. "We will go to Miami. Then we will seek asylum from our backers overseas," he said. "Tell them to fly to Miami."

Now, that was interesting, Dutch thought as he watched the taller man hesitate and then go back into the cockpit. He had a hunch that the gentlemen with the stage props were Central American natives. But obviously they had no wish to be connected with any of the Central American countries. And that talk of comrades overseas sounded very familiar. As almost everyone knew, there were foreign interests at work all over Central America.

The taller man was back in a minute. "They are turning toward Miami," he told his companion.

"*Bueno!*" The short man sounded relieved. "Come."

He forced the stewardess to her feet and dragged her along with him as he urged the tall man toward the cockpit. "We will explain the demands the pilot is to present to the American authorities," the short one murmured.

Dutch's eyes opened. "How much courage do you have, Mrs. van Meer?" he asked Dani without turning his head. His voice was low enough that only she could hear it.

She tensed. What in the world did he mean? "I'm no coward," she managed.

"What I have in mind could get you killed."

Her heart leaped. "The stewardess!"

He looked down at her. His eyes were dark and quiet and his face was like so much granite. "That will depend on you. When we approach that airport I want you to distract the man with the syringe. Just distract him. Force him to move that syringe for just a fraction of a second."

"Why do anything?" she asked softly. "You said that they'd leave—"

"Because they're desperate now," he said quietly. "And I have no doubt whatsoever that one of their demands is going to be for automatic weapons. Once they have those, we've lost any chance of escape.''

''The authorities won't give them weapons,'' she said.

''Once they've used that acid on a couple of people they will,'' he said.

She shuddered again. She could taste her own fear, but Dutch seemed oddly confident. He also seemed to know what he was doing. She looked up into his eyes with returning faith. No, she told herself, she'd been reading him wrong. All that time he'd been quiet, he'd been thinking. And now she trusted him instinctively.

''You could be killed,'' he repeated, hating the words even as he said them. How could he put her in danger? But how could he not take the chance? ''There's a risk; I won't minimize it.''

She sighed. ''Nobody would miss me, except maybe you and Harriett,'' she said dryly.

He felt odd. She didn't say it in a self-pitying way. It was just a simple statement of fact. Nobody gave a damn. He knew how that felt himself, because outside the group nobody cared about him, either. Except for Dani. And he cared about her, too. He was suddenly vulnerable because of her, he realized.

She looked up at him with wide gray eyes that had seen too little living to be closed forever.

''There's a chance I could manage it alone,'' he began slowly.

''I'm not afraid,'' she said. ''Well, that is, I am afraid, but I'll do whatever you tell me to.''

So Gabby wasn't a freak after all, he told himself,

gratified to find Dani so much like his best friend's wife. This little dove had teeth, just as he'd suspected.

He smiled faintly. "Okay, tiger. Here's what I want you to do...."

She went over it again and again in her mind in the minutes that followed. She chewed her lower lip until it was sore, and then chewed it some more. She had to get it right the first time. The poor stewardess wouldn't have a second chance. If they failed—and she still didn't realize how Dutch was going to get to that man in time—the stewardess would die.

She agonized over it until the captain announced that the plane was on its approach to Miami. He cautioned the passengers to stay calm and not panic, and to stay in their seats once the plane was on the ground. He sounded as strained as Dani felt. That hand grenade was the most terrifying part of all, and she wondered how Dutch was going to prevent the second man from throwing it.

The plane circled the airport and went down, landing roughly this time, bumping around as it went toward the terminal. Dani got her first glimpse of Miami and thought ironically that she sure was getting to see a lot of the world!

As soon as the plane came to a halt, Dutch touched her arm and looked down at her. Dani closed her eyes on a brief prayer.

The man with the syringe had just moved back into the cabin. He looked taut and nervous as well. The stewardess looked as though she'd given up all hope of living and had resigned herself to the horror of the acid. Her eyes were blank.

"Uh, señor...?" Dani called, getting halfway out of her seat.

The short man jumped at the sound of her voice and his arm tightened around the stewardess. "What you want?" he growled.

"I...oh, please..." Dani clutched the back of the seat and her gray eyes widened as she fought to make the words come out. "I have to go...to the rest room, please..."

The short man cursed. He called something in another language to the man in the cockpit, who looked out, angrily.

"I have to!" Dani pleaded, looking and sounding convincing.

The tall man muttered something and the short one laughed curtly. "All right," he said after a minute, during which Dani aged five years. "Come on, then."

She slipped over Dutch, and while she was moving, his hand went slowly to his inside jacket pocket.

Dani moved into the aisle and started carefully toward the rest room on the other side of the man with the syringe. Two more steps, she told herself. Her heart pounded, and she kept her eyes cast downward in case the man saw the terror in them and reacted too quickly. One more step. Please don't fail me, she said silently to Dutch. This is insane, I'm only twenty-six, I don't want to die, I've only just gotten married!

One more step. And she stopped and swayed, putting a hand to her temple. "I'm so sick!" And it was almost the truth. She deliberately let herself fall toward him.

It was enough. It was enough. He instinctively

moved to catch her, and at that instant Dutch threw the knife. The syringe went to the floor as the hijacker caught his middle. Dutch was out of his seat in a heartbeat. It was 'Nam all over again. Angola. Rhodesia. He ignored Dani, who was watching with incredulous eyes, tore the stewardess out of the hijacker's helpless grasp, threw her into a seat and kicked the hypodermic out of the way. He was through the cockpit door seconds after he'd thrown the knife, ignoring the groaning bald man on the floor as he went for the taller man.

"I will throw it, señor!" the man threatened, and grasped the firing pin of the grenade.

"Go ahead," Dutch said, and kept going. With two movements of his hands, so quick that the pilot didn't even see them, the hijacker went down with the grenade in his hand.

"He's pulled the pin!" the young copilot yelled, and there was pandemonium in the airplane.

"For God's sake," Dutch growled, retrieving it, "what are you afraid of, flying bits of plastic?" And he tossed the cheap imitation into the pilot's lap.

The copilot started to dive for it, but the pilot, a man in his late forties, just laughed. He turned toward Dutch and grinned.

"I should have realized why he was so nervous."

The copilot was still gaping. "It's a fake!"

"Keep it for a souvenir." The pilot sighed, tossing it to his colleague. "How's Lainie?"

"If you mean the stewardess, she's okay," Dutch said. "But his buddy isn't. You'd better get a doctor out here."

"Right away. Hey. Thanks," the pilot said with a quiet smile.

Dutch shrugged. "Pure self-interest," he said. "He was holding up my coffee."

"I'll buy you a cup when we get out of here," the captain offered.

Dutch grinned. "Take you up on that."

He left the cockpit. "It wasn't a live grenade," he called, the authority in his voice pacifying the nervous passengers. "It's all over, just sit quietly."

Dani was sitting on the floor, staring horrified at the groaning man with the knife in his stomach while she tried to deal with what was happening. She looked up at the stranger she'd married without even recognizing him. Who was he?

Dutch was sorry she'd had to see it, but there was no other way to do it. He bent and caught her by the arms and pulled her up gently.

"He'll be okay," he said. "No sweat. Let's get off this thing." He pulled her toward the door. Two other flight attendants came rushing from the back of the plane, embracing the stewardess, apologizing for not being able to help.

"It's okay," the little blond said shakily. "I'm fine."

She turned to Dutch, all blue eyes and gratitude. "Thank you. Thank you both!"

"All in a day's work," Dutch said carelessly. "How about getting this door open? That man needs a medic."

The groaning man got their attention. One of the flight attendants bent over him, and the copilot was just frog-marching the second terrorist, whose hands were belted together behind him, into the service compartment.

"Wait and I'll show you to the office," the captain called to Dutch. "We'll need to speak to the police, I'm sure."

"Okay," Dutch told him. He propelled Dani, who was still half shocked, down the stairs with him, out into the darkness. "Oh," he said, turning and addressing the male flight attendant, "would you please get the lady's books and purse out of seat 7B and bring them to the office?"

"Be glad to, sir," came the reply.

Dani was still shocked, but her mind registered what he'd just said. In the middle of all the furor he'd remembered her blessed books. She looked up at him uncomprehendingly, her eyes wide and frightened and uncertain and still bearing traces of sick terror.

"I had to," he said quietly as he recognized the look. "I couldn't have reached him in time."

"Yes, I—I realize that. I've just never seen anybody...like that."

"You were superb," he said. "I can think of only one other woman who would have kept her head so well."

She wondered whom he meant, but there were more immediate questions. "What...what you did," she faltered as they waited for the captain. "You said you were a soldier."

He turned her gently and held her in front of him, holding her wary gaze. "I am. But not the kind you're thinking of. I make my living as a professional soldier. I hire out to the highest bidder,'' he told her bluntly, without pulling his punches, and watched the horror that filled her face. He hadn't realized how devastated she was going to be, or how he might feel when he saw the horror in her innocent face. Her reaction surprised him. It irritated him. What had she expected, for God's sake, a clerk?

"A mercenary," she said in a choked tone.

"Yes," he replied, his whole stance challenging.

But she didn't say anything more. She couldn't. Her dreams were lying around her feet, and she hurt all the way to her soul. This news was much more devastating than what she'd seen on the plane. She didn't lift her eyes again; she didn't speak. Seconds later the pilot, copilot and stewardess who'd been held prisoner joined them, and they went to the airport office. Dani walked apart from Dutch, not touching him. He noticed that, and his face was grim when they got into the building.

Minutes later they were sitting in a small office, going over and over what had happened for the airport security people and three men who looked very much like federal officers. It didn't take long, and they were told that they'd have to appear in court, but Dani hardly heard any of it. She was trying to deal with the realization that she was married to a professional mercenary soldier. And she didn't know what to do.

Her eyes studied him as he spoke to the other men. He didn't look like one. But the air of authority that had puzzled her, his confidence, the way he seemed to take command of things—yes, it made sense now.

She even knew when it had happened, back when that woman had made a fool of him. That was the beginning. And now he had a life-style he liked, and a biddable little wife who'd be waiting back at home while he went around the world looking for trouble.

She lifted the cup of coffee they'd brought her and sipped it quietly. No, sir, she thought, her eyes narrowing. No, sir, she wasn't going to be his doormat. She cared for him, but there had to be more to a relationship than sex. And if that was all he wanted from her, he could go away.

A cold sickness washed over her as she realized how much a part of her life he'd become. So quickly, he'd absorbed her. All she had to do was look at him and she ached to hold him, to be loved by that warm, powerful body. She knew so much about him, things she blushed even remembering. But none of it was real. She couldn't sit alone at home while he went out and risked his life. My God, she thought, no wonder he didn't want children! How could he have kids in his line of work? They'd never even see their father! As for Dani, how could she live with worry eating at her like an acid? Every time he left she'd be wondering if she'd ever see him again. She'd wonder, and not know, and eventually the not-knowing would kill her soul. No, she thought miserably. Better to have a sweet memory than a living nightmare. He'd have to divorce her. She knew already that he wouldn't give up his way of life. And she couldn't stay married to him under the circumstances. So there was nothing left. A dream, ending too soon.

After the meeting was over they walked quietly

outside the terminal. The captain followed them, along with the male flight attendant who brought Dani's purse and her sack of books.

"What now?" she asked helplessly.

"The airline will pay for hotel rooms," the captain said with a kind smile. "Tomorrow we'll fly you to Greenville."

Dutch looked hunted as he glanced over the captain's shoulder. "The press corps has taken up residence," he growled.

"No stomach for stardom?" the captain grinned.

"None whatsoever," came the taut reply. "Dani and I are catching the next flight out of here tonight," he added flatly. "I'm afraid that the international wire services will have a field day."

"Probably so," the captain agreed. "It seems our erstwhile hijackers have some interesting ties to a certain Central American dictator and a few communist strings as well." He sighed. "They'd have wanted weapons once we landed," he said, glancing at Dutch.

"Yes. And they'd have gotten them," the blond man said. He lit a cigarette.

"Used that knife very often?" the captain asked quietly.

Dutch nodded. "Far too often, in years past."

"Would you mind telling me what occupation you're in?" he was asked.

Dutch eyed him quietly. "Care to make an educated guess?"

"Covert operations."

He nodded, noticing Dani's hollow-eyed stare. He

looked down at her with unreadable eyes. "I'm a professional mercenary. My specialty is logistics, but I'm handy with small arms as well, and I have something of a reputation with that knife. I made it myself." He glanced at the captain. "When the surgeons get it removed, I'd like to have it back."

The captain nodded. "I'll have it gold-plated, if you like. You saved us one hell of a mess. Any time you need help, just let me know."

"That isn't likely, but thank you."

The captain walked away and Dutch smoked his cigarette quietly while the press converged on the pilot once he was alone.

"Is that why you wanted to avoid the press?" Dani asked hesitantly. He frightened her. Despite the fact that she'd read *The Dogs of War* twice and seen the film three times, she could hardly believe what she was hearing. It was like watching a movie. All of it. The hijacking, the way he'd handled the hijackers, the matter-of-fact way he'd dealt with all of it. Her eyes were glued to his face while she turned it all around in her mind. She was married to a soldier of fortune. Now what was she going to do?

He saw that look in her eyes and could have cursed. Fate was giving him a hard time.

"I don't like publicity," he said. "My private life is sacred."

"And where do I fit into your life?" she asked quietly. It was too soon to ask that, but things needed to be said now.

"You're my wife," he said simply.

"Why did you marry me?" she asked.

He looked hunted. His eyes narrowed, his jaw clenched. He took a deep puff of his cigarette before he replied. "I wanted you."

So that was all, she thought. It didn't hurt, although she was sure it was going to, when the numbness wore off. She was still in a state of shock. She had risked her life, seen a man wounded in front of her eyes, learned that her husband was a mercenary....

He was watching her face, and he felt a violence of emotion that made him dizzy. She was under his skin. In his very soul. How did he get her out?

"Yes, I thought so," she said too casually. She searched the face her hands had touched so lovingly. "And what did you expect that our married life would be like? That I'd sit home and wait while you went away and came home shot to pieces year after year?"

He felt shocked. Taken by surprise. He stared at her intently. "I thought...we'd each have our own lives. That we could enjoy each other. Belong to each other."

She shook her head. "No. I'm sorry. I couldn't live that way. You'd better divorce me."

It was almost comical. His spinster wife of a week was showing him the door. Him! Women had chased him for years. They'd practically hung out windows trying to snare him because of his very elusiveness. And this plain little frumpy bookseller was showing him the door!

"You needn't look so shocked," she told him. "I'm only saving myself a little heartache, that's all. I can't live with the knowledge that your life is constantly in danger. I'd be destroyed."

"I'm not suicidal, for God's sake," he began.

"You're not superhuman, either," she reminded him. "There are scars on you. I didn't realize what they were at the time, but now I know. And one day you'll stop a bullet. I don't want to be sitting alone waiting for the phone to ring. I'm strong. But I'm not that strong. I care too much."

It amazed him that he felt those last four words to the soles of his feet. She cared about him. Of course she did; it was written all over her, in the soft gray eyes that had worshipped him when he loved her, in the hands that had adored him. It was infatuation or hero worship, he knew, but it had been flattering. Now it meant something more to him. Now it mattered that she was turning him away.

"We'll talk when we get to Greenville," he said firmly.

"You can talk all you like," she said, walking away from him. "I've had my say."

"You little frump!" he burst out, infuriated.

"Look who's calling whom a frump!" she threw back, whirling, all big angry gray eyes behind her glasses and flying hair and flushed cheeks. "Who do you think you are, big, bad soldier. God's gift?"

He wanted to strangle her, but he laughed instead.

"And don't laugh at me," she fumed. "It was all a line, wasn't it? You told me I was beautiful to you, but I was just a pickup, something to play with between wars!"

"At first," he agreed. He finished his cigarette and ground it out under his shoe. "But not now."

"That's right, now I'm a liability," she told him. "I'm a holiday interlude that's over."

He shook his blond head. She got prettier by the day, he mused, watching her. He'd called her a frump only because he was so angry. He smiled slowly. "You aren't over, pretty girl."

"I'm a frump!" she yelled at him.

A passing flight attendant grinned at her. "Not quite," he murmured, and winked.

Dani picked up her bag of books and started walking toward the terminal.

"Where are you going?" Dutch asked.

"Back home," she told him. "I've got a bookstore to run."

"Stop."

She did, but she kept her back to him. "Well?"

He hesitated. It was uncharacteristic. He didn't know what to do next. If he pushed her, he could lose her. But he couldn't let go, either. She'd become important to him. He didn't want to think about never seeing her again.

"Thank about it for a while," he said finally. "For a few weeks, until I get back."

"Back?" She turned, not caring if he saw her pain. Tears bit at her eyelids and she felt sick all over.

Oh, God, it hurt to see her like this! He glared toward the horizon, jamming his hands into his pockets. He'd never seen that expression on a woman's face in his life. He'd come to the brink of death with cool disdain more times than he cared to remember, and now the look on a woman's face terrified him.

She fought to get herself under control. She took a

slow, deep breath. "I won't change my mind," she said, sure now that it would be suicide to stay with him.

"All the same, I'll be in touch."

"Suit yourself."

He met her eyes, searching them. "I'm already committed to this job. I can't back out." It was the first time in years that he'd explained himself, he realized.

"I don't want to know," she said firmly. "You have your life, and I have mine. If you'd told me in the very beginning, I wouldn't have come near you."

"I think I knew that," he said softly. He sketched her with his eyes, memorizing her. "Take care of yourself."

"I always have." She let her eyes love him one last time. She ached already at their parting. It would be like losing a limb. "You take care of yourself, too."

"Yes."

She stared at her wedding ring, and he saw the thought in her eyes.

"Leave it on," he said gently. "I—would like to think that you were wearing my ring."

The tears burst from her eyes. She didn't even look at him again, she turned and broke into a run, suitcases and all, crying so hard that she could hardly see where she was going. Behind her he stood quietly on the apron, alone, watching until she was out of sight.

Seven

Nothing was the same. The first day she was home Dani went into the bookstore the same as always, but her life was changed. Harriett Gaynor, her small, plump friend, gave her odd looks, and Dani was almost certain that Harriett didn't believe a word of the story her employer told her about the Mexican holiday. Then the next day the papers hit the stands.

"It's true!" Harriett burst out, small and dark-eyed, her black hair in tight curls around her elfin face. "It's all here in the paper, about the hijacking, look!"

Dani grimaced as she looked down at the newspaper Harriett had spread over the counter. There was a picture of the pilot, and a blurred one of the uninjured hijacker being carried off the plane. There wasn't a picture of Dutch, but she hadn't expected to see one. He seemed quite good at dodging the press.

"Here's something about the man who overpowered the hijacker..." Harriett frowned and read, catching her breath at the vivid account. She looked up at Dani. "You did that?"

"He said they would have asked for automatic weapons once we were in Miami," Dani said quietly.

Harriett put the paper down. "A professional mercenary." She stared at her best friend. "I don't believe it. Didn't you ask what he did before you married him?"

"If you saw him, you wouldn't be surprised that I didn't," Dani told her. She turned away. She didn't want to talk about Dutch. She wanted to forget. Even now, he was on his way to another conflict....

"No man is that good-looking," Harriett said. "Not even Dave." Dave, a pleasant man, wasn't half the scrapper his pint-sized wife was. "By the way, Mrs. Jones called to thank you for her autographed books."

"She's very welcome. It was nice, getting to meet some of the authors at the autographing." She checked the change in the cash register as they started to open the shop.

"Where is he now?" Harriett asked suddenly.

"Getting a good lawyer, I hope," Dani said, laughing even though it hurt to say it. "We're setting a new record for short marriages. One week."

"You might work it out," came the quiet reply.

Dani wouldn't look at her friend. "He makes his living risking his life, Harrie," she said. "I can't spend mine worrying about him. I'd rather get out while I still can."

"I suppose you know your own mind," Harriett

said, shrugging. "But when you decide to go adventuring, you sure go whole hog, don't you? Marrying strangers, overpowering hijackers..."

She went away muttering, and Dani smiled at her retreating back. Yes, she'd had an adventure all right. But now it was over, and she'd better tuck her bittersweet memories away in a trunk and get on with her life. The first step was to put Dutch out of her mind forever. The second was to stop reading the newspaper. From now on, every time she learned about a small foreign war, she'd see him.

Of course, it wasn't that easy. In the weeks that followed, everything conspired to remind her of him. Especially Harriett, who became heartily suspicious when Dani began losing her breakfast.

"It's the curse of Montezuma," Dani said shortly, glaring at her friend from a pasty face as she came out of the bathroom with a wet paper towel at her mouth.

"It's the curse of the flying Dutchman," came the dry reply.

Dani laughed in spite of herself, but it was brief. "I am not pregnant."

"I had a miscarriage," Harriett said quietly. "But I've never forgotten how it felt, or how I looked. You're white as a sheet, you tire so easily it isn't funny, and your stomach stays upset no matter what you do."

It was the same thing Dani had been dreading, hoping, terrified to admit. But she'd arrived at the same conclusion Harriett had. She sat down on the stool behind the counter with a weary sigh.

"You crazy child, didn't you even think about contraceptives?" Harriett moaned, hugging her.

Harriett, only four years her senior, sometimes seemed twice that. Dani let the tears come. She wept so easily these days. Last night a story on the news about guerrilla action in Africa had set her off when she spotted a blond head among some troops. Now, Harriett's concern was doing it, too.

"I'm pregnant," Dani whispered shakily.

"Yes, I know."

"Oh, Harrie, I'm scared stiff," she said, clutching the older woman. "I don't know anything about babies."

"There, there, Miss Scarlett, I doesn't know anything about birthin' babies my own self, but we'll muddle through somehow." She drew away, smiling with a genuine affection. "I'll take care of you." She searched Dani's eyes. "Do you want to have it?"

Dani shuddered. "I saw a film once, about how babies develop." She put her hand slowly, tenderly, to her flat abdomen. "They showed what happened when a pregnancy is terminated." She looked up. "I cried for hours."

"Sometimes it's for the best," Harriett said gently.

"In some circumstances," she agreed. "But I'll never see it as a casual answer to contraception. And as for me," she said shifting restlessly, "I...want his baby." She clasped her arms around herself with a tiny smile. "I wonder if he'll be blond?" she mused.

"He may be a she," came the dry reply.

"That's all right. I like little girls." She sighed

dreamily. "Isn't it amazing? Having a tiny life inside you, feeling it grow?"

"Yes," Harriett said wistfully. "It was the happiest time of my life."

Dani looked up and smiled. "You can share mine."

Harriett, tougher than nails, grew teary-eyed. She turned quickly away before Dani could see that vulnerability. "Of course I can. Right now you need to get to a doctor and see how far along you are."

"I already know," Dani said, remembering the morning in Dutch's room, the exquisite tenderness of that brief loving. "I know."

"You'll need vitamins," Harriett continued. "And a proper diet."

"And baby clothes and a baby bed..." Dani was dreaming again.

"Not until after the seventh month," Harriett said firmly. "You have to be realistic, too. Sometimes it happens, sometimes it doesn't. But it helps not to get too involved too soon."

"Spoilsport!" Dani burst out, half-irritated.

"The doctor will tell you the same thing," Harriett said. "Dani, I bought baby furniture when I was a month along. I miscarried at four months, and had all those bright new things to dispose of. Don't do it."

Dani immediately felt repentant. She hugged Harriett warmly. "Thank you for being my friend. For caring about me."

"Someone has to." She glowered up at Dani. "Are you going to tell him?"

"How?" Dani asked. "I don't even know his address."

"My God, she's married to a man and she doesn't know where he lives."

Dani laughed at the expression on Harriett's face. "Well, we didn't spend much time talking."

Harriett started at the young woman's belly. "So I noticed."

"Stop that!" Dani sighed wearily. "Besides, he said he never wanted children. He'd go right through the roof if he knew. It's just as well that the divorce go through without his finding out."

"How can you divorce a man you can't find?" Harriett asked reasonably.

"He's getting the divorce, not me. He has my address."

"Lovely. Shall we sell some books? Call the doctor first," Harriett said, and went back to her pricing.

Dani was healthy, and after her family doctor put her on prenatal vitamins, she began to bloom. Dr. Henry Carter laughed delightedly every visit she made to his office for checkups, pleased with her progress as well as her attitude toward being pregnant.

"You really love being pregnant, don't you?" he asked when she was having her third checkup, at a little over four and a half months.

"Every second!" She touched the swell of her abdomen. "I think he moved this morning," she added excitedly. "Little flutters, like a bird trying to get free."

"Yes," he said with a warm smile. "That's what

it feels like, I'm told. The first sign of a healthy baby. The tests we ran assured us of that.''

She'd liked the test—it was done with ultrasound, and they'd given her a polaroid picture of the baby's head, just visible in the X-ray–type sound scan.

"Has there been any word from your husband?" he added quietly.

Dani felt herself go cold. "No." She started down at her hands. "He might...never come back."

"I'm sorry. The reason I asked is because I'd like you to sign up for natural childbirth classes. Even if you don't want to have a natural delivery, they'll help you cope with labor,'' he explained. "They involve exercises that prepare you for childbirth. And, sadly, they require a partner.''

"Can—can Harriett do it?'' she asked.

He knew Harriett, and he grinned. "Best person I know for a coach. All she really has to do is stand beside you and tell you when to breathe.''

"She already does that very well,'' she said dryly.

"Okay. Next month I'll sign you up. You're doing fine. Get out of here. And don't exert yourself too much. The heat's terrible this summer.''

"Tell me about it,'' she murmured, sweating even in her loose sleeveless tent blouse and elastic-fronted skirt. "See you next time.''

She made another appointment and dawdled on her way back to work. It was a lovely summer day, the kind that lures dreamers to quiet ponds and butterfly-laden meadows full of flowers. She sang a little as she walked along, feeling the tiny flutters in her stomach and laughing as she went. What a beautiful world. How wonderful to be pregnant and healthy.

Finally, she gave in and went back to the bookstore, because she knew Harriett would worry if she was gone too long. She strolled lazily along the small shopping center in the heart of Greenville, oblivious to shoppers and the sounds of children playing on the sidewalk.

With a slow, dreamy smile, she opened the door of the shop and walked inside. And came face to face with Dutch.

He was wearing khakis—a bush shirt with slacks—and there was a new scar on one cheek. He looked as though he'd lost a little weight, although he was as handsome, as physically devastating, as ever. Harriett must have thought so, too, because she was openly staring at him, wide-eyed.

Dutch did some staring of his own. His eyes were on her stomach, and their expression was frankly terrified. He felt as if he'd never breathe again. He'd come back to see if they could work out a compromise, if she might be willing to rethink her position. Only to find—this!

Dani saw the stark terror in his eyes. If she'd hoped for any kind of reconciliation, she knew now that it was all a pipe dream. After all the long nights of remembering, worrying, hoping, praying, for him, of thinking how he'd react if she told him about the baby, now she knew.

It was too much all at once. The sight of him, the hunger for him, the weeks and months of worry. He began to blur, and then to darken. And she fainted at his feet.

She came to in the back of the shop, in a storeroom that Dani and Harriett used for lunch breaks. There was a big armchair there, and Dani was lying across it, her shoes off, a cold cloth on her forehead.

"...had a hard time of it," Harriett was saying grimly. "She's healthy enough, but she won't rest."

"I never should have married her," came the harsh reply.

"You're a prize, aren't you?" Harriett was saying. "That child has never had anything or anyone in her life to make her way easier. Her parents deserted her when she was just a baby; she doesn't even know where they are. She never really had a boyfriend of her own. She's had no one except me. And now you sweep her off her feet, get her pregnant, and walk out on her. Mister, you are a walking blond plague, and if there's one iota of human decency left in you, you'll do her a favor and get out of her life."

"And leave her at your mercy?" Dutch came back idly. "Like hell."

Oh, no, Dani thought sickly. She'd known that would happen. World War III. Dutch and Harriett were just alike....

"What kind of mercy would she get from you, you...!" Harriett retorted.

"No," Dani whispered hoarsely, opening her eyes to see them squared off, glaring at each other scant feet away. They both turned toward her. "No," she repeated more strongly. "If you two want to brawl, go stand in the street. You can't do it here. I can't cope.''

"I'm sorry, baby," Harriett said softly. "Are you all right?"

"I'm fine, thanks." She sat up, smoothing the wet cloth over her face while Dutch glared down at her with fierce anger in his dark eyes. His blond hair was slightly mussed, his handsome face harder than she remembered it. "Well, you needn't glare at me," she told him shortly. "I didn't get pregnant all alone, remember!"

Harriett had to hide a smile. "I'll leave you two to talk," she offered.

"We'll talk at home," Dani said firmly, glaring at Dutch. "Where I can throw things and scream. The store cramps my style."

She got up while Dutch tried not to grin at her fury. Glasses and all, she was something in a temper.

"Don't rush around; it isn't healthy," he said, taking her hand in his. He glanced at Harriett. "Can you manage for an hour or so?"

"Of course. Can you?" she returned.

He couldn't help the faint smile. "Yes, Mama," he said mockingly,. "I won't hurt your lamb."

He guided her out the door, letting her show him the way to her nearby apartment. It was up a flight of stairs, and he frowned as they climbed. He didn't like the stairs.

"You have to move," he said when she'd unlocked her apartment and they were inside in the white and yellow homey confines of the living room.

She turned and gaped at him. "What?"

"You have to move," he said shortly. "You can't be walking up and down stairs like...that." He indicated her belly.

"It isn't a that. It's a baby," she said firmly, planting her feet as she challenged him. "It's a boy, in fact, and I am going to call him Joshua Eric."

His face gave nothing away. His eyes went over her quietly, and for the first time in months he felt whole again. Leaving her had been the hardest thing he'd ever done. All the time he was away, he thought of her, longed for her, wanted her. He still wanted her. But she was pregnant. He didn't want a baby, he didn't want her pregnant. It brought back memories that were unbearable.

He hadn't even meant to come back; he hadn't wanted his life to change. And his worst fears had confronted him the instant he saw her.

"Do you have the divorce papers with you?" she asked calmly.

He sighed angrily and lit a cigarette without even asking if she minded. "You've put 'paid' to that, haven't you?" he asked, his voice as cold as his dark eyes. "How can I divorce you in that condition? You'll want child support, I imagine?"

He couldn't possibly have hurt her any more, not if he'd knocked her down. Quick tears welled in her eyes, and she glared at him through them.

"Get out!" she shot at him.

"Is it even mine?" he goaded, feeling trapped and straining at invisible bonds fiercely.

She picked up the nearest object, a small statuette

of some Greek figure, and flung it at him. "Damn you!"

He ducked and it hit the door, shattering into a hundred pieces.

"Get out of my apartment! Get out of my life!" she choked. "Oh, God, I hate you, I hate——!" The nausea hit her all at once. She turned, running for the bathroom, where she was horribly sick. She cried helplessly, oblivious to the tall man holding the wet cloth to her head and hating himself so much he wanted to jump off a building to make the guilt stop.

"I hate you," she whispered weakly when it was over and she could talk. Her head was leaning against the cold porcelain sink. She could hardly move.

"Yes." He bathed her face gently, her hands. Then he put the cloth aside and lifted her, carrying her into the bedroom. He laid her down and turned on the oscillating fan, positioning it so that it wouldn't blow directly on her.

"Go to sleep," he said quietly. "Then we'll talk."

"I—don't want to," she murmured drowsily, but she was drained and overwhelmed and so tired. Her eyes closed, and seconds later she drifted off.

Dutch sat down on the bed beside her, frightened and sick at what he'd done to her. His eyes ran lovingly over her body, and without conscious thought he eased up the hem of her maternity blouse and moved the elastic of her skirt down, and looked. Her belly was slightly swollen, round and womanly. So that was what pregnancy looked like. He winced, remembering another time, another pregnant woman. But Dani wasn't like that, he told himself. Never like that. His lean fingers touched the soft flesh gently, hesitantly. Yes, it was firm. His child was in there. His child. A boy, she'd said. Could she be so certain? Of course, there were tests they did now. His big hand smoothed over the swell, pressing, and all at once something fluttered against his fingers. He jerked them back with a gasp.

Dani had woken with the first light touch of his fingers, and she found the expressions that flickered on his face fascinating. But that last reaction amused her, and she laughed softly.

His eyes darted to hers. "What did I do?" he asked softly.

"The baby moved," she said simply.

"Moved?" He looked back down, frowning. Hesitantly, he reached down again. She took his fingers and placed them against the side of her belly. She pressed them close, and it happened again. And he laughed. Slowly. Softly. Delightedly.

"When they get bigger, they kick," she told him. "The doctor says the more active they are, the healthier they are. He moves a lot."

"I never knew...." He looked up from her belly to her rib cage. His hand moved up to the bunched top and he glanced up at her face with the question in his eyes. "I've never seen a pregnant woman this way."

"I don't mind if you look at me," she whispered, fascinated by the way he was reacting to her. There was something in his face, a kind of tenderness. She wondered what had soured him on pregnancy, and why he hated the thought of a child.

He lifted the blouse to under her chin and his body

stilled as his eyes sought the subtle changes in her breasts.

"You're bigger," he said quietly. "Darker... here." His fingers brushed an enlarged areole, making her tense with remembered pleasure.

"Little changes," she said, fighting for breath. "All that will increase as I get further along. It prepares me so that I can nurse him."

He felt a wild charge of emotion. It showed when he looked into her eyes. "I didn't think women did that anymore."

She smiled. "I want to do everything. I—" She laughed. "I love it. Being pregnant, I mean. I've never had anyone to fuss over, you see," she tried to explain. "Never had anyone of my own to worry about, to care about, to love. He'll be my whole world. I'll take care of him, and sit with him when he's sick, and play games with him when he's older. I'll take him everywhere with me, I'll—" She lowered her eyes at the expression on his face. "What you said, about child support. It's not necessary," she added proudly. "I make a comfortable living from the bookstore. I can take care of him. He'll be my responsibility."

He'd never felt so empty and alone in all his life. He stared at her belly, hearing the words and wanting all that tender caring for himself. But it wasn't possible. She didn't want him. She was telling him so.

He tugged the blouse back down. "You'll be a good mother," he said numbly.

"I'm sorry that you had to find it out this way,"

she murmured. "I would have written you, but I didn't even have your address."

He drew in a slow breath and got to his feet. He went to the window, smoking another cigarette. He looked so alone. So lost.

"You...weren't hurt?" she asked, averting her face so that he couldn't see her eyes.

"A few scratches." He stared at the glowing tip of the cigarette for a minute before his dark eyes went back out the window to the city traffic. He'd done nothing right since he got off the damned plane. He'd wanted to talk about reconciliation, but when he'd found her pregnant, he'd gone off the deep end. It was because of the memories, of course; they'd haunted him for so long. Perhaps he'd blown the whole incident out of proportion over the years.

He turned back to her, uneasy at the way she looked. That woman, Harriett, had mentioned how tired Dani was. Yes, she was tired. Run down. There had been a radiance in her when she'd come into the bookstore, but it was gone now. He'd taken it away with his cold attitude and stupid accusations. He'd hurt her. Again. And he hadn't meant to.

"What I said, before," he said hesitantly, glancing at her. His hand, holding the cigarette, moved aimlessly. "I know the baby's mine."

"Do you?" she asked with an empty smile as she sat up. "I might have had a legion of lovers since you left."

"I came back to see if we might salvage the marriage," he said after a minute, hoping for some reaction in her face, but there was nothing.

She looked up at him, schooling her features to remain calm. "And now?"

He shifted restlessly, pacing near the window, his blond head bowed, one hand in his pocket. "Now I don't know."

She swung her feet to the floor. "I haven't changed my mind, even if you've started to change yours," she said before he could speak. She looked at him with quiet gray eyes. "It's all I can do to manage carrying the baby and running my business so that I can support him. I can't have any additional pressure right now. I hope you understand."

"You keep referring to it as a 'he,' " he said curtly.

"He is a he," she told him. "They ran some tests."

He felt odd. A son. A little boy who might look like him. He stared at her as if he'd never seen a woman before, studying every line and curve of her body.

"Don't look so worried, Eric, I don't expect anything from you," she mused, getting slowly to her feet. "Now, if you've said all you came to say, I've got to work to do. I'll give you the name of my attorney...."

"No!" The word came out without conscious volition. They couldn't divorce. Hell, he didn't even want to think about it! She had his child, and he... wanted it!

She clenched her fingers together and glared at him. "I won't live with you," she said stubbornly.

His face hardened. "You will."

"Make me."

He stared at her. Mutinous bow mouth, stormy gray

eyes, flushed face. Pregnant. He started to laugh help-lessly, a deep, rich sound like velvet.

"I like you," he said absently. "I honestly like you. No deceit, no tricks, no lines, no backing away from trouble. You're a hell of a woman."

She shifted from one foot to the other. No, he wasn't going to get around her that way. "Remember me?" she asked coldly. "Miss Frump?"

He put out the cigarette, still smiling faintly, and moved toward her with a gleam in his eyes that made her back away.

"Sexy frump," he murmured dryly. "Very preg-nant, very desirable. And I don't want a divorce. I want you."

"I'm not for sale," she told him, moving backward until the wall stopped her. "Go away. Go blow up something."

"I don't blow up things, actually," he murmured, pinning her to the wall with a strong arm on either side of her. "I'm more into logistics and strategy."

"You'll get killed, anyway," she said.

He shrugged. "I could get hit by a car downstairs."

"Not quite as easily," she argued.

"I want you," he said quietly.

"Yes, I know," she replied softly. "But wanting isn't enough. You've already said you'd never fall in love again, so all you're offering me is your body, between wars. It's a gorgeous body, and in bed you're all any woman could ever want. But you're asking me to live with death, day in and day out, and I can't."

He drew in a breath and started to speak, but before

he could she took one of his hands and pressed it slowly against her belly.

"I have your son under my heart," she whispered, pressing his palm flat against her. "I can't live with the fear of losing both of you."

He frowned. "I don't understand."

"Eric, I could miscarry," she said, her voice soft with a fear he was just beginning to sense.

"Is it likely?" he asked.

"I'm healthy. So is the baby. But there are no guarantees," she said, lowering her eyes to his chest.

"It...frightens you, to think of losing him?" he asked hesitantly.

She looked up wide-eyed. "Of course it does!"

He was remembering another woman, another time, and he cursed himself for that lapse. Dani wanted the baby. It was written all over her.

"I can't worry about him and you as well," she said curtly. "And he deserves a chance. You're old enough to make your own mistakes, but I'm responsible for him now."

He stared down at her for a long time. Then he turned away with a sigh and lit still another cigarette.

"I've done it for so many years," he said after a minute, staring at the floor. "It's all I know."

"I'm not asking you to change," she reminded him.

He looked up. "We're married."

"We can get divorced."

"I don't want a damned divorce!" he burst out, his eyes black with anger.

She stood there staring at him helplessly, searching for the right words.

He sighed angrily. "I knew you'd be trouble the minute I saw you," he growled. "A frumpy little bookseller with the body and soul of an angel. And you're in my blood like poison. I'd have to die to get you out of my system!"

She lifted her shoulders and smiled ruefully. "Well, look at it this way, you'll never have to fight off other men."

He laughed softly, shaking his head. "Would you care to bet? The way you look right now…"

"I look pregnant," she said. "In two or three more months I'll look like a blimp."

"Not to me you won't."

He averted his eyes to his shoes. "Well, I'll go home and pack. And there are some people I want to see."

"Pack?"

He looked up. "I'm going to live with you," he said. "If you don't like it, that's tough. I am not," he continued, gathering steam, "going to have you working yourself to death and running up and down these damned stairs. Harriett's right. You need look-ing after. So I'm going to look after you. Until the baby comes, at least," he added. "After that we'll make whatever decisions have to be made."

She wanted to argue. But he looked very formi-dable. "But, your…your work…."

"To hell with my work," he bit off. He looked frankly dangerous. "I've got enough in foreign banks to buy this damned building you live in. I work because I like it, not because I need money.''

''But...''

''Shh. Talking is bad for the baby.'' He crushed out his cigarette. ''I'll get back Saturday.''

Things were happening too fast. She was shell-shocked. She watched him walk toward her.

''Little gray-eyed witch,'' he whispered. He pulled her gently against him and bent to tease her mouth with his. ''Open it,'' he murmured. ''I haven't kissed you in months.''

''I'll bet you've kissed other women,'' she said mutinously.

He lifted his head. ''Nope.'' He drew his knuckles over her flushed cheek. ''I haven't even looked at one. And yes, there are always women in the circles I move in. Beautiful women, with no principles and eyes like dollar signs. And all I could think of was how it felt with you, that morning when we made such exquisite love on my bed and created this little boy.''

Tears burst into her eyes, startling him. ''You know?'' she breathed.

''Of course. Didn't you?'' he asked, smiling at her.

''You're more experienced than I am,'' she hedged.

''Not in that kind of lovemaking,'' he murmured ruefully. ''I wasn't lying when I said I'd never experienced it before.''

''Do you mind very much, about the baby?'' she asked, because she had to know.

He smoothed away her frown with a lean forefinger. ''I have to get used to the idea, that's all. I've been a free spirit for a very long time. I've had no one.''

"Yes, I know." She studied his shirt buttons. "Eric, you don't have to do this. You don't have to come here...."

He stopped the sacrificing little speech with his mouth, opening hers to a delicate, gently probing kiss that had her going stiff with desire all too soon.

His fingers tangled in the short hair at the nape of her neck and eased her head back against the hard muscle of his upper arm. His other hand made slow, torturous forays against her collarbone, her shoulder, the side of her breast.

"Sadist," she whispered shakily as the magic worked on her.

He bit her lower lip gently. "Do you want to make love?"

Her eyes opened, looking straight into his face. "No."

He smiled, and his fingers brushed knowingly over her nipples. She flinched with sudden pleasure, and he laughed gently.

"Yes, you do," he murmured dryly.

"My mind doesn't want to," she amended, trying to save herself from the sensual prison he was trying to trap her in.

He kissed her eyes closed, and his hands slid to her stomach, cupping its firm warmth. "It won't make you miscarry," he whispered. "Not if I'm gentle enough. And I will be."

She trembled at the soft tone, and he smiled and pulled her into his arms, holding her.

"It isn't that," she whispered into his shoulder, eyes open and worried as they stared at the fabric of his shirt. "Don't make me care for you. It will make it all that much harder to let go. Just…just let me pretend that it's Mexico, and we're having a holiday. All right?"

He stood very still, smoothing her hair. "Dani…"

"Please!"

He sighed heavily and let her go. "All right. A holiday." His eyes dropped to her belly and he chuckled. "For the three of us."

"And—and no sex," she added, her eyes dark and frightened.

He searched them, seeing her fear of losing him. It bothered him, but he didn't quite know how to handle it. "Are you sure?" he asked. "We could enjoy each other."

"Yes, I know. But I don't want to."

She was imposing impossible limits on his self-control, but he couldn't turn his back on his responsibility to her. He shrugged, as if it didn't matter. "Okay," he said carelessly. "No sex."

She breathed more easily. She had expected him to argue. He brushed a kiss against her nose.

"Of course," he added, "you can always seduce me if you like."

"Thank you," she replied with a reluctant smile. "I'll keep that in mind."

He winked at her. "See you Saturday. Rest for another hour. I'll stop by your store and tell the mother hen where you are. And watch those damned stairs," he added firmly.

"Yes, your worship." She curtsied.

He laughed shortly as he went out the door, closing it quietly behind him. Dani stared at it for a long time before she went back to lie down. She wondered what she was letting herself in for. He wasn't going to be able to settle down, she was sure of it. It would mean only more heartache. But apparently he felt responsible and he wasn't going to let her out of his sight for five months. She grimaced at the thought of having to cope with Dutch and Harriett together. It was going to be a rough pregnancy.

Eight

Dutch thought that getting married might have been worth it all when he saw the shock on J.D.'s and Gabby's faces.

J.D. Brettman was big and dark. He was an ex-mercenary who now practiced law in Chicago. And Gabby Darwin Brettman had been his secretary before she married him. Dutch had heard a little about her from First Shirt, another member of the team, who'd told him how rough the courtship had been, and he'd met her once himself. Now he need advice, and he couldn't think of anyone better than J.D. to ask.

"Married." J.D. caught his breath. "You?"

Dutch shrugged. He looked up from his lit cigarette to catch the amused look in Gabby's green eyes, and he laughed in spite of himself. "It's your fault," he told her. "I never would have noticed her, but for you. Until J.D. married you, I thought all women were incapable of honesty.''

J.D. touched Gabby's cheek gently. ''She changed my own outlook,'' he said, and a look passed between them that embarrassed Dutch.

Dutch got up and went to the window, staring blankly out at Chicago. ''I don't know what to do,'' he confessed. ''I thought I would keep working and we'd each have our own lives. But she won't agree to that. She says she can't handle knowing what I'm doing when I'm away.''

J.D. got up. ''I'll make a pot of coffee. Gabby, keep Dutch company, will you?''

''Sure.'' She got up and went to the window, standing quietly beside the tall blond man, her arms folded over her chest. She looked at him. ''I was going to get out of J.D.'s life when I thought he might go back to it,'' she said honestly. ''I couldn't handle it, either.'' Her shoulders rose and fell. ''I'm not a coward, but the worry would have made one of me. If he'd been a policeman or worked in law enforcement, I suppose I'd have had to make the best of it. But the kind of work he did, and you do, isn't easy for a woman to cope with. It's extraordinarily dangerous.''

''Gabby,'' he said, staring out the window, ''how would you have felt if J.D. hadn't been able to give it up—and you were pregnant?''

Tears burst from her eyes. He looked down and saw them, and his face contorted. ''Oh, God,'' he breathed roughly.

She turned away. ''I'm sorry,'' she said. ''I want a baby so much. But J.D. and I haven't been able to have one. If I were pregnant, and he went off to a war, I think I'd die in my sleep.''

He started to speak and couldn't. He lifted the cigarette to his lips, anguish in his eyes.

''I meant to tell you,'' J.D. said minutes later, after he'd brought the coffee, ''that Apollo's been cleared of any criminal charges.''

''You got him off?'' Dutch asked with a smile, feeling happy for their old friend and comrade.

J.D. nodded. ''It took a little work. But he was innocent; that helped.'' He pursed his lips and glanced at Dutch. ''He's opened his own business.''

''Oh? Doing what?'' Dutch asked.

''A consulting firm. He specializes in teaching anti-terrorism tactics to international corporations. And already he's got more work than he can handle.'' He leaned back against the sofa. ''It's exciting work. Even a little risky. He asked if you might be interested. He needs someone experienced in tactics and strategy.''

''A desk job,'' Dutch scoffed.

''Not at all. Go see him.''

Dutch met J.D.'s level gaze. ''I don't know if I can settle down.''

''I didn't know, either.'' He glanced at Gabby, who was writing letters at the small desk, her long hair around her shoulders. ''But it wasn't hard to decide which meant more, a few wild thrills, or her. She's my world,'' he added in a tone that made Dutch look away.

He leaned forward, staring at the carpet. ''Dani's pregnant.''

J.D. hesitated. "Is it yours?"

He nodded and smiled. "No doubt about it."

Later, he went to see Apollo Blain, the tall black man who'd been part of their small unit since J.D. and First Shirt had formed it years ago. Apollo grinned at him from behind his big desk, looking urbane and capable and prosperous.

"Tired of planning battles?" Apollo chuckled as he shook Dutch's outstretched hand. "Help me save paunchy executives from terrorists. It's a hell of a lot safer, and the pay's good."

"J.D. said I might like it," Dutch sighed, settling back in an armchair. "I got married."

"You?" Apollo gaped at him. He felt his own forehead. "My God, I must have an awful fever. I thought you just said you were married."

"I am. And I've got a son on the way," came the amused reply.

"I'd better lie down."

"Not until we discuss this job," Dutch returned.

"Are you really interested?" Apollo asked seriously.

Dutch nodded. "I don't know if I can stick it out. That's up front. But I think I need to try, for her sake."

Apollo whistled. "I'd like to meet this lady. Anything like Gabby?"

Dutch smiled. "Quite a lot."

"I hope there aren't any more of them running around loose." Apollo shuddered. "Even First Shirt's on the verge, with Gabby's mother. Anyway, enough about that. Here's what I had in mind, if you'd like to give it a shot...."

Dutch lit a cigarette and listened quietly. He nodded. Yes, it sounded like an interesting job. Outwitting terrorists. He smiled. Perhaps he might even enjoy it. He leaned back and crossed his legs as Apollo's deep voice outlined the project.

When Dani told her best friend what was happening, Harriett had little to say about it, except to mutter something about a strong cage and a thin whip.

"He's not at all difficult when you know him." Dani grinned impishly. "And you have to admit, he's rather extraordinarily handsome."

"Handsome doesn't have anything to do with it," Harriett said curtly. And then she smiled. And growled wolfishly. And went off grinning.

Dani stared after Harriett, her own smile being slowly replaced by a frown. Her hand went absently to the swell of her stomach and she walked back behind the counter slowly.

It all seemed like a dream, somehow. The only reality left in her life was the baby. How in the world was she going to cope with a husband who felt trapped? She couldn't forget the look on his face when he'd seen that she was pregnant, couldn't forget what he'd said to her. He'd apologized, but still she couldn't forget. He didn't want this baby for some reason, and although he desired Dani, he didn't love her. His feelings were superficial at best, nothing that a marriage could be built on.

Her eyes went to the order sheet on the counter and

she stared at it blankly, oblivious to the sound of Harriett helping a new customer find the books she wanted. Harriett had been right; she should have kept her head in Mexico. How incredible that level headed Dani had gone off the deep end and married a stranger. It wasn't like her.

And now he felt responsible for what he'd done, and he was going to take care of her. She almost cried. Not because he loved her, but because the baby was his fault. She stared at her neat, short nails. How could she bear seeing him day after day, knowing that only the baby held him to her, that when it was all over, he'd be gone again. Perhaps he'd be killed. Her eyes closed in agony.

"Stop it," Harriett whispered sharply, pausing by the counter. "Stop tormenting yourself. At least he cares enough to look after you, doesn't he?"

Her eyelids lifted, and her anguished gray eyes were fogged from tears. "Does he?"

"He was snarling like a mountain lion," Harriett said, "when he stopped by here on this way to the airport. But it wasn't all guilt, you know. He's really worried about you."

Dani sighed thoughtfully. "He was terrified when he saw I was pregnant, Harrie," she murmured. "And when we got back to my apartment...he said some harsh things."

"None of which he meant, I imagine." Harriett patted her hand. "But you've got to stop worrying. It isn't healthy."

"He said he had to see some people," Dani said tightly.

"So that's it." Harriett glanced toward the browsing customer. "If he said he'd be back, he will. You can't put a rope around a man like that."

"I'd die if I lost him," she whispered, closing her eyes. "I offered him a divorce, and he wouldn't take it. I can't bear being nothing more than a responsibility."

"Once he gets to know you, that might change. Have you thought of it that way?" Harriett asked with a quiet smile. "Now, get busy. That's the best therapy I know for worry. Okay?"

"Okay." But as the days went by, the worries grew. What if he didn't come back at all? What if the people he was seeing told him of another mission, and he couldn't resist taking it?

Friday afternoon, when she left, she asked Harriett to open up the next morning so that she could sleep late. She was tired, and the worry wasn't helping. Harriett started to say something, but apparently thought better of it.

Something woke Dani. A movement beside her, a heavy weight on the bed. She came awake slowly, her face pale and drawn from lack of rest, her eyes heavily shadowed.

Dutch stared at her with unconcealed anxiety. She looked even worse than when he'd left. His eyes went slowly down her body to the swell of her stomach and they darkened. He didn't touch her this time. She didn't want that, he recalled bitterly, she didn't want him in any physical way anymore.

Dani blinked and almost reached out to touch him.

Was he real? Her eyes wandered over his broad shoulders in the tan raincoat he was wearing. His blond hair was damp, too, curling a little around the sides of his face, and she wondered if their child would inherit that slight waviness.

"I didn't expect you so early," she said drowsily. "Is it raining?"

"Cats and dogs." He stood up, moving away from the bed. "Harriett's watching the store, I gather?"

"Yes. Would you like some breakfast?" she asked, although the thought of food was giving her problems already.

"I had it on the plane," he said. He lit a cigarette and glanced at her. "Can you eat anything?"

She shook her head. "Not now, I can't. I have toast when I get up."

"I'll go make some."

She gaped at him, and he laughed reluctantly.

"Well, I can toast bread, you know," he said. "We used to take turns with chow when the group and I were on a mission."

Her eyes lowered quickly to the bedspread. She touched the design in the white chenille. "The... people you had to see?" Her glance skipped to his hard face and down again. "I'm sorry. That's none of my business." She got up, standing slowly because any movement could trigger the nausea.

He felt as if he'd taken a hard blow in the stomach. Not her business! For God's sake, didn't she even care?

He turned, striding angrily into the kitchen while

she sighed miserably, wondering what she'd done, and made her way into the bathroom.

The toast was on the table when she joined him. She'd thrown on a sleeveless flowered dress and came barefoot into the room, her hair gently brushed, her face white and drawn. He was wearing jeans and a brown knit shirt that made him look even more vital, tanned and powerful than usual.

"Thank you," she said as she sat down.

"You don't look well," he said bluntly.

"I'm pregnant."

"Yes, I noticed that."

She looked up and caught an amused gleam in his dark eyes.

"I don't ever feel well in the morning," she returned. "It's normal. And as for looking well," she added with a glare, "as you like to remind me, I never have looked well. I'm frumpy."

"Talk about bad moods," he murmured, leaning back to smoke his cigarette with an amused smile on his firm mouth. "Eat your toast, little shrew."

She glared at him. "You don't have to feel responsible for me," she said coldly. "I've already told you, it isn't necessary for you to stay here. I can have the baby all by myself."

"Sure you can," he scoffed, his eyes narrowing. "That's why you look so healthy."

"I'd be healthier if you'd go away!" she shot back. She left the toast, started to get up and suddenly sat down again, swallowing rapidly.

Dutch went to fetch a damp cloth and held it to her face, her throat, her mouth, kneeling beside her.

"All right now?" he asked in a tone so tender, it brought quick tears to her eyes.

"Yes," she whispered miserably.

His hand sought her belly and pressed there protectively. "This is mine," he said softly, holding her gaze. "I put it there. And until it's born, and the danger is all over, I'm going to stay with you."

The tears overwhelmed her. "Oh, please go away," she whispered brokenly. "Please..."

He pulled her gently against him, her face against his, his arms warm and strong at her back. He smelled of spicy cologne and cigarette smoke, and her body reacted to him with a crazy surge of pleasure that she tried to fight down. It wasn't permanent, she had to keep reminding herself, it was only temporary, until the baby was born. She'd better not get too attached to the feel of his arms.

"I was going to wait until later to discuss this with you," he said after a minute, "but I think we'd better talk now. Come here."

He lifted her in his arms and stood up in one smooth motion, carrying her back into the bedroom.

He laid her down against the pillows and leaned over her, searching her wide gray eyes behind the glasses.

"You're killing me," she whispered achingly.

"I can see that," he said quietly. "It isn't making my life any easier. I can't love you," he said tersely, and his face was hard. "I'm sorry. I'm...very fond of you," he added, brushing the tears from her cheeks. He took off her glasses and laid them aside, wiping the tear tracks away with a corner of the sheet.

"But what there was in me of love died long ago. I can't afford the luxury of caring, not in my line of work."

Her eyes closed and her voice was hoarse with pain. "I love you," she said helplessly, her voice strained.

"I know," he replied. Her eyes opened, and he searched them. What the hell! She needed to know. Perhaps it would help her to understand. He took a sharp breath. "The woman, the one I loved so desperately...she became pregnant with my child," he said coldly. "The day she left me she told me she'd had an abortion. She laughed about it. How absurd, she said, to think that she'd want a child of mine!" His hands gripped her arms fiercely, but she didn't notice it at all. Her shocked eyes were fixed on his tortured face. "She got rid of it," he said harshly, "like so much garbage!"

Now she understood. Now it all made sense. She reached up hesitantly and touched his face.

"I'm raw from thinking about it," he whispered roughly, "from the memories. When I saw you pregnant with my child it all came back like a fever." His eyes blazed. "You don't know me. What I am now, she made me..."

Her fingers touched his hard mouth, feeling its warmth. Everything soft and womanly inside her reached out. Poor, storm-battered man, she thought achingly. Poor, tortured man.

"My parents hated me," he ground out. "They died hating me!"

"Come here." She reached up, drawing him down

with her, holding him. He shuddered, and her eyes closed. Perhaps he didn't love her, but he needed her. She knew that even if he didn't. Her arms enfolded him—loving, comforting arms. Her hands smoothed his cool blond hair, and she nuzzled her cheek against it.

"Parents never hate children," she said quietly. "Not really."

"How would you know?" he growled harshly. "Didn't yours desert you?"

She took a slow breath, clinging to him. "Yes." She shifted under his formidable weight. "They were very young. Just children themselves. The responsibility must have been terrible." She held him closer. "They tried to contact me once. My aunt...told them I was dead." He stiffened and she swallowed hard. "I found out only when she was dying herself. It was too late then."

"Dani..."

"We can't go back, either of us," she continued quietly. Her hand brushed the nape of his neck. "We have to do the best we can with what we have."

"Are you sorry that I made you pregnant?" he asked in a tone so quiet she barely heard it.

"I've already told you that I'm happy," she said, and smiled against his cool skin. "I've never had anyone of my own."

It was a long minute before he lifted his head. He drew in a slow, calming breath and met her eyes. His own were stormy, turbulent; his face was terrible with remembered pain.

"I would never hurt you," she said. "Never, in

any way, even if I had the ability. She was a horrible woman, and you were young and vulnerable. But I'm sure your parents understood, even if they were hurt. And I will never believe that they didn't love you," she said, her face soft and caring.

His jaw tautened. He got to his feet and turned away. A long moment later he fumbled to light a cigarette.

Dani, blind without her glasses, didn't see the betraying movement of his hands. She tugged her glasses back on and sat up, straightening her dress, which had ridden up her legs.

"I have to get to the store," she said after the long silence began to grate on her nerves. "Harriett has an appointment to get her hair cut at noon."

He turned, scowling. "You're in no condition to go to work," he said curtly.

She looked up, eyebrows raised. "Fudge! I'm a little shaky on my legs, that's all." She got up, daring him to stop her. "I've got a business to take care of."

"You've got a baby to take care of," he corrected. "Call Harriett and tell her to close up when she leaves."

She glared at him. "No."

He shrugged and watched her pull out a slip and hose, and she thought the matter was settled.

He waited until she started to pull the dress over her head. Then he put down his cigarette and moved forward. Before she had time to react he stripped her, quickly and deftly, and put her under the covers. Then he took her clothes, tossed them into the closet, locked the closet, and pocketed the key.

She lay there with the covers around her neck, staring at him with eyes like saucers. It had happened so quickly, she'd had not time to retaliate.

He picked up the phone and asked for the number of her bookstore. Blankly, she told him. He finished dialing.

"Harriett? This is Dutch. Dani said to close up the shop when you leave. She's staying in bed today. Yes, that's right. Yes, I will." He hung up and retrieved his cigarette. "Now," he told Dani, "you'll stay right there until I say you can get up."

"I won't!" she returned.

"All right," he said easily, sliding one hand into his pocket. "Get up."

She started to, remembered her unclothed condition, and sank back against the pillows. "I want my clothes."

"You can have them tomorrow."

"I want them now."

"Go back to sleep. It's only nine," he said. "I'll clean up the kitchen."

He started out of the room and she stared at him uncomprehendingly, her eyes wide and uncertain. He turned and looked at her, the cigarette in his hand sending up curls of gray smoke.

"You're very much like Gabby," he said quietly.

He was gone before she could reply. Was Gabby the woman in his past? she wondered miserably. She took off her glasses and turned her face into her pillow as fresh tears came. She was sure that he hated her. Why else would he have said such a thing to her?

Eventually, she slept. It was late afternoon when

she awoke, to find her clothes at the foot of the bed and a note under the pillow. Drowsily, she unfolded the paper and read it.

You can have your clothes, but don't leave the apartment, it said in a bold black scrawl. *I have gone to do some shopping. Back by five. Dutch.*

She glanced at the clock beside the bed. It was almost five now. She scrambled out of bed quickly to dress before he got back.

When he came in, with a bag of groceries in one powerful arm, she was curled up on the sofa with her ledgers spread around her. He glared and she glared back.

"Well, somebody has to do the paperwork," she said stubbornly. "And you won't let me do my job."

"Tit for tat," he said carelessly. "You won't let me do mine."

"I won't get killed selling books," she returned.

"I like the idea of being a father now that I'm getting used to it," he said as he put down the bag on the kitchen table. "I'm not going to let you risk losing him."

"You make me sound as if I didn't care about him at all," she snapped.

He started putting food into the refrigerator. "Stop trying to pick fights with me," he said pleasantly. "I won't argue with you."

"I'm not picking a fight," she said tautly. She just found it hard to believe that he was really concerned about her. She put her paperwork aside and padded into the kitchen to get something cold to drink. The heat was stifling, and the little air conditioner in the window was barely adequate.

He turned, frowning at her damp skin. "Are you hot?" he asked gently. "I'll get a bigger air conditioner delivered."

"No, you won't," she said stubbornly. "I like the one I've got."

He took her by the arms and held her in front of him. "You won't win," he said quietly. "So stop trying. I have to go to Chicago on Monday."

She wouldn't look up. "Work?" she asked, trying to sound as if she didn't care.

"Work," he agreed. His hands smoothed up and down her soft arms. "I'm not making any promises."

"Have I asked for any?" she murmured, lifting her eyes.

"You wouldn't," he said, as if he knew. "You're too proud to ask for anything that isn't freely given." He bent and started to kiss her, but she turned her face away.

He felt a tremor of hurt and anger go through him. His hands clenched, and he moved away from her with a new and unexpected pain eating at him.

He sighed angrily. How the hell had she gotten so far under his skin? He wanted to throw things.

"I'm not leaving the country," he said curtly. "An old friend of mine has opened a consulting firm. He teaches counterterrorism tactics to corporate executives. He needed someone experienced in tactics, and asked if I'd be interested." He shrugged. "So I told him yes."

It shocked her that he'd even consider changing his

profession. Did the baby mean so much? Yes, she thought, probably it did. There were deep scars on his heart. Perhaps he'd never truly get over them. She didn't have the beauty or the sophistication to capture his heart. It wasn't enough that he desired her. Desire was something a man could feel for almost anybody, frumpy or not.

"It's a long way to commute," she said quietly.

"Yes." He moved toward her, but this time he didn't come too close. He studied her, and she looked back, noticing how very tall he was, how powerfully built. He had a face a movie star would have envied— even features, dark velvet eyes, chiseled lips.

"We discussed this a long time ago," he said. "I don't mind commuting. I think it's best, for now, that you stay here. You'd be alone a good bit of the time in Chicago, although I'm sure Gabby wouldn't mind looking in on you."

"Gabby?" She stared at him.

"Gabby Brettman," he said. "She's married to one of my best friends, a trial lawyer." His firm mouth relaxed into a smile. "Gabby followed J.D. through a Central American jungle with an AK-47 under one arm. She actually shot a terrorist with it and saved his life. A hell of a woman, Gabby."

So Gabby hadn't been the woman from his past! And he admired her—he'd said that Dani was much like Gabby. She blushed.

"Now you make the connection, is that it?" he asked softly. "For God's sake, what did you think I meant when I compared you to her?"

Her eyes fell to his chest. "I thought...she was the

woman who betrayed you," she said miserably, and went back to the sofa.

"You don't read me any better than I read you," he said after a minute. "Suppose you come to Chicago with me for a few days? Meet my friends. Learn a little about me."

The invitation excited her, but she hesitated. "I don't know."

"My apartment has two bedrooms," he said icily. "You won't have to sleep with me."

"I can't imagine why you'd want to," she laughed bitterly, curling up on the sofa with her ledgers. "There are a lot of pretty women in the...Eric!"

He was beside her, over her, the ledgers scattered onto the floor as he pinned her down. His eyes glittered, his chest rose and fell harshly. He held her wrists over her head and looked as if he could do her violence.

"I'd never do that to you," he said harshly. "Never! What kind of man do you think I am?"

Tears stung her eyes. "You're hurting me," she whispered unsteadily.

He loosened her wrists, but he didn't let go of them. "I'm sorry," he muttered, still glaring into her white face. "I've hardly done anything else, have I? I picked you up, got you pregnant, forced you into marriage without telling you the truth about myself...and lately all I've done is blame you for it."

Her eyes closed. The tears ran from beneath her lids, and he caught his breath.

"Don't cry," he said with reluctant concern. "Dani, don't cry. I'm sorry. *Lieveling,* I'm sorry, I'm sorry..." he told her over and over again, his mouth searching across her wet cheek to her mouth. He took it gently, opening it to the moist possession of his own, while his hands freed her wrists and moved to cup her face. "*Lieveling,*" he breathed against her mouth. His body stretched full length over hers, his forearms catching the bulk of his weight. His heart pounded, his breath came unevenly. He wanted her. He wanted her!

She felt him begin to tremble, and against her hips she felt the helpless reaction of his body to her soft yielding. She hadn't wanted this to happen; she hadn't wanted to give in to something purely physical. But it had been months since she'd known the possession of that hard, expert body, and his mouth was driving her mad with its taunting hunger. She reached up hesitantly and slid her arms around his neck.

"Let me have you, Dani," he murmured into her open mouth. He shifted so that his hands could ease up her dress. "Let me have you."

She wanted to stop. But his hands were touching her soft body now, teasing it into reckless abandon, his mouth probing hers in a kiss so deep it became an act of intimacy in itself. Her body moved against his, her hands trembled and clenched on his shoulders and she moaned.

"Yes," he said, his voice urgent now, shaking. "Yes."

"Here...?" she managed in a last attempt at sanity.

"Here," he groaned, pressing her into the cushions with the gentle, carefully controlled weight of his body. "Here...!"

It was as it had been that morning in Mexico. He was breathlessly tender with her, each motion slow and sweet and reverent. His hands trembled as they touched her, guided her. His voice was passionate as he reverted to Dutch, whispering in her ear.

His mouth moved to hers, open and tender and trembling on her own as he began with aching tenderness to possess her.

Her mouth opened, her eyes widened. "Eric...!"

"Shhh," he whispered huskily. He watched her as he moved, tender motions that wouldn't harm his child, arousing motions that made her gray eyes dilate, that made her heart beat wildly against his hairmatted chest.

"Oh!" she cried out, a whisper of sound that he took into his mouth.

"Gentle violence," he said into her parted lips. "Rock with me. Take my body, and give me yours. Be my lover now."

"I...love you!" she whimpered helplessly. "I love you!"

It shattered what little was left of his control, to hear her cry it out so huskily, to see it in her eyes as she looked at him with all the barriers down. His mouth crushed softly into hers and his hands held her. He heard her fluttering little cries, felt the wildness in her body, the heat of it burning his hands. He wanted to look, but it was happening for him, too, the tender explosions that were so much more terrible than the fierce passion he'd known before with women. He thought he might die....

He was aware of her in every cell as they lay trembling together in the aftermath. His hands stroked along her relaxed body, feeling its softness in a kind of dazed reality.

"Dani?" he whispered as his eyes opened and he saw the back of the sofa.

"Yes." Her voice sounded like velvet.

"I...didn't meant to do it," he said hesitantly. "I didn't plan it."

"I know." She kissed him. Her lips touched his eyes, his eyebrows, his straight nose, his cheeks, his mouth, his chin.

He loved the softness of her mouth on his face. His eyes closed, so that she could kiss his eyelids, too. He smiled, feeling sated, loved. Profound, he thought dizzily. This, with her, was so much more than a brief merging of bodies. His hands touched her belly and felt his child move.

He laughed softly, delightedly. "He kicks," he whispered. "No more bird flutters."

"He's very strong, the doctor says," she whispered back.

He lifted his head and looked at her, at the tiny line of freckles over her nose. Sometime in the last feverish few minutes her glasses had been removed. He glanced around and saw them on the coffee table and smiled.

"I'd forgotten where we were." He sighed, kissing her again. His hands slid up her sides, and his thumbs moved over her breasts, feeling their swollen softness. "Will you let me watch you nurse him?" he asked lazily, and laughed when she blushed. "Will you?"

"Yes," she said, and buried her red face against his throat.

He kissed her forehead, her closed eyes. "Dani, is it gentle explosions for you, the way it is for me?" he asked hesitantly. "Do you feel what the French call the little death when the moment comes?"

Her breath caught. "Yes," she whispered. She clung to him. "I didn't know…"

"It was never like that for me," he told her softly, and his arms slid further around her. "Never, with anyone, the way it is with you." He shuddered.

Yes, but it was only physical, she thought miserably, and closed her eyes. Still, it was better than nothing. She smoothed the hair at his nape. It was a start.

They went to Chicago on Monday, after Dutch had taken time to call Dr. Carter to make sure it was safe for Dani to make the trip. He watched her closely, with narrowed dark eyes, every step she took. It was almost amusing, the care he was taking of her. Amusing…and very flattering. Perhaps he was growing fond of her, at least.

He hadn't loved her again. Afterward, he'd been protective and gentle, but he hadn't touched her as a lover. She wondered why, but she didn't provoke him by asking. She'd long since decided to take one day at a time, to accept what he could give without asking for more. Somehow she'd learn to live with him. Because she couldn't leave him now.

Nine

Dani wasn't sure what she'd expected Dutch's friends to look like. But when she was introduced to J.D. and Gabby Brettman and Apollo Blain, her face must have given her away.

"Yep—" Apollo nodded as he shook her shyly outstretched hand "—I told you, J.D., she expected us to look like the cover of *Soldier of Fortune* magazine."

Dani blushed and burst out laughing. "Well, I've never seen professional mercenaries before," she explained. "Anyway, at least I didn't come in looking for camouflage netting, did I?" she asked reasonably.

Apollo chuckled. "Nope, little mama, I guess not."

She lowered her eyes with a self-conscious smile, feeling Dutch's arm come around her shoulders.

"Animals." Gabby glared at the men. "Shame on you."

"Well, we're curious," J.D. said defensively. He studied Dani through eyes as dark as Dutch's. All three men were wearing lightweight suits, and Gabby was in a green-patterned dress. Dani felt as though she stood out like a sort thumb in her maternity garb.

"Of course we are," Apollo seconded. "After all, it took some kind of woman to catch Dutch, didn't it?"

"I won't argue with that." Gabby grinned. "Come on, Dani, you can help me in the kitchen while these three talk shop."

"I think I'd better," Dani confided, throwing an impish smile at Dutch. "At least I know a potato from a head of lettuce, even if I don't know an AK-47 from an Uzi."

Dutch smiled at her, possession in his whole look. She followed Gabby into the kitchen. "What can I do?" Dani asked helpfully.

"You can tell me how you did it!" Gabby burst out delightedly, smiling from a radiant face. "Dutch, married! Honestly, J.D. and I almost fainted!"

"It's a long story," Dani murmured dryly, sensing a comrade in Gabby. She sat down at the kitchen table. "It isn't love, though, you know," she added quietly.

Gabby studied her. "For you it is. Yes, it shows. Are you happy with him?"

"As happy as I can expect to be," Dani said. "I can't hope to hold him, of course. He's very protective, and he wants the baby. But it isn't in him to love."

Gabby poured two cups of coffee, checked the

timer on her microwave and sat back down. She pushed a mug of black coffee toward Dani and offered the cream and sugar.

"You know about Melissa?" she asked after a minute.

Dani knew instinctively whom she meant. "The woman from his past?"

Gabby nodded. "I wouldn't know, but Dutch was badly wounded once, and he blurted out the whole story to J.R. Dutch doesn't know," she added, lifting her eyes to Dani's. "J.D. didn't let on. But that woman...!"

"He told me all of it," Dan said quietly, sipping her coffee. "He was devastated when he found out I was pregnant."

"Did you know what he did for a living when you married him?" Gabby asked.

Dani smiled ruefully and shook her head. "I found out when the airplane we were coming home on was hijacked."

Gabby forced air through her lips. "What an interesting way to find out."

"Yes." She lowered her eyes to her cup. "He thought we could make a go of it, each leading our own lives. I didn't. I walked off and left him." She sighed. "Several weeks later I learned that I was pregnant. He came back...." She laughed. "We've been going around and around ever since."

"I remember the first time I ever heard of Dutch," Gabby recalled. "J.D.'s sister Martina had been captured by terrorists and we went to Italy to see about the ransom. Dutch was J.D.'s go-between." She looked up. "J.D. wouldn't even introduce me to him. He said Dutch hated women."

"He told me so," Dani said, smiling. "When did you get to meet him?"

"At the wedding, when I married J.D. He wasn't at all what I expected. At first I was a little nervous around him," Gabby said. "Then I got to know him—as well as he lets outsiders know him." She held Dani's curious eyes. "He talked to me about you when he was here before. He wanted to know how I'd feel if I were pregnant and J.D. couldn't give up the old life. I cried."

Dani drew in a shaky breath. "I've done my share of crying. I don't know what to do. I don't feel that I have the right to ask him to change his life for me. But I can't live with what he does." Her eyes were wide with fear and love. "I'm crazy about him. I'd die if anything happened to him."

"That's how I feel about J.D.," Gabby said quietly. "I envy you that baby," she added with a sad smile. "J.D. and I have tried..." Her thin shoulders rose and fell. "I can't seem to get pregnant."

"I had a girlfriend who couldn't get pregnant at first," Dani said, recalling an old friend from years past. She grinned. "Five years after she got married she had triplets, followed by twins the next year."

Gabby burst out laughing. "What a delightful prospect!"

"What's all the noise in here?" J.D. asked, opening the kitchen door. "Are we eating tonight?" he asked Gabby.

She got up and kissed him tauntingly on his hard

mouth. "Yes, we're eating tonight, bottomless pit. And we're laughing about triplets."

His eyes widened. "What?"

"Tell you later. Let's eat!"

It was late when Dani and Dutch got back to his elegant lakeside apartment. She hadn't expected such luxury, and it emphasized once again the difference between her life-style and his. During dinner the conversation had inevitably gone back to old times and comrades whose names Dani didn't recognize. And then mention was made of the new job Apollo had offered Dutch, and Dani listened with wide eyes as it was outlined. It wasn't as dangerous as what he was doing now, of course, she reminded herself. There wasn't half the risk. She'd have to get used to it. She could, too, if she tried.

"I don't think I can manage a desk job," he told her as if he sensed her deep, frightening thoughts.

She turned from the window, where she was watching the lights of cars far below, and the city lights near the river. "Yes, I know that."

He looked at her for a long time, hands in his pockets, eyes narrow and dark and searching. "But I'm going to try."

She nodded. "I won't ask you for anything more than that," she said then. "I'll settle for whatever you can give me. I...have very little pride left." She sighed and she seemed to age. "I'd like to go to bed now, Eric. I'm so tired."

"It's been a long day. You can have whichever bedroom you like."

She looked at him across the room, started to

speak, and then smiled faintly and walked down the hall.

"Dani…"

She didn't turn. "Yes?"

There was a long, trembling silence. "My room is the first door to the left," he said thickly. "The bed…is large enough for all three of us."

Tears stung her eyes. "If you don't mind," she whispered.

"Mind!" He was behind her, beside her; he had her in his arms, close and warm and protected. His mouth found hers in a single graceful motion. She clung. He lifted her, devoured her. His dark eyes sought hers as he kissed her.

"Now?" he whispered, trembling.

"Now," she moaned huskily.

He bent to her mouth again and she trembled with delicious anticipation as he carried her slowly into his bedroom and closed the door behind them.

Two weeks later she had to go back home for her checkup, and to hire someone else to help Harriett at the bookstore. Dutch flew back with her since the weekend was coming up. But he had to be in Chicago for a conference on Monday.

"I don't like leaving you here," he said curtly, glaring around at her small apartment. She'd become so much a part of his life that it felt odd to leave her behind.

She didn't want the parting, either, but she hadn't switched to a Chicago doctor yet, and she needed to be sure about the baby.

"Don't worry about me," she told him, holding his big hand in hers as she walked him to the door. "I'll be fine. The nights will last forever, but I'll manage," she teased.

He didn't smile. He touched her cheek, feeling tremors all the way to his soul. It was because of the baby that he felt this uneasy, he told himself. Only because of the baby. "I'll be back day after tomorrow," he said. "We'll spend the week here, getting things in order. Tell Harriett I said to look after you."

"Harrie will." She smiled. "Do I get a good-bye kiss?"

He pulled her against his tall frame. "I wonder if I'll make it out the door if I kiss you?" he murmured with a dry smile. "Come here."

He drew her up on her tiptoes and covered her smiling mouth with his. It was like flying, he mused, eyes closing as he savored the taste of her. Flying, floating. She made his head light. He lifted his lips finally and searched her loving eyes. It didn't bother him so much these days, that adoration. Perhaps he'd gotten used to it.

He brushed a last kiss against her lips. "Behave. And watch these steps, okay?"

"Okay. 'Bye."

He touched her hair. " 'Bye." He walked away without looking back. She closed the door, and realized she hadn't felt so alone since her parents had walked away from her years and years ago.

Ten

Harriett was all ears, fascinated by the news that Dani's unlikely husband was actually going to try to settle down.

"He must feel something for you," she said, smiling at Dani. "I don't care what you say, no man is going to go to those lengths just because of a purely physical involvement."

Dani had been afraid to think that, much less say it. But she stared at Harriett for a long time, wondering.

"In some ways you're still very naive, my friend," Harriett said with a wicked grin. "He's hooked. He just hasn't realized it yet."

If only it were true, Dani thought, praying for a miracle. If only he liked the job Apollo offered him. Even moving to Chicago wouldn't be any hardship. Harriett and Dave would visit. And she could come back to Greenville from time to time. Harriett could be godmother. She smiled.

With her mind on Dutch, not on what she was doing, she went to step up on the long ladder against the wall to get a book from a high shelf. She was halfway up when she slipped. Terrified, screaming as she hit the floor, she looked up at Harriett, her face white.

"Oh, God, the baby!" she sobbed, clutching her stomach.

"It's all right," Harriett said quickly, soothing her. "It's all right, I'll get an ambulance. Lie still! Are you hurt anywhere?"

"I don't know!"

Harriett ran for the phone. Dani lay there, panic-stricken, clutching her stomach. No, please don't let me lose my baby, she prayed. Her eyes closed and tears bled from them as the first pain began to make itself felt in her leg, in her back. Please, please, please!

The next few minutes were a nightmare of waiting, worrying. The ambulance came, the attendants got her on the stretcher, took her to the hospital, and into the emergency room, with Harriett right behind. She hardly knew Harriett was there, she was so afraid of losing the baby.

She was examined by the emergency room doctor, who would tell her nothing. Then the tests began and went on and on until finally they took her to a room and left her shaking with worry. Her doctor would talk to her when they got the test results, she was informed.

She cried and cried. Harriett tried to soothe her, but it was useless. She was feeling a dragging pain in her lower stomach, and she knew she was going to lose the baby. She was going to lose her baby! Harriett asked her for something, a name in Chicago to call, to tell Dutch. Numbly, she gave her J.D. Brettman's name and closed her eyes. It was no use, she wanted to say. Dutch would come, but only out of responsibility...and then she remembered the other time, the other pregnant woman, and she was terrified of what he might do.

Dr. Carter came walking in a few hours later, took one look at her and went back out to call for a sedative. He came in again, took her hand and nodded Harriett toward the door. He didn't speak until she was gone.

"The baby's going to be fine," he said. "So are you. Now, calm down."

The tears stopped, although her eyes remained wet and red. "What?"

"The baby's all right." He smiled, his blue eyes twinkling. "Babies are tough. They've got all that fluid around them, wonderful protection. Of course, you're bruised a little here and there, but bruises heal. You'll be fine."

She leaned back with a sigh. "Thank God," she said. "Oh, thank God. But—but these dragging pains," she added, pressing her stomach.

"False labor. A few twinges are normal," he said, grinning. "Now, stop worrying, will you?"

The nurse came in with a syringe, but before she could go any farther, the door flew open and a blond man burst into the room with eyes so wild that both doctor and nurse actually backed up a step.

"Eric!" Dani whispered, astonished at the look on his face.

He went to her, a wet, disheveled raincoat over his gray suit. He was wild-eyed, flushed as if he'd been running, and half out of breath.

"You're all right?" he asked unsteadily, touching her as if he expected to find broken limbs. "The baby's all right?"

"Yes," she whispered. "Eric, it's all right!" she repeated softly, and the look on his face was the answer to a prayer. "It's all right, I just fell off the ladder, but I'm—"

"Oh, God." He sat down beside her. The hands that touched her trembled, and there was a look in his eyes that struck her dumb. He caressed her face and suddenly bent, burying his face in her throat. "Oh, God." He was shaking!

Her arms went up and around him, hesitantly, her hands smoothing his hair, comforting him. She felt something wet against her throat and felt her own eyes being to sting.

"Oh, darling," she whispered, holding him closer. Her eyes closed as the enormity of what he felt for her was laid bare, without a word being spoken. She laughed through her tears. She could conquer the world now. She could do anything! He loved her!

"Reaction," the doctor said, nodding. He took the syringe from the nurse. "Pregnancy is hard on fathers, too," he murmured dryly. "Off with that coat, young man." He removed the raincoat, and the suit-

coat, then rolled up the sleeve of the shirt without any
help from Dutch, who wouldn't let go of Dani, and
jabbed the needle into the muscular arm. "I'll have a
daybed rolled in here, because you aren't driving anywhere. Dani, I think you'd do without a sedative now,
am I right?" he added with a grin.

"Yes, sir," she whispered, smiling dreamily as she
rocked her husband in her arms.

He nodded and went out with the nurse, closing the
door behind him.

"I love you," Dani whispered adoringly. "I love
you, I love you, I love you...."

His mouth stopped the words, tenderly seeking,
probing, and his lips trembled against hers.

He lifted his head to look at her, unashamedly letting her see the traces of wetness on his cheeks. "J.D.
came himself to tell me after Harriett called." He
touched her face hesitantly. "I went crazy," he confessed absently. "J.D. got me a seat on the next plane.
I ran out of the terminal and took a cab away from
some people.... I don't even remember how I got
here." He bent and brushed his mouth softly against
hers as he let the relief wash over him. His wife. His
heart. "I was...I was going to call you tonight. I
wanted to tell you how much I like what I'll be doing.
I found us a house," he added slowly. "On the beach,
with a fenced yard. It will be nice, for the baby."

"Yes, darling," she whispered softly.

He brushed the hair back from her face. "I was so
afraid of what I'd find in here," he said unsteadily.
"All I could think was that I'd only just realized what

I felt for you, and so quickly it could have ended. I would have been alone again."

"As long as I'm alive, you'll never be alone," she whispered.

He touched her mouth, her throat, her swollen stomach. "Danielle, I love you," he whispered breathlessly, admitting it at last, awe in his whole look.

"Yes, I know," she answered on a jubilant little laugh.

He laughed, too. "I've never said that before. It isn't hard." He looked into her eyes. "I love you."

She smiled, stretching. "I love you, too. Ooh," she groaned, touching her back. "I'm bruised all over. That stupid ladder!"

"No more stupid ladders," he said firmly. "We're moving to Chicago, where I can watch you. Harriett can visit."

Her eyes searched his. "This is what you really want?"

"How can I take care of you from across the world?" he asked reasonably. His voice was slowing, and he looked drowsy. "Anyway, I was getting too old for it. And I like the challenge of teaching techniques I've learned." He kissed her softly again. "J.D. told me I could do it. When he and Gabby got married, he decided that marriage was more exciting than dodging bullets. I think he has something there."

He looked down at her stomach and the last of the barriers came down. "He's going to be all right, they're sure?" he asked touching the swell.

Her lips parted, smiling. She sat up and touched his face with soft, loving hands. "I'm giving you a baby," she whispered, smiling. "A healthy, strong boy. The doctor said so."

He started to speak, and couldn't. And tried again. "I'll take care of you both," he whispered.

She reached forward and caught his full lower lip gently between her teeth. "I'll take care of you, just as soon as they let me out of here," she teased.

He chuckled softly, putting a hand to his temple. "I may need taking care of. My God, what was in that syringe?"

"A sedative. They brought it for me, but I guess they decided you needed it more."

He smiled ruefully. "I'd like to talk some more, but I think I'd feel better lying down."

Dr. Carter came in with a nurse and a spare bed even as the words were echoing in the room. He glanced at his watch and grinned at Dutch. "I thought you'd be about ready for this. Lie down, father-to-be, and you can both have a nice nap until supper. Feeling okay now, Dani?" he asked.

"Just wonderful." She sighed, trading soft looks with her drowsy husband. The nurse was eyeing him wistfully, and Dani only smiled with confidence of a woman who is deeply loved. As Dutch lay down her eyes closed on the smile he gave her. Minutes later she was asleep, with the future lying open and bright ahead.

Eleven

The christening took place six months later, with little two-month-old Joshua van Meer cradled in his mother's arms. At Dani's side Dutch burned with pride in his young son, and amused looks passed among an odd group on the front pew of the Presbyterian church in the outskirts of Chicago.

Harriett felt uneasy, sitting next to them all, and Dane had actually started to get up except that she'd caught him in time. What a collection of unusual men, she thought, gaping. There was an older, wiry little man sitting beside a wiry, tough-looking woman and they were holding hands. There were two black men, a tall, dignified one and a shorter, grinning one. There was a huge dark-eyed, dark-headed man sitting beside a green-eyed brunette who was obviously pregnant. On the other side was a swarthy Latin, arms folded, looking elegant. Harriett turned her attention back to the minister, who had taken the child in his arms and was walking it up and down the rows of pews. Harriett smiled. Her godchild. Dani had wanted her to stand with them during the ceremony, but she'd twisted her ankle getting on the airplane, and could hardly manage to stand. Just as well, she thought with a smile at the big blond Dutchman. She and that handsome giant were too much alike to ever get along. But even she had to admit that he was a terrific husband and father. A surprisingly domestic man, all around. A really normal man. Except for his friends here.

After the ceremony was over, the group beside Harriett sat still. She wondered for a wild minute if they were escaped fugitives, because they seemed to be looking around them all the time.

Dani rushed forward and hugged her. "Wasn't Joshua good?" she asked enthusiastically, kissing the white-clad baby in her arms. He cooed up at her. "I was so proud of him! Harrie, you haven't met our friends. Gabby!"

Gabby Darwin Brettman drew her tall husband along with her, beaming as she made faces at the baby.

"Isn't he gorgeous! I want a girl myself," Gabby said, her bright green eyes gleaming, "but J.D.'s holding out for a boy."

"I don't care what it is, as long as it's ours," J.D. grinned. "Hi, Dani. Nice ceremony. Dutch didn't even pass out; I was proud of him."

"Imagine Dutch married." The wiry old man shook his head. "And with a child!"

"Could have knocked me over with a feather when I found out," the tall black man joined in.

"Hush, First Shirt," Gabby growled at the older man. "And shame on you, Apollo," she told the tall black man. "Dutch just had to find the right girl, that's all."

Apollo shrugged. "Well, I'm glad he did," he told Dani with twinkling eyes, "because he's sure made the best vice-president any consulting firm could ask for. Shirt, when are you going to give in and join up? Semson and Drago already did. And I need someone to teach defensive driving."

"You corporate tycoons give me a pain," First Shirt scoffed. "Besides, Mrs. Darwin and I are contemplating a merger." He grinned at the blushing widow beside him, who was Gabby's mother, from Lytle, Texas. "We're going to raise cattle and sand."

"I owe it all to J.D.," Apollo said, smiling warmly at the big, dark man beside Gabby. "He got me off. Years of hiding, over. I'm glad you decided to go into law, J.D."

"So am I," J.D. replied. He looked up as Dutch joined them. "I was just coming to find you. Gabby and I are starting natural childbirth classes. Any advice?"

Dutch grinned as he put an affectionate arm around Dani. "Sure. Go buy a can of tennis balls."

Gabby stared at him. "Tennis...balls?"

"Tennis balls." He leaned forward conspiratorially. "They're for your backache. J.D. is supposed to roll them up and down your spine."

"It really does help," Dani said. She bent and

kissed her son. "The best part is when you get to hold him for the first time."

"Yes," Dutch agreed. "Let's go grill some steaks," he said. "Everybody know how to get to our place?"

"Sure," Apollo said. "I'll lead the ones who don't. You got enough steaks?"

"Shirt and Mrs. Darwin brought a boxful. If we make you stand last in line, there should be enough to go around," he said with a grin.

Apollo glared at him. "I don't eat that much!"

"Only half a ham at a time," Dutch shot back. "Remember Angola, when you ate the rabbit I'd just snared?"

"Oh, yeah, remember 'Nam, when you ate the snake I caught?"

"It's a christening," J.D. said, separating them. "We're supposed to forget old grudges at a time like this."

They both turned at him. "Yeah?" Apollo asked. "Well, you're the turkey that ate the box of cookies my mother sent me...."

"And the plum pudding I scrounged from the camp cook," Dutch added in the same breath.

J.D. drew Gabby beside him. "You can't pick on a man with a pregnant wife."

"I had one of my own until two months ago," Dutch returned.

"Well, I'm not standing too close to you guys," Apollo said gruffly, eyeing them. "It might be contagious."

"You won't get pregnant, Apollo, honest," Dutch said with a wicked grin.

Apollo glared at him and moved away. "Funny man. You know I meant this marriage virus."

"Some virus." J.D. grinned, hugging Gabby close. "What a way to go!"

Dani was laughing wildly, along with Gabby and the others. She moved close to Dutch and nuzzled her dark head against his shoulder. "I'm starved. Let's go home. We've got all kinds of stuff to eat."

"Yes, well, let's just make sure Apollo doesn't get there before us," J.D. teased.

Apollo glared at him. "I'm returning the Christmas present I bought you."

"It's almost March," J.D. reminded him.

"That gives you ten months to look forward to not getting one," Apollo said smugly.

"Come on," Dutch chuckled. "Let's go celebrate."

"Yes," Dani said, so that only Dutch could hear. "I have a different kind of celebration in mind for later," she murmured. "My doctor said I could."

Dutch's eyes lit up as he studied her bright eyes. "Did he? Hmmm," he murmured, drawing her close to his side and smiling down at the baby sleeping in her arms. "Well, we'll have to think up some new things to try, won't we?" he asked, watching her with smug delight. He whispered into her ear, and despite months of marriage and a baby, she colored delightfully.

She felt more alive than she ever had in her life. She looked up at him with such love that the roomful of people seemed to disappear. His fingers touched her mouth.

"Tonight," he whispered, holding her gaze, "I'll love you the way I loved you that morning in Veracruz."

"You'll get me pregnant again," she whispered, her heart throbbing wildly.

His own breath caught. "We'll talk about it tonight."

"Yes." She searched his eyes slowly. "No regrets?"

He shook his head. "Not one. Watching that baby being born was the most exciting thing I've ever done; next to loving you," he added softly.

She reached up and touched his hard cheek gently. He smiled, and for a moment, they were alone in the world.

* * * * *

Enamored

To my Alice with love

Prologue

The gentle face on the starched white pillow was pale and very still. The man looking down at it scowled with unfamiliar concern. For so many years, his emotions had been caged. Tender feelings were a luxury no mercenary could afford, least of all a man with the reputation of Diego Laremos.

But this woman was no stranger, and the emotions he felt when he looked at her were still confused. It had been five years since he'd seen her, yet she seemed not to have aged a day. She would be twenty-six now, he thought absently. He was forty.

He hadn't expected her to be unconscious. When the hospital had contacted him, he almost hadn't come. Melissa Sterling had betrayed him years before. He wasn't anxious to renew their painful acquaintance, but out of curiosity and a sense of duty, he'd made the trip to southern Arizona. Now he was here, and it was not a subterfuge, a trap, as it had been before. She was injured and helpless; she was alive, though he'd given her up for dead all those long years ago. The cold emptiness inside him was giving way to memories, and that he couldn't allow.

He turned, tall and dark and immaculate in his charcoal-gray suit, to stare out the window at the well-kept grounds beyond the second-floor room Melissa Sterling occupied. He had a mustache now that he hadn't sported during the turbulent days she'd shared with him. He was a little more muscular, older. But age had only emphasized his elegant good looks, made him more mature. His dark eyes slid to the bed, to the slender body of this woman, this stranger, who had trapped him into marriage and then deserted him.

Melissa was tall for a woman, although he towered above her. She had long, wavy blond hair that had once curled below her waist. That had been cut, so that now it curved around her wan oval face. Her eyes were blue-shadowed, closed, her perfect mouth almost as white as her face, her straight nose barely wrinkling now and again as it protested the air tubes taped to it. She seemed surrounded by electronic equipment, by wires that led to various monitors.

An accident, the attending physician had said over a worse-than-poor telephone conversation the day before. An airplane crash that, by some miracle, she and the pilot and several other passengers on the commuter flight from Phoenix had survived. The plane had gone down in the desert outside Tucson, and she'd been brought here to the general hospital, unconscious. The emergency room staff had found a worn, carefully folded paper in her wallet that contained the only evidence of her marital status. A marriage license, written in Spanish; the fading ink stated that she was the *esposa* of one Diego Alejandro Rodriguez Ruiz Laremos of Dos Rios, Guatemala. Was Diego her husband, the physician had persisted, and if so, would he authorize emergency surgery to save her life?

He vaguely recalled asking if she had no other relatives, but the doctor had told him that her pitifully few belongings gave no evidence of any. So Diego had left his Guatemalan farm in the hands of his hired militia and flown himself all the way from Guatemala City to Tucson.

He'd had no sleep in the past twenty-four hours. He'd been smoking himself to death and reliving a tormenting past.

The woman in the bed stirred suddenly, moaning. He turned just as her eyes opened and then closed quickly again. They were gray. Big and soft, a delicate contrast to her blond fairness; her gray eyes were the only visible evidence of Melissa's Guatemalan mother, whose betrayal had brought anguish and dishonor to the Laremos family.

His black eyes ran slowly over her pale, still features and he wondered as he watched how he and Melissa had ever come to this....

One

It was a misty rain, but Melissa Sterling didn't mind. Getting soaked was a small price to pay for a few precious minutes with Diego Laremos.

Diego's family had owned the *finca*, the giant Guatemalan farm that bordered her father's land, for four generations. And despite the fact that Melissa's late mother had been the cause of a bitter feud between the Laremos family and the Sterlings, that hadn't stopped Melissa from worshiping the son and heir to the Laremos name. Diego seemed not to mind her youthful adoration, or if he did, he was kind enough not to mock her for it.

There had been a storm the night before, and Melissa had ridden down to Mama Chavez's small house to make sure the old woman was all right, only to find that Diego, too, had been worried about his old nurse and had come to check on her. Melissa liked to visit her and listen to tales of Diego's youth and hear secret legends about the Maya.

Diego had brought some melons and fish for the old woman, whose family tree dated back to the very beginning of the Mayan empire, and now he was escorting Melissa back to her father's house.

Her dark eyes kept running over his lean, fit body, admiring the way he sat on his horse, the thick darkness of his hair under his panama hat. He wasn't an arrogant man, but he had a cold, quiet authority about him that bordered on it. He never had to raise his voice to his servants, and Melissa had only seen him in one fight. He was a dignified, self-contained man without an apparent weakness. But he was mysterious. He often disappeared for weeks at a time, and once he'd come home with scars on his cheek and a limp. Melissa had been curious, but she hadn't questioned him. Even at twenty, she was still shy with men, and especially with Diego. He'd rescued her once when she'd gotten lost in the rain forest searching for some old Mayan ruins, and she'd loved him secretly ever since.

"I suppose your grandmother and sister would die if they knew I was within a mile of you," she sighed, brushing back her long wavy blond hair as she glanced at him with a hesitant smile that was echoed in the soft gray of her eyes.

"They bear your family no great love, that is true," he agreed. The distant mountains were a blue haze in front of them as they rode. "It is difficult for my family to forget that Edward Sterling stole my father's *novia* on the eve of their wedding and eloped with her. My father spoke of her often, with grief. My grandmother never stopped blaming your family for his grief.''

''My father loved her, and she loved him,'' Melissa defended. ''It was only an arranged marriage that your father would have had with her, anyway, not a love match. Your father was much older than my mother, and he'd been a widower for years.''

''Your father is British,'' he said coldly. ''He has never understood our way of life. Here, honor is life itself. When he stole away my father's betrothed, he dishonored my family.'' Diego glanced at Melissa, not adding that his father had also been counting on her late mother's inheritance to restore the family fortunes. Diego had considered his father's attitude rather mercenary, but the old man had cared about Sheila Sterling in his cool way.

Diego reined in his mount and stared at Melissa, taking in her slender body, in jeans and a pink shirt unbuttoned to the swell of her breasts. She attracted him far more than he wanted to admit. He couldn't allow himself to become involved with the daughter of the woman who'd disgraced his family.

''Your father should not let you wander around in this manner,'' he said unexpectedly, although he softened the words with a faint smile. ''You know there has been increased guerrilla activity here. It is not safe.''

''I wasn't thinking,'' she replied.

''You never do, *chica*,'' he sighed, cocking his hat over one eye. ''Your daydreaming will be your downfall one day. These are dangerous times.''

"All times are dangerous," she said with a shy smile. "But I feel safe with you."

He raised a dark eyebrow. "And that is the most dangerous daydream of all," he mused. "But no doubt you have not yet realized it. Come; we must move on."

"In just a minute." She drew a camera from her pocket and pointed it toward him, smiling at his grimace. "I know, not again, you're thinking. Can I help it if I can't get the right perspective on the painting of you I'm working on? I need another shot. Just one, I promise." She clicked the shutter before he could protest.

"This famous painting is taking one long time, *niña*," he commented. "You have been hard at it for eight months, and not one glimpse have I had of it."

"I work slow," she prevaricated. In actual fact, she couldn't draw a straight line without a ruler. The photo was to add to her collection of pictures of him, to sit and sigh over in the privacy of her room. To build dreams around. Because dreams were all she was ever likely to have of Diego, and she knew it. His family would oppose any mention of having Melissa under their roof, just as they opposed Diego's friendship with her.

"When do you go off to college?" he asked unexpectedly.

She sighed as she pocketed the camera. "Pretty soon, I guess. I begged off for a year after school, just to be with Dad, but this unrest is making him more stubborn about sending me away. I don't want to go to the States. I want to stay here."

"Your father may be wise to insist," Diego murmured, although he didn't like to think about riding
around his estate with no chance of being waylaid by
Melissa. He'd grown used to her. To a man as worldly
and experienced and cynical as Diego had become
over the years, Melissa was a breath of spring air. He
loved her innocence, her shy adoration. Given the
chance, he was all too afraid he might be tempted to
appreciate her exquisite young body, as well. She was
slender, tall, with long, tanned legs, breasts that had
just the right shape and a waist that was tiny, flaring
to full, gently curving hips. She wasn't beautiful, but
her fair complexion was exquisite in its frame of long,
tangled blond hair, and her gray eyes held a kind of
serenity far beyond her years. Her nose was straight,
her mouth soft and pretty. In the right clothes and
with the right training, she would be a unique hostess,
a wife of whom a man could be justifiably proud....

That thought startled Diego. He had had no inten-
tion of thinking of Melissa in those terms. If he ever
married, it would be to a Guatemalan woman of good
family, not to a woman whose father had already once
disgraced the name of Laremos.

"You're always at home these days," Melissa said
as they rode along the valley, with the huge Atitlán
volcano in the distance against the green jungle. She
loved Guatemala, she loved the volcanos and the
lakes and rivers, the tropical jungle, the banana and
coffee plantations and the spreading valleys. She especially loved the mysterious Mayan ruins that one
found so unexpectedly. She loved the markets in the
small villages and the friendly warmth of the Guate-

malan people whose Mayan ancestors had once ruled here.

"The *finca* demands much of my time since my father's death," he replied. "Besides, *niña*, I was getting too old for the work I used to do."

She glanced at him. "You never talked about it. What did you do?"

He smiled faintly. "Ah, that would be telling. How did your father fare with the fruit company? Were they able to recompense him for his losses during the storm?"

A tropical storm had damaged the banana plantation in which her father had a substantial interest. This year's crop had been a tremendous loss. Like Diego, though, her father had other investments—such as the cattle he and Diego raised on their adjoining properties. But as a rule, fruit was the biggest money-maker.

She shook her head. "I don't know. He doesn't share business with me. I guess he thinks I'm too dumb to understand." She smiled, her mind far away on the small book she'd found recently in her mother's trunk. "You know, Dad is so different from the way he was when my mother knew him. He's so sedate and quiet these days. Mama wrote that he was always in the thick of things when they were first married, very daring and adventurous."

"I imagine her death changed him, little one," he said absently.

"Maybe it did," she murmured. She looked at him curiously. "Apollo said that you were the best there was at your job," she added quickly. "And that someday you might tell me about it."

He said something under his breath, glaring at her. "My past is something I never expect to share with anyone. Apollo had no right to say such a thing to you."

His voice chilled her when it had that icily formal note in it. She shifted restlessly. "He's a nice man. He helped Dad round up some of the stray cattle one day when there was a storm. He must be good at his job, or you wouldn't keep him on."

"He is good at his job," he said, making a mental note to have a long talk with the black American ex-military policeman who worked for him and had been part of the band of mercenaries Diego had once belonged to. "But it does not include discussing me with you."

"Don't be mad at him, please," she asked gently. "It was my fault, not his. I'm sorry I asked. I know you're very close about your private life, but it bothered me that you came home that time so badly hurt." She lowered her eyes. "I was worried."

He bit back a sharp reply. He couldn't tell her about his past. He couldn't tell her that he'd been a professional mercenary, that his job had been the destruction of places and sometimes people, that it had paid exceedingly well, or that the only thing he had put at risk was his life. He kept his clandestine operations very quiet at home; only the government officials for whom he sometimes did favors knew about him. As for friends and acquaintances, it wouldn't do for them to know how he earned the money that kept the *finca* solvent.

He shrugged indifferently. *"No importa."* He was

silent for a moment, his black eyes narrow as he glanced at her. "You should marry," he said unexpectedly. "It is time your father arranged for a *novio* for you, *niña*."

She wanted to suggest Diego, but that would be courting disaster. She studied her slender hands on the reins. "I can arrange my own marriage. I don't want to be promised to some wealthy old man just for the sake of my family fortunes."

Diego smiled at her innocence. "Oh, *niña*, the idealism of youth. By the time you reach my age, you will have lost every trace of it. Infatuation does not last. It is the poorest foundation for a lasting relationship, because it can exist where there are no common interests whatsoever."

"You sound so cold," she murmured. "Don't you believe in love?"

"Love is not a word I know," he replied carelessly. "I have no interest in it."

Melissa felt sick and shaky and frightened. She'd always assumed that Diego was a romantic like herself. But he certainly didn't sound like one. And with that attitude he probably wouldn't be prejudiced against an arranged, financially beneficial marriage. His grandmother was very traditional, and she lived with him. Melissa didn't like the thought of Diego marrying anyone else, but he was thirty-five and soon he had to think of an heir. She stared at the pommel on her saddle, idly moving the reins against it. "That's a very cynical attitude."

He looked at her with raised black eyebrows. "You and I are worlds apart, do you know that? Despite your Guatemalan upbringing and your excellent Spanish, you still think like an Anglo."

"Perhaps I've got more of my mother in me than you think," she confessed sheepishly. "She was Spanish, but she eloped with the best man at her own wedding."

"It is nothing to joke about."

She brushed back her long hair. "Don't go cold on me, Diego," she chided softly. "I didn't mean it. I'm really very traditional."

His dark eyes ran over her, and the expression in them made her heart race. "Yes. Of that I am quite certain," he said. His eyes slid up to hers again, holding them until she colored. He smiled at her expression. He liked her reactions, so virginal and flattering. "Even my grandmother approves of the very firm hand your father keeps on you. Twenty, and not one evening alone with a young man out of the sight of your father."

She avoided his piercing glance. "Not that many young men come calling. I'm not an heiress and I'm not pretty."

"Beauty is transient; character endures. You suit me as you are, *pequeña*," he said gently. "And in time the young men will come with flowers and proposals of marriage. There is no rush."

She shifted in the saddle. "That's what you think," she said miserably. "I spend my whole life alone."

"Loneliness is a fire which tempers steel," he counseled. "Benefit from it. In days to come it will give you a serenity which you will value."

She gave him a searching look. "I'll bet you haven't spent your life alone," she said.

He shrugged. "Not totally, perhaps," he said, giving away nothing. "But I like my own company from time to time. I like, too, the smell of the coffee trees, the graceful sweep of the leaves on banana trees, the sultry wind in my face, the proud Maya ruins and the towering volcanoes. These things are my heritage. Your heritage," he added with a tender smile. "One day you will look back on this as the happiest time of your life. Don't waste it."

That was possible, she mused. She almost shivered with the delight of having Diego so close beside her and the solitude of the open country around them. Yes, this was the good time, full of the richness of life and love. Never would she wish herself anywhere else.

He left her at the gate that led past the small kitchen garden to the white stucco house with its red roof. He got down from his horse and lifted her from the saddle, his lean hands firm and sure at her small waist. For one small second he held her so that her gaze was level with his, and something touched his black eyes. But it was gone abruptly, and he put her down and stepped back.

She forced herself to move away from the tangy scent of leather and tobacco that clung to his white shirt. She forced herself not to look where it was unbuttoned over a tanned olive chest feathered with black hair. She wanted so desperately to reach up and kiss his hard mouth, to hold him to her, to experience all the wonder of her first passion. But Diego saw only a young girl, not a woman.

"I will leave your mare at the stable," he promised as he mounted gracefully. "Keep close to home from now on," he added firmly. "Your father will tell you, as I already have, that it is not safe to ride alone."

"If you say so, Señor Laremos," she murmured, and curtsied impudently.

Once he would have laughed at that impish gesture. But her teasing had a sudden and unexpected effect. His blood surged in his veins, his body tautened. His black eyes went to her soft breasts and lingered there before he dragged them back to her face. *"¡Hasta luego!"* he said tersely, and wheeled his mount without another word.

Melissa stared after him with her heart in her throat. Even in her innocence, she'd recognized the hot, quick flash of desire in his eyes. She felt the look all the way to her toes and burned with an urge to run after him, to make sure she hadn't misunderstood his reaction. To have Diego look at her in that way was the culmination of every dream she'd ever had about him.

She went into the house, tingling with banked-down excitement. From now on, every day was going to be even more like a surprise package.

Estrella had outdone herself with supper. The small, plump *Ladina* woman had made steak with peppers and cheese and salsa, with seasoned rice to go with it, and cool melon for a side dish. Melissa hugged her as she sniffed the delicious aroma of the meal.

"*Delicioso,*" she said with a grin.

"Steak is to put on a bruised eye," Estrella sniffed. "The best meat is iguana."

Melissa made a face. "I'd eat snake first," she promised.

Estrella grinned wickedly. "You did. Last night."

The younger woman's eyes widened. "That was chicken."

Estrella shook her head. "Snake." She laughed when Melissa made a threatening gesture. "No, no, no, you cannot hit me. It was your father's idea!"

"My father wouldn't do such a thing," she said.

"You do not know your father," the *Ladina* woman said with a twinkle in her eyes. "Get out now, let me work. Go and practice your piano or Señora Lopez will be incensed when she comes to hear you on Friday."

Melissa sighed. "I suppose she will, that patient soul. She never gives up on me, even when I know I'll never be able to run my cadences without slipping up on the minor keys."

"Practice!"

She nodded, then changed the subject. "Dad didn't phone, I suppose?" she asked.

"No." Estrella glanced at Melissa with one of her black eyes narrowed. "He will not like you riding with Señor Laremos."

"How did you know I was?" Melissa exclaimed. These flashes of instant knowledge still puzzled her as they had from childhood. Estrella always seemed to know things before she actually heard about them formally.

"That," the *Ladina* woman said smugly, "is my secret. Out with you. Let me cook."

Melissa went, hoping Estrella wasn't planning to share her knowledge with her father.

And apparently the *Ladina* woman didn't, but Edward Sterling knew anyway. He came back from his business trip looking preoccupied, his graying blond hair damp with rain, his elegant white suit faintly wrinkled.

"Luis Martinez saw you out riding with Diego Laremos," he said abruptly, without greeting her. Melissa sat with her hands poised over the piano in the spacious living room. "I thought we'd had this conversation already."

Melissa drew a steadying breath and put her hands in her lap. "I can't help it," she said, giving up all attempts at subterfuge. "I suppose you don't believe that."

"I believe it," he said, to her surprise. "I even understand it. But what I don't understand is why Laremos encourages you. He isn't a marrying man, Melissa, and he knows what it would do to me to see you compromised." His face hardened. "Which is what disturbs me the most. The whole Laremos family would love to see us humbled. Don't cut your leg and invite a shark to kiss it better," he added with a faint attempt at humor.

She threw up her hands. "You won't believe that Diego has no ulterior motives, will you? That he genuinely likes me?"

"I think he likes the adulation," he said sharply. He poured brandy into a snifter and sat down, crossing his long legs. "Listen, sweet, it's time you knew the truth about your hero. It's a long story, and it isn't pretty. I had hoped that you'd go away to college, and no harm done. But this hero worship has to stop. Do you have any idea what Diego Laremos did for a living until about two years ago?"

She blinked. "He traveled on business, I suppose. The Laremoses have money—"

"The Laremoses have nothing, or had nothing," he interrupted curtly. "The old man was hoping to marry Sheila and get his hands on her father's supposed millions. What Laremos didn't know was that Sheila's father had lost everything and was hoping to get *his* hands on the Laremoses' banana plantations. It was a comedy of errors, and then I found your mother and that was the end of the plotting. To this day, none of your mother's people will speak to me, and the Laremoses only do out of politeness. And the great irony of it is that none of them know the truth about each other's families. There never was any money—only pipe dreams about mergers."

"Then, if the Laremoses had nothing," Melissa ventured, "why do they have so much these days?"

"Because your precious Diego had a lot of guts and few equals with an automatic weapon," Edward Sterling said bluntly. "He was a professional soldier."

Melissa didn't move. She didn't speak. She stared blankly at her father. "Diego isn't hard enough to go around killing people."

"Don't kid yourself," came the reply. "Haven't you even realized that the men he surrounds himself with at the Casa de Luz are his old confederates? That man they call First Shirt, and the black ex-soldier, Apollo Blain, and Semson and Drago...all of them are ex-mercenaries with no country to call their own. They have no future except here, working for their old comrade.''

Melissa felt her hands trembling. She sat on them. It was beginning to come together. The bits and pieces of Diego's life that she'd seen and wondered about were making sense now—a terrible kind of sense.

"I see you understand," her father said, his voice very quiet. "You know, I don't think less of him for what he's done. But a past like his would be rough for a woman to take. Because of what he's done, he's a great deal less vulnerable than an ordinary man. More than likely his feelings are locked in irons. It will take more than an innocent, worshiping girl to unlock them, Melissa. And you aren't even in the running in his mind. He'll marry a Guatemalan woman, if he ever marries. He won't marry you. Our unfortunate connection in the past will assure that, don't you see?''

Her eyes stung with tears. Of course she did, but hearing it didn't help. She tried to smile, and the tears overflowed.

"Baby." Her father got up and pulled her gently into his arms, rocking her. "I'm sorry, but there's no future for you with Diego Laremos. It will be best if you go away, and the sooner the better.''

Melissa had to agree. "You're right." She dabbed at her tears. "I didn't know. Diego never told me about his past. I suppose he was saving it for a last resort,'' she said, trying to bring some lightness to the moment. "Now I understand what he meant about not knowing what love was. I guess Diego couldn't afford to let himself love anyone, considering the line of work he was in.''

"I don't imagine he could,'' her father agreed. He smoothed her hair back. "I wish your mother was still alive. She'd have known what to say.''

"Oh, you're not doing too bad,'' Melissa told him. She wiped her eyes. "I guess I'll get over Diego one day.''

"One day,'' Edward agreed. "But this is for the best, Melly. Your world and his would never fit together. They're too different.''

She looked up. "Diego said that, too.''

Edward nodded. "Then Laremos realizes it. That will be just as well. He won't put any obstacles in the way.''

Melissa tried to forget that afternoon and the way Diego had held her, the way he'd looked at her. Maybe he didn't know what love was, but something inside him had reacted to her in a new and different way. And now she was going to have to leave before she could find out what he felt or if he could come to care for her.

But perhaps her father was right. If Diego felt anything, it was physical, not emotional. Desire, in its place, might be exquisite, but without love it was just a shadow. Diego's past had shocked her. A man like that—was he even capable of love?

Melissa kept her thoughts to herself. There was no

sense in sharing them with her father and worrying him even more. "How did it go in Guatemala City?" she asked instead, trying to divert him.

He laughed. "Well, it's not as bad as I thought at first. Let's eat, and I'll explain it to you. If you're old enough to go to college, I suppose you're old enough to be told about the family finances."

Melissa smiled at him. It was the first time he'd offered that kind of information. In an odd way, she felt as if her father accepted the fact that she was an adult.

Two

Melissa hardly slept. She dreamed of Diego in a confusion of gunfire and harsh words, and she woke up feeling that she'd hardly closed her eyes.

She ate breakfast with her father, who announced that he had to go back into the city to finalize a contract with the fruit company.

"See that you stay home," he cautioned her as he left. "No more tête-à-têtes with Diego Laremos."

"I've got to practice piano," she said absently, and kissed his cheek as he went out the door. "You be careful, too."

He drove away, and she went into the living room where the small console piano sat, opening her practice book to the cadences. She grimaced as she began to fumble through the notes, all thumbs.

Her heart just wasn't in it, so instead she practiced a much-simplified bit of Sibelius, letting herself go in the expression of its sweet, sad message. She was going to have to leave Guatemala, and Diego. There was no hope at all. She knew in her heart that she was never going to get over him, but it was only beginning to dawn on her that the future would be pretty bleak if she stayed. She'd wear herself out fighting his indifference, bruise her heart attempting to change his will. Why had she ever imagined that a man like Diego might come to love her? And now, knowing his background as she did, she realized that it would take a much more experienced, sophisticated woman than herself to reach such a man.

She got up from the piano, closing the lid, and sat down at her father's desk. There were sheets of white bond paper still scattered on it, along with the pencil he'd been using for his calculations. Melissa picked up the pencil and wrote several lines of breathless prose about unrequited love. Then, impulsively, she wrote a note to Diego asking him to meet her that night in the jungle so that she could show him how much she loved him until dawn came to find them....

Reading it over, she laughed at the very idea of sending such a message to the very correct, very formal Señor Diego Laremos. She crumpled it on the desk and got up, pacing restlessly. She read and went back to the piano, ate a lunch that she didn't really taste and finally decided that she'd go mad if she had to spend the rest of the afternoon just sitting around. Her father had said not to leave the house, but she couldn't bear sitting still.

She saddled her mare and, after waving to an exasperated, irritated Estrella, rode away from the house and down toward the valley. She wondered at the agitated way Estrella, with one of the vaqueros at her side, was waving, but she soon lost interest and quickened her pace. She didn't want to be called back like a delinquent child. She had to ride off some of her nervous energy.

She was galloping down the hill and across the valley when a popping sound caught her attention. Startled, her mare reared up and threw Melissa onto the hard ground.

Her shoulder and collarbone connected with some sharp rocks, and she grimaced and moaned as she tried to sit up. The mare kept going, her mane flying in the breeze, and that was when Melissa saw the approaching horseman, three armed men hot on his heels. Diego!

She couldn't believe what she was seeing. It was unreal, on this warm summer afternoon, to see such violence in the grassy meadow. So the reports about the guerrillas and the political unrest were true. Sometimes, so far away from Guatemala City, she felt out of touch with the world. But now, with armed men flying across the grassy plain, danger was alarmingly real. Her heart ran wild as she sat there, and the first touch of fear brushed along her spine. She was alone and unarmed, and the thought of what those men might do to her if Diego fell curled her hair. Why hadn't she listened to the warnings?

The popping sound came again, and she realized that the men were shooting at Diego. But he didn't look back. His attention was riveted now on Melissa, and he kept coming, his mount moving in a weaving pattern to make less of a target for the pistols of the men behind him. He circled Melissa and vaulted out of the saddle, some kind of small, chubby-looking weapon in his hands.

"Por Dios—" He dropped to his knees and fired off a volley at the approaching horsemen. The sound deafened her, bringing the taste of nausea into her throat as she realized how desperate the situation really was. "Are you wounded?"

"No, I fell. Diego—"

"Silencio!" He fired another burst at the guerrillas, who had stopped suddenly in the middle of the valley to fire back at him. He pushed Melissa to the ground with gentle violence and aimed again, deliberately this time. He didn't want her to see it, but her life depended on whether or not he could stop his pursuers. He couldn't bear the thought of those brutal hands on her soft skin.

The firing from the other side stopped abruptly. Melissa peeked up at Diego. He didn't look like the man she knew so well. His deeply tanned face was steely, rigid, his hands incredibly steady on the small weapon.

He cursed steadily in Spanish as he surveyed his handiwork, terrible curses that shocked Melissa. She tried not to cry out in fear. The smell of gunsmoke was acrid in her nostrils, her ears were deafened by the sound of the small machine gun.

Diego turned then to sweep Melissa up in his arms, holding the automatic weapon in the hand under her knees. He got her out of the meadow with quick, long strides, his powerful body absorbing her weight as if he didn't even feel it. He darted with her into the thick jungle at the edge of the meadow and kept going. Over his shoulder she saw the horses scatter, two of the riders bent over their saddles as if in pain, the third one lying still on the ground. Diego's horse was long gone, like Melissa's.

Now that they were temporarily out of danger, relief made her body limp. She'd been shot at. She'd actually been shot at! It seemed like some impossible nightmare. Thank God Diego had seen her. She shuddered to think what might have happened if those men had come upon her and she'd been alone.

"Were you hit?" Diego asked curtly as he laid her down against a tree a good way into the undergrowth. "You're bleeding."

"I fell off," she faltered, her eyes helpless on his angry face as he bent over her. "I hit...something. Diego, those men, are we far enough away...?"

"For the moment, yes," he said shortly. "Until they get reinforcements, at least. Melissa, I told you not to go riding alone, did I not?" he demanded.

His eyes were black, and she thought she'd never really seen him before. Not the real man under the lazy good humor, the patient indulgence. This man was a stranger. The mercenary her father had told her about. The unmasked man.

"Where are your men?" she asked huskily, her body becoming rigid as his lean fingers went to the front of her blouse and started to unbutton it. "Diego, no!" she burst out in embarrassment.

He glowered at her. "The bleeding has to be

stopped," he said curtly. "This is no time for outraged modesty. Lie still."

While the wind whispered through the tall trees, she fought silently, but he moved her hands aside with growing impatience and peeled the blouse away from the flimsy bra she was wearing. His black eyes made one soft foray over the transparent material covering her firm young breasts, and then glanced at her shoulder, which was scratched and bleeding.

"We are cut off," he muttered. "I made the mistake of assuming a few rounds would frighten off a guerrilla who was scouting the area around my cattle pens. He left, but only to come back with a dozen or so of his amigos. Apollo and the rest of my men are at the casa, trying to hold them off until Semson can get the government troops to assist them. Like a fool, I allowed myself to be cut off from the others and pursued."

"I suppose you'd have made it back except for me," she murmured quietly, her pale gray eyes apologetic as she looked up at him.

"Will you never learn to listen?" he asked coldly. He had his handkerchief at the scraped places now and was soothing away the blood. He grimaced. "This will need attention. It's a miracle that your breast escaped severe damage, *niña*, although it is badly bruised."

She flushed, averting her eyes from his scrutiny. Very likely, a woman's naked body held no mysteries for Diego, but Melissa had never been seen unclad by a man.

Diego ignored her embarrassment, spreading the

handkerchief over the abrasions and refastening her blouse to hold it in place. Nothing of what he was feeling showed in his expression, but the sight of her untouched, perfect young body was making him ache unpleasantly. Until now it had been possible to think of Melissa as a child. But after tonight, he'd never be able to think of her that way again. It was going to complicate his life, he was certain of it. "We must get to higher ground, and quickly. I scattered them, but depend on it, they will be back." He helped her up. "Can you walk?"

"Of course," she said unsteadily, her eyes wide and curious as she looked at the small bulky weapon he scooped up from the ground. He had a cartridge belt around his shoulder, over his white shirt.

"An Uzi," he told her, ignoring her fascination. "An automatic weapon of Israeli design. Thank God I listened to my old instincts and carried it with me this afternoon, or I would already be dead. I am deeply sorry that you had to see what happened, little one, but if I had not fired back at them…"

"I know that," she said. She glanced at him, then away, as he led her deeper into the jungle. "Diego, my father told me what you used to do for a living."

He stopped and turned around, his black eyes intent on hers because he needed to know her reaction to the discovery. He searched her expression, but there was no contempt, no horror, no shock. "To discourage you, I presume, from any deeper relationship with me?" he asked unexpectedly.

She blushed and lowered her gaze. "I guess I've been pretty transparent all the way around," she said bitterly. "I didn't realize everybody knew what a fool I was making of myself."

"I am thirty-five years old," he said quietly. "And women have been, forgive me, a permissible vice. Your face is expressive, Melissa, and your innocence makes you all the more vulnerable. But I would hardly call you a fool for feeling an—" he hesitated over the word "—attraction. But this is not the time to discuss it. Come, *pequeña*, we must find cover. We have little time."

It was hard going. The jungle growth of vines and underbrush was thick, and Diego had only his knife, not a machete. He was careful to leave no visible trace of the path they made, but the men following them were likely to be experienced trackers. Melissa knew she should be afraid, but being with Diego made fear impossible. She knew that he'd protect her, no matter what. And despite the danger, just being with him was sheer delight.

She watched the muscles in his lean, fit body ripple as he moved aside the clinging vines for her. Once, his dark eyes caught hers as she was going under his arm, and they fell on her mouth with an expression that made her blood run wild through her veins. It was only a moment in time, but the flare of awareness made her clumsy and self-conscious. She remembered all too well the feel of his hard fingers on her soft skin as he'd removed the blood and bandaged the scrapes. She thought of the time ahead, because darkness would come soon. Would they stay in the jungle overnight? And would he hold her in the night, safe in his arms, against his warm body? She trembled at the delicious image, already feeling the muscles of his arms closing around her.

He paused to look at the compass in the handle of his knife, checking his bearings.

"There are ruins very near here," he murmured. "With luck, we should be able to get to them before dark." He looked up at the skies, which were darkening with the threat of a storm. "Rain clouds," he mused. "We shall more than likely be drenched before we reach cover. Your father is not at home, I assume?"

"No," she said miserably. "He'll be worried sick. And furious."

"Murderously so, I imagine," he said with an irritated sigh. "Oh, Melissa, what a situation your impulsive nature has created for us."

"I'm sorry," she said gently. "Really I am."

He lifted his head and stared down into her face with something like arrogance. "Are you? To be alone with me like this? Are you really sorry, *querida*?" he asked, and his voice was like velvet, deep and soft and tender.

Her lips parted as she tried to answer him, but she was trembling with nervous pleasure. Her gray eyes slid over his face like loving hands.

"An unfair question," he murmured. "When I can see the answer. Come."

He turned away from her, his body rippling with desire for her. He was too hot-blooded not to feel it when he looked at her slender body, her sweet innocence like a seductive garment around her. He wanted her as he'd never wanted another woman, but to give in to his feelings would be to place himself at the mercy of her father's retribution. He was already concerned about how it would look if they were forced to bed down in the ruins. Apollo and the others would come looking for him, but the rain would wash away the tracks and slow them down, and the guerrillas would be in hot pursuit, as well. He sighed. It was going to be difficult, whichever way they went.

The rain came before they got much further, drenching them in wet warmth. Melissa felt her hair plastered against her scalp, her clothing sticking to her like glue. Her jeans and boots were soaked, her shirt literally transparent as it dripped in the pounding rain.

Diego's black hair was like a skullcap, and his very Spanish features were more prominent now, his olive complexion and black eyes making him look faintly pagan. He had Mayan blood as well as Spanish because of the intermarriage of his Madrid-born grandparents with native Guatemalans. His high cheekbones hinted at his Indian ancestry, just as his straight nose and thin, sensual lips denoted his Spanish heritage. Watching him, Melissa wondered where he had inherited his height, because he was as tall as her British father.

''There,'' he said suddenly, and they came to a clearing where a Mayan temple sat like a gray sentinel in the green jungle. It was only partially standing, but at least one part of it seemed to have a roof.

Diego led her through the vined entrance, frightening away a huge snake. She shuddered, thinking of the coming darkness, but Diego was with her. He'd keep her safe.

Inside, it was musty and smelled of stone and dust, but the walls in one side of the ruin were almost intact, and there were a few timbers overhead that time hadn't completely rotted.

Melissa shivered. ''We'll catch pneumonia,'' she whispered.

''Not in this heat, *niña*,'' he said with a faint smile. He moved over to a vine-covered opening in the stone wall. At least he'd be able to see the jungle from which they'd just departed. With a sigh, he stripped off his shirt and hung it over a jutting timber, stretching wearily.

Melissa watched him, her gaze caressing the darkly tanned muscles and the faint wedge of black hair that arrowed down to the belt around his lean waist. Just looking at him made her tingle, and she couldn't hide her helpless longing to touch him.

He saw her reaction, and all his good intentions melted. She looked lovely with her clothing plastered to her exquisite body, and through the wet blouse he could see the very texture of her breasts, their mauve tips firm and beautifully formed. His jaw tautened as he stared at her.

She started to lift her arms, to fold them over herself, because the way he was looking at her frightened her a little. But he turned abruptly and started out.

''I'll get some branches,'' he said tersely. ''We'll need something to keep us from getting filthy if we have to stay here very long.''

While he was gone, Melissa stripped off her blouse

and wrung it out. It didn't help much, but it did remove some of the moisture. She dabbed at her hair and pushed the strands away from her face, knowing that she must look terrible.

Diego came back minutes later with some wild-banana leaves and palm branches that he spread on the ground to make a place to sit. He was wetter than ever, because the rain was still coming down in torrents.

"Our pursuers are going to find this weather difficult to track us through," he mused as he pulled a cigarette lighter from his pocket and managed to light a small cheroot. He eased back on one elbow to smoke it, studying Melissa with intent appreciation. She'd put the blouse back on, but even though it was a little drier, her breasts were still blatantly visible through it.

"I guess they will," she murmured, answering him.

"It embarrasses you, *niña*, for me to look at you so openly?" he asked quietly.

"I don't have much experience..." She faltered, blushing.

He blew out a thick cloud of smoke while his eyes made a meal of her. It was madness to allow himself that liberty, but he couldn't seem to help himself. She was untouched, and her eyes were shyly worshipful as she looked at his body. He wanted more than anything to touch her, to undress her slowly and carefully, to show her the delight of making love. His heart began to throb as he saw images of them together on the makeshift bedding, her body receptive to his, open to his possession.

Melissa was puzzled by his behavior. He'd always been so correct when they'd been together, but he wasn't bothering to disguise his interest in her body, and the look on his face was readable even to a novice.

"Why did you become a mercenary?" she asked, hoping to divert him.

He shrugged. "It was a question of finances. We were desperate, and my father was unable to face the degradation of seeking work after having had money all his life. I had a reckless nature, and I enjoyed the danger of combat. After I served in the army, I heard of a group that needed a small-arms expert for some 'interesting work.' I applied." He smiled in reminiscence. "It was an exciting time, but once or twice I had a close call. The others slowly drifted away to other occupations, other callings, but I continued. And then I began to slow down, and there was a mistake that almost cost me my life." He lifted the cheroot to his lips. "I had enough wealth by then not to mind settling down to a less demanding life-style. I came home."

"Do you miss it?" she asked softly, studying his handsome face.

"On occasion. There were good times. A special feeling of camaraderie with men who faced death with me."

"And women, I guess," she said hesitantly, her face more expressive than she realized.

His black eyes ran over her body like hands, slow

and steady and frankly possessive. "And women," he said quietly. "Are you shocked?"

She swallowed, lowering her eyes. "I never imagined that you were a monk, Diego."

He felt himself tautening as he watched her, longed for her. The rain came harder, and she jumped as a streak of lightning burst near the temple and a shuddering thunderclap followed it.

"The lightning comes before the noise," he reminded her. "One never hears the fatal flash."

"How encouraging," she said through her teeth. "Do you have any more comforting thoughts to share?"

He smiled faintly as he put out the cheroot and laid it to one side. "Not for the moment."

He took her by the shoulders and laid her down against the palms and banana leaves, his lean hands on the buttons of her shirt once more. This time she didn't fight and she didn't protest, she simply watched him with eyes as big as saucers.

"I want to make sure the bleeding has stopped," he said softly. He pulled the edges of the blouse open and lifted the handkerchief that he'd placed over the cut. His black eyes narrowed, and he grimaced. "This may leave a scar," he said, tracing the wound with his forefinger. "A pity, on such exquisite skin."

Her breath rattled in her throat. The touch of his hand made her feel reckless. All her buried longings were coming to the surface during this unexpected interlude with him, his body above her, his chest as bare and brawny as she'd dreamed it would be.

"I have no healing balm," he said softly, searching

her eyes. "But perhaps *pequeña*, I could kiss it better...."

Even as he spoke, he bent, and Melissa moaned sharply as she felt the moist warmth of his mouth on her skin. Her hands clenched beside her, her back arched helplessly.

Startled by such a passionate reaction from a girl so virginal, he lifted his head to look at her. He was surprised, proud, when he saw the pleasure that made her cheeks burn, her eyes grow drowsy and bright, her lips part hungrily. It made him forget everything but the need to make her moan like that yet again, to see her eyes as she felt the first stirrings of passion in her untried body. The thought of her innocence and his resolve not to touch her vanished like the threat of danger.

He slid one hand under the nape of her neck to support it, his fingers spreading against her scalp as he bent again. His lips touched her tenderly, his tongue lacing against the abrasions, trailing over her silky skin. She smelled of flowers, and the scent of her went to his head. His free hand went under her back and found the catch of her bra, releasing it. He pulled the straps away from her shoulder and lifted her gently to ease the wispy material down her arms along with her blouse, leaving her bare and shivering under his quiet, experienced eyes. He hadn't meant to let it happen, but his hunger for her had burst its bonds. He couldn't hold back. He didn't want to. She was his. She belonged to him.

He stopped her impulsive movement to cover herself by shaking his head. "This between us will be a

secret, something for the two of us alone to share,"
he whispered. His dark eyes went to her breasts, adoring them. "Such lovely young breasts," he breathed,
bending toward them. "So sweet, so tempting, so exquisitely formed..."

His lips touched the hard tip of her breast, and she
went rigid. His arm went under her to support her
back, and his free hand edged between them, raising
sweet fires as it traced over her rib cage and belly
before it went up to tease at the bottom swell of her
breasts and make her ache for him to touch her completely. His mouth eased down onto her breast, taking
it inside, savoring its warm softness as the rain pelted
down overhead and the thunder drowned out the
threat of the world around them. Their drenched
clothing was hardly a barrier, their bodies sliding
damply against each other in the dusty semidarkness
of the dry ruin.

He felt her begin to move against him with helpless
longing. She wasn't experienced enough to hide her
desire for him or to curb her headlong response. He
delighted in the shy touch of her hands on his chest,
his back, in her soft cries and moans as he moved his
mouth up to hers finally and covered her soft lips,
pressing them open in a kiss that defied restraint.

She arched against him, glorying in the feel of skin
against wet skin, her bareness under his, the hardness
of his muscles gently crushing her breasts. Her nails
dug helplessly into his back while she felt the hunger
in the smoke-scented warmth of his open mouth on
hers, and she moaned tenderly when she felt the probing of his tongue.

He was whispering something in husky Spanish, his mouth insistent, his hands suddenly equally insistent with other fastenings, hard and swift and sure.

She started to protest, but he brushed his mouth over hers. His body was shuddering with desire, and he sat up, his eyes fiercely possessive as he began to remove the rest of her clothing.

"Shhh," he whispered when she started to speak. "Let me tell you how it will be. My body and yours," he breathed, "with the rain around us, the jungle beneath us. The sweet fusion of male and female here, in the Mayan memory. Like the first man and woman on earth, with only the jungle to hear your cries and the aching pleasure of my skin against yours, my hands holding you to me as we drown in the fulfillment of our desire for each other."

The soft deepness of his voice drugged her. Yes, she wanted that. She wanted him. She arched as his hands slid down her yielding body, his lips softly touching her in ways she'd never dreamed of. The scent of the palm leaves and the musty, damp smell of the ruins in the rain combined with the excitement of Diego's feverish lovemaking.

She watched him undress, her shyness buried in the fierce need for fulfillment, her eyes worshiping his lean, fit body as he lay down beside her. He let her look at him, taking quiet pride in his maleness. He coaxed her to touch him, to explore the hard warmth of his body while he whispered to her and kissed her and traced her skin with exquisite expertise, all restraint, all reason burned away in the fires of passion.

She gave everything he asked, yielded to him completely. At the final moment, when there was no turning back, she looked up at him with absolute trust, absorbing the sudden intrusion of his powerful body with only a small gasp of pain, lost in the tender smile of pride he gave at her courage.

"Virgin," he whispered, his eyes bright and black as they held hers. He began to move, very slowly, his body trembling with his enforced restraint. "And so we join, and you are wholly mine. *Mi mujer.* My woman."

She caught her breath at the sensations he was causing, her eyes moving and then darting away, her face surprised and loving and hungry all at the same time, her eyes full of wonder as they lifted back to his.

"Hold me," he whispered. "Hold tight, because soon you will begin to feel the whip of passion and you will need my strength. Hold fast, *querida*, hold fast to me, give me all that you are, all that you have...*adorada*," he gasped as his movements increased with shocking effect. "Melissa *mía!*"

She couldn't even look at him. Her body was climbing to incredible heights, tautening until the muscles seemed in danger of snapping. She cried out something, but he groaned and clasped her, and all too soon she was reaching for something that had disappeared even as she sought to touch it.

She wept, frustrated and aching and not even able to explain why.

He kissed her face tenderly, his hands framing it, his eyes soft, wondering. "You did not feel it?" he whispered, making her look at him.

"It was so close," she whispered back, her eyes frantic. "I almost...oh!"

He smiled with aching tenderness, his body moving slowly, his head lifting to watch her face. "Ah, yes," he whispered. "Here. And here...gently, *querida*. Come up and kiss me, and let your body match my rhythm. Yes, *querida*, yes, like that, like—" His jaw clenched. He shouldn't be able to feel it again so quickly. He watched her face, felt her body spiraling toward fulfillment. Even as she cried out with it and whispered to him he was in his own hot, black oblivion, and this time it took forever to fall back to earth in her arms.

They lay together in the soft darkness with the rain pelting around them, sated, exquisitely fatigued, her shirt and his pulled over them for a damp blanket. He bent to kiss her lazily from time to time, his lips soft and slow, his smile gentle. For just a few minutes there was no past, no future, no threat of retribution, no piper to pay.

Melissa was shocked by what had happened, so in love with him that it had seemed the most natural thing on earth at the time to let him love her. But as her reason came back, she became afraid and apprehensive. What was he thinking, lying so quietly beside her? Was he sorry or glad, did he blame her? She started to ask him.

And then reality burst in on them in the cruelest way of all. Horses' hooves and loud voices had been drowned out by the thunder and the rain, but suddenly a small group of men was inside the ruin, and at the head of them was Melissa's father.

He stopped dead, staring at the trail of clothing and the two people, obviously lovers, so scantily covered by two shirts.

''Damn you, Laremos!'' Edward Sterling burst out. ''Damn you, what have you done?''

Three

Melissa knew that as long as she lived there would be the humiliation of that afternoon in her memory. Her father's outrage, Diego's taut shouldering of the blame, her own tearful shame. The men quickly left the ruins at Edward Sterling's terse insistence, but Melissa knew they'd seen enough in those brief seconds to know what had happened.

Edward Sterling followed them, giving Melissa and Diego time to get decently covered. Diego didn't speak at all. He turned his back while she dressed, and then he gestured with characteristic courtesy for her to precede him out of the entrance. He wanted to speak, to say something, but his pride was lacerated at having so far forgotten himself as to seduce the daughter of his family's worst enemy. He was appalled at his own lack of control.

Melissa went out after one hopeful glance at his rigid, set features. She didn't look at him again.

Her father was waiting outside. The rain had stopped and his men were at a respectful distance.

"It wasn't all Diego's fault," Melissa began.

"Yes, I'm aware of that," her father said coldly. "I found the poems you wrote and the note asking Laremos to meet you so that you could—how did you put it?—'prove your love' for him."

Diego turned, his eyes suddenly icy, hellishly accusing. "You planned this," he said contemptuously. "*Dios mío*, and like a fool I walked into the trap..."

"How could I possibly plan a raid by guerrillas?" she asked, trying to reason with him.

"She certainly used it to her advantage," Edward Sterling said stiffly. "She was warned before she left the house that there was trouble at your estate, Estrella told her as she rode out of the yard, and she went in that general direction."

Melissa defended herself weakly. "I didn't hear Estrella. And the poems and the note were just daydreaming...."

"Costly daydreaming," her father replied. He stared at Diego. "No man with any sense of honor could refuse marriage in the circumstances."

"What would you know of honor?" Diego asked icily. "You, who seduced my father's woman away days before their wedding?"

Edward Sterling seemed to vibrate with bad temper. "That has nothing to do with the present situation. I won't defend my daughter's actions, but you must admit, Señor Laremos, that she couldn't have found herself in this predicament without some co-operation from you!''

It was a statement that turned Diego's blood molten, because it was an accusation that was undeniable. He was as much to blame as Melissa. He was trapped, and he himself had sprung the lock. He couldn't even look at her. The sweet interlude that had been the culmination of all his dreams of perfection had turned to ashes. He didn't know if he could bear to go through with it, but what choice was there? Another dishonor on the family name would be too devastating to consider, especially to his grandmother and his sister.

"I will not shirk my responsibility, *señor*," Diego said with arrogant disdain. "You may rest assured that Melissa will be taken care of."

Melissa started to speak, to refuse, but her father and Diego gave her such venomous looks that she turned away and didn't say another word.

The guerrillas had been dealt with. Apollo Blain, tall and armed to the teeth at the head of a column led by the small, wiry man Laremos called First Shirt, was waiting in the valley as the small party approached.

"The government troops are at the house, boss," Shirt said with a grin.

Apollo chuckled, his muscular arms crossed over the pommel of his saddle. "Cleaning house, if you'll forgive the pun. Glad to see you're okay, boss man. You, too, Miss Sterling."

"Thanks," Melissa said wanly.

"With your permission, I will rejoin my men," Diego said with cool formality, directing the words to Edward. "I will make the necessary arrangements for the service to take place with all due haste."

"We'll wait to hear from you, *señor*," Edward said tersely. He motioned to his men and urged his mount into step beside Melissa's.

"I don't suppose there's any use in trying to explain?" she asked miserably, too sick to even look back toward Diego and his retreating security force.

"None at all," her father said. "I hope you love Laremos. You'll need to, now that he's well and truly hamstrung. He'll hate both of us, but I won't let you be publicly disgraced, even if it is your own damned fault."

Tears slid down her cheeks. She stared toward the distant house with a sick feeling that her life was never going to be the same again. Her hero-worshiping and daydreaming had led to the end she'd hoped for, but she hadn't wanted to trap Diego. She'd wanted him to love her, to want to marry her. She had what she thought she desired, but now it seemed that the Fates were laughing at her. She remembered a very old saying that had never made sense before: *Be careful what you wish for, because you might get it.*

Weeks went by while Melissa was feted and given party after party with a stiff-necked Señora Laremos and Juana, Diego's sister, at her side. Their disapproval and frank dislike had been made known from the very beginning, but like Diego, they were making the most of a bad situation.

Diego himself hardly spoke to Melissa unless it was necessary, and when he looked at her she felt chilled to the bone. That he hated her was all too apparent. As the wedding approached, she wished with all her heart that she'd listened to her father and had never left the house that rainy day.

Her wedding gown was chosen, the Catholic church in Guatemala City was filled to capacity with friends and distant kin of both the bride's and groom's families. Melissa was all nerves, even though Diego seemed to be as nonchalant as if he were going to a sporting event, and even less enthusiastic.

Diego spoke his vows under Father Santiago's quiet gaze with thinly veiled sarcasm and placed the ring upon Melissa's finger. He pushed back the veil and looked at her with something less than contempt, and when he kissed her it was strictly for the sake of appearances. His lips were ice-cold. Then he bowed and led her back down the aisle, his eyes as unfeeling as the carpet under their feet.

The reception was an ordeal, and there was music and dancing that seemed to go on forever before Diego announced that he and his bride must be on their way home. He'd already told Melissa there would be no honeymoon because he had too much work and not enough free time to travel. He drove her back to the casa, where he deposited her with his cold-eyed grandmother and sister. And then he packed a bag and left for an extended business trip to Europe.

Melissa missed her father and Estrella. She missed the warmth of her home. But most of all, she missed the man she'd once loved, the Diego who'd teased her and laughed with her and seemed to enjoy having her with him for company when he'd ridden around the estate. The angry, unapproachable man she'd married was a stranger.

It was almost six weeks from the day she and Diego had been together when Melissa began to feel a stirring inside, a frightening certainty that she was pregnant. She was nauseated, not just at breakfast but all the time. She hid it from Diego's grandmother and sister, although it grew more difficult all the time.

She spent her days wandering miserably around the house, wishing she had something to occupy her. She wasn't allowed to take part in any of the housework or to sit with the rest of the family, who made this apparent by simply leaving a room the moment she entered it. She ate alone, because the *Señora* and the *Señorita* managed to change the times of meals from day to day. She was avoided, barely tolerated, actively disliked by both women, and she didn't have the worldliness or the sophistication or the maturity to cope with the situation. She spent a great deal of time crying. And still Diego stayed away.

"Is it so impossible for you to accept me?" she asked Señora Laremos one evening as Juana left the sitting room and a stiff-backed *señora* prepared to follow her.

Señora Laremos gave her a cold, black glare from eyes so much like Diego's that Melissa shivered. "You are not welcome here. Surely you realize it?" the older woman asked. "My grandson does not want you, and neither do we. You have dishonored us yet again, like your mother before you!"

Melissa averted her face. "It wasn't my fault," she said through trembling lips. "Not completely."

"Had it not been for your father's insistence, you would have been treated like any other woman whose favors my son had enjoyed. You would have been adequately provided for—"

"How?" Melissa demanded, her illusions gone at the thought of Diego's other women, her heart broken. "With an allowance for life, a car, a mink coat?" Her chin lifted proudly. "Go ahead, *Señora*. Ignore me. Nothing will change the fact that I am Diego's wife."

The older woman seemed actually to vibrate with anger. "You impudent young cat," she snarled. "Has your family not been the cause of enough grief for mine already, without this? I despise you!"

Melissa didn't blink. She didn't flinch. "Yes, I realize that," she said with quiet pride. "God forbid that in your place I would ever be so cruel to a guest in my home. But then," she added with soft venom, "I was raised properly."

The Señora actually flushed. She went out of the room without another word, but afterward her avoidance of Melissa was total.

Melissa gave up trying to make them accept her now that she realized the futility of it. She wanted to go home to see her father, but even that was difficult to arrange in the hostile environment where she lived. She settled for the occasional phone call and had to pretend, for his sake, that everything was all right. Perhaps when Diego had time to get used to the situation, everything would be all right. That was the last hope she had—that Diego might relent. That she might be able to persuade him to give her a chance to be the wife she knew she was capable of being.

Meanwhile, the sickness went on and on, and she knew that soon she was going to have to see a doctor. She grew paler by the day. So pale, in fact, that Juana risked her grandmother's wrath to sneak into Melissa's room one night and ask how she was.

Melissa gaped at her. "I beg your pardon?" she asked tautly.

Juana grimaced, her hands folded neatly at her waist, her dark eyes oddly kind in her thin face. "You seem so pale, Melissa. I wish it were different. Diego is—" she spread her hands "Diego. And my grandmother nurses old wounds that have been reopened by your presence here. I cannot defy her. It would break her heart if I sided with you against her."

"I understand that," Melissa said quietly, and managed a smile. "I don't blame you for being loyal to your grandmother, Juana."

Juana sighed. "Is there something, anything, I can do?"

Melissa shook her head. "But thank you."

Juana opened the door, hesitating. "My grandmother will not say so, but Diego has called. He will be home tomorrow. I thought you might like to know."

She was gone then, as quickly as she'd come. Melissa looked around the neat room she'd been given, with its dark antique furnishings. It wasn't by any means the master bedroom, and she wondered if Diego would even keep up the pretense of being married to her by sleeping in the same room. Somehow she doubted it. It would be just as well that way, because she didn't want him to know about the baby. Not until she could tell how well he was adapting to married life.

She barely slept, wondering how it would be to see him again. She overslept the next morning and for once was untroubled by nausea. She went down the hall and there he was, sitting at the head of the table. The whole family was together for breakfast for once.

Her heart jumped at just the sight of him. He was wearing a lightweight white tropical suit that suited his dark coloring, but he looked worn and tired. He glanced up as she entered the room, and she wished she hadn't worn the soft gray crepe dress. It had seemed appropriate at the time, but now she felt over-dressed. Juana was wearing a simple calico skirt and a white blouse, and the *señora* had on a sedate dark dress.

Diego's eyes went from Melissa's blond hair in its neat chignon to her high-heeled shoes in one light-ning-fast, not-very-interested glance. He acknowl-edged her with cool formality. "Señora Laremos. Are you well?"

She wanted to throw things. Nothing had changed, that was obvious. He still blamed her. Hated her. She was carrying his child, she was almost certain of it, but how could she tell him?

She went to the table and sat down gingerly, as far away from the others as she could without being too obvious. "Welcome home, *señor*," she said in a sub-dued tone. She hardly had any spirit left. The weeks

of avoidance and cold courtesy and hostility had left
their mark on her. She was pale and quiet, and something stirred in Diego as he looked at her. Then he
banked down the memories. She'd trapped him. He
couldn't afford to let himself forget that. First Sheila,
then Melissa. The Sterlings had dealt two bitter blows
to the Laremos honor. How could he even think of
forgiving her?

Still, he thought, she looked unwell. Her body was
thinner than he remembered, and she had a peculiar
lack of interest in the world around her.

Señora Laremos also noticed these things about her
unwanted houseguest but she forced herself not to
bend. The girl was a curse, like her mother before
her. She could never forgive Melissa for trapping Diego in such a scandalous way, so that even the servants whispered about the manner in which the two
of them had been found.

"We have had our meal," the *Señora* said with
forced courtesy, "but Carisa will bring something for
you if you wish, Melissa."

"I don't want anything except coffee, thank you,
señora." She reached for the silver coffeepot with a
hand that trembled despite all her efforts to control it.
Juana bit her lip and turned her eyes away. And Diego
saw his sister's reaction with a troubled conscience.
For Juana to be so affected, the weeks he'd been away
must have been difficult ones. He glanced at the *señora* and wondered what Melissa had endured. His
only thought had been to get away from the forced
intimacy with his new wife. Now he began to wonder
about the treatment she'd received from his family

and was shocked to realize that it was only an echo of his own coldness.

"You are thinner," Diego said unexpectedly. "Is your appetite not good?"

She lifted dull, uninterested eyes. "It suffices, *señor*," she replied. She sipped coffee and kept her gaze on her cup. It was easier than trying to look at him.

He hated the guilt that swept over him. The situation was her fault. She'd baited a trap that he'd fallen headlong into. So why should he feel so terrible? But he did. The laughing, shy young woman who'd adored him no longer lived in the same body with this quiet, unnaturally pale woman who wouldn't look at him.

"Perhaps you would like to lie down, Melissa," the *señora* said uneasily. "You do seem pale."

Melissa didn't argue. It was obvious that she wasn't welcome here, either, even if she had been invited to join the family. "As you wish, *señora*," she said, her tone emotionless. She got up without looking at anyone and went down the long, carpeted hall to her room.

Diego began to brood. He hardly heard what his grandmother said about the running of the estate in his absence. His mind was still on Melissa.

"How long has she been like this, *abuela*?" he asked unexpectedly. "Has she no interest in the house at all?"

Juana started to speak, but the *señora* silenced her. "She has been made welcome, despite the circumstances of your marriage," the *señora* said with dignity. "She prefers her own company."

"Excuse me," Juana said suddenly, and she left the table, her face rigid with distaste as she went out the door.

Diego finished his coffee and went to Melissa's room. But once outside it, he hesitated. Things were already strained. He didn't really want to make it any harder for her. He withdrew his hand from the door-knob and, with a faint sigh, went back the way he'd come. There would be time later to talk to her.

But business interceded. He was either on his way out or getting ready to leave every time Melissa saw him. He didn't come near her except to inquire after her health and to nod now and again. Melissa began to stay in her room all the time, eating her food on trays that Carisa brought and staring out the window. She wondered if her mind might be affected by her enforced solitude, but nothing really seemed to matter anymore. She had no emotion left in her. Even her pregnancy seemed quite unreal, although she knew it was only a matter of time before she was going to have to see the doctor.

It was storming the night Diego finally came to see her. He'd just come in from the cattle, and he looked weary. In dark slacks and an unbuttoned white shirt, he looked very Spanish and dangerously attractive, his black hair damp from the first sprinkling of rain.

"Will you not make even the effort to associate with the rest of us?" he asked without preamble. "My grandmother feels that your dislike for us is growing out of proportion."

"Your grandmother hates me," she said without

inflection, her eyes on the darkness outside the window. "Just as you do."

Diego's face hardened. "After all that has happened, did you expect to find me a willing husband?"

She sighed, staring at her hands in her lap. "I don't know what I expected. I was living on dreams. Now they've all come true, and I've learned that reality is more than castles in the air. What we think we want isn't necessarily what we need. I should have gone to America. I should never have...I should have stopped you."

He felt blinding anger. "Stopped me?" he echoed, his deep voice ringing in the silence of her room. "When it was your damnable scheming that led to our present circumstances?"

She lifted her face to his. "And your loss of control," she said quietly, faint accusation in her voice. "You didn't have to make love to me. I didn't force you."

His temper exploded. He didn't want to think about that. He lapsed into clipped, furious Spanish as he expressed things he couldn't manage in English.

"All right," she said, rising unsteadily to her feet. "All right, it was all my fault—all of it. I planned to trap you and I did, and now both of us are paying for my mistakes." Her pale eyes pleaded with his unyielding ones. "I can't even express my sorrow or beg you enough to forgive me. But Diego, there's no hope of divorce. We have to make the best of it."

"Do we?" he asked, lifting his chin.

She moved closer to him in one last desperate effort to reach him. Her soft eyes searched his. She looked young and very seductive, and Diego felt himself caving in when she was close enough that he could smell the sweet perfume of her body and feel her warmth. All the memories stirred suddenly, weakening him.

She sensed that he was vulnerable somehow. It gave her the courage to do what she did next. She raised her hands and rested them on his chest, against the cool skin and the soft feathering of hair over the hard muscles. He flinched, and she sighed softly as she looked up at him.

"Diego, we're married," she whispered, trying not to tremble. "Can't we...can't we forget the past and start again...tonight?"

His jaw went taut, his body stiffened. No, he told himself, he wouldn't allow her to make him vulnerable a second time. He had to gird himself against any future assaults like this.

He caught her shoulders and pushed her away from him, his face severe, his eyes cold and unwelcoming. "The very touch of you disgusts me, Señora Laremos," he said with icy fastidiousness. "I would rather sleep alone for the rest of my days than to share my bed with you. You repulse me."

The lack of heat in the words made them all the more damning. She looked at him with the eyes of a bludgeoned deer. Disgust. Repulse. She couldn't bear any more. His grandmother and sister like hostile soldiers living with her, then Diego's cold company, and now this. It was too much. She was bearing his child, and he wouldn't want it, because she disgusted him. Tears stung her eyes. Her hand went to her mouth.

"I can't bear it," she whimpered. Her face contorted and she ran out the door, which he'd left open, down the hall, her hair streaming behind her. She felt rather than saw the women of the house gaping at her from the living room as she ran wildly toward the front door with Diego only a few steps behind her.

The house was one story, but there was a long drop off the porch because of the slope on which the house had been built. The stone steps stretched out before her, but she was blinded by tears and lost her footing in the driving rain. She didn't even feel the wetness or the pain as she shot headfirst into the darkness and the first impact rocked her. Somewhere a man's voice was yelling hoarsely, but she was mercifully beyond hearing it.

She came to in the hospital, surrounded by white-coated figures bending over her.

The resident physician was American, a blond-haired, blue-eyed young man with a pleasant smile. "There you are," he said gently when she stirred and opened her eyes. "Minor concussion and a close call for your baby, but I think you'll survive."

"I'm pregnant?" she asked drowsily.

"About two and a half months," he agreed. "Is it a pleasant surprise?"

"I wish it were so." She sighed. "Please don't tell my husband. He'll be worried enough as it is," she added, deliberately misleading the young man. She didn't want Diego to know about the baby.

"I'm sorry, but I told him there was a good chance you might lose it," he said apologetically. "You were in bad shape when they brought you in, *señora*. It's a miracle that you didn't lose the baby, and I'd still like to run some tests just to make sure.''

She bit her lower lip and suddenly burst into tears. It all came out then, the forced marriage, his family's hatred of her, his own hatred of her. "I don't want him to know that I'm still pregnant," she pleaded. "Oh, please, you mustn't tell him, you mustn't! I can't stay here and let my baby be born in such hostility. They'll take him away from me and I'll never see him again. You don't know how they hate me and my family!"

He sighed heavily. "You must see that I can't lie about it."

"I'm not asking you to," she said. "If I can leave in the morning, and if you'll just not talk to him, I can tell him that there isn't going to be a baby."

"I can't lie to him," the doctor repeated.

She took a slow, steadying breath. She was in pain now, and the bruises were beginning to nag her. "Then can you just not talk to him?"

"I might manage to be unavailable," he said. "But if he asks me, I'll tell him the truth. I must."

"Isn't a patient's confession sacred or something?" she asked with a faint trace of humor.

"That's so, but lying is something else again. I'm too honest, anyway," he said gently. "He'd see right through me."

She lay back and touched her aching head. "It's all right," she murmured. "It doesn't matter."

He hesitated for a minute. Then he bent to examine her head and she gave in to the pain. Minutes later he gave her something for it and left her to be transported to a private room and admitted for observation overnight.

She wondered if Diego would come to see her, but she was half-asleep when she saw him standing at the foot of the bed. His face was in the shadows, so she couldn't see it. But his voice was curiously husky.

"How are you?" he asked.

"They say I'll get over it," she replied, turning her head away from him. Tears rolled down her cheeks. At least she still had the baby, but she couldn't tell him. She didn't dare. She closed her eyes.

He stuck his hands deep in his pockets and looked at her, a horrible sadness in his eyes, a sadness she didn't see. "I...am sorry about the baby," he said stiffly. "One of the nurses said that your doctor mentioned the fall had done a great deal of damage." He shifted restlessly. "The possibility of a child had simply not occurred to me," he added slowly.

As if he'd been home enough to notice, she thought miserably. "Well, you needn't worry about it anymore," she said huskily. "God forbid that you should be any more trapped than you already were. You'd have hated being tied to me by a baby."

His spine stiffened. He seemed to see her then as she was, an unhappy child who'd half worshiped him, and he wondered at the guilt he felt. That annoyed him. "Grandmother had to be tranquilized when she knew," he said curtly, averting his eyes. "*Dios mío*, you might have told me, Melissa!"

"I didn't know," she lied dully. Her poor bruised face moved restlessly against the cool pillow. "And it doesn't matter now. Nothing matters anymore."

She sighed wearily. "I'm so tired. Please leave me in peace, Diego." She turned her face away. "I only want to sleep."

He stared down at her without speaking. She'd trapped him and he blamed her for it, but he was sorry about the baby, because he was responsible. He grimaced at her paleness, at the bruising on her face. She'd changed so drastically, he thought. She'd aged years.

His eyes narrowed. Well, hadn't she brought it on herself? She'd wanted to marry him, but she hadn't considered his feelings. She'd forced them into this marriage, and divorce wasn't possible. He still blamed her for that, and forgiveness was going to come hard. But for a time she had to be looked after. Well, tomorrow he'd work something out. He might send her to Barbados, where he owned land, to recover. He didn't know if he could bear having to see the evidence of his cruelty every day, because the loss of the child weighed heavily on his conscience. He hadn't even realized that he wanted a child until now, when it was too late.

He didn't sleep, wondering what to do. But when he went to see her, she'd already solved the problem. She was gone...

As past and present merged, Diego watched Melissa's eyes open suddenly and look up at him. It might have been five years ago. The pain was in those soft gray eyes, the bitter memories. She looked at him and shuddered. The eyes that once had worshiped him were filled with icy hatred. Melissa seemed no happier to see him than he was to see her. The past was still between them.

Four

Melissa blinked, moving her head jerkily so she could see him. Her gaze focused on his face, and then she shivered and closed her eyes. He pulled himself erect and turned to go and get a nurse. As he left the room, his last thought was that her expression had been that of a woman awakening not from, but into, a nightmare.

When Melissa's eyes opened again, there was a shadowy form before her in crisp white, checking her over professionally with something uncomfortably cold and metallic.

"Good," a masculine voice murmured. "Very good. She's coming around. I think we can dispense with some of this paraphernalia, Miss Jackson," he told a white-clad woman beside him, and proceeded to give unintelligible orders.

Melissa tried to move her hand. "Pl-please." Her

voice sounded thick and alien. "I have...to go home."

"Not just yet, I'm afraid," he said kindly, smiling.

She licked her lips. They felt so very dry. "Matthew," she whispered. "My little boy. At a neighbor's. They won't know..."

The doctor hesitated. "You just rest, Mrs. Laremos. You've had a bad night of it—"

"Don't...call me that!" she shuddered, closing her eyes. "I'm Melissa Sterling."

The doctor wanted to add that her husband was just outside the door, but the look on her face took the words out of his mouth. He said something to the nurse and quickly went back out into the hall.

Diego was pacing, and smoking like a furnace. He'd shed his jacket on one of the colorful seats in the nearby waiting room. His white silk shirt was open at the throat and his tie was lying neatly on his folded jacket. His rolled-up sleeves were in dramatic contrast to his very olive skin. His black eyes cut around to the doctor.

"How is she?" he asked without preamble.

"Still a bit concussed." The doctor leaned against the wall, his arms folded. He was almost as tall as Diego, but a good ten years younger. "There's a problem." He hesitated, because he knew from what Diego had told him that he and Melissa had been apart many years. He didn't know if the child was her husband's or someone else's, and situations like this could get uncomfortable. He cleared his throat. "Your wife is worried about her son. He's apparently staying at a neighbor's house."

Diego felt himself go rigid. A child. His heart seemed to stop beating, and for one wild moment he enjoyed the unbounded thought that it was his child. And then he remembered that Melissa had lost his child and that it was impossible for her to have conceived again before she'd left the *finca*. They had only slept together the one time.

That meant that Melissa had slept with another man. That she had become pregnant by another man. That the child was not his. He hated her in that instant with all his heart. Perhaps she was justified in her revenge. To be fair, he'd made her life hell during their brief marriage. And now she'd had her revenge. She'd hurt him in the most basic way of all.

He had to fight not to turn on his heel and walk away. But common sense prevailed. The child wasn't responsible for its circumstances. It would be alone and probably frightened. He couldn't ignore it. "If you can find out where he is, I will see about him," he said stiffly. "Will Melissa be all right?"

"I think so. She's through the worst of it. There was a good deal of internal bleeding. We've taken care of that. There was a badly torn ligament in her leg that will heal in a month or so. And we had to remove an ovary, but the other one was undamaged. Children are still possible."

Diego didn't look at the doctor. His eyes were on the door to Melissa's room. "The child. Do you know how old he is?"

"No. Does it matter?"

Diego shook himself. What he was thinking wasn't remotely possible. She'd lost the child he'd given her.

She'd been taken to the hospital after a severe fall, and the doctor had told him there was little hope of saving it. It wasn't possible that they'd both lied. Of course not.

"I'll try to find the child's whereabouts," the doctor told Diego. "Meanwhile, you can't do much good here. By tomorrow she should be more lucid. You can see her then."

Diego wanted to tell him that if she was lucid Melissa wouldn't want to see him at all. But he only shrugged and nodded his dark head.

He left a telephone number at the nurse's station and went back to his hotel, glad to be out of Tucson's sweltering midsummer heat and in the comfort of his elegant air-conditioned room. A local joke had it that when a desperado from nearby Yuma had died and gone to hell, he'd sent back home for blankets. Diego was inclined to believe it, although the tropical heat of his native Guatemala was equally trying for Americans who settled there.

He much preferred the rain forest to the desert. Even if it was a humid heat, there was always the promise of rain. He wondered if it ever rained here. Presumably it did, eventually.

His mind wandered back to Melissa in that hospital bed and the look on her face when she'd seen him. She'd hidden well. He'd tried every particle of influence and money he'd possessed to find her, but without any success. She'd covered her tracks well, and how could he blame her? His treatment of her had been cruel, and she hadn't been much more than a child hero-worshiping him.

But Diego thought about the baby with bridled fury. They were still married, despite her unfaithfulness, and there was no question of divorce. Melissa, who was also Catholic, would have been no more amenable to that solution than he. But it was going to be unbearable, seeing that child and knowing that he was the very proof of Melissa's revenge for Diego's treatment of her.

The sudden buzz of the telephone diverted him. It was the doctor, who'd obtained the name and address of the neighbor who was caring for Melissa's son. Diego scribbled the information on a pad beside the phone, grateful for the diversion.

An hour later he was ushered into the cozy living room of Henrietta Grady's house, just down the street from the address the hospital had for Melissa's home.

Diego sat sipping coffee, listening to Mrs. Grady talk about Melissa and Matthew and their long acquaintance. She wasn't shy about enumerating Melissa's virtues. "Such a sweet girl," she said. "And Matthew's never any trouble. I don't have children of my own, you see, and Melissa and Matthew have rather adopted me."

"I'm certain your friendship has been important to Melissa," he replied, not wanting to go into any detail about their marriage. "The boy…"

"Here he is now. Hello, my baby."

Diego stopped short at the sight of the clean little boy who walked sleepily into the room in his pajamas. "All clean, Granny Grady," he said, running to her. He perched on her lap, his bare toes wiggling, eyeing the tall, dark man curiously. "Who are you?" he asked.

Diego stared at him with icy anger. Whoever Melissa's lover had been, he obviously had a little Latin blood. The boy's hair was light brown, but his skin was olive and his eyes were dark brown velvet. He was captivating, his arms around Mrs. Grady's neck, his lean, dark face full of laughter. And he looked to be just about four years old. Which meant that Melissa's fidelity had lasted scant weeks or months before she'd turned to another man.

Mrs. Grady lifted the child and cuddled him while Matthew waited for the man to answer his question.

"I'm Matthew," he told Diego, his voice uninhibited and unaccented. "My mommy went away. Are you my papa?"

Diego wasn't sure he could speak. He stared at the little boy with faint hostility. "I am your mama's husband," he said curtly, aware of Matthew's uncertainty and Mrs. Grady's surprise.

Diego ignored the looks. "Your mama is going to be all right. She is a little hurt, but not much. She will come home soon."

"Where will Matt go?" the boy asked gently.

Diego sighed heavily. He hadn't realized how much Melissa's incapacity would affect his life. She was his responsibility until she was well again, and so was this child. It was a matter of honor, and although his had taken some hard blows in years past, it was still as much a part of him as his pride. He lifted his chin. "You and your mama will stay with me," he said stiffly, and the lack of welcome in his voice made the little boy cling even closer to Mrs. Grady. ''But in the meantime, I think it would be as well if you stay here.'' He turned to Mrs. Grady. ''This can be arranged? I will need to spend a great deal of time at the hospital until I can bring Melissa home, and it seems less than sensible to uproot him any more than necessary.''

''Of course it can be arranged,'' Mrs. Grady said without argument. ''If there's anything else I can do to help, please let me know.''

''I will give you the number of the phone in my hotel room and at the hospital, should you need to contact me.'' He pulled a checkbook from the immaculate gray suit jacket. ''No arguments, please,'' he said when she looked hesitant about accepting money. ''If you had not been available, Melissa would certainly have had to hire a sitter for him. I must insist that you let me pay you.''

Mrs. Grady gave in gracefully, grateful for his thoughtfulness. ''I would have done it for nothing,'' she said.

He smiled and wrote out a check. ''Yes. I sensed that.''

''Is Matt going to live with you and Mama?'' Matthew asked in a quiet, subdued tone, sadness in his huge dark eyes.

Diego lifted his chin. ''Yes,'' Diego said formally. ''For the time being.''

''My mommy will miss me if she's hurt. I can kiss her better. Can't I go see her?''

It was oddly touching to see those great dark eyes filled with tears. Diego had schooled himself over the

years to never betray emotion. But he still felt it, even
at such an unwelcome time.

Mrs. Grady had put the boy down to pour more
coffee, and Diego studied him gravely. "There is a
doctor who is taking very good care of your mother.
Soon you may see her. I promise."

The small face lifted warily toward him. "I love
Mama," he said. "She takes me places and buys me
ice cream. And she lets me sleep with her when I get
scared."

Diego's face became, if anything, more reserved
than before, Mrs. Grady noticed. A flash of darkness
in his eyes made her more nervous than before. How
could Melissa have been married to such a cold man,
a man who seemed unaffected even by his own son's
tears? "How about a cartoon movie before bedtime?"
Mrs. Grady asked Matthew, and quickly put on a
Winnie the Pooh video for him to watch. The boy
sprawled in an armchair, clapping his hands as the
credits began to roll.

"*Gracias,*" Diego said as he got gracefully to his
feet. "I will tell Melissa of your kindness to her son."

Mrs. Grady tried not to choke. "Excuse me, *señor*,
but Matthew is surely your son, too?"

The look in his eyes made her regret ever asking
the question. She moved quickly past him to the door,
making a flurry of small talk while her cheeks burned
with her own forwardness.

"I hope everything goes well with Melissa," she
said, flustered.

"Yes. So do I." Diego glanced back at Matthew,
who was watching television. His dark eyes were

quiet and faintly bitter. He didn't want Melissa's child. He wasn't sure he even wanted Melissa. He'd come out of duty and honor, but those were the only things keeping him from taking the first flight home to Guatemala. He felt betrayed all over again, and he didn't know how he was going to bear having to look at that child every day until Melissa was well enough to leave him.

He went back to the hospital, pausing outside Melissa's room while he convinced himself that upsetting her at this point would be unwise. He couldn't do that to an injured woman, despite his outrage. After a moment he knocked carelessly and walked in, tall and elegant and faintly arrogant, controlling his expression so that he seemed utterly unconcerned.

Which was quite a feat, considering that inside he felt as if part of him had died over the past five years. Melissa couldn't possibly know how it had been for him when she'd first vanished from the hospital, or how his guilt had haunted him. Despite his misgivings, he'd searched for her, and if he'd found her he'd have made sure that their marriage worked. For the sake of his family's honor, he'd have made her think that he was supremely contented. And after they'd had other children, perhaps they'd have found some measure of happiness. But that was all supposition, and now he was here and the future had to be faced.

The one thing he was certain of was that he could never trust her again. Affection might be possible after he got used to the situation, but love wasn't a word he knew. He'd come close to that with Melissa before she'd forced him into an unwanted marriage. But she'd nipped that soft feeling in the bud, and he'd steeled himself in the years since to be invulnerable to a woman's lies. Nothing she did could touch him anymore. But how was he going to hide his contempt and fury from her when Matthew would remind him of it every day they had to be together?

Five

Melissa watched Diego come in the door, and it was like stepping back into a past she didn't even want to remember. She was drowsy from the painkillers, but nothing could numb her reaction to her first sight of her husband in five years.

She seemed to stop breathing as her gray eyes slid drowsily over his tall elegance. Diego. So many dreams ago, she'd loved him. So many lonely years ago, she'd longed for him. But the memory of his cold indifference and his family's hatred had killed something vulnerable in her. She'd grown up. No longer was she the adoring woman-child who'd hung on his every word. Because of Matthew, she had to conceal from Diego the attraction she still felt for him. She was helpless and Diego was wealthy and powerful. She couldn't risk letting him know the truth about the little boy, because she knew all too well that Diego would toss her aside without regret. He'd already done that once.

Even now she could recall the disgust in his face when he'd pushed her away from him that last night she'd spent under his roof.

Her eyes opened again and he was closer, his face as unreadable as ever. He was older, but just as masculine and attractive. The cologne he used drifted down to her, making her fingers curl. She remembered the clean scent of him, the delicious touch of his hard mouth on her own. The mustache was unfamiliar, very black and thick, like the wavy, neatly trimmed hair above his dark face. He was older, yes, even a little more muscular. But he was still Diego.

"Melissa." He made her name a song. It was the pronunciation, she imagined, the faint accent, that gave it a foreign sound.

She lowered her eyes to his jacket. "Diego."

"How are you feeling?"

He sounded as awkward as she felt. She wondered how they'd found him, why they'd contacted him. She was still disoriented. Her slender hand touched her forehead as she struggled to remember. "There was a plane crash," she whispered, grimacing as she felt again the horrible stillness of the engine, the sudden whining as they'd descended, her own screaming.

"You must try not to think of it now." He stood over her, his hands deep in his pockets.

Then, suddenly, she remembered. "Matthew! Oh, no. Matthew!"

"*¡Cuidado!*" he said gently, pressing her back into

the pillows. "Your son is doing very well. I have been to see him."

There was a flicker of movement in her eyelids that she prayed he wouldn't see and become curious about. She stared at him, waiting. Waiting. But he made no comment about the child. Nothing.

His back straightened. "I have asked Mrs. Grady to keep him until you are well enough to be released."

She wished she felt more capable of coping. "That was kind of you," she said.

He turned to her again, his head to one side as he studied her. He decided not to pull any punches. "You will not be able to work for six weeks. And Mrs. Grady seemed to feel that you are in desperate financial straits."

Her eyes closed as a wave of nausea swept over her. "I had pneumonia, back in the spring," she said. "I got behind with the bills..."

"Are you listening to me, Señora Laremos?" he asked pointedly, emphasizing the married name he knew she hated. "You are not able to work. Until you are, you and the child will come home with me."

Her eyes opened then. "No!"

"It is decided," he said carelessly.

She went rigid under the sheet. "I won't go to Guatemala, Diego," she said with unexpected spirit. In the old days, she had never fought him. "Not under any circumstances."

He stared at her, his expression faintly puzzled. So the memories bothered her, as well, did they? He lifted his chin, staring down his straight nose at her.

"Chicago, not Guatemala," he replied quietly. "Retirement has begun to bore me." He shrugged. "I hardly need the money, but Apollo Blain has offered me a consultant's position, and I already have an apartment in Chicago. I was spending a few weeks at the *finca* before beginning work when the hospital authorities called me about you."

Apollo. That name was familiar. She remembered the mercenaries with whom Diego had once associated himself. "He was in trouble with the law."

"No longer. J.D. Brettman defended him and won his case. Apollo has his own business now, and most of the others work for him. He is the last bachelor in the group. The others are married, even Shirt."

She swallowed. "Shirt is married?"

"To a wiry little widow. Unbelievable, is it not? I flew to Texas three years ago for the wedding."

She couldn't look at him. She knew somehow that he'd never told his comrades about his own marriage. He'd hated Melissa and the very thought of being tied to her. Hadn't he said so often enough?

"I'm very happy for them," she said tautly. "How nice to know that some people look upon marriage as a happy ending, not as certain death."

His gaze narrowed, his dark eyes wary on her face. "Looking into the past will accomplish nothing," he said finally. "We must both put it aside. I cannot desert you at such a time, and Mrs. Grady is hardly able to undertake your nursing as well as your son's welfare."

She didn't miss the emphasis he put on the reference to Matthew. He had to believe she'd betrayed

him, and she had no choice but to let him think it.
She couldn't fight him in her present condition.

Her gray eyes held his. "And you are?"

"It is a matter of honor," he said stiffly.

"Yes, of course. Honor," she said wearily, wincing
as she moved and felt a twinge of pain. "I hope I can
teach Matthew that honor and pride aren't quite as
important as compassion and love."

The reference to her own lack of honor made his
temper flare. "Who was his father, Melissa?" he
asked cuttingly, his eyes hard. He hadn't meant to ask
that, the words had exploded from him in quiet fury.
"Whose child is he?"

She turned her head back to his. "He's my child,"
she said with an indignant glare. Gone were the days
when she'd bowed down to him. Gone were the old
adulation and the pedestal she'd put him on. She was
worlds more mature now, and her skin wasn't thin
anymore. "When you pushed me away, you gave up
any rights you had to dictate to me. His parentage is
none of your business. You didn't want me, but
maybe someone else did."

He glared, but he didn't fire back at her. How could
he? She'd hit on his own weakness. He'd never gotten
over the guilt he'd felt, both for the loss of control
that had given her a weapon to force him into marriage and for causing her miscarriage.

He stared out the window. "We cannot change
what was," he said again.

Melissa hated the emotions that soft, Spanish-
accented voice aroused in her, and she hated the hun-

ger she felt for his love. But she could never let him know.

She stared at her thin hands. "Why did they contact you?"

He went back to the bed, his eyes quiet, unreadable. "You had our marriage license in your purse."

"Oh."

"It amazes me that you would carry it with you," he continued. "You hated me when you left Guatemala."

"No less than you hated me, Diego," she replied wearily.

His heart leaped at the sound of his name on her lips. She'd whispered it that rainy afternoon in the mountains, then moaned it, then screamed it. His fist clenched deep in his pocket as the memories came back, unbidden.

"It seemed so, did it not?" he replied. He turned away irritably. "Nevertheless, I did try to find you," he added stiffly. "But to no avail."

She stared at the sheet over her. "I didn't think you'd look for me," she said. "I didn't think you'd mind that I was gone, since I'd lost the child," she added, forcing out the lie, "and that was the only thing you would have valued in our marriage."

He averted his head. He didn't tell her the whole truth about the devastation her disappearance had caused him. He was uncertain of his ability to talk about it, even now, without revealing his emotions. "You were my wife," he said carelessly, glancing her way with eyes as black as night. "You were my responsibility."

"Yes," she agreed. "Only that. Just an unwelcome duty." She grimaced, fighting the pain because her shot was slowly wearing off. Her soft gray eyes searched his face. "You never wanted me, except in one way. And after we were married, not even that way."

That wasn't true. She couldn't know how he'd fought to stay out of her bedroom for fear of creating an addiction that he would never be cured of. She was in his blood even now, and as he looked at her he ached for her. But he'd forced himself to keep his distance. His remoteness, his cutting remarks, had all been part of his effort to keep her out of his heart. He'd come closer to knowing love with her than with any of the women in his past, but something in him had held back. He'd lived alone all his life, he'd been free. Loving was a kind of prison, a bond. He hadn't wanted that. Even marriage hadn't changed his mind. Not at first.

"Freedom was to me a kind of religion," he said absently. "I had never foreseen that I might one day be forced to relinquish it." He shifted restlessly. "Marriage was never a state I coveted."

"Yes, I learned that," she replied. She grimaced as she shifted against the pillow. "What did they...do to me? They won't tell me anything."

"They operated to stop some internal bleeding." He stood over her, his head at a faintly arrogant angle. "There is a torn ligament in your leg which will make you uncomfortable until it heals, and some minor bruises and abrasions. And they had to remove one of your ovaries, but the physician said that you can still bear a child.''

Her face colored. "I don't want another child."

He stared down at her with faint distaste. "No doubt the one your lover left you with is adequate, is he not, *señora*?" he shot back.

She wanted to hit him. Her eyes flashed wildly and her breath caught. "Oh, God, I hate you," she breathed huskily, and her face contorted with new pain.

He ignored the outburst. "Do you need something else for the discomfort?" he asked unexpectedly.

She wanted to deny it, but she couldn't. "It... hurts." She touched her abdomen.

"I will see the nurse on my way out. I must get more clothes for Matthew."

She felt drained. "I'd forgotten. My apartment. There are clothes in the tall chest of drawers for him."

"The key?" he asked.

"In my purse." She didn't really want Diego in her apartment. There were no visible traces of anything, but he might find something she'd overlooked. But what choice did she have? Matthew had to be her first consideration.

He brought it to her, took the key she extended, then replaced the pitiful vinyl purse in her locker. The sight of her clothing was equally depressing. She had nothing. His dark eyes closed. It hurt to see her so destitute when she was entitled to his own wealth. Diego knew that Melissa's father had gone bankrupt just before his death.

The apartment she shared with Matthew was as dismal as the clothing he'd seen in her locker at the hospital. The landlady had eyed him with suspicion and curiosity until he'd produced his checkbook and asked how much his *wife* owed her. That had shaken the woman considerably, and there had been no more questions or snide remarks from her.

Diego searched through the apartment until he found a small vinyl bag, which he packed with enough clothing to get Matthew through the next few days. But he knew already that he was going to have to do some shopping. The child's few things looked as if they'd been obtained at rummage sales. Probably they had, he thought bitterly, because Melissa had so little. His fault. Even that was his fault.

He looked in another chest of drawers for more gowns and underthings for Melissa, and stopped as he lifted a gown and found a small photograph tucked there. He took it out carefully. It was one that Melissa had taken of him years before. He'd been astride one of his stallions, wearing a panama hat and dark trousers with a white shirt unbuttoned over his bronzed chest with its faint feathering of black hair. He'd been smiling at her as he'd leaned over the neck of the horse to stroke its waving mane. On the back of it was written: Diego, Near Atitlán. There was no date, but the photo was worn and wrinkled, as if she'd carried it with her for a long time. And he remembered to the day when she'd taken it—the day before they'd taken refuge in the Mayan ruins.

He slowly put it back under the gown and found something else. A small book in which were tucked

ENAMORED

flowers and bits of paper and a thin silver bookmark. He recognized some of the mementos. The flowers he'd given her from time to time or picked for her when they'd walked across the fields together. The bits of paper were from things he'd scribbled for her, Spanish words that she'd been trying to master. The bookmark was one he'd given her for her eighteenth birthday. He frowned. Why should she have kept them all these years?

He put them back, folded the gown gently over them and left the drawer as he'd found it, forcing himself not to consider the implications of those revealing mementos. After all, she might have kept them to remind her more of his cruelty than of any feeling she had had for him.

He went shopping the next morning. He knew Melissa's size, but he'd had to call Mrs. Grady to ask for Matthew's. It disturbed him to buy clothes for another man's child, but he found himself in the toy department afterward. Before he could talk himself out of it he'd filled a bag with playthings for the child, chiding himself mentally for doing something so ridiculous.

But Matthew's face when he put the packages on the sofa in Mrs. Grady's apartment was a revelation. Diego smiled helplessly at the child's unbridled delight as he took out building blocks and electronic games and a small remote-controlled robot.

"He's had so little, poor thing," Mrs. Grady sighed, smiling as she watched the boy go feverishly from one toy to another, finally settling down with a small computerized teddy bear that talked. "Not

Melly's fault, of course. Money was tight. But it's nice to see him with a few new things.''

"*Sí.*" Diego watched the little boy and felt a sudden icy blast of regret for the child he'd caused Melissa to lose. He remembered with painful clarity what he'd said to her the night she'd run out into the rain and pitched down the steps in the wet darkness. *Dios,* would he never forget? He turned away. "I must go. Melissa needed some new gowns. I am taking them to the hospital for her."

"How is she?"

"Much better, *gracias*. The doctor says I may take her home in a few more days." He looked down at the heavyset woman. "Matthew will be going with us to Chicago. I know he will miss you, and Melissa and I are grateful for the care you have taken of him."

"It was my pleasure," she assured him.

"Thank you for my toys, mister," Matthew said, suddenly underfoot. His big dark eyes were happy. He lifted his arms to Diego to be picked up; he was used to easy affection from the adults around him. But the tall man went rigid and looked unapproachable. Matthew stepped back, the happiness in his eyes fading to wary uncertainty. He shifted and ran back to his toys without trying again.

Diego hated the emotions sifting through his pride, the strongest of which was self-contempt. How could he treat a child so coldly—it wasn't Matthew's fault, after all. But years of conditioning had made it impossible for him to bend. He turned to the door, avoiding Mrs. Grady's disapproving glance, made his goodbyes and left quickly.

Back at the hospital, while Diego went to get himself a cup of coffee, Melissa had a nurse help her into one of the three pastel gowns Diego had brought. She was delighted with the pink one. It had a low bodice and plenty of lace, and she thought how happy it would have made her years ago to have Diego buy her anything. But he'd done this out of pity, she knew, not out of love.

She thanked him when he came back. "You shouldn't have spent so much..." She faltered, because she knew the gowns were silk, not a cheap fabric.

He only shrugged. "You will be wearing gowns for a time," he said, as if that explained his generous impulse. He sat down in the armchair in the corner with a Styrofoam cup of coffee, which he proceeded to sip. "I bought a few things for your son," he added reluctantly. He crossed his long legs. "And a toy or so." He caught the look in her eyes. "He went from one to the other like a bee in search of the best nectar," he mused with stiff amusement.

Melissa almost cried. She'd wanted to give the child so many things, but there hadn't been any money for luxuries.

"Thank you for doing that for him," Melissa said quietly. "I didn't expect that you'd do anything for him under the circumstances, much less buy him expensive toys." Her eyes fell from his cold gaze. "I haven't been able to give him very much. There's never been any money for toys."

She was propped up in bed now, and her hair had been washed. It was a pale blonde, curling softly toward her face, onto her flushed cheeks. She was lovely, he thought, watching her. There was a new maturity about her, and the curves he remembered were much more womanly now. His eyes dropped to the low bodice of the new gown he'd bought her, and they narrowed on the visible swell of her pink breasts.

She colored more and started to pull up the sheet, but his lean, dark hand prevented her.

"There is no need for that, Melissa," he said quietly. "You certainly do not expect me to make suggestive remarks to you under the circumstances?"

She shifted. "No. Of course not." She sighed. "I didn't expect you to buy me new gowns," she said, hoping to divert him. She didn't like the way it affected her when he looked at her that way. "Couldn't you find mine?" And as she asked the question, she remembered suddenly and with anguish what she'd hidden under those gowns. Had he seen— He turned away so that she couldn't see his expression. "One glance in the drawer was enough to convince me that they were unsuitable, without disturbing them," he said with practiced carelessness. "Do you not like the new ones?"

"They're very nice," she said inadequately. Silk, when she could barely afford cotton. Of course she liked them, but why had he been so extravagant?

"Has it been like this since you came to America?" he asked, glancing at her. "Have you been so hard-pressed for money?"

She didn't like the question. She stared at her folded hands. "Money isn't everything," she said.

"The lack of it can be," he replied. He straightened, his eyes narrow and thoughtful. "The child's father—could he not help you financially?"

She gritted her teeth. This was going to be intolerable. She lifted her cold gaze to his. "No, he couldn't be bothered," she said tersely. "And you needn't look so self-righteous and accusing, Diego. I don't believe for a minute that you've spent the last five years without a woman."

He didn't answer her. His expression was distant, impassive. "Has Matthew seen his father?" he persisted.

She didn't answer him. She didn't dare. "I realize that you must resent Matthew, but I do hope you don't intend taking out your grievances on him," she said.

He glared at her. "As if I could treat a child so."

"I was little more than a child," she reminded him. "You and your venomous family had no qualms about treating me in just such a way."

"Yes," he admitted, as graciously as he could. He put his hands in his pockets and studied her. "My grandmother very nearly had a breakdown when you vanished. She told me then how you had been treated. It was something of a shock. I had not considered that she might feel justified in taking her vengeance out on you. I should have realized how she'd react, but I was feeling trapped and not too fond of you when I left the Casa de Luz."

Before Melissa could respond to his unexpected confession, the door opened and a nurse's aide came in with a dinner tray. She smiled at Diego and put a tray in front of Melissa. Oh, well, Melissa thought as she was propped up and her food containers were opened for her, she could argue with him later. He didn't seem inclined to leave her anytime soon.

"You eat so little," he remarked when she only picked at her food.

She glanced at him. He sat gracefully in an upholstered armchair beside the window, his long legs crossed. He looked very Latin like that, and as immaculate as ever. She had to drag her eyes away before her expression told him how attractive she still found him.

"I'm not very hungry."

"Could you not eat a thick steak smothered in mushrooms and onions, *chiquita*?" he murmured, his black eyes twinkling gently for the first time since she'd opened her eyes and seen him in her room. "And fried potatoes and thick bread?"

"Stop," she groaned.

He smiled. "As I thought, it is the food that does not appeal. When you are released I will see to it that you have proper meals."

"I have a job," she began.

"Which you cannot do until you are completely well again," he reminded her. "I will speak to your employer."

She sighed. "It won't help. They can't afford to hold the position open for six weeks."

"Is there someone who can replace you?"

She thought of her young, eager assistant. "Oh, yes."

"Then there should be no problem."

She glared at him over the last sip of milk. "I

won't let you take me over," she said. "I'm grateful for your help, but I want no part of marriage ever again."

"I want it no more than you do, Melissa," he said carelessly, with forced indifference. "But for the time being, neither of us has any choice. As for divorce—" he shrugged "—that is not possible. But perhaps a separation or some other arrangement can be made when you are well. Naturally I will provide for you and the child."

"You will like hell," she said, shocking him not only with her unfamiliar language but with the very adult and formidable anger in her gray eyes. "This isn't Guatemala. In America women have equal rights with men. We aren't property, and I'm perfectly capable of providing for Matthew and myself."

His dark eyebrows lifted. "Indeed?" he asked lightly. "And this is why I found you living in abject poverty with a child who wears secondhand clothing and had not one new toy in his possession?"

She wanted to climb out of bed and hit him over the head with her tray. Her eyes told him so. "I won't live with you."

He shrugged. "Then what will you do, *niña*?" he asked.

She thought about that for a minute and fought back tears of helpless rage. She lay back on the pillows with a heavy sigh. "I don't know," she said honestly.

"It will only be a temporary arrangement," he reminded her. "Just until you are well again. You might like Chicago," he added. "There is a lake and a beach, and many things for a small boy to explore."

She made a face. "Matt and I will catch pneumonia and die if we have to spend a winter there," she said shortly. "Neither of us has ever been out of southern Arizona in the past f—" she corrected herself quickly "—three years."

He didn't notice the slip. He was studying her slender body under the sheets. She thought that he'd spent the past five years womanizing. Little did she know that the memory of her had destroyed any transient desire he might have felt for any other woman. Even now his dreams were filled with her, obsessed with her. So much love in Melissa, but he'd managed to kill it all. Once, he'd been sure she wanted to love him, but now he couldn't really blame her for her reticence. And his own feelings had been in turmoil ever since he'd learned about the child.

"It is spring," he murmured. "By winter, much could happen."

"I won't live in Guatemala, Diego," she repeated. "And not with your grandmother and sister under any circumstances."

He ran a restless hand through his hair. "My grandmother lives in Barbados with her sister," he said. "She still grieves for the great-grandchild she might have had if not for our intolerable coldness to you. My sister is married and lives in Mexico City."

"Did they know you were coming here?" she asked casually, though she didn't feel casual about it. The *señora* had been cruel, and so, despite her reluctance to side with her grandmother, had Juana.

"I telephoned them both last night. They wish you well. Perhaps one day there may be the opportunity for them to ask your pardon for the treatment you received."

"Juana tried to be kind," she said. She traced a thread on the sheet. "Your grandmother did not. I suppose I can understand how she felt, but it didn't make it any easier for me to stay there."

"And you blame me for leaving you at her mercy, ¿Es verdad?"

"Yes, as a matter of fact, I do," she replied, looking up. "You never allowed me to explain. You automatically convicted me on circumstantial evidence and set out to make me pay for what you thought I did. And I paid," she added icily. "I paid in ways I won't even tell you."

"But you had your revenge, did you not?" he returned with an equally cold laugh. "You took a lover and had his child."

She forced a smile to her pale lips. "You're so good at getting at the truth, Diego," she said mildly. "I'm in awe of your ability to read minds."

"A pity I had no such ability when you left the hospital without even being discharged and vanished," he replied. "There was a military coup the same day you left, and there were several deaths."

As he spoke she saw the flash of emotion in his black eyes. She hadn't noticed before how haunted he looked. There was a deep, dark coldness about him, and there were new lines in his lean face. He looked his age for once, and the old lazy indifference she remembered seemed gone forever. This remote, polite man was nothing like the man she'd known in Guatemala. He'd changed drastically.

Then what he had said began to penetrate her tired mind. She frowned. ''Several deaths?'' she asked suddenly.

He laughed bitterly. ''During the time the coup was accomplished there were a few isolated fatalities, and one of the bodies could not be identified.'' His eyes went cold at the memory. ''It was a young girl with blond hair.''

''You thought it was me?'' she exclaimed.

He took a slow, deep breath. It was a minute before he could answer her. ''Yes, I thought…it was you.''

Six

Diego's quiet confirmation took Melissa's breath away. She knew about the coup, of course. It was impossible not to know. But at the time her only thought had been of escape. She hadn't considered that depriving Diego of knowledge of her whereabouts might lead to the supposition that she was dead. She'd only been concerned about hiding her pregnancy from him.

"I find it very hard to believe you were concerned."

"Concerned!" He turned around, and the look in his black eyes was the old one she remembered from her teens, the one that could make even the meanest of his men back away. His eyes were like black steel in his hard face. "Shall I tell you what that young woman looked like, *niña*?"

She couldn't meet his eyes. "I can imagine how she looked," she said. "But you'll never make me believe it mattered to you. I expect you were more angry than relieved to discover that it wasn't me. How did you discover it?" she added.

"Your father told me," he said, moving restlessly to the window. "By that time you had successfully made it into the United States, and all my contacts were unable to track you down."

She wanted to ask a lot more questions, but this wasn't the time. She had other concerns. The main one was how she was going to manage living with him until she was fully recovered. And more importantly, how she was going to protect Matthew from him.

"I don't want to go with you, Diego," she said honestly. "I will, because I've no other choice. But you needn't expect me to worship the ground you walk on the way I used to. I've stopped dreaming in the past five years."

"And I have barely begun," he replied, his voice deep and soft. His gaze went over her slowly. "Perhaps it is as well that we meet again like this. Now you are old enough to deal with the man and not the illusion." He got to his feet with the easy grace Melissa remembered from the past. "I will return later. I must check on Matthew."

She turned under the sheet to keep her restless hands busy. "Tell him I love him and miss him very much, and that I'll be home soon, will you?"

"Of course." He hesitated, feeling awkward. "The

child misses you, too." He smiled faintly. "He said if he could be allowed to visit you he would kiss the hurts better."

Tears sprang to her eyes and suddenly she felt terribly alone. She dabbed at the tears with the sheet, but Diego drew out a spotless white handkerchief and wiped them away. The handkerchief smelled of the cologne he favored and brought back vivid memories of him. Her eyes lifted, and she gazed at him. For one long instant, time rolled away and she was a girl with the man she loved more than her own life.

"*Enamorada,*" he breathed huskily, his black eyes unblinking, smoldering. "If you knew how empty the years have been—"

The sudden opening of the door was like a gunshot. Melissa glanced that way as a smiling nurse's aide came into the room to check her vital signs. Diego smiled at the woman, his expression only slightly strained, and left with a brief comment about the time. Melissa clutched his handkerchief tightly in her hand, wanting nothing more than the luxury of tears. She was in pain and helpless, and she was much too vulnerable with Diego. She didn't dare let him see how she felt or make one slip that would give away Matthew's parentage. She had to bank down her hidden desire and hide it from him—now more than ever.

She was grateful Diego had left, because the look in his black eyes when he'd held that handkerchief to her eyes had brought back the most painful kind of memories. He still wanted her, if that look was anything to go by, even though he didn't love or trust her. Perhaps that might have been enough for her, but it wouldn't be for Matthew. Matthew deserved a father, not a reluctant guardian. It would be hardest for him, because of Diego's resentment. But telling Diego the truth could cost her the child, and at a time when she wasn't capable of fighting for him. She'd have to bide her time. Meanwhile, at least she could be temporarily free of financial terrors. And that was something.

Several days later, Melissa was released from the hospital and Diego took her to the hotel where he was staying. He had chartered a plane to take Melissa to Chicago the next day, a luxury she was reluctantly grateful for.

She pleaded to let her come along when he went to Mrs. Grady's to pick up Matthew, but he wouldn't allow it. She was too weak, he insisted. So he went to get the boy and Melissa lay smoldering quietly in one of the big double beds in the exquisite hotel suite, uncomfortable and angry.

It only took a few minutes. The door was unlocked and Matthew ran toward her like a little tornado, crying and laughing as he threw himself onto her chest and held her, mumbling and muttering through his tears.

"Oh, my baby," she cooed, smiling as she smoothed his brown hair and sighed over him. It was difficult to reach out because her stitches still pulled, but she didn't complain. She had her baby back.

Diego, watching them, glared at the sight of her

blond head bent over that dark one. He was jealous of the boy, and more especially of the boy's father. He hated the very thought of Melissa's body in another man's arms, another man's bed. He hated the thought of the child she'd borne her lover.

Melissa laughed as Matt lifted his electronic bear and made it talk for her.

"Isn't he nice?" Matt asked, all eyes. "My… your…Mr. Man bought him for me."

"Diego," she prompted.

"Diego," Matthew parroted. He glanced at the tall man who'd been so quiet and distant all the way to the hotel. Matt wasn't sure if he liked Diego or not, but he was certain that the tall man didn't like him. It was going to be very hard living with a man who made him feel so unwelcome.

Melissa touched the pale little cheek. "You need sunshine, my son," she murmured. "You've spent too much time indoors."

Diego put down the cases and lit a small cheroot, pausing to open the curtains before dropping into an easy chair to smoke it at the table beside the window. "I have engaged a sitter for Matthew, since I will be away from the apartment a good deal when we get to Chicago," he told Melissa. "Perhaps the sitter will take him to the park or the beach."

Melissa felt the hair on the back of her neck bristle. Here she'd been the very model of a protective, caring mother, making sure Matt was always supervised, and now Diego came along and thought he could shift responsibility onto a total stranger about whom she knew nothing.

She clasped Matt's waist tightly. "No," she said firmly. "If he goes anywhere, it will be with me."

Diego's eyebrows lifted. She was overly protective of the child, that was obvious. Mrs. Grady had intimated something of the sort; now he could see that the older woman had been right. Something would have to be done about that, he decided. It wasn't healthy for a mother to be so sheltering. A boy who clung to his mother's apron could hardly grow into a strong man.

He crossed his legs and smoked his cheroot while his narrowed eyes surveyed woman and child. "Will you condemn him to four walls and your own company?"

She sat up, wincing as she piled pillows behind her. "I'll be able to get up and around in no time," she protested.

"Oh, yes," he agreed blandly, watching her struggle. "Already you can sit up by yourself."

She gave him her best glare. "I can walk, too."

"Not without falling over," he murmured, watching the cheroot with a faint smile as he recalled her last attempt to use her damaged leg.

"I'll hold you up, Mama," Matt assured her. "I'm very strong."

"Yes, I know you are, my darling," she said, her voice soft and loving. The man sitting in the chair felt an explosive anger that she cared so much for another man's child.

''What would you like for dinner?'' he asked suddenly, getting up. ''I can get room service to bring a tray.''

''Steak and a salad for me, please,'' she said.

''Matt wants a fish.'' The little boy looked up, nervous and unsure, clinging to his mother's arm.

''They may not have fish, Matt,'' Melissa began.

''They have it,'' Diego said stiffly. ''I had fish last night.''

''Coffee for me, and milk for Matt,'' she said, turning away from the coldness of Diego's face as he looked at her son.

He nodded, a bare inclination of his head, and went to telephone.

''Mr. Man doesn't like Matt,'' Matthew said with a sad little sigh. ''Doesn't he have any children?''

Melissa wanted to cry, but she knew that wouldn't solve anything. She only hoped Diego didn't hear the little boy as she shushed him and shook her head.

Diego didn't turn or flinch, but he heard, all right. It made the situation all the more difficult. He hadn't realized how perceptive children were.

Dinner was served from a pushcart by a white-coated waiter, and Matthew took his to the far side of the table, as if he wanted a buffer between himself and the tall man who didn't like him. Diego sat beside Melissa, and she tried not to smell the exotic cologne he wore or notice the strength of his powerful, slender body next to hers. He was the handsomest man she'd ever seen, and as he cut his steak she had to fight not to slide her fingers over the dark, lean hand holding the knife.

Diego finished first and went to the lobby on the pretext of getting Melissa something to read. In fact he wanted to get away from the boy's sad little face, with its big, haunting black eyes. He hated his own reactions because they were hurting that innocent little child who, under different circumstances, might have been his own.

He went to the lounge and had a whiskey sour, ignoring the blatant overtures of a slinky blonde who obviously found him more than attractive. He finished his drink and his cheroot and went back upstairs, taking a magazine for Melissa and a coloring book and crayons for Matt.

Melissa had Matt curled up beside her on the couch, and they both tensed the minute he walked in. His chin lifted.

"I brought a coloring book for the boy," he said hesitantly.

Matt didn't move. He looked up, waiting, without any expression on his face.

Diego took the book and the crayons and offered them to him, but still Matt didn't make a move.

"Don't you want the book, Matt?" Melissa asked softly.

"No. He doesn't like Matt," Matt said simply, lowering his eyes.

Diego frowned, torn between pain and his desire for vengeance. The child touched him in ways he had never dreamed of. He saw himself in the little boy, alone and frightened and sad. His own childhood had been an unhappy one, because his father had never truly loved his mother. His mother had known it, and suffered for it. She had died young, and his father had become even more withdrawn. Then, when his father had met the lovely Sheila, the older man's attitude had changed for the better. But the change had been short-lived—and that loss of hope Diego owed to Melissa's family, because his father had died loving Sheila Sterling, loving her with a hopeless passion that he was never able to indulge. The loss had warped him and Diego had seen what loving a woman could do to a man, and he had learned from it. Allowing a woman close enough to love was all too dangerous.

But the boy…it was hardly his fault. How could he blame Matt for Melissa's failings?

He put the coloring book and the crayons gently on the table by the sofa and handed Melissa the women's magazine he'd bought for her. Then he went back to his chair and sat smoking his cheroot, glancing through a sheaf of papers in a file.

"I'm going to read, Matt," Melissa said gently, nudging him to stand up. "You might as well try out your crayons. Do you remember how to color?"

Matt glanced at the man, who was oblivious to them both, and then at the crayons and coloring book. "It's all right?" he asked his mother worriedly.

"It's all right," she assured him.

He sighed and got down on the floor, sprawling

with crayons everywhere, and began to color one of his favorite cartoon characters.

Diego looked up then and smiled faintly. Melissa, watching him, was surprised by his patience. She'd forgotten how gentle he could be. But then it had been a long time since she and Diego had been friends.

They had an early night. Melissa almost spoke when Diego insisted that Matt pick up his crayons and put them away neatly. But she didn't take the child's side, because she knew Diego was right. Often she was less firm with Matt than she should be because she was usually so tired from her job.

She helped Matt into his pajamas and then looked quickly at Diego, because there were two double beds. She didn't want to be close to her estranged husband, but she didn't know how to say it in front of Matt.

Diego stole her thunder neatly by suggesting that the boy bunk down with her. It was only for the one night, because there were four bedrooms in the Chicago apartment. Matt would have his own room. Yes, Melissa thought, and that's when the trouble would really start, because she and Matt had been forced to share a room. She could only afford a tiny efficiency apartment with a sofa that folded out to make a bed. Matt wasn't used to being alone at night, and she wondered how they were going to cope.

But she didn't want to borrow trouble. She was tired and nervous and apprehensive, and there was worse to come. She closed her eyes and went to sleep. And she didn't dream.

The next morning, they left for Chicago. Despite the comfort of the chartered Lear jet, Melissa was still sore and uncomfortable. She had her medicine, and the attending physician at the hospital had referred her to a doctor in Chicago in case she had any complications. If only she could sit back and enjoy the flight the way Matthew was, she thought, watching his animated young face as he peered out the window and asked a hundred questions about airplanes and Chicago. Diego unbent enough to answer a few of them, although he did it with faint reluctance. But Matt seemed determined now to win him over, and Diego wasn't all that distant this morning.

Back in the old days in Guatemala, Melissa had never thought about the kind of father Diego would make. In her world of daydreams, romance had been her only concern, not the day-to-day life that a man and a woman had to concern themselves with after the wildness of infatuation wore off. Now, watching her son with his father, she realized that Diego really liked children. He was patient with Matthew, treating each new question as if it were of the utmost importance. He hadn't completely gotten over the shock of the child, she knew, and there was some reserve in him when he was with this boy he thought was another man's son. But he was polite to the child, and once or twice he actually seemed amused by Matt's excitement.

He was the soul of courtesy, but Melissa couldn't help thinking he'd much rather be traveling alone. Nevertheless, he carried her off the plane and to a waiting limousine for the trip to the Lincoln Park apartment he maintained, and she had to grind her teeth to keep from reaching up and kissing his hard, very masculine mouth as he held her. She hoped he didn't see how powerfully his nearness affected her. She was still vulnerable, even after all the years apart, but she didn't dare let him see it. She couldn't let him destroy her pride again as he had once before.

The apartment was a penthouse that overlooked the park and the shoreline, with the city skyline like a gray silhouette on the rainy horizon. Melissa was put to bed at once in one of the guest bedrooms and told to rest while Matthew explored the apartment and Diego introduced Melissa to Mrs. Albright, who was to do the baby-sitting as well as the cooking and cleaning. Apollo had recommended the pleasant, heavyset woman, and she'd been taking care of the apartment for Diego for over a year now.

Mrs. Albright was middle-aged and graying, with a sweet face and a personality to match. She took Melissa coffee and cake in bed and set about making her as comfortable as possible, insisting that she stay in bed to recuperate from the long flight. Then she took Matt off to the kitchen to spoil him with tiny homemade cream cakes and milk while she listened to his happy chatter about the flight from Tucson.

Once the boy and Melissa were settled, Diego picked up the phone and punched in a number.

Melissa heard him, but she couldn't make out many of the words. It sounded as though he were speaking to Apollo, and in fact he was, because Apollo showed up at the apartment an hour later with a slender, petite black woman.

Diego introduced the tall, muscular black man in the gray suit. "This is Apollo Blain. Perhaps you remember him." Apollo smiled and nodded, and Melissa smiled back. "And this is Joyce Latham, Apollo's secretary."

"Temporarily," Apollo said with a curt nod in Joyce's direction.

"That's right, temporarily," Joyce said in a lilting West Indian accent, glaring up at the tall man. "Just until the very second I can find anybody brave enough to take my place."

Apollo glowered down at her. "Amen, sister," he bit off. "And with any luck I'll get somebody who can remember a damned telephone number long enough to dial it and who can file my clients alphabetically so I can find the files!"

"And maybe I'll get a boss who can read!" Joyce shot back.

"Enough!" Diego laughed, getting between them. "Melissa has survived one disaster. She doesn't need to be thrust into a new one, *por favor*."

Apollo grinned sheepishly. "Sorry. I got carried away." He shot a speaking glance at Joyce.

"Me, too," she muttered, shifting so that she was a little away from him. Her features weren't pretty, but her eyes were lovely, as deep and black as a bottomless pool, and her coffee-with-cream complexion was blemishless. She had a nice figure, probably, but the floppy uninspired blue dress she was wearing hid that very well.

"It's nice to meet you," Melissa told the woman, smiling. "I remember Apollo from years ago, of course. How long have you worked for him?"

"Two weeks too long," Joyce muttered.

"That's right, two weeks and one day too long," Apollo added. "Dutch and J.D. are coming over later, and Shirt says he and his missus are going to fly up to see you next week. It'll be like a reunion."

"I remember our last reunion," Diego said, smiling faintly. "We were evicted from the suite we occupied at three in the morning."

"And one of us was arrested," Apollo said smugly.

"That so?" Joyce asked him. "How long did they keep you in jail?"

He glared. "Not me. Diego."

"Diego?" Melissa stared at him in disbelief. The cool, careless man she knew wasn't hotheaded enough to land himself in jail. But perhaps she didn't really know him at all.

"He took exception to some remarks about his Latin heritage," Apollo explained with a glance at Diego, whose expression gave nothing away. "The gentleman making the remarks was very big and very mean, and to make a long story short, Diego assisted the gentleman into the hotel swimming pool through a plate-glass window."

"It was a long time ago." Diego turned as Matthew came running into the room.

"You have to come see my drawing, Mama," the

boy said urgently, tugging at his mother's hand. "I drew a puppy dog and a bee! Come look!"

"*Momento*, Matthew," Diego said firmly, holding the boy still. He introduced the visitors, who smiled down warmly at the child. "You can show your drawings to Mama in a moment, when our visitors have gone, all right, little one?"

"All right." Matthew sighed. He smiled at his mama and went shyly past the visitors and back to his crayons.

Apollo said, "He's a mirror image of you..." The last word trailed away under the black fury of Diego's eyes. He cleared his throat. "Well, we'd better get back to work. We'll be over with the others tonight. But we won't stay long. We don't want to wear out the missus, and don't lay on food. Just drinks. Okay?"

"And we'll come in separate cars next time," Joyce grumbled, darting a glance at the black man. "His idea of city driving is to aim the car and close his eyes."

"I could drive if you could stop putting your hands over your eyes and making those noises," he shot back.

"I was trying to say my prayers!"

"See you later," Apollo told Melissa and Diego. He took Joyce by the arm and half led, half dragged her out of the apartment.

"Don't they make a sweet couple?" Melissa murmured dryly when they'd gone. "I wonder if they both carry life insurance...?"

Diego smiled faintly at the mischief in her eyes. "An interesting observation, Señora Laremos. Now, if there is nothing I can do for you, you can praise your son's art while I get back to work."

Her pale gray eyes searched his face, looking for revelations, but there were none in that stony countenance. "It offended you that Apollo mentioned a resemblance."

"The boy's father obviously had some Ladino blood," he countered without expression. He put his hands in his pockets, and his black eyes narrowed. "You will not divulge your lover's identity, even now?"

"Why should it matter to you?" she asked. "I had the impression when I left Guatemala that it would be too soon if you never saw me again."

"I tried to talk to you at the time. You would not listen, so I assumed that my feelings would have no effect on you."

"Do you have any feelings?" she asked suddenly. "My father said once that if you did it would take dynamite to get to them."

He stood watching her, his slightly wavy black hair thick and clean where it shone in the light, his eyes watchful. "Considering the line of work I was in, Melissa, is that so surprising? I could not afford the luxury of giving in to my emotions. It has been both a protection and a curse in later years. Perhaps if I had not been so reticent with you the past five years would not have been wasted."

Her pulse jumped, but she kept her expression calm

so he wouldn't see how his words affected her. "I understood," she replied. "Even though I was young, I wasn't stupid."

"Had you no idea what would happen when you led me into that sweet trap, Melissa?" he asked with a bitter laugh.

"It wasn't a trap," she said doggedly. "I'd written a lot of silly love poems and scribbled some brazen note to you that I meant to destroy. I'd never have had the nerve to send it to you." She colored faintly at the memory. "I tried to tell you, and my father, that it was a mistake, but neither of you would listen." Her fingers toyed with the hem of her pink blouse. "I loved you," she said under her breath. Her eyes were closed, and she missed the expression that washed over his face. "I loved you more than my own life, and Dad was on the verge of sending me away to college. I knew that I'd never see you again. Every second I had with you was precious, and that's why I gave in. It wasn't planned, and it wasn't meant to be a trap." She laughed coldly. "The irony of it all is that I was stupid enough to believe that you might come to love me if we lived together. But you left me with your family and went away, and when you came back and I tried so desperately to catch your attention—" She couldn't go on. The memory of his contemptuous rejection was too vivid. She averted her eyes. "I knew then that I'd been living in a daydream. I had what I wanted, but through force, not through choice. Leaving was the first intelligent decision I made."

He felt as if she'd hit him with a rock. "Are you telling me that you didn't have marriage in mind?"

"Of course I had marriage in mind, but I never meant you to be forced into it!" she burst out, tears threatening in her eyes. "I loved you. I was twenty and there'd never been another man, and you were my world, Diego!"

His tall, elegant body tautened. He'd never let himself think about it, about what had motivated her. Perhaps, deep inside, he'd known all along how she felt but hadn't been able to face it. He drew a thin cheroot from his pocket and lit it absently. "I went to see your father after he confirmed that you were still alive. He told me nothing, except that you despised me and that you never wanted to see me again." He lifted his gaze and stared at her. "I was determined to hear that for myself, of course, so I kept searching. But to no avail."

"I used my maiden name when I applied for United States citizenship," she explained, "and I lived in big cities. After I was settled, I contacted my father and begged him not to let you know where I was. Later, when the attorney called and told me about my father's death, I grieved. But I didn't have enough money to go to the funeral. Even then, I pleaded with the lawyer not to reveal my whereabouts. I didn't really think you'd come looking for me when you knew I'd—" she forced out the lie "—lost the baby, but I had to be sure."

"You were my responsibility," he said stiffly. "You still are. Our religion does not permit divorce."

"My memory doesn't permit reconciliation," she said shortly. "I'll stay here until I'm able to work again, but that's all. I'm responsible for myself and my son. You have no place in my life, or in my heart, anymore."

He fought back the surge of misery her statement engendered. "And Matthew?"

She pushed back her hair. "Matthew doesn't concern you. He thinks you hate him, and he's probably right. The sooner I get him away from here the better."

He turned gracefully, staring hard at her. "Did you expect that I could accept him so easily? He is the very proof that your emotions were not involved when we were together. If you had loved me, Melissa, there could never have been another man. Never!"

And that was the crux of the entire problem, she thought. He didn't realize that he was stating a fact. If he'd trusted her, he'd have known that she loved him too much to take a lover. But he didn't trust her. He didn't know her. He'd never made the effort to know her in any way except the physical.

She lay back on the pillows, exhausted. "I can't fight, Diego. I'm too tired."

He nodded. "I know. You need rest. We can talk when you are more fit."

"I hope you didn't expect me to fall in line like the little slave I used to be around you," she said, lifting cold eyes to his.

"I like very much the way you are now, *niña*," he said slowly, his accent even more pronounced than usual. His dark eyes smoldered as he drew them over her body. "A woman with fire in her veins is a more interesting proposition than a worshipful child."

"You won't start any fires with me, *señor*," she said haughtily.

"*¿Es verdad?*" He moved slowly to the bed and, leaning one long arm across her, stared into her eyes from scant inches away. "Be careful before you sling out challenges, my own," he said in the deep, soft voice she remembered so well whispering Spanish love words in the silence of the Mayan ruins. "I might take you up on them." He bent closer, and she could almost feel the hard warmth of his mouth against her parted lips, faintly smoky, teasing her mouth with the promise of the kisses she'd once starved for.

She made a sound deep in her throat, a tormented little sob, and turned her face against the pillow, closing her eyes tight. "No," she whispered. "Oh, don't!"

She felt his breath against her lips. Then, abruptly, he pushed away, shaking the bed and stood up. He turned away to light a cheroot. "There is no need for such virginal terror," he said stiffly as he began to smoke it. "Your virtue is safe with me. I meant only to tease. I lost my taste for you the day I learned just how thirsty you were for vengeance."

She was grateful for his anger. It had spared her the humiliation of begging for his kisses. Because she wasn't looking at his face, she didn't realize that her rejection had bruised his ego and convinced him that she no longer wanted his kisses.

He got control over his scattered emotions. ''The man who replaced me in your affections—Matthew's father—where is he now, Melissa?''

Her eyes closed. She prayed for deliverance, and it came in the form of Matthew, who came running in to see why Mama hadn't come to look at his drawings. Melissa got up very slowly and allowed Matt to lead her into his bedroom, her steps hesitant and without confidence. She didn't look at Diego.

That night, Mrs. Albright bathed Matthew and put him to bed so that Diego and Melissa would be free to greet their guests. Melissa's leg still made walking difficult, as did the incision where her ovary had been removed. She managed to bathe and dress alone, but she was breathless when Diego came to carry her into the living room.

He stopped in the doorway, fascinated by the picture she made in the pale blue silky dress that emphasized her wavy blond hair, gray eyes and creamy complexion. She'd lost weight, but she still had such a lovely figure that even her slenderness didn't detract from it.

Diego was wearing a dark suit, and his white shirt emphasized his very Latin complexion and his black hair and eyes. It was so sweet just to look at him, to be with him. Melissa hadn't realized how empty the years without him had been, but now the impact of his company was fierce.

She had barely a minute to savor it before the doorbell rang and the guests came in. Apollo and Joyce were together, if reluctantly, and Melissa mused that since the black man hated his secretary so much it was odd that he'd bring her along on a social call. Behind them was a slender blond man with the masculine perfection of a movie star and a mountain of a man with dark, wavy hair.

Diego introduced the blond man. "Eric 'Dutch' van Meer. And this—" he smiled toward the big man "—is Archer, better known as J.D. Brettman. Gentlemen, my wife, Melissa."

They smiled and said all the right things, but Melissa could tell that they were surprised that Diego had never mentioned her. They apologized for not bringing their wives, Danielle and Gabby, but their children had given each other a virus and they were at home nursing them. Melissa would be introduced to them at a later time.

Melissa smiled back. "I'll look forward to that," she said politely. These men made her oddly nervous, because she didn't know them as she knew Apollo. They formed into a group and began talking about work, and Melissa felt very isolated from her husband as he spoke with his old comrades. She could see the real affection he felt for them. What a pity that he had none to give her. But what should she have expected under the circumstances? Diego was responsible for her, as he'd said. He was only her caretaker until she was well again, and she'd better remember that. There might be the occasional flare-up of the old attraction, but she couldn't allow herself to dream of a reconciliation. It was dangerous to dream—dreams could become a painful reality.

Joyce had eased away from the others to sit beside Melissa on the huge corner sofa. "I feel as out of place as a green bean in a gourmet ice-cream shop," she mumbled.

Melissa laughed in spite of herself. "So do I, so let's stick together," she whispered.

Joyce straightened the skirt of her beige dress. Her long hair was a little unkempt, and she slumped. Melissa thought what a shame it was that the woman didn't take care with her appearance. With a little work, she could be a knockout.

"How did you wind up working for Apollo?" Melissa asked.

The other woman smiled ruefully. "I was new to the city—I moved here from Miami—and I signed up with a temporary agency." She glanced at Apollo with more warmth than she seemed to realize. "They sent me to him and he tried to send me right back, but the agency was shorthanded, so he was stuck with me."

"He doesn't seem to mind too much," Melissa murmured dryly. "After all, most bosses don't take their secretaries along on social engagements."

Joyce sighed. "Oh, that. He thought you might feel uncomfortable around all these men. Since the wives couldn't come, here I am." She grinned. "I'm kind of glad that I was invited, you know. I'm not exactly flooded with social invitations."

"I know what you mean," Melissa said, smiling. "Thanks for coming."

As Apollo had promised, they didn't stay long. But as the men said their goodbyes and left, J.D. Brettman shot an openly curious glance in Melissa's direction.

Later, when the guests had gone, Melissa asked Diego about it as he removed his jacket and tie and loosened the top buttons of his shirt.

"Why was Mr. Brettman so curious about me?" she asked gently.

He poured himself a brandy, offered her one and was refused, and dropped gracefully into the armchair across from her. "He knew there was a woman somewhere in my life," he said simply. "There was a rumor to the effect that I had hurt one very badly." He shrugged. "Servants talk, you see. It was known that you fell and were rushed to the hospital." As he lifted the brandy to his lips, his eyes had a sad, faraway look. "I imagine it was said that I pushed you."

"But you didn't!"

His dark eyes caught hers. "Did I not?" His chin lifted, and he looked very Latin, very attractive. "It was because of me that you ran into the night. I was responsible."

She lowered her gaze. "I'm sorry that people thought that about you. I was too desperate at the time to think how it might look to outsiders."

"No importa," he said finally. "It was a long time ago, after all."

"I need to check on Matthew. Mrs. Albright left with the others." She started to stand, but the torn

ligament was still tricky and painful, like the incision.
She stood very still to catch her breath and laughed
self-consciously. "I guess I'm not quite up to the hun-
dred-yard dash."

He got up lazily and put his snifter down. His arms
went under her, lifting her with ridiculous ease. "You
are still weak," he murmured as he walked down the
long hall. "It will take time for you to heal properly."

She had to fight not to lay her cheek against his
shoulder, drinking in the scent of his cologne, savoring the warmth of his body and its lean strength as
he carried her. "I like your old comrades," she remarked quietly.

"They like you." He carried her through the open
door to Matthew's room and let her slide gently to
her feet. The little boy was sleeping, his long lashes
black against his olive skin, his dark hair disheveled
on the white pillow. Diego stared down at him quietly.

Melissa saw the look on his face and almost blurted
out the truth. It took every ounce of willpower in her
to keep still.

"There is so little of you in him," he said, his
voice deep and softly accented. "Except for his hair,
which has traces of your fairness in it." He turned,
his eyes challenging. "His father was Ladino, Melissa?"

She went beet red. She tried to speak, but the words
wouldn't come.

"You loved me, you said," he persisted. His eyes

narrowed. "If that was so, then how could you give yourself, even to avenge the wounds I caused you?"

She knew she was barely breathing. She felt and looked hunted.

"What was his name?" he asked, moving closer so that he towered over her, warming her, drowning her in the exquisite scent of the cologne he wore.

Her lips parted. "I…you don't need to know," she whispered.

He framed her face with his dark, lean hands, holding her eyes up to his. "Where did you meet him?"

She swallowed. His black eyes filled the world. In the dim light from Matthew's lamp, he seemed huge, dangerous. "Diego…"

"Yes," he breathed, bending to her soft mouth. "Yes, say it like that, *querida*. Say my name, breathe it into my mouth.…"

He brushed her lips apart with the soft drugging pressure of his own, teasing, cherishing. Her nervous hands lingered at his hard waist, lost in the warmth of his body under the silky white shirt. She hadn't meant to give in so easily, but the old attraction was every bit as overwhelming as it had been years ago. She was powerless to stop what was happening.

And he knew it. He sighed gently against her mouth, tilting her head at a more accommodating angle. Then the gentleness left him. She felt his mouth growing harder, more insistent. He whispered something in Spanish, and his hands slid into her hair, dragging her mouth closer under his. He groaned and she moved against him, her body trembling with the need to be close to him, to hold him. Her arms slid around him, and suddenly his arms were around her, molding her body to his with a pressure that was painful heaven.

She gasped under his demanding mouth and he stopped at once. He lifted his head, and his eyes were fierce and dark, his breathing as quick as hers.

"I hurt you?" he asked roughly. And then he seemed to come to his senses. He released her slowly, moving away. He turned his eyes briefly to the still-sleeping child. "I must ask your pardon for that," he said stiffly. "It was not intended."

She dropped her gaze to the opening of his white shirt, where dark olive skin and black hair peeked out. "It's all right," she said hesitantly, but she couldn't look up any farther than his chin.

He shifted restlessly, his body aching for the warm softness of hers, his mind burning with confused emotions. He raised her head. "Perhaps it would be wise for you to go to bed."

She wasn't about to argue. "No, I...you don't need to carry me," she protested when he moved toward her. "I can manage. I need to start exercising my leg. But thanks anyway."

He nodded, standing aside to let her leave. His dark eyes followed her hungrily, but when she was out of sight they turned to the sleeping child. His face was so like Melissa's, he thought quietly. But the boy's Spanish heritage was evident. He wondered if Melissa still loved the boy's father or thought about him.

The bitterness he felt drove him from the child's room and into his study. And not until he had worked himself into exhaustion did he fall into his bed to sleep.

Seven

The atmosphere at breakfast was strained. Melissa had hardly slept, remembering with painful clarity her headlong response to Diego's ardor. If only she could have kept up the front, convinced him that she wasn't attracted to him anymore. She'd almost accomplished that, and then he'd come too close and her aching heart had given in.

She felt his eyes on her as she tried to eat scrambled eggs and bacon. Matthew, too, was unusually silent. He was much more careful of his behavior at the table than he'd ever been when he and Melissa had lived by themselves. Probably, she thought sadly, because he felt the tension and was reacting to it.

"You are quiet this morning, Señora Laremos," Diego said gently, his black eyes slow and steady on her pale face as she toyed with her toast. "Did you not sleep well?"

He was taunting her, but she was too weary to play the game. "No," she confessed, meeting his searching gaze squarely. "In fact, I hardly slept at all, if you want the truth."

He traced the rim of his coffee cup with a finger, and his gaze held hers. "Nor did I, to be equally frank," he said quietly. "I have been alone for many years, Melissa, despite the opinion you seem to have of me as a philandering playboy."

She lifted her coffee cup to her lips for something to do. "You were never lacking in companionship in the old days."

"Before I married you, surely," he agreed. "But marriage is a sacred vow, *niña*."

"I'm not a girl," she retorted.

His chiseled lips tugged into a reluctant smile. "Ah, but you were, that long-ago summer," he recalled, his eyes softening with the memory. "Girlish and sweet and bright with the joy of life. And then, so soon, you became a sad, worn ghost who haunted my house even when you were not in it."

"I should have gone to college in America," she replied, glancing at a quiet but curious Matthew. "There was never any hope for me where you were concerned. But I was too young and foolish to realize that a sophisticated man could never care for an inexperienced, backward child."

"It was the circumstance of our marriage which turned me against you, Melissa," he said tersely. "And but for that circumstance, we might have come together naturally, with a foundation of affection and comradeship to base our marriage on.''

''I would never have been able to settle for crumbs, Diego,'' she said simply. ''Affection wouldn't have been enough.''

''You seemed to feel that desire was enough, at the time,'' he reminded her.

Wary of Matt's sudden interest, she smiled at the child and sent him off to watch his cartoons with his breakfast only half eaten.

''He's little, but he hears very well,'' she told Diego curtly, her gray eyes accusing. ''Arguments upset him.''

''Was I arguing?'' he asked with lifted eyebrows.

She finished her coffee and put the cup down. ''Won't you be late for work?''

''By all means let me relieve you of my company, since you seem to find it so disturbing,'' he said softly. He removed a drop of coffee from his mustache with his napkin and got to his feet. *''Adiós.''*

She looked up as he started to the front door, mingled emotions tearing at her.

Diego paused at the door, glaring toward Matthew, who'd just turned the television up very loud. He said something to the boy, who cut down the volume and glared accusingly at the tall man.

''If you disturb the other tenants, little one, we will all be evicted,'' Diego told him. ''And forced to live on the street.''

''Then Matt can go home with Mama,'' the child said stubbornly, ''and go away from you.''

Diego smiled faintly at that show of belligerence. Even at such a young age, the boy had spirit. It wouldn't do to break it, despite the fact that he was another man's child. Matt had promise. He was intelligent and he didn't back down. Despite himself, Diego was warming to the little boy.

Impulsively he went to the television and went down on one knee in front of the dark-eyed child. Melissa, surprised, watched from the doorway.

"On the weekend, we might go to the zoo," Diego told the boy with pursed lips and a calculating look in his black eyes. "Of course, if you really would rather leave me, little one, I can go to see the lions and tigers alone—"

Matt blinked, his eyes widening. "Lions and tigers?"

Diego nodded. "And elephants and giraffes and bears."

Matt moved a little closer to Diego. "And could I have cotton candy? Billy's dad took him to the zoo and he got cotton candy and ice cream."

Diego smiled gently. "We might manage that, as well."

"Tomorrow?"

"A few days past that," Diego told him. "I have a great deal to do during the week, and you have to take care of your Mama until she gets well."

Matt nodded. "I can read her a story."

Melissa almost giggled, because Matt's stories were like no one else's, a tangle of fairy-tale char-

acters and cartoon characters from television in unlikely situations.

"Then if you will be good, *niño*, on Saturday you
and I will go see the animals."

Matt looked at Melissa and then at Diego again,
frowning. "Can't Mama come?"

"Mama cannot walk so much," Diego explained
patiently. "But you and I can, *sí*?"

Matt shifted. He was still nervous with the man,
but he wanted very much to go to the zoo. "*Sí*," he
echoed.

Diego smiled. "It is a deal, then." He got to his
feet. "No more loud cartoons," he cautioned, shaking
his finger at the boy.

Matt smiled back hesitantly. "All right."

Diego glanced at Melissa, who was standing in the
doorway in her pink silk gown and her long white
chenille housecoat, with no makeup and her soft
blond hair curling around her pale face. Even like
that, she was lovely. He noticed the faint surprise in
her gray eyes, mingled with something like...hope.

His black eyes held hers until she flushed, and her
gaze dropped. He laughed softly. "Do I make you
shy, *querida*?" he asked under his breath. "A mature
woman like you?"

She shifted. "Of course not." She flushed even
more, looking anywhere but at him.

He opened the front door, his glance going from
the child back to her. "Stay in bed," he said. "The
sooner the leg is better, the sooner we can begin to
do things as a family."

"It's too soon," she began.

"No. It is five years too late." His eyes flashed at her. "But you are my responsibility, and so is Matt. We have to come to terms."

"I've told you I can get a job—"

"No!"

She started to say something, but he held up a hand and his eyes cut her off.

"*¡Cuidado!*" he said softly. "You said yourself that arguing is not healthy for the child. *¡Hasta luego!*"

He was gone before she could say another word.

It was a hectic morning. Diego had hardly gotten to the office before he and Dutch had to go out to give a demonstration to some new clients. When they got back, voices were raised behind the closed office door. Diego hesitated, listening to Joyce and Apollo in the middle of a fiery argument over some filing.

Dutch came down the hall behind him, a lighted cigarette in his hand, looking as suave as ever. He glanced at Diego with a rueful smile.

"Somehow combat was a little easier to adjust to than that," he said, indicating the clamor behind the closed office door. "I think I'll smoke my cigarette out here until they get it settled or kill each other."

Diego lit a cheroot and puffed away. "Perhaps someday they will marry and settle their differences."

"They'd better settle them first," Dutch remarked. "I've found that marriage doesn't resolve conflicts. In fact, it intensifies them."

Diego sighed. "Yes, I suppose it does." His dark

eyes narrowed thoughtfully. Last night seemed more and more like a dream as the din grew. Would he and Melissa become like that arguing couple in the office? Matthew was their unresolved conflict, and despite his growing interest in the child, he still couldn't bear the thought of the man who'd fathered him.

"Deep thoughts?" Dutch asked quietly.

The other man nodded. "Marriage is not something I ever coveted. Melissa and I were caught in a—how do you say?—compromising situation. Our marriage was a matter of honor, not choice."

"She seems to care about you," the other man ventured. "And the boy—"

"The boy is not mine," Diego said harshly, his black eyes meeting the equally dark ones of the other man.

"My God." Dutch stared at him.

"She left me after I cost her our child," Diego said, his eyes dark and bitter with the memories. "Perhaps she sought consolation, or perhaps she did it for revenge. Whatever the reason, the child is an obstacle I cannot overcome." His eyes fell to the cheroot in his hand. "It has made things difficult."

Dutch was silent for a long moment. "You're very sure that she lost your child?"

That was when Diego first began to doubt what he'd been told five years ago. When Dutch put it into words, he planted a seed. Diego stared back at him with knitted brows.

"There was a doctor at the hospital," he told Dutch. "I tried later to find him, but he had gone to

South America to practice. The nurse said Melissa was badly hurt in the fall, and Melissa herself told me the child was dead.''

"You got drunk at our last reunion," Dutch recalled. "And I put you to bed. You talked a lot. I know all about Melissa."

Diego averted his eyes. "Do you?" he asked stiffly.

"And you can take the poker out of your back," Dutch said. "You and I go back a long way. We don't have many secrets from each other. Things were strained between you and her. Isn't it possible that she might have hidden her pregnancy from you for fear that you'd try to take the boy from her?"

Diego stared at him, half-blind with shock. "Melissa would not do such a thing," he said shortly. "It is not her nature to lie. Even now, she has no heart for subterfuge."

Dutch shrugged. "You could be wrong."

"Not in this. Besides, the years are wrong," he said heavily. "Matthew is not yet four."

"I see."

Diego took another draw on his cheroot. Inside the office, the voices got louder, then stopped when the telephone rang. "I had my own suspicions at first, you know," he confessed. "But I soon forgot them."

"You might take a look at his birth certificate, all the same," Dutch suggested. "Just to be sure."

Diego smiled and said something polite. In the back of his mind there were new doubts. He wasn't certain about anything anymore, least of all his feel-

ings for Melissa and his stubborn certainty that he
knew her. He was beginning to think that he'd never
known her at all. He'd wanted her, but he'd never
made any effort to get to know her as a person.

When Diego came home, Matthew was sprawled
on the bed and Melissa was reading to him. He
paused in the doorway to watch them for a few seconds, his eyes growing tender as they traced the
graceful lines of Melissa's body and then went to
Matt, becoming puzzled and disturbed as he really
looked at the child for the first time.

Yes, it could be so. Matthew could be his child.
He had to admit it now. The boy had his coloring,
his eyes. Matt had his nose and chin, but he had the
shape of his mother's eyes, and his hair was only a
little darker than hers. Except that the years were
wrong—Matt would have to be over four years old if
he was truly Diego's son. Melissa had said that he
was just past three. But Diego knew so little about
children of any age, and there was always the possibility that she hadn't told the exact truth. Little things
she'd said, slips she'd made, could reveal a monu-
mental deception.

She didn't lie as a rule, but this was an extraordi-
nary situation. After all, she'd had more than enough
reason to want to pay him back for his cruelty. And
was she the kind of woman who could go from him
to another man so easily? Had she? Or had she only
been afraid, as Dutch had hinted—afraid of losing her
son to his real father? She might think Diego capable
of taking Matt away from her and turning her out of

their lives. His jaw tautened as he remembered his treatment of her and exactly why she had good reason to see him that way. If he didn't know Melissa, then she certainly didn't know him. He'd never let her close enough to know him. What if he did let her come close? He turned away from the door, tempted for the first time to think of pulling down the barriers he'd built between them. He was alone, and so was she. Was there any hope for them now?

Melissa hobbled to the supper table with Matt's help. She looked worried, and Diego wondered what had upset her.

He didn't have to wait long. Halfway through the first course, she got up enough nerve to ask him a question that had plagued her all day.

"Do you think I might get a job when the doctor gives me the all-clear?" Melissa asked cautiously.

He put down his coffee cup and stared at her. "You have a job already, do you not?" he asked, nodding toward a contented Matthew, who was obviously enjoying his chicken dish.

"Of course, and I love looking after him and having time to spend with him for a change," she confessed. "But..." She sighed heavily. "I feel as if I'm not pulling my weight," she said finally. "It doesn't seem fair to make you support us."

He looked, and was, surprised at the remark. He leaned back in his chair, looking very Latin and faintly arrogant. "Melissa, you surely remember that I was a wealthy man in Guatemala. I work because I enjoy it, not because I need to. I have more than enough in Swiss banks to support all of us into old age and beyond.''

''I didn't realize that.'' She toyed with her fork. ''Still, I don't like feeling obligated to you.''

His eyes flashed. ''I am your husband. It is my duty, my obligation, my responsibility, to take care of you.''

''And that's an archaic attitude,'' Melissa muttered, her own temper roused. ''In the modern world, married people are partners.''

''José's mama and papa used to fight all the time,'' Matthew observed with a wary glance at his mother. ''And José's papa went away.''

Diego drew in a sharp breath. ''*Niñito*,'' he said gently, ''your mama and I will inevitably disagree from time to time. Married people do, *comprende*?''

Matthew moved a dumpling around on his plate with his fork. ''*Yo no sé*,'' he murmured miserably, but in perfect Spanish.

Diego frowned. He got up gracefully to kneel beside Matthew's chair. ''*¿Hablas español?*'' he asked gently, using the familiar tense.

''*Sí*,'' Matthew said, and burst into half a dozen incomplete fears and worries in that language before Diego interrupted him by placing a long finger over his small mouth. His voice, when he spoke, was more tender than Melissa had ever heard it.

''*Niño*,'' he said, his deep voice soothing, ''we are a family. It will not be easy for any of us, but if we try, we can learn to get along with each other. Would it not please you, little one, to have time to spend with Mama, and a nice place to live, and toys to play with?''

Matt looked worried. ''You don't like Matt,'' he mumbled.

Diego took a slow breath and ran his hand gently over the small head. ''I have been alone for a long time,'' he said hesitantly. ''I have had no one to show me how to be a father. It must be taught, you see, and only a small boy can teach it.''

''Oh,'' Matt said, nodding his head. He shifted restlessly, and his dark eyes met Diego's. ''Well...I guess I could.'' His brows knitted. ''And we can go to the zoo and to the park and see baseball games and things?''

Diego nodded. ''That, too.''

''You don't have a little boy?''

Diego hated the lump in his throat. It was as if the years of feeling nothing at all had caught up with him at last. He felt as if a butterfly's wings had touched his heart and brought it to life for the first time. He looked at the small face, so much like his own, and was surprised at the hunger he felt to be this child's father, his real father. The loneliness was suddenly unbearable. ''No,'' he said huskily. ''I have...no little boy.''

Melissa felt tears running hot down her shocked face. It was more than she'd dared hope for that Diego might be able to accept Matt, to want him, even though he believed he was another man's child. It was the first step in a new direction for all of them.

''I guess so,'' Matthew said with the simple acceptance of childhood. "And Mama and I would live with you?"

"*Sí*."

"I always wanted a papa of my own," Matthew confessed. "Mama said my own papa was a very brave man. He went away, but Mama used to say he might come back."

That broke the spell. Diego's face tautened as it turned to Melissa, his black eyes accusing, all the tenderness gone out of him at once as he considered that his whole line of thought might have been a fabrication, created out of his own loneliness and need and guilt.

"Did she?" he asked tersely.

Melissa fought for control, dabbing at the tears. "Matt, wouldn't you like to go and play with your bear?"

"Okay." He jumped down from his chair with a shy grin at Diego and ran off to his room. Except for the first night, he'd given them no trouble about sleeping alone. He seemed to enjoy having a room of his very own.

Diego's face was without a trace of emotion when he turned to her. "His father is still alive?" he said tersely.

She dropped her eyes to the table while her heartbeat shook her. "Yes."

"Where is he?"

She shook her head, unable to speak, to tell any more lies.

He took an angry breath. "Until you can trust me, how can we have a marriage?"

She looked up. "And that works both ways. You never trusted me. How can you expect me to trust you, Diego?"

"I was not aware that he spoke such excellent Spanish," he remarked after a minute, lessening the tension.

"It seemed to come naturally to him," she said. "It isn't bad for a child to be bilingual, especially in Tucson, where so many people speak Spanish anyway. Most of his friends did."

He leaned back in his chair, his dark eyes sliding carelessly over Melissa's body. "You grow more lovely with each passing day," he said unexpectedly.

She flushed. "I didn't think you ever looked at me long enough to form an opinion."

He lit a cheroot, puffing on it quietly. "Things are not so simple anymore, are they? The boy is insecure."

"I'm sorry I argued with you," she said sadly. "I made everything worse."

"No. You and I are both responsible for that." He shrugged. "It is not easy, is it, *pequeña*, to forget the past we share?"

"Guatemala seems very far away sometimes, though." She leaned back. "What about the *finca*, Diego?"

"I have given that more thought than you realize, Melissa," he replied. He studied his cheroot. "It is growing more dangerous by the day to try to hold the estate, to provide adequate protection for my workers. I loathe the very thought of giving it up, but it is becoming too much of a financial risk. Now that I have you and the boy to consider, I have decided that I may well have to sell it.''

''But your family has lived there for three generations,'' she protested. ''It's your heritage.''

''*Niña,* it is a spread of land,'' he said gently. ''A bit of stone and soil. Many lives have been sacrificed for it over the years, and more will be asked. I begin to think the sacrifices are too many.'' He leaned forward suddenly, his black eyes narrow. ''Suppose I asked you to come with me to Guatemala, to bring Matthew, to raise him there.''

Her breathing stopped for an instant. She faltered, trying to reconcile herself to the fear his words had fostered.

He nodded, reading her apprehension. ''You see? You could no more risk the boy's life than I could.'' He sat back again. ''It is much more sensible to lease or sell it than to take the risk of trying to live there. I like Chicago, *niña.* Do you?''

''Why, yes,'' she said slowly. ''I suppose I do. I don't know about the winter....''

''We can spend the winter down in the Caribbean and come back in the spring. Apollo is thinking of expanding the company, Blain Security Consultants, to include antiterrorism classes in that part of the world.'' He smiled. ''I can combine business with pleasure.''

''You haven't told me about the kind of work you

do," she reminded him. She wanted to know. This was one of the few times he'd ever let down his guard and talked to her, sharing another part of his life. It was flattering and pleasant.

"I teach tactics," he said. He put out the cheroot. "Dutch and I share the duties, and I also teach defensive driving to the chauffeurs of the very rich." He looked up at her. "You remember that I raced cars for a few years."

"My father mentioned it once," she said. Her eyes ran over his dark face. "You can't live without a challenge, can you? Without some kind of risk?"

"I have grown used to surges of adrenaline over the years," he mused, smiling. "Perhaps I have become addicted." He shrugged. "It is unlikely that I will make you a rich widow in the near future, Señora Laremos," he added mockingly, thinking bitterly of the boy's father.

"Money was never one of my addictions," she said with quiet pride. She got to her feet slowly. "But think what you like. Your opinion doesn't matter a lot to me these days, *Señor*."

"Yet it did once," he said softly, rising to catch her gently by the waist and hold her in front of him. "There was a time when you loved me, Melissa."

"Love can die, like dreams." She sighed wistfully, watching the quick rise and fall of his chest. "It was a long time ago, and I was very young."

"You are still very young, *querida*," he said, his voice deep and very quiet. "How did you manage, alone and pregnant, in a strange place?"

"I had friends," she said hesitantly. "And a good job, working as an assistant buyer for a department store's clothing department. Then I got pneumonia and everything fell apart."

"Yet you have managed enough time with Matthew to teach him values and pride and honor in his heritage."

She smiled. "I wanted him to be a whole person," she said. She looked up, searching the dark eyes so close to hers. "You blame me, don't you? For betraying you..."

Her humility hurt him. It made him feel guilty for the things he'd said to her. He sighed wearily. "Was it not I who betrayed you?" he breathed, and bent to her mouth.

He'd never kissed her in quite that way before. She felt the soft pressure of his mouth with wonder as he cherished it, savored it in a silence ablaze with shared pleasure.

"But, Matthew..." she whispered.

"Kiss me, *querida*," he whispered, and his mouth covered hers again as he drew her against his lean, hard body and his lips grew quietly insistent.

She felt the need in him. Her legs trembled against his. Her mouth followed where his led, lost in its warm, bristly pressure. She put her arms around him and moved closer until she felt him stiffen, until she felt the sudden urgency of his body and heard him groan.

"No," he whispered roughly, pushing her away. His eyes glittered. His breathing was quick and unsteady. "No half measures. I want all of you or nothing. And it is too soon, is it not?"

She wanted to say no, but of course it was too soon, and not just physically. There were too many wounds, too many questions. She lowered her eyes to his chest. "I won't stop you," she said, shocking herself as well as the man standing so still in front of her. "I won't say no."

His fingers contracted, but only for an instant. "It has been a long time," he said in a deep, soft voice. "I do not think that I could be gentle with you the first time, despite the tenderness I feel for you." He shuddered almost imperceptibly. "My possession of you would be violent, and I could not bear to hurt you. It is not wise to let this continue." He let her go and moved away, with his back to her, while he lit another cheroot.

She watched him with curious eyes. Her body trembled with frustration, her leg ached. But she wanted nothing more in life than his body over hers in the sweet darkness.

"I want you," she whispered achingly.

He turned, his black eyes steady and hot. "No less than I want you, I assure you," he said tersely. "But first there must be a lowering of all the barriers. Tell me about Matthew's father, Melissa."

She wanted to. She needed to. But she couldn't tell him. He had to come to the realization himself, he had to believe in her innocence without having proof. "I can't," she moaned.

"Then know this: I have had enough of subterfuge

and pretense. Until you tell me the truth, I swear that I will never touch you again.''

She exhaled unsteadily. He was placing her in an intolerable position. She couldn't tell him the truth. She didn't trust him enough, and obviously he didn't trust her enough. If he loved her, he'd trust her enough to know that Matthew was his. But that had always been the problem—she loved too much and he loved too little. He was hot-blooded, and he desired her. But desire was a poor foundation for marriage. It wouldn't be enough.

Diego watched the expressions pass over her face. When he saw her teeth clench, he knew that he'd lost the round. She wasn't going to tell him. She was afraid. Well, there was still one other way to get at the truth. As Dutch had mentioned, there would surely be a birth certificate for Matthew. He would write to the Arizona Bureau of Vital Statistics and obtain a copy of it. That would give Diego the truth about Matt's age and his parentage. Diego had to know, once and for all, who Matthew's father was. Until he did, there was no hope of a future for him and Matthew and Melissa.

''It is late,'' he said without giving her a chance to say anything else. ''You had better get some sleep.''

Melissa hesitated, but only for an instant. It was disappointing. She felt they'd been so close to an understanding. She nodded, turning toward her room without another word.

It was like sitting on top of a bomb for the next few days. Melissa was more aware of Diego than ever before, but he was polite and courteous and not much more. The nights grew longer and longer.

But if she was frustrated, her son wasn't. Diego seemed to have a new shadow, because Matthew followed him everywhere when he wasn't working. Rather than resenting it, Diego seemed to love it. He indulged the child as never before, noticed him, played with him. His efforts were hesitant at first because he'd never spent much time around children. But as time wore on he learned to play, and the child became a necessary part of his day, of his life.

They went to the zoo that weekend, leaving Melissa with the television and a new videocassette of an adventure movie for company. They stayed until almost dark, and when they came back Matthew seemed a different boy. Oddly enough, Diego was different, too. There was an expression on his face and in his black eyes that Melissa didn't understand.

"We saw a cobra!" Matt told Melissa, his young face alive with excitement. "And a giraffe, and a lion, and a monkey! And I had cotton candy, and I rode a train, and a puppy dog chased me!" He giggled gleefully.

"And Papa is worn to a nub," Diego moaned, dropping wearily onto the sofa beside Melissa with a weary grin. "*Dios mío*, I almost bought a motorcycle just to keep up with him!"

"I wore Papa out," Matt chuckled, "didn't I, Papa?"

Melissa glanced from one of them to the other, curiosity evident in her gray eyes.

"Matthew's papa isn't coming back," Diego told her. He lit a cheroot with steady hands, his black eyes daring her to challenge the statement. "So I'm going to be his papa and take care of him. And he will be my son."

"I always wanted a papa of my own," Matthew told Melissa. He leaned his chin on the arm of the sofa and stared at her. "Since my papa's gone away, I want Diego."

Melissa drew a slow breath, barely breathing as all the things she'd told Matt about his father came back with vivid clarity. She prayed that he hadn't mentioned any of them to Diego. Especially the photograph…why in heaven's name had she shown Matt that photo!

But Diego looked innocent, and Matthew was obviously unruffled, so there couldn't have been any shared secrets. No. Of course not. She was worrying over nothing.

"Did you have a good time?"

Matt grinned. "We had a really good time, and tomorrow we're going to church."

Melissa hoped she wouldn't pass out. It wouldn't be good to shock the child. But her eyes looked like saucers as they slid to Diego's face.

"A child should be raised in the church," he said tersely. "When you are able, you may come with us."

"I'm not arguing," she said absently.

"Good, because it would avail you nothing. Matt,

suppose you watch television while I organize something for us to eat? Do you want a fish?''

''Yes, please,'' the child said with a happy laugh, and ran to turn on cartoons.

''And you, *querida*?'' he asked Melissa, letting his dark eyes slide over her gray slacks and low-cut cream sweater with soft desire.

''I'd like a chef's salad,'' she murmured. ''There's a fish dinner in the freezer that Matt can have, and the salad's already made. I prepared it while you were gone. There's a steak I can grill for you....''

''I can do it.'' He got up, stretching lazily, and her eyes moved over him with helpless longing, loving the powerful lines of his tall body.

''I need to move around, though,'' she murmured. She got up and stood for a minute before she started to walk. The limp was still pronounced, but it didn't hurt half as bad to move as it had only a week ago. She laughed at her own progress.

''How easily the young heal,'' Diego remarked with a smile.

''I'm not that young, Diego,'' she said.

He moved close to her, taking her by the waist to lazily draw her body to him, holding her gently. ''You are when you laugh, *querida*,'' he said, smiling. ''What memories you bring back of happy times we shared in Guatemala.''

The smile faded. ''Were there any?'' she asked sadly.

He searched her soft gray eyes. ''Do you not remember how it was with us, before we married? The comradeship we had, the ease of being together?''

"I was a child and you were an adult.'' She dropped her eyes. "I was bristling with hero-worship and buried in dreams.''

"And then we took refuge in a Mayan ruin.'' He was whispering so that Matt, who was engrossed in a television program, wouldn't hear. "And we became lovers, with the rain blowing around us and the threat of danger everywhere. Your body under my body, *Melissa mía*, your cries in my mouth as I kissed you...''

She moved away too fast and almost fell, her face beet red and her heart beating double time. "I—'' She had to try again because her voice squeaked. "I'll just fix the salad dressing, Diego.''

He watched her go with a faint, secretive smile. Behind him, Matt was laughing at a cartoon, and Diego glanced his way with an expression that he was glad Melissa couldn't see. Matt had told him about the photograph of his father while they'd been looking at a poster that showed banana trees.

Those funny-looking trees, Matt exclaimed, were in the photo his Mama had of his papa. And his papa was wearing a big hat and riding a horse.

Diego had leaned against a wall for support, and he didn't remember what he'd mumbled when Matt had kept on talking. But even though he'd sent for the birth certificate, it was no longer necessary. There couldn't be another photo like the one Matt described, and it was with amused fury that he realized the man he'd been jealous of was himself.

He was Matt's father. Matt was the child Melissa had sworn she'd lost. It even made sense that she'd hidden her pregnancy from him. She'd probably been afraid that he didn't care enough about her to let her stay after the child was born. More than likely she'd thought that Diego would take her baby from her and send her away. She'd run to keep that from happening.

She was still running. She hadn't told him the truth about Matt because she didn't trust him enough. Perhaps she didn't love him enough anymore, either. He was going to have to work on that. But at least he knew the truth, and that was everything. He looked at his son with fierce pride and knew that, whatever happened, he couldn't give up Matt. He couldn't give up Melissa, either, but he was going to have to prove that to her first.

After supper, Diego and Matthew sprawled on the carpet in front of the television. Melissa's eyes softened at the two of them, so alike, so dark and delightfully Latin, laughing and wrestling in front of the television. Diego was in his stocking feet, his shirt unbuttoned in front, his hair disheveled, his eyes laughing at his son. He looked up with the laughter still in his face and saw Melissa watching him. For an instant, something flared in his eyes and left them darkly disturbing. She flushed and looked away, and she heard him laugh. Then Matthew attacked him again and the spell was broken. But it left Melissa shaken and hungry. Diego was accepting Matt, and that should have satisfied her. But it didn't. She wanted Diego to love her. When, she wondered bitterly, had she ever wanted anything else? But it seemed as impossible now as it had in the past. He wanted her, but perhaps he had nothing left to offer.

Diego was involved with work for the next few weeks. The atmosphere at the apartment was much less strained. Matt played with Diego, and the two of them were becoming inseparable. And Diego looked at Melissa with lazy indulgence and began to tease her gently now and again. But the tension between them was growing, and her nervousness with him didn't help. She couldn't understand his suddenly changed attitude toward Matt and herself. Because she couldn't figure out the reason behind his turnaround, she didn't trust it.

When the time came for her final checkup, Diego took time off from work to take her to the doctor.

She was pronounced cured and released from the doctor's care. He told her to progress slowly with her rapidly healing leg but said she was fit to work again.

When she told Diego that and started hinting at wanting to get a job, he felt uneasy. She'd run away from him once, and he was no longer able to hide his growing affection for the boy. What if she knew that he suspected the truth? Would she take Matt and run again, fearing that Diego might be trying to steal him away from her? His blood ran cold at the prospect, but he wasn't confident enough to put the question to her. He might force her hand if he wasn't careful. The thing was, how was he going to keep her?

He worried the question all the way back to the apartment, reserved and remote as he pondered. He went back to work immediately after dropping her off at the apartment. He didn't even speak as he went out the door. His withdrawal worried Melissa.

"You need some diversion, Mrs. Laremos," Mrs. Albright chided as she fixed lunch for them. "Staying around this apartment all the time just isn't healthy."

"You know, I do believe you're right," Melissa agreed with a sigh. "I think I'll call Joyce and take her out to lunch tomorrow. I might even get a job."

"Your husband won't like that, if you don't mind my saying so, ma'am," Mrs. Albright murmured as she shredded carrots for a salad.

"I'm afraid he won't," Melissa said. "But that isn't going to stop me."

She dropped a kiss on Matthew's dark head as he sat engrossed in a children's program on the educational network and went into Diego's study to use the phone.

It was bad luck that she couldn't remember the name of Apollo's company. Diego surely had it written down somewhere. She didn't like going into his desk, but this was important. She opened the middle drawer and found a black book of numbers. But underneath it was an open envelope that caught her attention.

With a quick glance toward the door and a pounding heart, she drew it out and looked at it. The return address was the Arizona Bureau of Vital Statistics. Her cold, nervous hands fumbled it open, and she drew out what she'd been afraid she'd find—a copy of Matthew's birth certificate. Under father, Diego's full name and address were neatly typed.

She sighed, fighting back tears. So he knew. But he hadn't said anything. He'd questioned her and promised her that he wouldn't come near her again until she told him the truth about Matthew. Why? Did it matter so much to his pride? Or was he just buying time to gain Matthew's affection before he forced Melissa out of their lives? Perhaps despite what he'd said about Guatemala he meant to take Matthew there and leave Melissa behind. His lack of ardor since he and Matt had gone to the zoo, his lack of attention to her, made her more uncertain than ever. And today, his remoteness when the doctor had said she could work. Was he thinking about throwing her out now that she no longer needed his support?

She was frightened, and her first thought was to pack a case and get Matthew far away, as fast as possible. But that would be irrational. She had to stop and think. She had to be logical, not make a spur-of-the-moment decision that she might come to regret.

She put the birth certificate back into the envelope and replaced it carefully, facedown under the black book, and closed the drawer. She didn't dare get a number out of it now because Diego would know that she'd been into his desk drawer.

Then she remembered that Mrs. Albright would

surely have his number. She went into the kitchen and asked the woman.

"Oh, certainly, Mrs. Laremos," she smiled. "It's listed under Blain Security Consultants, Incorporated, in the telephone directory." She eyed Melissa curiously. "Are you all right? You seem very pale."

"I'm fine." Melissa forced a smile. "It's just a little hard to get around. The ligament is healed, but my leg is stiff. They wanted me to have physical therapy, but I settled for home exercises instead. I'm sure it will limber up once I start them."

"My sister had a bad back, and the doctor put her on exercises," Mrs. Albright remarked. "They helped a great deal. I'm sure you'll do fine, ma'am."

"Yes. So am I. Thank you."

She went into the living room and looked up the number, dialing it with shaky hands.

Joyce's musical voice answered after the second ring. "Blain Security Consultants. How may we help you?"

"You can come out to lunch with me tomorrow and help me save my sanity," Melissa said dryly. "It's Melissa, Diego's wife."

"Yes, I recognized your voice, Melissa," Joyce said with a laugh. "And I'd be delighted to go to lunch with you. Shall I pick you up at your apartment about 11:30? If my boss will let me—"

Apollo's deep, angry voice sounded from a distance. "Since when do I deny you a lunch hour, Miss Latham? By all means, if that's Melissa, you can take her to lunch. Stop making me out to be an ogre."

"I'd never do such a thing, Mr. Blain," Joyce assured him stiffly. "It would be an insult to the ogre."

There was a muttered curse, and a door slammed. Joyce sighed and Melissa hid a giggle.

"See you tomorrow," Joyce whispered. "I'd better get to work or I may wind up out the window on my head."

"It sounds that way, yes. Have a nice day."

"You too!"

That evening, Diego came home late. He was just in time to kiss Matthew good night. Melissa, watching them from the doorway, saw the affection and pride in his dark face as he looked at his son. How long had he known? Perhaps he'd suspected it from the beginning. She sighed, thinking how transparent she'd always been to him. She was so green, how could he help but know that she couldn't sleep with anyone except him? Probably he even knew how deeply she loved him. His cruelty in the past, his rejection, even his indifference, didn't seem to affect her feelings. She wondered where she was going to get the strength to leave him. But if he was thinking about taking Matthew away from her, she wouldn't have any choice. He'd never made any secret of his opinion about love. He didn't believe in it. She had no reason to suspect that his feelings had changed over the years.

He loved Matthew, if he loved anyone. Melissa was a complication he didn't really seem to want. When he stood up and moved to the door, Melissa hid her eyes from him. She didn't want him to see the worry in them.

"Joyce said you're taking her out to lunch tomorrow," he remarked after she'd called another good night to Matthew and closed his bedroom door.

"Yes. I thought I might try getting out of the apartment a little bit," she said. "It's...lonely here."

He stopped at her bedroom door, his eyes dark and quiet. "It will not always be like this," he said. "When time permits, now that you are able to get around, we will find some things that we can do as a family."

She smiled wistfully. "You don't need to feel obligated to include me."

He frowned. "Why?"

She'd forgotten how clever he was. She averted her eyes. "Well, boys like to be with men sometimes without women along, don't they?"

He eyed her curiously. He'd expected her to say more than that. He felt irritable at his own disappointment. What had he expected? She'd held out so long now that he didn't really expect her to give in. He was giving way slowly to a black depression. He'd left her alone, hoping she'd come to him and tell him the truth, and she hadn't. Suppose he'd misjudged her feelings? What if she didn't care? What if she left him, now that she didn't need him to take care of her?

He barely remembered that she'd asked him a question. "I suppose it is good for Matthew to spend some time with just me," he answered her wearily. His face mirrored his fatigue. There were new, harsh lines on it. He studied her slowly for a moment before he turned away. "I have had a long day. If you don't mind, Señora Laremos, I prefer sleep to conversation."

"Of course. Good night," she said, surprised by his tone as well as by the way he looked.

He nodded and went down the hall. She watched him, her eyes wistful and soft and full of regret. Love wasn't the sweet thing the movies made of it, she thought bitterly. It was painful and long-suffering for all its sweetness. He wanted Matthew, but did he want her? She wondered what she was going to do.

She turned away and went into her own bedroom, looking at herself in the mirror. She looked thinner and older, and there were new lines in her face. Did Diego ever think about the past, she wondered, about the times the two of them had gone riding in the Guatemalan valleys and talked about a distant future? She thought of it often, of the way Diego had once been.

She opened her chest of drawers and pulled out the snapshot she'd taken of Diego the day before her father had found them in the hills. Her fingers touched the face lightly and she sighed. How long ago it all seemed, how futile. She'd loved him, and pain was the only true memory she had. If only, she thought, he'd loved her a little in return. But perhaps he really wasn't capable of it. She tucked the photo away and closed the drawers. Dreams were no substitute for reality.

Eight

The restaurant that Joyce and Melissa went to was small and featured French cuisine. Melissa picked her way through a delicious chicken-and-broccoli crepe and a fresh melon while Joyce frowned over her elaborate beef dish.

"You're very quiet for someone who wanted to talk," Joyce remarked fifteen minutes into the exquisite meal, her dark eyes quietly scrutinizing Melissa's face.

Melissa sighed. "I've got a problem."

Joyce smiled. "Who hasn't?"

"Yes. Well, mine is about to make me pack a bag and leave Chicago."

Joyce put down her fork. "In that case, I'm all ears."

Melissa picked up her coffee cup and sipped the

sweet, dark liquid. "Matthew is Diego's son," she said. "The son I told him I lost before I ran away from him five years ago."

"That's a problem?" Joyce asked blankly.

"I didn't think he knew. He didn't seem to like Matt at first, but now they're inseparable. I thought that maybe he was beginning to accept Matt even though he thought he was another man's son. But yesterday I found a copy of Matthew's birth certificate in his desk drawer."

"If he knows, everything will be all right, won't it?" Joyce asked her.

"That's just it," Melissa said miserably. "It was important to me that he'd believe Matt was his son, without proof, that he'd believe I could never have betrayed him. But now I'll never be sure. And lately Diego acts as if he doesn't want me around. I even think I know why. He knows that Matt is his, and he hates me for letting him think I lost his child."

Joyce blinked. "Come again?"

"That's really a long story." Melissa smiled and stared into her coffee. "I thought I was justified at the time not to tell him or get in touch with him. The way he used to feel about me, I was sure he'd try to take Matt away."

"Maybe he would have," the other woman said gently. "You can't blame yourself too much. You must have had good reasons."

Melissa lifted tortured eyes. "Did I? Oh, there's been fault on both sides, you know. But now that he knows Matt is his, he has to be thinking about all the time he's missed with his son. He has to blame me for that, even though I had provocation. And now I'm afraid that he may be trying to win Matt away from me. He may take him away!''

"That is pure hysteria," Joyce said firmly. "Get hold of yourself, girl! You can't run away this time. You've got to stay and fight for your son. Come to think of it," she added, "you might try fighting for your husband as well. He married you. He had to care about you."

Melissa grimaced as she fingered her cup. "Diego didn't really want to marry me. We were found in a compromising situation, which he thought I planned, and he was forced to marry me. He and his family made me feel like a leper, and when I discovered that I was pregnant, I couldn't bear the thought of bringing up my child in such an atmosphere of hatred. So I let him think I lost the baby and I ran away."

"There's no chance that he loves you?"

She smiled wistfully. "Diego was a mercenary for even longer than the rest of the group. He told me once that he didn't believe in love, that it was a luxury he couldn't afford. He wants me. But that's all."

Joyce studied her friend's sad expression. "You and I are unlucky in love," she said finally. "I work for a man who hates me and you live with a man who doesn't love you."

"You hate Apollo, too," Melissa pointed out.

Joyce smiled, her eyes wistful. "Do I?"

"Oh." Melissa put the cup down. "I see."

"I give him the response he expects to keep him

from seeing how I really feel. Look at me," she moaned. "He's a handsome, rich, successful man. Why would he want someone as plain and unattractive as I am? I wish I were as pretty as you are."

"Me? Pretty?" Melissa was honestly astounded.

Joyce glowered at her. "Do you love Diego?"

It was a hard question to answer honestly, but in the end she had to. "I always have," she confessed. "I suppose I always will."

"Then why don't you stop running away from him and start running toward him?" Joyce suggested. "Running hasn't made you very happy, has it?"

"It's made me pretty miserable. But how can I stay with a man who doesn't want me?"

"You could make him want you." She reached out and touched Melissa's hand. "Is he worth fighting for?"

"Oh, yes!"

"Then do it. Stop letting the past create barriers."

Melissa frowned slightly. "I don't know very much about how to vamp a man."

Joyce shrugged. "Neither do I. So what? We can learn together."

This was sounding more delightful by the minute. Melissa was nervous, but she knew that Diego wanted her, and the knowledge gave her hope. "I suppose we could give it a try. If things don't work out—"

"Trust me. They'll work out."

"Then if I have to do it, so do you." Melissa pursed her lips. "Did you know that I was an assistant buyer for a clothing store? I have a passable eye for fashion, and I know what looks good on people. Suppose we go shopping together. I'll show you what to buy to make you stand out."

Joyce raised her eyebrows. "Why?"

"Because with very little work you could be a knockout. Think of it, Apollo on his knees at your desk, sighing with adoration," she coaxed.

Joyce grimaced. "The only way he'd be on his knees at my desk would be if I kicked him in the stomach."

"Pessimist! You're the one giving the pep talk. Suppose we both listen to you and try to practice what you preach?"

The other woman sighed. "Well, what have we got to lose, after all?"

"Not much, from where I'm sitting. How about Saturday morning? You can take me to the right department stores, and I'll make suggestions."

"I do have a little in my savings account," Joyce murmured. She smiled. "All right. We'll do it."

"Great!" Melissa started on her dessert. "Amazing how good this food tastes all of a sudden. I think I feel better already."

"So do I. But if Apollo throws me out the window, you're in a lot of trouble."

"He won't. Eat up."

Melissa's head was full of ideas. Joyce had inspired her. She hadn't really tried to catch Diego's eye since they'd been back together. Even in the old days she'd never quite lived up to her potential. She wasn't any more experienced now, but she was well-traveled and

she'd learned a lot from listening to other women talk
and watching them in action as they attracted men.
She was going to turn the tables on her reluctant husband and see if she couldn't make him like captivity.
Whether or not the attempt failed, she had to try.
Joyce was right. Running away had only complicated
things. This time, she had to stand and fight.

While she was out, she'd bought a memory card
game for Matthew, and when Diego came home that
night she was sprawled on the carpet with her son.
She made a pretty picture in a clinging beige sleeveless blouse and tight jeans. Diego paused in the doorway, and when she saw him she rolled onto her side,
striking a frankly seductive pose.

"Good evening, Señor Laremos," she murmured.
"Matthew has a new game."

"I can remember where the apple is," Matthew
enthused, jumping up to hug his father and babble
excitedly about the game and how he'd already beaten
Mama once.

"He has a quick mind," Diego remarked as he
studied the large pile of matched cards on Matthew's
side of the playing area and the small one on Melissa's.

"Very quick," she agreed, laughing at Matthew's
smug little face. "And he's modest, too."

"I know everything," Matthew said with innocent
certainty. "Will you play with us, Papa?"

"After dinner, niño," the tall man agreed. "I must
change, and there is a phone call I have to make."

"Okay!" Matthew went back to turning over cards.

"Only two," Melissa cautioned. "It's cheating if you keep peeking under all of them."

"Yes, Mama."

She took her turn, aware that Diego's eyes were on the deep vee of her blouse, under which she was wearing nothing at all.

She sat up again, glancing at him. "Is something wrong, *señor*?"

"Of course not. Excuse me." He turned, frowning, and went off toward his bedroom. Melissa smiled secretively as she watched Matthew match two oranges.

Dinner was noisy because Mrs. Albright had taken Matthew down to the lobby to meet her daughter and grandson, who were just back from a Mexican trip, and the daughter had given Matt a small wooden toy, a ball on a string that had to be bounced into the cup it was attached to. Matt was overjoyed with both his new friend and his toy.

"Ah," Diego smiled. "Yes, these are very common in my part of the world, and your mother's," he added with a smile at Melissa. "Are they not, *querida*? I can remember playing with one as a child myself."

"Where we lived there were no toy stores," she told Matthew. "We lived far back in the country, near a volcano, and there were ancient Mayan ruins all around." She colored a little, remembering one particular ruin. She looked at Diego and found the same memory in his dark eyes as they searched hers.

"*Sí,*" he said gently. "The ruins were...potent."

Her lips parted. "Five years," she said, her eyes

more eloquent than she knew. "And sometimes it seems like days."

"Not for me," he said abruptly, drawing his eyes back to his coffee cup. "It has not been easy, living through the black time that came afterward."

Matthew was trying to play with his toy, but Melissa took it and put it firmly beside his plate, indicating that he should eat his food first. He grimaced and picked up his fork.

"Did you never think of contacting me?" he asked unexpectedly, and his eyes narrowed. It disturbed him more and more, thinking about all he'd missed. Understanding the reason for Melissa's actions didn't make the lack of contact with his child any easier to bear. He'd missed so much of the boy's life, all the things that most fathers experienced and cherished in memory. Matt's first word, his first step, the early days when parents and children became bonded. He'd had none of that.

Melissa sighed sadly, remembering when Matthew had been born and how desperately she'd wanted Diego. But he hadn't wanted her. He'd made it so plain after their marriage, and even after her fall down the steps he'd been unapproachable. "I thought about it once," she said quietly, wondering if he was going to accuse her of denying him his rights. She wouldn't have had a reply. "But you'd made it clear that I had no place in your life, Diego, that you only married me to spare your family more disgrace."

He studied his cup. "You never considered that I

might have had a change of heart, Melissa? That I might have regretted, bitterly, my treatment of you?''

"No," she said honestly. Her pale eyes searched his dark ones. "I didn't want to play on your guilt. It was better that I took care of myself." She dropped her gaze to the table. "And Matt."

"It must have been difficult when he was born," he probed, trying to draw her out.

She smiled faintly, remembering. "Something went wrong," she murmured. "They had to do a cesarean section."

He caught his breath. "My God. And you had no one to turn to."

She looked at Matthew warmly. "I managed very well. I had neighbors who were kind, and the company I worked for was very understanding. My boss made sure my insurance paid all my bills, and he even gave me an advance on my salary so that we had enough to eat."

His fingers contracted around the cup almost hard enough to break it. It didn't bear thinking about. Melissa must have been in severe pain, alone and with an infant to be responsible for. His eyes closed. It hurt him terribly to think that if he'd been kinder to her he could have shared that difficulty with her. He could have been there when she'd needed someone, been there to take care of her. His anguish at being denied all those years with Matt seemed a small thing by comparison.

"It wasn't so bad, Diego," she said softly, because

there was pain in his face. ''Really it wasn't. And he was the sweetest baby—''

Diego got up abruptly. ''I have phone calls to make. Please excuse me.''

Melissa watched him, aching for him. His stiff back said it all. She realized then that it wasn't so much her predicament as missing the birth of his son that had hurt him. She felt guilty about that, too, but there was nothing to be done about it now.

Diego went into the study and closed the door, leaning heavily back against it. He couldn't stand the anguish of knowing what she'd suffered because of him. If only he could talk to her. Bare his heart. Tell her what he really felt, how much she and the boy meant to him. He wondered sometimes if he was still capable of real emotion. His past had been so violent, and tenderness had no place in it. He was only now learning that he was capable of it, with his child and even with Melissa, who more and more was becoming the one beautiful thing in his life. The longer they stayed together, the harder it became for him to hide his increasing hunger for her. Not that it was completely physical now, as it had been in the very beginning in Guatemala. No. It was becoming so much more. But he was uncertain of her. She changed before his eyes, first resentful, then shy and remote, and now she seemed oddly affectionate and teasing.

That, of course, could be simply a kind of repayment, for his having taken care of her and Matt and given them a home when she'd needed time to heal.

Was that it? Was it gratitude, or was it something more? He couldn't tell.

But perhaps it was too soon. She didn't trust him enough to tell him about Matthew. When she did, there might be time for such confessions.

Melissa went back into the living room with Matthew and spread the memory cards out on the floor. They were into the second round before Diego came in again. He'd taken off his jacket and tie and rolled up the sleeves of his white shirt. It was unbuttoned in front, and Melissa's eyes went helplessly to the hair-covered expanse of brown muscle.

He noticed her glance and delighted in her response to him. No woman had ever made him feel as masculine and proud as Melissa. Her soft eyes had a light in them when she looked at him that made his body sing with pleasure. Desire was the one thing he was certain of. She couldn't begin to hide it from his experienced eyes.

"Play with us, Papa!" Matthew called, inviting the tall man down onto the carpet with them.

"We'll make room for you," Melissa said, smiling softly. She moved toward Matthew, making a space beside her where she was lying on her stomach and lifting cards.

"Perhaps for a moment or two," Diego agreed. He took off his shoes and slid alongside Melissa, the warm, cologne-scented length of his body almost touching hers. "How does one play this game?"

They explained it to him and watched him turn over two cards that matched. Matthew laughed and

Melissa groaned as he pulled them near him and made a neat stack.

He smiled at Melissa with a wicked twinkle in his black eyes. "I was watching from the doorway," he confessed. "Although not so much the cards as—" his gaze went to her derriere, so nicely outlined in the tight jeans "—other things."

She flushed, but her gaze didn't falter. "Lecher," she accused in a whisper, teasing.

That surprised and delighted him. His gaze dropped to her smiling mouth, and he bent suddenly and brushed his lips over hers in a whisper of pressure.

Matthew laughed joyfully. "Bobby's mama and daddy used to kiss like that, only Bobby said his mama used to kiss his daddy all the time."

Diego chuckled. "Your mama is not up to kissing me, niño. She is weak from her accident."

Melissa glanced at him mischievously. "Matt, will you go to the kitchen and bring me a cold soft drink, please? And be careful not to open it, okay?"

"Okay!" He jumped up and ran from the room.

Melissa smiled at Diego wickedly. "So I'm too weak to kiss you, am I, señor?" she murmured with soft bravado, enjoying the dark, glittering pleasure she read in his faintly shocked eyes.

She rolled over, pushing him gently onto the carpet. He chuckled with open delight as she bent over him and kissed him with a fervor that dragged a reluctant groan from his lips before his arms reached up and gathered her against him.

"Too weak, am I?" Melissa breathed into his hard mouth.

His hand contracted in her soft, wavy blond hair, and the bristly pressure of his mouth grew rough as he turned her gently and eased her down onto the carpet. She could feel the fierce thunder of his heartbeat against her breasts as her arms curled around his neck and she sighed into his hungry mouth. Her blood sang at the sweet contact. He lifted his head abruptly, and she saw the savage desire in the black eyes that stared unblinking into hers.

"*¡Cuidado,*" he murmured. "You tempt fate."

"Not fate," she whispered unsteadily. "Only you, *señor.*" Her hand slid under his shirt, against his body, her fingers spearing into the dark hair that covered his warm muscles. He stiffened, and she sighed contentedly. "Well, if you don't want to be assaulted, keep your shirt buttoned."

He laughed, thrown completely off balance by the way she was acting with him. "*Dios*, what has become of my shy little jungle orchid?"

"She grew up." Her soft eyes searched his. "You don't mind...?"

He pressed her hand against his chest. "No," he said quietly. "Do what you please, little one. So long as you do not mind the inevitable consequence of such actions as this. You understand?"

"I understand," she whispered, her eyes warm with secrets.

As she spoke, she drew one of Diego's hands to her body and sat up gracefully. Holding his eyes, she

pressed his palm against her blouse where there was
no fabric to conceal the hard thrust of her body.

His breath sighed out as his hand caressed her. "Is
this premeditated?" he asked roughly.

"Oh, yes," she confessed, leaning her head against
his shoulder because his touch was so sweet. "Diego—"

He drew his hand away. "No. Not here."

She looked up at him. "Not interested?" she asked
bravely.

His jaw clenched. "Sweet idiot," he breathed. "If
I held you against me now, my interest would be all
too apparent. But this is not the game we need to be
playing at the moment."

She cleared her throat, aware of where they were.
"Yes. Of course." She smiled, avoiding his eyes, and
turned over again as Matt came rushing back into the
room with her soft drink. She opened it after thanking
the laughing little boy. Then sighing, she turned back
to the game.

Diego lounged nearby, watching but not partici-
pating. The look in his dark eyes was soft and dangerous, and he hardly glanced away from Melissa for
the rest of the evening. But his attitude was both curious and remote. He seemed to suspect her motives
for this new ardor, and she lost her nerve because of
it, withdrawing into her shell again. There were times
when Diego seemed very much a stranger.

Matthew was put to bed eventually. Melissa kept
her expression hidden from Diego but felt her knees
knocking every time he came close. She wished she

knew if her forwardness had offended him, but she was too shy to ask him. While he was bidding Matthew good night, she called her own good night and went into her room. She locked it for the first time since she'd come to the apartment, and only breathed again when she heard his footsteps going down the hall. To her secret chagrin, the steps didn't even hesitate at her door.

On Saturday, Melissa and Joyce spent the entire day buying clothes and having their hair done. The colors she pointed Joyce toward were flamboyant and colorful, bringing attention to her lovely figure and making the most of her exquisite complexion.

"These are sexy clothes," Joyce said, her misgivings evident as she tried on a dress with a halter top that clung like ivy to her slender body. The color was a swirl of reds and yellows and oranges and whites, and it suited her beautifully. "I'll never be able to pull this off."

"Of course you will," Melissa assured her. "All you really need is a little self-confidence. The clothes will give you that and improve your posture, too. You'll feel slinky, so you'll walk like a cat. Try it and see."

Joyce laughed nervously, but when she got a look at herself in one of the exclusive boutique's full-length mirrors, she blinked and drew in her breath. It was as if she suddenly felt reborn. She began to walk, hesitantly at first, then with more and more poise, until she was moving like the graceful West Indian woman she was.

"Yes!" Melissa laughed, clapping her hands. "Yes, that's exactly what I expected. You have a natural grace of carriage, but you've been hiding it in drab, loose clothing. You have a beautiful figure. Show it off!"

Joyce could hardly believe what she was seeing. She tried on another outfit and a turban, and seemed astonished by the elegant creature who looked out of the mirror at her.

"That can't be me," she murmured.

"But it is." Melissa grinned. "Come on. You've got the clothes. Now let's get the rest of the image."

She took Joyce to a hairstylist who did her hair in a fashionable cut that took years off her age and gave her even more poise, drawing her long hair back into an elegant bun with wisps around her small ears. She looked suddenly like a painting, all smooth lines and graceful curves.

"Just one more thing," Melissa murmured, and took her friend to the cosmetics department.

Joyce was given a complete make-over, with an expert cosmetician to show her which colors of powder to have mixed especially for her and which lipsticks and eye shadows and blushers to set off her creamy, blemishless complexion.

"That is not me," Joyce assured her image when the woman was finished and smiling contentedly at her handiwork.

"Poor Apollo," Melissa said with a faint smile. "Poor, poor man. He's done for."

Joyce's heart was in her big eyes. "Is he really?"

"I would say so," Melissa assured her. "Now. Let's get my wardrobe completed and then we'll get to work on the menu for a dinner party Monday night. But you can't wear any of your new clothes or makeup until then," she cautioned. "It has to be a real surprise."

Joyce grinned back at her. "Okay. I can hardly wait!"

"That makes two of us!"

Melissa still had a little money in her own bank account, which she'd had Diego move to Chicago from Tucson. She drew on that to buy some new things of her own. She had her own hair styled, as well, and opted for the makeup job. She tingled with anticipation and fear. Diego wasn't the same easygoing man she'd known in Guatemala. He was much more mature, and his experience intimidated her. If only she could get her nerve back. She had to, because he seemed determined not to make the first move.

By the time she and Joyce finished and went back to the apartment, it was almost dark and Melissa was limping a little.

"You've overdone it," Joyce moaned. "Oh, I hope all this hasn't caused a setback!"

"I'm just sore," Melissa assured her. "And it was fun! Wait until next week, and then the fireworks begin. Don't you dare go near the office like that."

"I wouldn't dream of shocking Apollo into a nervous breakdown," the other woman promised. "I'll go home and practice slinking. Melissa, I can never thank you enough.''

Melissa only smiled. "What are friends for? You gave me the pep talk. The least I could do was help you out a little. You look great, by the way. Really pretty.''

Joyce beamed. "I hope that wild man at the office thinks so.''

"You mark my words, he will. Good night.''

"Good night.''

Melissa let herself into the apartment. Mrs. Albright had the evening off, and it was a shock to find Diego and their son in the kitchen with spicy smells wafting up from the stove.

Diego was wearing Mrs. Albright's long white apron over his slacks and sports shirt, and little Matthew was busily tearing up lettuce to make a salad.

"What are you doing?" Melissa burst out after she'd deposited her packages on the living-room sofa.

"Making dinner, *querida*," Diego said with a smile. "Our son is preparing a heart-of-lettuce salad, and I am making chili and enchiladas. Did you and Joyce have a good time?''

"A wonderful time. My goodness, can't I help?''

"Of course. Set the table, if you please. And do not disturb the cooks," he added with a wicked glance.

She laughed softly, moving to his side. She reached up impulsively and brushed a kiss against his hard cheek. "You're a darling. Can I have the van Meers and the Brettmans and Apollo and Joyce to dinner Monday night?''

Diego caught his breath at her closeness and the unexpected kiss. ''Little one, you can have the boy's club wrestling team over if this change in you is permanent.''

''Have I changed?'' she mused, her pale gray eyes searching his as she clung to his arm and smiled, encouraged by his smile and the softness in his dark eyes.

''More than you realize, perhaps. The leg, it is not painful?''

''A little stiff, that's all.''

''Papa, something is burning,'' Matthew pointed out.

Diego jerked his attention back to the heavy iron skillet he was using, and he began to stir the beef quickly. ''The cook had better return to the chili, *amada*, or we will all starve. Dessert must wait, for the moment,'' he added in a tone that made her toes curl.

''As you wish, *señor*. She laughed softly, moving away reluctantly to put the dishes and silverware on the table.

It was the best meal she could remember in a long time, and dinner brought with it memories of Guatemala and its spicy cuisine. She and Diego talked, but of work and shopping trips and how much Diego had enjoyed the trip to the zoo with Matthew, who enthused about seeing a real lion. For the first time, there were no arguments.

When the little boy was put to bed, Melissa curled up on the sofa to watch a movie on cable while Diego apologetically did paperwork.

"This is new to me," he murmured as he scribbled notes. "But I find that I like the involvement in Apollo's company, as well as the challenge of helping businessmen learn to combat terrorism."

"I suppose it's all very hush-hush," she ventured.

"Assuredly so." He chuckled. "Or what would be the purpose in having such a business to teach survival tactics, hmm?"

She pushed her hair away from her face. "Diego...how do you think Apollo really feels about Joyce?"

He looked up. "No, no," he cautioned, waving a lean finger at her with an indulgent smile. "Such conversations are privileged. I will not share Apollo's secrets with you."

She colored softly. "Fair enough. I won't tell you Joyce's."

"You look just as you did at sixteen," he said softly, watching her, "when I refused to take you to the bull ring with me. You remember, *querida*? You would not speak to me for days afterward."

"I'd have gone to a snake charmer's cell to be with you in those days," she confessed quietly. "I adored you."

"I knew that. It was why I was so careful to keep you at arm's length. I succeeded particularly well, in fact, until we were cut off by a band of guerrillas and forced to hide out in a Mayan ruin. And then I lost my head and satisfied a hunger that had been gnawing at me for a long, long time.''

''And paid the price,'' she added quietly.

He sighed. ''You paid more than I did. I never meant to hurt you. It was difficult knowing that my own lack of control had led me to that precipice and pushed me over. I should never have accused you of trapping me.''

''But there was so much animosity in our pasts,'' she said. ''And you didn't love me.''

His dark eyes narrowed. ''I told you once that my emotions were deeply buried.''

''Yes. I remember. You needn't worry, Diego,'' she said wearily. ''I know you don't have anything to offer me, and I'm not asking for anything. Only for a roof over my head and the chance to raise my son without having to go on welfare.'' Her pale eyes searched his hard face. ''But I'll gladly get a job and pull my weight. I want you to know that.''

He glared at her. ''Have I asked for such a sacrifice?''

''Well, you aren't getting any other benefits, are you?'' she muttered. ''All I'm giving you is two more mouths to feed and memories of the past that must be bitter and uncomfortable.''

He got up, holding his paperwork in one clenched fist. He stared at her angrily. ''You build walls, when I seek only to remove barriers. We still have a long way to go, *querida*. But before we can make a start, you have to learn to trust me.''

"Trust is difficult," she retorted, glaring at him. "And you betrayed me once."

"Yes. Did you not betray me with Matthew's father?"

She started to speak and couldn't. She turned and left the room, her new resolve forgotten in the heat of anger. They seemed to grow farther apart every day, and she couldn't get through to Diego, no matter how hard she tried.

Perhaps the dinner party would open a few doors. Meanwhile, she'd bide her time and pray. He had to care a little about her. If not, why would the past even matter to him? The thought gave her some hope, at least.

Nine

The one consolation Melissa had after a sleepless night was the equally bloodshot look of Diego's eyes. Apparently their difference of opinion the night before had troubled him as much as it had her. And until the argument, things had been going so well. Was Diego right? Was she building walls?

She dressed for church and helped Matthew into the handsome blue suit that Diego had insisted they buy him. She didn't knock on the door of Diego's room as they went into the living room. He was already there, dressed in a very becoming beige suit.

He turned, his dark eyes sweeping over the pale rose dress she wore, which emphasized the soft curves of her body. In the weeks of her recovery, her thinness had left her. She looked much healthier now, and her body was exquisitely appealing. He almost ground his teeth at the effect just gazing at her had on him.

"You look lovely," he said absently.

"I'd look lovelier if I got more sleep," she returned. "We argue so much lately, Diego."

He sighed, moving close to her. Matthew took advantage of their distraction to turn on an educational children's program and laugh with delight at some rhymes.

"And at a time when we should have laid the ghosts to rest, *sí*?" he asked. His lean hands rested gently on her shoulders, caressing her skin through the soft fabric. His black eyes searched hers restlessly. "A little trust, *niña*, is all that we need."

She smiled wistfully. "And what neither of us seem to have."

He bent to brush his mouth softly over her lips. "Let it come naturally," he whispered. "There is still time, is there not?"

Tears stung her eyes at the tenderness in his deep voice. She lifted her arms and twined them around his neck, her fingers caressing the thick hair at the back of his head. "I hope so," she whispered achingly. "For Matthew's sake."

"For his—and not for ours?" he asked quietly. "We lead separate lives, and that cannot continue."

"I know." She leaned her forehead against his firm chin and closed her eyes. "You never really wanted me. I suppose I should be grateful that you came when I went down in the crash. I never expected you to take care of Matt and me."

He touched her hair absently. "How could I leave you like that?" he asked.

''I thought you would when you knew about Matt,'' she confessed.

He tilted her chin and looked into her eyes. His were solemn, unreadable. ''Melissa, I have been alone all my life, except for family. Every day I lived as if death were at the door. I never meant to become involved with you. But I wanted you, little one,'' he whispered huskily. ''Wanted you obsessively, until you were all I breathed. It was my own loss of control, my guilt, which drove us apart. I could not bear to be vulnerable. But I was.'' He shrugged. ''That was what sent me from the casa. It was the reason I lied the night you ran out into the rain and had to be taken to the hospital. Repulse me?'' He laughed bitterly. ''If only you knew. Even now, I tremble like a boy when you touch me....''

Her heart jerked at his admission, because she could feel the soft tremor that ran through his lean body. But after all, it was only desire. And she wanted, needed, so much more.

''Would desire be enough, though?'' she asked sadly, watching him.

He touched her soft cheek. ''Melissa, we enjoy the same things. We like the same people. We even agree on politics. We both love the child.'' He smiled. ''More importantly, we have known each other for oh, so long, *niña*. You know me to the soles of my feet, faults and all. Is that not a better basis for marriage than the desire you seem to think is our only common ground?''

"You might fall in love with someone—" she began.

He touched her mouth with a lean forefinger. "Why not tempt me into falling in love with you, *querida*?" he murmured. "These new clothes and the way you play lately have more effect than you realize." He bent toward her.

She met his lips without restraint, smiling against their warmth. "Could you?"

"Could I what?" he whispered.

"Fall in love with me?"

He chuckled. "Why not tempt me and see?"

She felt a surge of pure joy at the sweetness of the way he was looking at her, but before she could answer him, Matt wormed his way between them and wanted to know if they were ever going to leave to go to church.

They went to lunch after mass and then to a movie that Matt wanted to see. For the rest of the day, there was a new comradeship in the way Diego reacted to her. There were no more accusations or arguments. They played with Matt and cooked supper together for the second night in a row. And that night, when Matt was tucked up and Melissa said good night to Diego, it was with real reluctance that she went to her room.

"*Momento, niña,*" he called, and joined her at her door. Without another word, he drew her gently against him and bent to kiss her with aching tenderness. "Sleep well."

She touched his mouth with hers. "You...too."

Her eyes asked a question she was too shy to put into words, but he shook his head.

"Not just yet, my own," he breathed. His black eyes searched hers. "Only when all the barriers are down will we take that last, sweet step together. For now it is enough that we begin to leave the past behind. Is it tomorrow night that our guests are expected?"

The sudden change of subject was rather like jet lag, she thought amusedly, but she adjusted to it. "Yes. Mrs. Albright and I will no doubt spend the day in the kitchen, but I've already called Gabby and Danielle and Joyce, and they've accepted. I'm looking forward to actually meeting the other wives, although we've talked on the phone quite a lot. I like them."

"I like you," he said unexpectedly, and smiled. "Dream of me," he whispered, brushing his mouth against hers one last time. Then he was gone, quietly striding down the hall to his study.

Melissa went into her room, but not to sleep. She did dream of him, though.

The next day was hectic. That evening, Melissa dressed nervously in one of her new dresses. It was a sweet confection in tones of pink, mauve and lavender with a wrapped bodice and a full skirt and cap sleeves. It took five years off her age and made her look even more blond and fair than she was.

She was trying to fasten a bracelet when she came out of her bedroom. Diego was in the living room, sipping brandy. He watched her approach with a familiar darkness in his eyes, an old softness that brought back so many memories.

"Allow me," he said, putting the brandy snifter down to fasten the bracelet for her. He didn't release her arm when he finished. He frowned, staring at the bracelet.

She knew immediately why he was staring. The bracelet was a tiny strand of white gold with inlaid emeralds, an expensive bit of nothing that Diego had given her when she'd graduated from high school. She colored delicately, and his eyes lifted to hers.

"So long ago I gave you this, *querida*," he said softly. He lifted her wrist to his lips and kissed it. His mustache tickled her delicate skin. "It still means something to you—is that why you kept it all these years, even when you hated me?" he probed.

She closed her eyes at the sight of the raven-black head bent over her hand. "I was never able to hate you, though," she said with a bitter laugh. Tears burned her eyes. "I tried, but you haunted me. You always have."

He drew in a steadying breath as his black head lifted and his eyes searched hers. "As you haunted me," he breathed roughly. "And now *niña*? Do you still care for me, a little, despite the past?" he added, hoping against hope for mere crumbs.

"You needn't pretend that you don't know how I feel about you," she said, her chin trembling under her set lips. "You're like an addiction that I can't quite cure. I gave you everything I had to give, and still it wasn't enough...!'' Tears slipped from her eyes.

"Melissa, don't!'' He caught her to him in one smooth, graceful motion, his lean hand pressing her face into his dark dinner jacket. "Don't cry, little one, I can't bear it.''

"You hate me!''

His fingers contracted in her hair and his eyes closed. "No! *Dios mío, amada,* how could I hate you?'' His cheek moved roughly against hers as he sought her mouth and found it suddenly with his in the silence of the room. He kissed her with undisguised hunger, his hands gentle at her back, smoothing her body into his, caressing her. "Part of me died when you left. You took the very color from my life and left me with nothing but guilt and grief.''

She hardly heard him. His mouth was insistent and she needed him, wanted him. She was reaching up to hold him when the doorbell sounded loudly in the silence.

He drew his head back reluctantly, and the arms that held her had a faint tremor. "No more deceptions,'' he said softly. "We must be honest with each other now. Tonight, when the others leave, we have to talk.''

She touched his mouth, tracing the thick black mustache. "Can you bear total honesty, Diego?'' she asked huskily.

"Perhaps you underestimate me.''

"Didn't I always?'' she sighed.

He heard voices out in the hall and released Melissa to take her hand and lead her toward the group. "When our guests leave, there will be all the time in the world to talk. Matthew has gone to bed, but you might check on him while I pass around drinks to our visitors. Mrs. Albright mentioned that his stomach was slightly uneasy."

"I'll go now." Melissa felt his fingers curl around hers with a thrill of pleasure and gazed up at him. She found his dark eyes smiling down into hers. It had been a long time since they'd been close like this, and lately it had been difficult even to talk to him. She returned the pressure of his hand as they joined a shell-shocked Apollo and a smug Joyce. The West Indian woman didn't even look like Joyce. She was wearing one of the dresses she and Melissa had found while they'd been shopping. It was a cinnamon-and-rust chiffon that clung lovingly to her slender figure, with a soft cowl neckline. Her feet were in strappy high heels. Her hair was pulled back with wisps at her ears, and she was wearing the makeup she'd bought at the boutique. She was a knockout, and Apollo's eyes were registering that fact with reluctance and pure malice.

"Now what did I tell you?" Melissa asked, gesturing at Joyce's dress. "You're just lovely!"

"Indeed she is." Diego lifted her hand to his lips and smiled at her while Apollo shifted uncomfortably and muttered, "Good evening," to his host and hostess.

"I'm just going to look in on Matthew. I'll be right back," Melissa promised, excusing herself.

The little boy was oddly quiet, his eyes drowsy. Melissa pushed back his dark hair and smiled at him.

"Feel okay?" she asked.

"My tummy doesn't," he said. "It hurts."

"Where does it hurt, baby?" she asked gently, and he indicated the middle of his stomach. She asked as many more questions as she could manage and decided it was probably either a virus or something he'd eaten. Still, it could be appendicitis. If it was, it would get worse very quickly, she imagined. She'd have to keep a careful eye on him.

"Try to sleep," she said, her voice soft and loving. "If you don't feel better by morning, we'll see the doctor, all right?"

"I don't want to see the doctor," Matthew said mutinously. "Doctors stick needles in people."

"Not all the time. And you want to get better, don't you? Papa mentioned that we might go to the zoo again next weekend," she whispered conspiratorially. "Wouldn't you like that?"

"Oh, yes," he said. "There are bears at the zoo."

"Then we'll have to get you better. Try to get some sleep, and maybe you'll feel better in the morning."

"All right, Mama."

"I'm just down the hall, and I'll leave your door open a crack. If you need me, call, okay?" She kissed his forehead and paused to smile at him before leaving. But she was almost sure it was a stomach virus. Mrs. Albright's grandson had come down with it just after Matthew had been downstairs to visit him again two days before. It was just a twenty-four-hour bug, but it could make a little boy pretty miserable all the same.

She wiped the frown off her face when she got into the living room. Gabby and J.D. Brettman had arrived by now, and Diego put a snifter of brandy into Melissa's hand and drew her to his side while they talked about Chicago and the business. His arm was possessive, and she delighted in the feel of it, in the feel of him, so close. Her love for him had grown by leaps and bounds in the past few weeks. She wondered if she could even exist apart from him now. Minutes later, Eric van Meer and his wife, a rather plain brunette with glasses and a lovely smile, joined the group. Melissa was surprised; she'd expected Dutch to show up with some beautiful socialite. But as she got to know Danielle, his interest in her was apparent. Dani was unique. So was Gabby.

"Let's let the girls talk fashion for a while. I've got something I need to kick over with you two before we eat," Apollo said suddenly, smiling at the wives and pointedly ignoring Joyce as he moved the men to the other side of the room.

"Just like men," Gabby sighed with a wistful glance at her enormous husband's back. "We're only afterthoughts."

"Someday I'll strangle him," Joyce was muttering to herself. "Someday I'll kick him out the window suspended by the telephone cord and I'll grin while I cut it."

"Now, now." Danielle chuckled. "That isn't a wholesome mental attitude."

Joyce's eyes were even blacker than usual. "I hate him!" she said venomously. "That's wholesome."

Gabby grinned. "He's running scared, haven't you noticed?" she whispered to Joyce. "He's as nervous as a schoolboy. You intimidate him. He comes from sharecroppers down South, and your parents are well-to-do. In a different way, J.D. was much the same before we married. He seemed to hate me, and nothing I did suited him. He fought to the bitter end. Apollo is even less marriage-minded than Dutch, and Dani could write you a book on reluctant husbands. Dutch hated women!"

"He thought he did," Dani corrected with a loving glance at her handsome husband. "But perhaps all they really need is the incentive to become husbands and fathers."

Melissa nodded. "Diego is very good with Matthew, and I never even knew that he liked children in the old days in Guatemala."

"It must have been exciting, growing up in Central America," Gabby remarked.

Melissa's eyes were soft with memories. "It was exciting living next door to Diego Laremos," she corrected. "He was my whole world."

Gabby's eyes narrowed as she studied the blond woman. "And yet the two of you were apart for a long time."

Melissa nodded. "It was a reluctant marriage. I left because I thought he didn't want me anymore, and now we're trying to pick up the pieces. It isn't easy," she confided.

"He's a good man," Gabby said, her green eyes quiet and friendly. "He saved my life in Guatemala when J.D. and I were there trying to rescue J.D.'s sister. Under fire he's one of the coolest characters I've ever seen. So are J.D. and Apollo."

"I suppose it's the way they had to live," Joyce remarked. Her eyes slid across the room to Apollo, and for one instant, everything she felt for the man was in her expression.

Apollo chose that moment to let his attention be diverted, and he looked at the West Indian woman. The air fairly sizzled with electricity, and Joyce's breath caught audibly before she lowered her eyes and clenched her hands in her lap.

"Excuse me, ma'am," Mrs. Albright said from the doorway in time to save Joyce from any ill-timed comments. "But dinner is served."

"Thank you, Mrs. Albright." Melissa smiled and went to Diego's side, amazed at how easy it was to slip her hand into the bend of his elbow and draw him with her. "Dinner, darling," she said softly.

His arm tautened under her gentle touch. "In all the time we have been together," he remarked as they went toward the elegant dining room, "I cannot remember hearing you say that word."

"You say it all the time," she reminded him with a pert smile. "Or the Spanish equivalent, at least, don't you?"

He shrugged. "It seems to come naturally." He pressed her hand against his sleeve, and the look he bent on her was full of affection.

She nuzzled his shoulder with her head, loving the new sense of intimacy she felt with him.

Behind them, the other husbands and wives exchanged expressive smiles. Bringing up the rear, Joyce was touching Apollo's sleeve as if it had thorns on it, and Apollo was as stiff as a man with a poker up his back.

"Relax, will you?" Apollo muttered at Joyce.

"You're a fine one to talk, iron man."

He turned and gazed down at her. They searched each other's eyes in a silence gone wild with new longings, with shared hunger.

"God, don't look at me like that," he breathed roughly. "Not here."

Her lips parted on a shaky breath. "Why not?"

He moved toward her and then abruptly moved away, jerking her along with him into the dining room. He was almost frighteningly stern.

It was a nice dinner, but the guests—two of them at least—kept the air sizzling with tension. When they'd eaten and were enjoying after-dinner coffee from a tray in the living room, the tension got even worse.

"You're standing on my foot," Joyce said suddenly, bristling at Apollo.

"With feet that size, how is that you can even feel it?" he shot back.

"That's it. That's it! You big overstuffed facsimile of a Chicago big shot, who do you think you're talking to?"

"A small overstuffed chili pepper with delusions of beauty," he retorted, his eyes blazing.

Joyce tried to speak but couldn't. She grabbed her purse and, with a terse, tear-threatening good night to the others, ran for the door.

"Damn it!" Apollo went after her out the door, slamming it behind him, while the others paused to exchange conspiratorial smiles and then continue their conversation.

When Apollo eventually came back into the apartment to say good night, he was alone. He looked drawn and a little red on one cheek, but his friends were too kind to remark on it. He left with a rather oblivious smile, and the others said their good nights shortly thereafter and left, too.

The door closed, and Melissa let Diego lead her back into the living room, where there was still half a pot of hot coffee.

"We can drink another cup together," he said, "while Mrs. Albright clears away the dishes."

She poured and watched him add cream to his coffee, her eyes soft and loving. "It went well, don't you think?"

He lifted an eyebrow and smiled. "Apollo and Joyce, you mean? I expect he has met his match there. Properly attired, she has excellent carriage and a unique kind of beauty."

"I thought so, too." She laughed. "I think she hit him. Did you notice his cheek?"

"I was also noticing the very vivid lipstick on his mouth," he mused with a soft chuckle. He leaned back in his chair with a sigh. "Poor man. He'll be married before he knows it."

She balanced her cup and saucer on her lap. "Is that how you think of marriage? As something to cause a man to be pitied?"

"Oh, yes, at one time I felt exactly that way," he admitted. He lit a cheroot and blew out a cloud of smoke. "I even told you so."

"I remember." She smiled into her coffee as she sipped it. "I was young enough and naive enough to think I could make you like it."

"Had I given you the chance, perhaps you might have," he said. His dark eyes narrowed. "I cannot remember even once in my life thinking of children and a home when I was escorting a woman, do you know? Even with you, it was your delectable body I wanted the most, not any idea of permanence. And then I lost my head and found myself bound to you in the most permanent way of all. I hated you and your father for that."

"As I found out," she said miserably.

"It was only when you lost the baby that I came to my senses, as odd as that may sound," he continued, watching her face. "It was then that I realized how much I had thrown away. I had some idea of my grandmother's resentment of you when I left you at the casa and took myself away from your influence. Perhaps I even hoped that my family's coldness would make you leave me." He dropped his dark eyes to his shoes. "I had lived alone so long, free to do as I wanted, to travel as I pleased. But the weeks grew endless without you, and always there was the memory of that afternoon in the rain on our bed of leaves.'' He sighed heavily. ''I came home hoping to drive you away before I capitulated. And then you came to me, and because I was so hungry for you, I told you that you repulsed me. And I pushed you away.'' His eyes closed briefly.

She felt a stirring of compassion for what he'd gone through, even though her own path hadn't been an easy one.

''When you left, how did you manage?'' he asked.

''By sheer force of will, at first.'' She sighed. ''I had to go through a lot of red tape to get to stay in the United States, and when Matthew came along, it got rough. I made a good salary, but it took a lot of money to keep him in clothes and to provide for a baby-sitter. Without Mrs. Grady, I really don't know what I'd have done.''

His chin lifted, and he studied her through narrow dark eyes. ''Did you never wonder about me?''

''At first I wondered. I was afraid that you'd try to find me.'' She twisted her wedding band on her finger. ''Then, after I got over that, I wondered if you were with some other woman, having a good time without me.''

He scowled. ''You thought me a shallow man, *niña*.''

Her thin shoulders lifted, then fell. ''You said yourself that you didn't love me or need me, that I was a nuisance you'd been saddled with. What else was I to think, Diego? That you were pining away for love of me?''

He took a draw from his cheroot and quietly put it out with slow, deliberate movements of his hand. "When I began selling my services abroad for a living, it was to help my family out of a financial bind," he began. "Because your mother had run away with your father, taking her dowry from us, the family fortunes suffered and we were in desperate need. After a while I began to enjoy the excitement of what I did, and the risk. Eventually the reason I began was lost in the need for adventure and the love of freedom and danger. I suppose I fed on adrenaline."

"There's something your family never knew about my mother's dowry, Diego," Melissa said. "She didn't have one."

He scowled. "What is this? My father said—"

"Your father didn't know. My grandfather was in financial straits himself. He was hoping for a merger between his fruit company and your family's banana plantations to help him get his head above water." She smiled ironically. "There was never any dowry. That was one reason she ran away with my father, because she felt guilty that her father was trying to use her in a dishonest way to make money. My father's father died soon afterward, and my father inherited his fortune. That's where our money came from, not from my mother's dowry."

"*Dios mío,*" he breathed, putting his face in his hands. "*Dios,* and my family blamed your father all those years for our financial problems."

"He thought it best not to tell you," she said. "The wounds were deep enough, and your father said some harsh things to him after he and my mother were married. I suppose he rubbed salt in the wounds, because my father never forgave him."

"You make me ashamed, Melissa," he said finally, lifting his dark head. "I seem to have given you nothing but heartache."

"I wasn't blameless," she said. "The poems and the note I wrote so impulsively were genuine, you know. All I lacked was the courage to send them to you. I knew even then that a sophisticated man would never want an unworldly girl like me. I wasn't even pretty," she said wistfully.

"But you were exquisite," he said. He looked and sounded astonished at her denial of her own beauty. "A tea rose in bud, untouched by sophistication and cynicism. I adored you. And once I tasted your sweetness, *amada*, I was intoxicated."

"Yes, I noticed that." She sighed bitterly.

"I fought against marriage, that is true," he admitted. "I fought against your influence, and to some extent I won. But even as you ran from my bedroom that last night at the casa, I knew that I had lost. I was going after you, to tell you that I had meant none of what I said. I was going to ask you to try to make our marriage work, Melissa. And I would have tried. At least I was fond of you, and I wanted you. There was more than enough to build a marriage on." He didn't add how that feeling had grown over the years until now the very force of it almost winded him when he looked at her. He couldn't tell her everything just yet.

She searched his dark, unblinking eyes. "I was too young, though," she said. "I would have wanted things you couldn't have given me. You were my idol, not a flesh-and-blood man. You were larger than life, and how can a mere mortal woman live up to such a paragon? Oh, no, *señor*. I prefer you as you are now. Flesh and blood and sometimes a little flawed. I can deal with a man who is as human as I am."

He began to smile, and the warmth of his lips was echoed in his quiet, possessive gaze. "Can you, *enamorada*?" he asked. "Then come here and show me."

Her heart skipped with pure delight. "On the couch?" she asked, her eyebrows raised. "With the door wide open and Mrs. Albright in the kitchen?"

He chuckled softly. "You see the way you affect my brain, Melissa. It seems to stop working when I am in the same room with you."

"All finished, except for the coffee things," Mrs. Albright said cheerfully as she came into the room.

"Leave the coffee things until tomorrow," Diego said, smiling at her. "You have done quite enough, and your check this week will reflect our appreciation. Now go home and enjoy your own family. *¡Buenas noches!*"

"Thank you, *señor*, and *buenas noches* to you, too. Ma'am." She nodded to Melissa, got her coat from the closet and let herself out of the apartment.

Diego's eyes darkened as they slid over Melissa
with an expression in them that could have melted
ice. "Now," he said softly. "Come here to me, little
one."

She got up, her heartbeat shaking her, and moved
toward him. Diego caught her around the waist and
pulled her down into his lap with her blond head in
the crook of his arm and his black eyes searing down
into hers.

"No more barriers," he breathed as he lowered his
head, drowning her in his expensive cologne and the
faint tobacco scent of his mouth. "No more subterfuge, no more games. We are husband and wife, and
now we become one mind, one heart, one body...
amada!"

His mouth moved hungrily on hers and she clung
to him warmly, delighting in his possessive hold, in
the need she could sense as well as feel. He was going
to possess her, but she was no longer a twenty-year-
old girl with stars in her eyes. She was a woman, and
fully awakened to her own wants and needs.

She bit his lower lip, watching to see his expression. He chuckled softly, arrogance in every line of
his dark face.

"So," he breathed. "You are old enough now for
passion, is that what you are telling me with this provocative caress? Then beware, *querida*, because in
this way my knowledge is far superior to yours."

Her breath quickened. "Show me," she whispered,
curling her fingers into the thick hair at the nape of
his neck. "Teach me."

"It will not be as tender as it was the first time, *amada*," he said roughly, and something dark kindled in his eyes. "It will be a savage loving."

"Savage is how I feel about you, *señor*," she whispered, lifting her mouth to tease his. "Savage and sweet and oh, so hungry!"

He allowed the caress and repeated it against her starving mouth. "Then taste me, *querida*," he whispered as he opened her lips with his and his arms contracted. "And let us feast on passion."

She moaned, because the pleasure was feverish. He bruised her against him, and she felt his hand low on her hips, gathering them against the fierce tautness of his body. She began to tremble. She'd lived on dreams of him for years, but now there was the remembered delight of his mouth, of his body. He wanted her, and she wanted him so much it was agonizing. She clung, a tiny cry whispering into his mouth as she gave in completely, loving him beyond bearing.

He rose gracefully, lifting her easily as he got up. He lifted his head only a breath away, holding her eyes as he walked down the hall with her, his gaze possessive, explosively sweet.

"No quarter, *enamorada*," he whispered huskily. "This night, I will show no mercy. I will fulfil you and you will complete me. I will love you as I never dreamed of loving a woman in the darkness."

She trembled at the emotion in his deep, softly accented voice. "You don't believe in love," she whispered shakily.

His dark eyes held her wide gray ones. "Do I not, Melissa? Wait and see what I feel. By morning you may have learned a great deal more about me than you think you know."

She buried her face in his throat and pressed closer, shuddering with the need to give him her heart along with her body.

"*Querida...*" he breathed. His arms tightened bruisingly.

At the same time, a childish voice cried out in the darkness, and that sound was followed by the unmistakable sound of someone's dinner making a return appearance.

Ten

Matthew was sick twice. Melissa mopped up after him with the ease of long practice and changed his clothes and his sheets after bathing him gently with soap and warm water.

He cried, his young pride shattered by his loss of control. "I'm sorry," he wailed.

"For what, baby?" she said gently, kissing his forehead. "Darling, we all get sick from time to time. Mrs. Albright's grandson had this virus, and I'm sure that's where you caught it, but you'll be much better in the morning. I'm going to get you some cracked ice so that you don't get dehydrated, and perhaps Papa will sit with you until I get back."

"Of course," Diego said, catching Melissa's hand to kiss it gently as she went past him. "Make a pot of coffee for us, *amada*."

"You don't need to sit up, too," she said. "I can do it."

His dark eyes searched hers. "This is what being a father is all about, is it not? Sharing the bad times as well as the good? What kind of man would I be to go merrily to my bed and leave you to care for a sick little boy?"

She could barely breathe. He was incredible. She touched his mouth with her forefinger. "I adore you," she breathed, and left before she gave way to tears.

When she came back, with the coffee dripping and its delicious aroma filling the kitchen, she was armed with a cup of cracked ice and a spoon. Diego was talking to Matthew in a low voice. It was only when Melissa was in the room that she recognized the story he was telling the boy. It was "Beauty and the Beast," one of her own favorites.

"And they lived happily ever after?" Matthew asked, looking pale but temporarily keeping everything down.

"Happiness is not an automatic thing in the real world, *mi hijo*," Diego said as Melissa perched on the side of the bed and spooned a tiny bit of cracked ice into Matthew's mouth. "It is rather a matter of compromise, communication and tolerance. Is this not so, Señora Laremos?"

She smiled at him. He was lounging in the chair beside the bed with his shirt unbuttoned and his sleeves rolled up, looking very Latin and deliciously masculine with the shirt and slacks outlining every powerful muscle in his body.

"Yes. It is so," she agreed absently, but her eyes were saying other things.

He chuckled deeply, and the message in his own eyes was more than physical.

She gave Matthew the ice and took heart when it stayed in his stomach. In a little while he dozed off, and Melissa pushed the disheveled dark hair away from his forehead and adored him with her eyes.

"A fine young man," Diego said softly. "He has character, even at so early an age. You have done well."

She glanced at him with a smile. "He was all I had of—" She bit her tongue, because she had almost said "of you."

But he knew. He smiled, his eyes lazily caressing her. "I have waited a long time for you to tell me. Do you not think that this is the proper time, *querida*? On a night when we meant to love each other in the privacy of my bedroom and remove all the barriers that separate us? Here, where the fruit of our need for each other sleeps so peacefully in the security of our love for him?"

She drew in a steadying breath. "Did you know all the time?" she asked.

"No," he said honestly, and smiled. "I was insanely jealous of Matt's mythical father. It made me unkind to him at first, and to you. But as I grew to know him, and you, I began to have my suspicions. That was why I sent for his birth certificate."

"Yes, I saw it accidentally in your desk," she confessed, and noted the surprise in his face.

"But before I saw it," he continued softly, "Matthew described to me a photograph of his father that you had shown him." He smiled at her flush. "Yes, *niña*. The same photograph I had seen in your drawer under your gowns, and never told you. So many keepsakes. They gave me the only hope I had that you still had a little affection for me."

She laughed. "I was afraid you'd seen them." She shook her head. "I cared so much. And I was afraid, I've always been afraid, that you might want Matt more than you wanted me." She lowered her eyes. "You said that love wasn't a word you knew. But Matt was your son," she whispered, admitting it at last, "and you'd have wanted him."

"Him, and not you?" he asked softly. He leaned forward, watching her. "Melissa, I have not been kind to you. We married for the worst of reasons, and even when I found you again I was still fighting for my freedom. But now..." He smiled tenderly. "*Amada*, I awaken each morning with the thought that I will see you over the breakfast table. At night I sleep soundly, knowing that you are only a few yards away from me. My day begins and ends with you. And in these past weeks, you have come to mean a great deal to me. I care very much for my son. But Melissa, you mean more to me than anything on earth. Even more than Matthew."

She gnawed her lower lip while tears threatened. She took a slow, shuddering breath. "I wanted to tell you before I left Guatemala that I hadn't lost the baby. But I couldn't let him be born and raised in such an atmosphere of hatred.'' She looked down at the carpet. "He was all I had left of you, and I wanted him desperately. So I came to America, gave birth to him and raised him.'' Her eyes found his. "But there was never a day, or a night, or one single second, when you weren't in my thoughts and in my heart. I never stopped loving you. I never will.''

"Amada," he breathed.

"Matthew is your son,'' she said simply, smiling through tears. "I'm sorry I didn't trust you enough to tell you.''

"I'm sorry I made it so difficult.'' He leaned forward and took her hand in his, kissing the palm softly, hungrily. "We made a beautiful child together,'' he said, lifting his dark eyes to hers. "He combines the best of both of us.''

"And we can look into his face and see generations of Sterlings and Laremoses staring back at us,'' she agreed. Her soft eyes held his. "Oh, Diego, what a waste the past years have been!''

He stood up, drawing her into his arms. He held her and rocked her, his voice soft at her ear, whispering endearments in Spanish while she cried away the bitterness and the loneliness and the pain.

"Now, at last, we can begin again,'' he said. "We can have a life together, a future together.''

"I never dreamed it would happen.'' She wiped at her eyes. "I almost ran away again. But then Joyce reminded me that I'd done that before and solved nothing. So I stayed to fight for you.''

He laughed delightedly. "So you did, in ways I

never expected. I had married a child in Guatemala. I hardly expected the woman I found in Tucson.''

"I couldn't believe it when I saw you there," she said. "I'd dreamed of you so much, wanted you so badly, and then there you were. But I thought you hated me, so I didn't dare let you see how I felt. And there was Matt."

"Why did you not tell me the truth at the beginning?" he asked quietly.

"Because I couldn't be sure that you wouldn't take him away from me." She sighed. "And because I wanted you to trust me, to realize all by yourself that I'd loved you far too much to betray you with another man."

"To my shame, I believed that at first," he confessed. "And blamed myself for being so cruel to you that I made you hate me enough to run away."

"I never hated you," she said, loving his face with her eyes. "I never could. I understood, even then. And it was my own fault. The note, the poems, and I gave in without even a fight…"

"The fault was mine as well, for letting my desire for you outweigh my responsibility to protect you." He sighed heavily. "So much tragedy, my own, because we abandoned ourselves to pleasure. At the time, consequences were the last thought we had, no?"

"Our particular consequence, though, is adorable, don't you think, *esposo mío*?" she smiled at their sleeping son.

He followed her glance. *"Muy adorable."* His eyes caressed her. "Like his oh-so-beautiful *madrecita.*"

Touched by the tenderness in his deep voice, she reached up and kissed him, savoring the warm hunger of his embrace. Matthew stirred, and she sat back down beside him, watching his eyes open sleepily.

"Feeling better?" she asked gently.

"I'm hungry," he groaned.

"Nothing else to eat just yet, young man," she said, smiling. "You have to make sure your tummy's settled. But how about some more cracked ice?"

"Yes, please," he mumbled.

Diego got up and took the cup and the spoon from her. "I could use some coffee, *querida,*" he suggested.

"So could I. I'll get it."

She left him there after watching the tender way he fed ice to Matthew, the wonder of fatherhood and the pride of it written all over his dark face. Melissa had never felt so happy in all her life. As she left the room she heard his voice, softly accented, exquisitely loving, telling the little boy at last that he was his real papa. Tears welled up in her eyes as she left them, and she smiled secretly through them, bursting with joy.

It was a long night, but the two of them stayed with the little boy. Melissa curled up on the foot of his bed finally to catch a catnap, and Diego slept sprawled in the chair. Mrs. Albright found them like that the next morning and smiled from the doorway. But Matthew was nowhere in sight.

Frowning, she went toward the kitchen, where there was a strange smell...

"Matthew!" she gasped at the doorway.

"I'm hungry," Matthew muttered, "and mama and papa won't wake up."

He was standing in his pajamas at the stove, bare-foot, cooking himself two eggs. Unfortunately, he had the heat on high and several pieces of eggshell in the pan, and the result was a smelly black mess.

Mrs. Albright got it all cleared away and picked him up to carry him back to bed. "I'll get your break-fast, my lamb. Why were you hungry?"

"My supper came back up again," he explained.

Mrs. Albright nodded wisely. "Stomach bug."

"A very bad bug," he agreed. "Papa is my real papa, you know, he said so, and we're going to live with him forever. Can I have some eggs?"

"Yes, lamb, in just a minute," she promised with a laugh as they went into the bedroom.

"Matthew?" Melissa mumbled as she looked up and saw Mrs. Albright bringing Matthew into the room.

Diego blinked and yawned as Mrs. Albright put the boy back in bed. "Where did you find him?" he asked, his face unshaven and his eyes bleary.

"In the kitchen cooking his breakfast," Mrs. Albright chuckled, registering their openly horrified ex-pressions. "It's all right now. I've taken care of everything. I'll get him some scrambled eggs and toast if you think it's safe. I'd bet that it is, if my opinion is wanted. He looks fit to me."

"You should have seen him last night," Melissa said with a drowsy smile. "But if he thinks he's hungry, he can have some eggs."

"You two go and get some sleep," Mrs. Albright said firmly. "Matthew's fine, and I'll look out for him. I'll even call the office for you, *señor*, if you like, and tell them where you are."

"That would be most kind of you." He yawned, taking Melissa by the hand. "Come along, Señora Laremos, while I can stand up long enough to guide us to bed."

"*¡Buenas noches!*" Matthew grinned.

"*¡Buenos días!*" Melissa corrected with a laugh. "And eat only a little breakfast, okay?" She threw him a kiss. "Good night, baby chick."

She followed Diego into his bedroom and got into the bed while he locked the door. She hardly felt him removing her dress and hose and shoes and slip. Seconds later, she was asleep.

Sunshine streamed lazily through the windows when she stretched under the covers, frowning as she discovered that she didn't have a stitch of clothing on her body.

Diego came into the bedroom from the bathroom with a towel around his lean hips and his hair still damp.

"Awake at last," he murmured dryly. He reached down and jerked the covers off, his dark eyes appreciative of every soft, pink inch of her body as he looked at her openly for the first time in five years.

The impact of it was in his eyes, his face. "*Dios mío*, what a beautiful sight," he breathed, smiling at her shy blush.

As he spoke, he unfastened his towel and threw it carelessly on the floor. "Now," he breathed, easing down beside her. "This is where we meant to begin last night, is it not, *querida*?"

She knew it was incredible to be shy with him, but it had been five years. She lowered her eyes to his mouth and looped her arms around his neck and shifted to accommodate the warm weight of his muscular body. She shivered, savoring the abrasive pleasure of his chest hair against her soft breasts, the hardness of his long legs tangling intimately with hers.

Tremors of pleasure wound through her. "Sweet," she whispered shakily, drawing him closer. Her mouth nipped at his, pleaded, danced with it. "It's so sweet, feeling you like this."

"An adequate word for something so wondrous," he whispered, smiling against her eager mouth. He touched her, watching her eyes dilate and her body stiffen. "There, *querida*?" he asked sensuously. "Softly, like this?" He did it again, and she shuddered deliciously and arched. A sensual banquet, after years of starvation.

"You...beast," she chided. Her nails dug into his shoulders as she watched the face above hers grow dark with passion, his eyes glittering as he bent to her body.

"A feast fit for a starving man," he whispered as his lips traced her soft curves, lingering to tease and nip at the firm thrust of her breasts, at her rib cage, her flat belly. And all the while he talked to her, described what he felt and what he was doing and what he was going to do.

She moved under the exploration of his hands, her eyes growing darker and wilder as he kindled the flames of passion. Once she looked directly into his eyes as he moved down, and she saw the naked hunger in them as his body penetrated hers for the first time in more than five years.

She cried, a keening, husky, breathless little sound that was echoed in her wide eyes and the stiffening of her welcoming body. She cried in passion and in pain, because at first there was the least discomfort.

"Ah, it has been a long time, has it not?" he whispered softly, delighting in the pleasure he read in her face. "Relax, my own." His body stilled, giving hers time to adjust to him, to admit him without discomfort. "Relax. Yes, *querida*, yes, yes..." His eyes closed as he felt the sudden ease of his passage, and his teeth ground together at an unexpected crest of fierce pleasure. He shuddered. "Exquisite," he groaned, opening his eyes to look at her as he moved again, his weight resting on his forearms. "Exquisite, this...with you...this sharing." His eyes closed helplessly as his movements became suddenly harsh and sharp. "Forgive me...!"

But she was with him every step of the way, her fit young body matching his passion, equaling it. She adjusted her body to the needs of his, and held him and watched him and gloried in his fulfillment just before she found her own and cried out against his shoulder in anguished completion.

He shuddered over her, his taut body relaxing slowly, damp, his arms faintly tremulous. She bit his shoulder and laughed breathlessly, feeling for the first time like a whole woman, like a wife.

"Now try to be unfaithful to me," she dared him, whispering the challenge into his ear. "Just try and I'll wear you down until you can hardly crawl away from my bed!"

He nipped her shoulder, laughing softly. "As if I could have touched another woman after you," he whispered. "*Querida*, I took my marriage vows as seriously as you took yours. Guilt and anguish over losing you made it impossible for me to sleep with anyone else." He lifted his damp head and searched her drowsy, shocked eyes. "*Amada*, I love you," he said softly. He brushed her mouth with his. "I do not want anyone else. Not since that first time with you, when I knew that your soul had joined with mine so completely that part of me died when you left."

She hid her face against him, weeping with joy and pain and pleasure. "I'm sorry."

"It is I who am sorry. But our pain is behind us, and now our pleasure begins. This is only the start, this sweet sharing of our bodies. We will share our lives, Melissa. Our sorrow and our joy. Laughter and tears. For this is what makes a marriage."

She reached up and kissed his dark cheek. "I love you so much."

"As I love you." He twined a strand of her long

blond hair around his forefinger. His eyes searched hers. He bent, and his mouth opened hers. Seconds later she pulled him down to her again, and he groaned as the flare of passion burned brightly again, sending them down into a fiery oblivion that surpassed even the last one.

Mrs. Albright was putting supper on the table when they reappeared, freshly showered and rested and sharing glances that held a new depth of belonging.

Matthew was still in his room. They ate supper alone and then went to see him, delighting in the strength of their attachment to each other, delighting in their son.

"Tomorrow I will bring you a surprise when I come home from work. What would you like?" Diego asked his son.

"Only you, Papa," the little boy laughed, reaching up to be held and hugged fiercely.

"In that case, I shall bring you a battleship, complete with crew," his Papa chuckled with a delighted glance toward Melissa, who smiled and leaned against him adoringly.

Diego went to work reluctantly the next morning to find Apollo like a cat with a bad leg and Joyce as cold as if she'd spent two days in a refrigerator.

"How's Matthew?" Apollo asked when Diego entered the office.

"He's much better, thanks, but his mama and I are still trying to catch up on our sleep," Diego laughed, and told him about Matthew's attempt to make breakfast.

Joyce laughed. "I hope your fire insurance is paid up."

Apollo stared at her with unconcealed hunger. "Don't you have something to do?" he asked curtly.

"Of course, but I have to work for you instead," she said with a sweet smile. She was wearing another one of the new outfits, and she looked very pretty in a red-and-orange print that showed off her figure to its best advantage. Apollo could hardly keep his eyes off her, which made for a long and confusing work-day.

When Diego went home that afternoon, Apollo was at the end of his rope. He glared at Joyce and she glared back until they both had to look away or die from the electricity in their joined gaze.

"You look nice," he said irritably.

"Thank you," she said with equal curtness.

He drew in an angry breath. "Oh, hell, we can't go on like this," he muttered, going around the desk after her. He caught her by the arms and pulled her against him, his mind registering that she barely came up to his shoulder and that she made him feel violently masculine. "Look, it's impossible to treat each other this way after what happened at the Laremoses two nights ago. I'm going crazy. Just looking at you makes my body ache."

She drew in a steadying breath, because he was affecting her, too. "What do you want to do about it?" she asked, certain that he was thinking along serious lines and wondering how she was going to bear it if he wasn't.

He tilted her mouth up to his and kissed her, long and hard and hungrily. She moaned, stepping closer, pushing against him. His arms swallowed her and he groaned.

"I won't hurt you," he promised huskily, his black eyes holding hers. "I swear to God, I won't. I'll take a long time..."

She could barely make her mind work. "What?"

"I'll get you a better apartment, in the same building as mine," he went on. "We'll spend almost every night together, and if things work out, maybe you can move in with me eventually."

She blinked. "You...want me to be your mistress?"

He scowled. "What's this mistress business? This is America. People live together all the time—"

"I come from a good home and *we* don't live together," she said proudly. "We get married and have babies and behave like a family! My mother would shoot you stone-cold dead if she thought you were trying to seduce me!"

"Who is your mama, the Lone Ranger?" he chided. "Listen, honey, I can have any woman I want. I don't have to go hungry just because my little virgin secretary has too many hang-ups to—oof!"

Joyce surveyed her handiwork detachedly, registering the extremely odd look on Apollo's face as he bent over the stomach she'd put her knee into. He was an interesting shade of purple, and it served him right.

"I quit, by the way," Joyce said with a smile he

couldn't see. She turned, cleaned out her desk drawer efficiently and picked up her purse. There wasn't much to get together. She felt a twinge of regret because she loved the stupid man. But perhaps this was best, because she wasn't going to be any man's kept woman, modern social fad or not.

"Goodbye, boss," she said as she headed for the door. "I hope you have better luck with your next secretary."

"She can't...be worse...than you!" he bit off, still doubled over.

"You sweet man," she said pleasantly as she paused in the doorway. "It's been a joy working for you. I do hope you'll give me a good reference."

"I wouldn't refer you to hell!"

"Good, because I don't want to go anyplace where I'd be likely to run into you!" She slammed the door and walked away. By the time she was in the elevator going down, the numbness had worn off and she realized that she'd burned her bridges. There were tears welling up in her eyes before she got out of the building.

She wound up at Melissa's apartment, crying in great gulps. Diego took one look at her and poured her a drink, then left the women alone in the living room and went off to play the memory game with his son.

"Tell me all about it," Melissa said gently when Joyce managed to stop crying.

"He wants me to be his mistress," she wailed, and buried her face in the tissue Melissa had given her.

"Oh, you poor thing." Melissa curled her feet under her on the sofa. "What did you tell him, as if I didn't know?"

"It wasn't so much what I told him as what I did," Joyce confessed. She grinned sheepishly. "I kicked him in the stomach."

"Oops."

"Well, he deserved it. Bragging about how many women he could get if he wanted them, laughing at me for being chaste." Joyce lifted her chin pugnaciously. "My mother would die if she heard him say such a thing. She has a very religious background, and I was raised strictly and in the church."

"So was I, so don't apologize," Melissa said softly. "Let me tell you, I learned the hard way that it's best to save intimacy for marriage. I'm a dinosaur, I suppose. Where I grew up, the family had its own special place. No member of the family ever did anything to besmirch the family name. Now honor is just a word, but at what cost?"

"You really are a dinosaur," Joyce sighed.

"Purely prehistoric," Melissa agreed. "What are you going to do, my friend?"

"What most dinosaurs do, I guess. I'm going to become extinct, at least as far as Apollo Blain is concerned. I resigned before I left." Her eyes misted again. "I'll never see him again."

"I wouldn't bet on it. Stay for supper and then we'll see what we can do about helping you get another job."

"You're very kind," Joyce said, "but I think it

might be best if I go back to Miami. Or even home to my mother.'' She shrugged. "I don't think I'll be able to fit into this sophisticated world. I might as well go back where I belong.''

"I'll have no one to talk to or shop with,'' Melissa moaned. "You can't! Listen, we'll dig a Burmese tiger trap outside Apollo's office door…''

"You're a nice friend,'' Joyce said, smiling. "But it really won't do. We'll have to think of something he can't gnaw through.''

"Let's have supper. Then we'll talk.''

Joyce shook her head. "I can't eat. I want to go home and have a good cry and call my mother. I'll talk to you tomorrow, all right? Meanwhile, thank you for being my friend.''

"Thank you for being mine. If you get too depressed, call me. Okay?''

Joyce got up, smiling. "Okay.''

Melissa walked her to the door and let her out. Then she leaned back against it, sighing.

Diego came into the hall with his eyebrows raised. "Trouble?''

"She quit. After she kicked your boss in the stomach,'' she explained. "I think he's probably going to be in a very bad mood for the rest of the week, although I'm only guessing,'' she added, grinning.

He moved toward her, propping his arms at either side of her head. He smiled. "Things are heating up,'' he remarked.

"And not only for Joyce and Apollo,'' she whispered, tempting him until he bent to her mouth and kissed her softly.

She nibbled his lower lip, smiling. ''Come here,'' she breathed, reaching around his waist to draw his weight down on hers.

He obliged her, and she could tell by his breathing as well as by the tautness of his body and his fierce heartbeat that he felt as great a need for her as she felt for him. She opened her mouth to the fierce pressure of his.

''Papa!''

Diego lifted his head reluctantly. ''In a moment, *mi hijo*,'' he called back. ''Your mother and I are discussing plans,'' he murmured, brushing another kiss against Melissa's eager mouth.

''What kind of plans, Papa, for a trip to the zoo?'' Matthew persisted.

''Not exactly. I will be back in a moment, all right?''

There was a long sigh. ''All right.''

Diego shifted his hips and smiled at Melissa's helpless response. ''I think an early night is in order,'' he breathed. ''To make up for our lack of sleep last night,'' he added.

''I couldn't possibly agree more,'' she murmured as his mouth came down again. It grew harder and more insistent by the second, but the sound of Mrs. Albright's voice calling them into the dining room broke the spell.

''I long for that ancient Mayan ruin where we first

knew each other," Diego whispered as he stood up and let her go.

"With armed guerrillas hunting us, spiders crawling around, snakes slithering by, and lightning striking all around," she recalled. She shook her head. "I'll take Chicago any day, Diego!"

He chuckled. "I can hardly argue with that. Let us eat, then we will discuss this trip to the zoo that our son seems determined to make."

There was a new temporary secretary at work for the rest of the week, but Apollo didn't give her a hard time. In fact, he looked haggard and weary and miserable.

"Perhaps you need a vacation, amigo," Diego said.

"It wouldn't hurt," Dutch nodded, propped gracefully against Apollo's desk with a lighted cigarette in one lean hand.

Apollo glowered at them. "Where would I go?"

Diego studied his fingernails. "You could go to Ferris Street," he remarked. "I understand the weather there is quite nice."

Ferris Street was where Joyce's apartment was, and Apollo glowered furiously at the older man.

"You could park your car there and just relax," Dutch seconded, pursing his lips. His blond hair looked almost silver in the light. "You could read a book or take along one of those little television sets and watch soap operas with nobody to bother you."

"Ferris Street is the end of the world," Apollo said. "You don't take a vacation sitting in your damned car on a side street in Chicago! What's the matter with you people?''

"You could entice women to sit in your car with you," Dutch said. "Ferris Street could be romantic with the right companion. You were a counterterrorist. You know how to appropriate people."

"This is true," Diego agreed. "He appropriated us for several missions, at times when we preferred not to go."

"Right on," Dutch said. He studied Apollo curiously. "I was like you once. I hated women with a hell of lot more reason than you've got. But in the end I discovered that living with a woman is a hell of a lot more interesting than being shot at."

"I asked her to live with me, for your information, Mr. Social Adviser," Apollo muttered. "She kicked me in the gut!"

"What about marriage?" Dutch persisted.

"I don't want to get married," Apollo said.

"Then it is as well that she resigned," Diego said easily. "She can find another man to marry and give her children—"

"Shut up, damn you!" Apollo looked shaken. He wiped the sweat off his forehead. "Oh, God, I've got to get out of here. You guys have things to do, don't you? I'm going for a walk!"

He started out the door.

"You might walk along Ferris Street," Dutch called after him. "I hear flowers are blooming all over the place."

"You might even see a familiar face," Diego added with a grin.

Apollo threw them a fiercely angry gesture and slammed the door behind him.

Dutch got off the desk and moved toward the door with Diego. "He'll come around," the blond man mused. "I did."

"We all come to it," Diego said. He smiled at the younger man. "Bring Dani to supper Saturday. And bring the children. Matthew would enjoy playing with your eldest."

Dutch eyed him. "Everything's okay now, I gather?"

Diego sighed. "My friend, if happiness came in grains of sand, I would be living on a vast desert. I have the world."

"I figured Matthew was yours," Dutch said unexpectedly. "Melissa didn't strike me as the philandering kind."

"As in the old days, you see deeply," Diego replied. He smiled at his friend. "And your Dani, she is content to stay with the children instead of working?"

"Until they're in school, yes. After that, I keep hearing these plans for a really unique used bookstore." Dutch grinned. "Whatever she wants. I come first, you know. I always have and I always will. It's enough to make a man downright flexible."

Diego thought about that all the way home. Yes, it did. So if Melissa wanted to work when Matthew started school, why not? He told her so that night as she lay contentedly in his arms watching the city lights play on the ceiling of the darkened room. She smiled and rolled over and kissed him. And very soon afterward, he was glad he'd made the remark.

Eleven

There were bells ringing. Melissa put her head under the pillow, but still they kept on. She groaned, reaching out toward the telephone and fumbled it under the pillow and against her ear.

"Hello?" she mumbled.

"Melissa? Is Diego awake?" Apollo asked.

She murmured something and put the receiver against Diego's ear. It fell off and she put it back, shaking his brown shoulder to make him aware of it.

"Hello," he said drowsily. "Who is it?"

There was a pause. All at once he sat straight up in bed, knocking off the pillow and stripping back the covers. "You what?"

Melissa lifted her head, because the note in Diego's voice sounded urgent and shocked. "What is it?" she whispered.

"You what?" Diego repeated. He launched into a wild mixture of Spanish and laughter, then reverted to English. "I wouldn't have believed it. When?"

"What is it?" Melissa demanded, punching Diego.

He put his hand over the receiver. "Apollo and Joyce are being married two days from now. They want us to stand up with them."

Melissa laughed delightedly and clapped her hands. "We'll all come," she said. "There'll be photographers and we'll bring the press!"

"Yes, we'll be delighted," Diego was telling Apollo. "Melissa sends her love to Joyce. We'll see you there. Yes. Congratulations! *¡Hasta luego!*"

"Married!" Melissa sighed, sending an amused, joyful glance at her husband. "And he swore he never would."

"He shouldn't have," Diego grinned. He picked up the phone again and dialed. "I have to tell Dutch," he explained. "I'll tell you later about how we suggested Apollo should take his vacation in his car on Ferris Street."

Melissa giggled, because she had a pretty good idea what kind of vacation they'd had in mind....

Two days later, a smiling justice of the peace married Apollo and Joyce in a simple but beautiful ceremony while Melissa, Diego, the Brettmans and the van Meers, Gabby's mother and First Shirt, Semson and Drago all stood watching. It was the first time the entire group had been together in three years.

Apollo, in a dark business suit, and Joyce, in a

white linen suit, clasped hands and repeated their vows with exquisite joy on their faces. They smiled at each other with wonder and a kind of shyness that touched Melissa's heart. Clinging to her husband's hand, she felt as if all of them shared in that marriage ceremony. It was like a rededication of what they all felt for their spouses, a renewal of hope for the future.

Afterward, all of them gathered at a local restaurant for the reception, and Apollo noticed for the first time the number of photographers who were enjoying hors d'oeuvres and coffee and soft drinks.

He frowned. "I don't mean to sound curious," he murmured to Diego and Dutch, "but there sure are a lot of cameras here."

"Evidence," Dutch said.

"In case you got cold feet," Diego explained, "we were going to blackmail you by sending photographs to all the news media showing that your courage had deserted you at the altar."

"You guys," Apollo muttered.

Joyce leaned against his shoulder and reached up to kiss his lean cheek warmly. "I helped pay for the photographers," she confessed. "Well, I had to have an ace in the hole, you know."

He just smiled, too much in love and too happy to argue.

Melissa and Diego left early, holding hands as they wished the happy couple the best, promised to have them over for dinner after the honeymoon and said goodbye to the rest of the gang.

Melissa sighed. "It was a nice wedding."

"As nice as our own?" he asked.

"Ours was a beautiful affair, but it lacked heart," she reminded him. "It was a reluctant marriage."

"Suppose we do it again?" he asked, studying her soft face. "Suppose we have a priest marry us all over again, so that we can repeat our vows and mean them this time?"

"My husband," she said softly, "each day with you is a rededication of our marriage and a reaffirmation of what we feel for each other. The words are meaningless without the day-to-day proving of them. And we have that."

His dark eyes smiled at her. "Yes, *querida*," he agreed quietly. "We have that in abundance."

She clung to his hand. "Diego, I had a letter yesterday. I didn't show it to you, but I think you expected it all the same."

He frowned. "Who was it from?"

"From your grandmother. There was a note from your sister enclosed with it."

He sighed. "A happy message, I hope?" he asked. He wasn't certain that his family had relented, even though they'd promised him they had.

She smiled at him, reading his uneasiness in his face. "An apology for the past and a message of friendship in the future. They want us to come and visit them in Barbados and bring Matthew. Your grandmother wants to meet her great-grandson."

"And do you want to go?" he asked.

She curled her fingers into his. "You said we might go down to the Caribbean for the summer, didn't you?'' she asked. "And combine business with pleasure? I'd like to make my peace with your people. I think you'd like that, too."

"I would. But there is so much to forgive, *querida*," he said softly, his dark face quiet and still. "Can you find that generosity in your heart?"

"I love you," she said, and the words were sweet and heady in his ears. "I'd do anything for you. Forgiveness is a small thing to ask for the happiness you've given me."

"And you have no regrets?" he persisted.

She nuzzled her cheek against his jacket. "Don't be absurd. I regret all those years we spent apart. But now we have something rare and beautiful. I'm grateful for miracles, because our marriage is certainly one."

He looked down at her bright head against his arm and felt that miracle right to his toes. He brought her hand to his lips and kissed it warmly. "Suppose we get Matthew and take him on a picnic?" he suggested. "He can feed the ducks and we can sit and plan that trip to Barbados."

Melissa pressed closer against Diego, all the nightmares of the past lost in the sunshine of the present. "I'd like that," she said. She watched the sky, thinking about how many times in the past she'd looked up and wondered if Diego was watching it as she was and thinking of her. Her eyes lifted to his smiling face. She laughed. The sound startled a small group of pigeons on the sidewalk, and they flew up in a cacophony of feathery music. Like the last of her doubts, they vanished into the trees and left not a trace of themselves in sight.

* * * * *

There are more
SOLDIERS OF FORTUNE
coming your way!

This May,

Silhouette Romance

presents a brand-new book in Diana Palmer's
passionate and adventurous series:
MERCENARY'S WOMAN
RS#1444

She was in danger and he fought to protect her.
But sweet-natured Sally Johnson dreamt of
spending forever in Ebenezer Scott's powerful
embrace. Would she walk down the aisle
as this tender mercenary's bride?

Soldiers of Fortune...prisoners of love.

Turn the page for an exciting preview of
MERCENARY'S WOMAN....

some painful emotional scars.

Chapter One

Ebenezer Scott stood beside his double-wheeled black pickup truck and stared openly at the young woman across the street while she fiddled under the hood of a dented, rusted hulk of a vehicle. Sally Johnson's long blond hair was in a ponytail. She was wearing jeans and boots and no hat. He smiled to himself as he remembered how many times in the old days he'd chided her about sunstroke. It had been six years since they'd even spoken. She'd been living in Houston until July, when she and her blind aunt and young cousin had moved back into the old, decaying Johnson homestead. He'd seen her several times since her return, but she'd made a point of not speaking to him. He really couldn't blame her. He'd left her with some painful emotional scars.

She was slender, but her trim figure still made his heartbeat jump. He knew how she looked under that loose blouse. His eyes narrowed as he recalled the shocked pleasure in her pale gray eyes when he'd touched her, kissed her, in those forbidden places. He'd meant to frighten her so that she'd stop teasing him, but his impulsive attempt to discourage her had succeeded all too well. She'd run from him then and she'd kept on running.

She was twenty-three now, a woman, probably an experienced woman. He mourned for what might have been if she'd been older and he hadn't just come back from leading a company of men into the worst bloodbath of his career. A professional soldier of fortune was no match for a young and very innocent girl. But, then, she hadn't known about his real life—the one behind the façade of cattle ranching. Not many people in this small town did.

Sally was a schoolteacher here in Jacobsville, Texas. He was retired, they called it. Actually, he was still on the firing line from time to time, but mostly he taught other men in the specialized tactics of covert operations on his ranch. Not that he shared that information. He still had enemies from the old days, and one of them had just been sprung from prison on a technicality, a man out for revenge and with more than enough money to obtain it.

Sally was rapidly losing patience with her vehicle. He watched her push at a strand of hair that had escaped from the long ponytail. She kept a beef steer or two. It must be a frugal existence for her, supporting not only herself, but her recently blinded aunt, and her six-year-old cousin as well.

He admired her sense of responsibility, even as he felt concern for her situation. He knew she had no idea why her aunt had been blinded in the first place, or that the whole family was in a great deal of danger. It was probably why Jessica had persuaded Sally to give up her first teaching job in Houston in June and come home with her and Stevie to Jacobsville. It was so they'd be near Ebenezer, and he realized Jessica knew he'd protect them. Sally had never been told what Jessica's profession actually was, any more than she knew what Jessica's late husband, Hank Myers, had once done for a living. But even if she had known, wild horses wouldn't have dragged Sally back here if Jessica hadn't pleaded with her, he mused bitterly. Sally had every reason in the world to hate him. But he was her best hope for survival. And she didn't even know it....

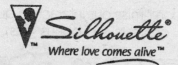